CERTAIN CURE

CERTAIN CURE

Where Science Meets Religion

A NOVEL

JENNIFER VALOPPI

Murray Hill Press

Published by Murray Hill Press, LLC
10800 Biscayne Blvd., Suite 820
Miami, FL 33161

Publisher's Cataloging-in-Publication Data
Valoppi, Jennifer.

Certain Cure (A Novel): Where Science Meets Religion / Jennifer Valoppi.–Miami, FL: Murray Hill Press, LLC, 2007.

p. ; cm.
ISBN: 978-0-9801682-0-4

1. Bible and science—Fiction. 2. Bible—Prophecies—Fiction. I. Title.

PS3622.A46 C47 2007
813/.6—dc22 2007941357

Book production and coordination by Jenkins Group, Inc. • www.bookpublishing.com
Cover concept by Steven Moseley
Cover layout and design by Barbara Hodge
Interior design and layout by Debbie Sidman

Printed in the United States of America
11 10 09 08 07 • 5 4 3 2 1

To my loving parents, Helen and Peter, who taught me a personal relationship with God is more important than any particular religion.

Acknowledgments

I am profoundly grateful to the many dear and wonderful friends who have given so generously of their time, energy and expertise.

From my earliest research they brought authenticity to the plot line; Dr. Barth Green, neurosurgeon, Dr. Al Eiber, radiologist, Dr. Elisa Krill Jackson, oncologist, Dr. Laurie Blach, oncologist, Dr. Mark Sinnreich, orthopedic surgeon and Millinda Sinnreich, RN, attorney Jeffrey Weiner, attorney Howard Srebnick, physicist Paul Bourgeois, computer expert Roger Bauman, Steve Miller, Director of Photography, Producer Michael Horowitz and John Mendola, NYPD.

I am deeply appreciative of attorneys Leslie Lott, Bill Tuttle and Steve Paul Mark, media expert Arielle Ford, my editor Daniel Zitin and literary agent Bob Diforio for helping this first time novelist navigate the literary world.

There are those who fit no specific category because they fill so many — you have been there to help me in so many ways and I cannot thank you enough for your brilliance, insight, encouragement and friendship; Dr. Diane Walder, Michael Naso, Bianca Erickson, Mel and Fran Harris, Jules Hamovitz, Larry Cucinella and my sister Helana Cucinella.

And to my family: My two young children, Julian and Jordan, have cheered me on every step of the way, even writing their own small books to provide inspiration; but it is their daily hugs and kisses that have done that all along; to my husband Christian, my step children Anna Lee and Mikhael and my entire family; your love and support bring meaning to life.

Author's Notes

We live in a modern, scientific world filled with facts and theories often portrayed as conflicting with spiritual and religious notions — where ancient prophecies are dismissed as little more than superstitions. In fact, many biblical prophecies are so far fetched it's hard to imagine how they could actually occur in a modern world — or is it?

As a veteran television journalist I have spent my career investigating and analyzing events of the day — intrigued by the way they impact our lives in ways we are often largely unaware. I can tell you that every time we experience a disaster, terrorist attack or "act of God" — something that seems to be of biblical proportions — there is a resurgent interest in "end days" prophecies. "Are these signs from God?" "Didn't Nostradamus predict that?" "Is that really in the bible?" These are all questions I have repeatedly heard.

Certain Cure is a thriller that bridges the gap between science and religion — where ancient Judeo-Christian prophecies intersect with modern quantum physics and nanotechnology, as the characters move through Manhattan — a world filled with signs and symbols, all warnings hidden in plain sight that must be deciphered and interpreted.

It's based on actual quotes from the Old and New Testaments. Some are obvious references; others not so obvious, so I have included a list of biblical citations at the end of the novel to help the reader better understand the context of the book.

Enjoy.

1

When Justin Cummings got up for school that morning his eyes were swollen and he had a bad case of the sniffles.

He couldn't remember ever feeling such a terrible pain. It cut like a knife turning deep in his gut.

He supposed his mother would say that life was filled with pain and joy and that at only fourteen years old, he had a lot more of both to look forward to. That didn't make him feel any better.

He was losing the great love of his life and there was nothing he could do about it.

Grams had a cold, for God's sake; it was just a simple cold. Or so they thought, before the doctor took that damn chest x-ray. Now they said she was dying.

It was inconceivable to Justin that a body could be snatched away when it was still so full of life. One day he and Grams were hanging out and laughing, and the next it was all coming to an abrupt end.

And he knew it was happening before anyone ever told him. He didn't know why, and he didn't know how he knew — perhaps he had dreamt it, but he knew his Grams was suddenly being pulled away.

Six months max was what the doctor had told the family; Grams should spend that time telling her family what she had intended to tell them over the next ten years. His mother, who knew everything, told him hope was not an option. Death was inevitable and it would not be pleasant.

He put on his gray pants and white oxford shirt. He pinched the knot of his navy and green striped tie, skewed to the side. He looked into the gilt-framed mirror at his gilded life now tarnished almost beyond recognition.

2

"I've got good news and bad news," Kyle said, walking into Helene Cummings's dressing room.

The makeup artist dusted a last blast of powder on Helene's nose as she unsnapped the protective apron covering her clothes.

"Don't use too much of that," Helene said. "It makes me look old." The makeup artist smiled and nodded amiably.

"Bad news first," she said.

"'Bup' is up 2 points — a 19 rating and 34 share. Now the suits will definitely want to move it to five days a week."

"Bup" was Kyle's pet name for Battle Ultimo Prime Time, an elaborate interactive tournament game that had been growing its numbers steadily over the first three months of its life. Born as a handheld video game played in cyberspace, it was the first such game to move to television — a big risk that was paying off big-time for the network.

Helene looked into the lighted mirror and smoothed the makeup under her eyes with her ring finger.

"So what?" she said. We're the lead-in to whatever show they have in that timeslot."

"I find it difficult to believe the network would want an adult talk show leading into an edgy new show for video game addicted teenagers. We're just not the same demo."

Helene knew he was right. The only thing more important than the ratings was the demographics, and Bup was a godsend for advertisers targeting the elusive 18–49 year old male who usually only frequented extreme sports programs and teenage reality shows. It was the network's best hope for revamping its fledgling primetime line up.

"Kyle, we're the hottest show on the air."

"Last season we never slipped below a 35 share. Last week we hit a 28."

"It was a re-run!" Helene protested.

"It was still a 28. Anyway, one of the studios has a talk show with a bunch of twenty-somethings under development. It would probably make more sense as a lead-in than us."

"We created this time slot," she yelled.

2

Getting a talk show into a network's prime-access time slot was itself an amazing feat, accomplished only after the New York station Helene worked for lost its network affiliation and in a desperate scramble for programming put her show on in the coveted 7 p.m. slot. Her news background, coupled with some gutsy shows on terrorists, escalated the numbers and her stock to such heights that one of the networks grabbed it up in syndication. But Helene knew too well that she could be on top today and be yesterday's news tomorrow. "You're the senior producer. What are you suggesting?" she said.

"We need to push the envelope. We need some hip, edgy shows to send a message to the powers that be — that you can be just as current as those twenty-somethings."

"We need to show them we're strong enough to be a great lead-in to anything."

"Exactly," Kyle said, sounding relieved.

"Don't worry. We'll do what we have to do to stay on top. I've taken this class before. What's everyone talking about today?"

"The United Nations meeting; we're already all over it, and the crying Virgin Mary statue in Harlem."

"So let's do something on that."

"I want the statue in here under controlled circumstances to see if it really cries. I also want the woman who owns it, but I can't get a response."

The stage manager stuck his head in the door. "One minute to air," he called out.

"Go on," Kyle said. "I'll talk to you in your IFB. And don't forget to keep the energy up. We're taping three shows today and we're on a tight schedule."

IFB stood for "interruptible feedback." It was an earpiece Helene wore in her right ear, so the producer could give her information and suggestions from the control room during the show.

"I'm right behind you," she said to the stage manager, as she walked the long corridor to the studio.

"Think edgy," Kyle yelled.

Helene walked past the flashing red "on air" sign and into a studio the size of a gymnasium as a stage manager held up an applause sign. Her set was in the center — a circle surrounded by floor to ceiling black retractable curtains. Half of the circle consisted of the stage and backdrop. The other half had risers with chairs. The audience was packed.

"Hello, hello" she said over the applause. "Thank you all so much for coming. It's a pleasure to have all of you here today."

She scanned the crowd for young faces. She knew Kyle was in the control room doing the same thing.

"So, we want edgy," she said quietly into the microphone clipped to her lapel, as she looked out at the mostly well kept, middle aged women and men.

At forty-six she was part of a generation that refused to get old, relinquish control, or admit they were losing their grasp on the reigns of the future.

She took her seat in the big round yellow chair on the stage.

"You never told me the good news," she whispered into the mike.

"A couple of kids had a Battle Ultimo tournament in the Bronx. One of them got shot."

"What's the good news?"

"Enough bad publicity on the game and maybe they'll cancel the show."

3

"If anyone in the world has something to be depressed about, it's me," Claire said out loud. "But I won't allow it. I'll fight this damn thing to the bitter end."

She propped herself up on the pillows of her hospital bed, raised the back a notch on the mechanical hand control, and attempted to drift off into her daily meditation. It wasn't so easy today.

She pictured her insides being eaten away by pasty brown globs of cancer cells. She tried to envision them flushed with healing flood waters of white light that cleansed them and turned them pink again, but she couldn't get that image to stick in her mind.

She just kept remembering that cough; a simple cough, a chest cold like she'd had a thousand times before. How was it possible that this time could be so different? She didn't believe it, not when Dr. Cohen pointed to the mass on the chest x-ray, not when he pulled out the CAT scan and said, "You also have multiple tumors in the liver. You're in a fairly advanced state of cancer. Our options are limited at this point."

"Our options are limited," kept floating in her head along with a thousand other words and pictures — images of her childhood, her child's childhood, her grandchild's childhood. She remembered the sensation of breast feeding, how the baby's mouth clung to her nipple with a warm, vacuum-like suction that tickled and taunted and wouldn't let go. She could feel the milk flowing through her glands and then, as if the milk were a narcotic, the infant's eyes would roll in the back of its head and the baby would drift off to sleep. Some women hated breast feeding. Not Claire. She loved the feeling of oneness with her child. Now, her child was a huge TV star who exceeded every dream Claire ever had for her.

I just can't believe God would bring me this far to drop me off now.

She returned to her mantra, gently chanting silently in her head, *ah-eng, ah-eng, ah-eng,* until it was all there was. She had been meditating for a long time, back to the days when the Beatles were hanging out with the Maharishi and Transcendental Meditation was a popular path to enlightenment. Claire had always been interested in her higher consciousness. She once trekked off to Nepal to meet an ascetic who lived on the top of a mountain;

the locals had said he could levitate. When she got there, he said levitation was a not a spectator sport.

She had visited the ancient ruins of Machu Picchu, high in the Andes of Peru, a vortex some believed, with a special energy, possibly left behind by visiting space aliens.

She took vitamins and ate mostly organic. For a while, she was on a strictly macrobiotic diet with brown rice and tofu and raw vegetables, modeled after eating habits in Asia, where many types of cancer barely existed. The diet was supposed to cure cancer, though the husband and wife who championed it both developed the disease.

Her torso ached from the damn tube that was stuck between her ribs, sucking fluid from her lungs. She opened her eyes to take a sip of medicinal green tea, and there stood the man who reminded her of all her troubles — patiently watching her from the doorway.

She hated him. She knew it wasn't his fault, but she still hated him.

"My beautiful Claire," Dr. Cohen said. "How are you today?"

"I'm in pain. I'm in a lot of pain. My side hurts, it's hard to breathe, my brain is like mush. I just hurt all over."

"It's from the operation, Claire. It's called 'pleurodesis,' or 'sclerosis of the pleura.' It always hurts, but at least the fever is gone. We drained some fluid out of your lungs, and that should make you feel better. It should make your breathing easier too. We put some talc in, to keep the fluid from coming back, but that always makes it hurt more. I'll get you some more pain medication."

"No, never mind. I think I like the pain. At least I know I'm still alive."

"I don't want you to be uncomfortable. Lung cancer is a tough one to tackle."

"I'm fine, Steve. I'll let you know if I need anything."

Dr. Cohen sat down on the side of the bed and took her left hand in his. "You know, it's really hard for me to see you hurting. We've been friends for a long time. You're one of the kindest, most admirable people I know. Your honesty, integrity, and character have been an inspiration to me for a long time. I don't know why things like this have to happen, but I want you to know that I truly wish we didn't have to go through this."

"But we do, Steve, and it's okay."

"And now we have to decide what to do next."

"It's not like I have a lot of choices," she said, coughing and wincing in pain with each exhalation.

"But you do have choices, Claire. If the chemo works, you can pick up three or four months."

"Three or four months? My ex-husband used to take that long just to make a decision. I want to be immortal. Can you make me immortal?"

Dr. Cohen grimaced. "No, Claire, I can't make you immortal. Unfortunately, in this battle it's the cancer cells that are immortal. I know three or four months doesn't sound like a long time, but a lot can happen in four months. The closer you get to the end, the more important those months will become."

"A lot can happen, huh? Like a cure? Is four months going to bring me a cure?"

"No, it's not."

"Then it's just four months of looking and feeling like shit, of looking and feeling like I should be dead but I won't be. I don't want my grandson to remember me that way."

"I understand, Claire, and it's entirely up to you. But Justin and Helene will love you no matter what you look like. The drugs today are really good. They only kill the divided cells. The problem is, that includes the blood cells, so you get fatigue, nausea, diarrhea, maybe some numbness in your fingers and toes."

"And hair loss. Don't forget the hair loss."

"Yes, hair loss. Well, I know a great wig maker."

"No thanks, Steve. I have my herbs and green tea and homeopathics. I'll meditate and do yoga and find my inner source to take over the healing. I'm going to make my exit my own way, with whatever's left of my own hair."

Unless, of course, my long shot comes through.

4

Robert Morgan could have been anyone, sitting on a newly refurbished park bench in Central Park, but he was *someone*, he told himself, fighting back the tears of depression that had come to define his life. He was looking out at the most beautiful part of the city. Central Park still had the breath of summer in its soft breeze — Indian summer they used to call it when he was a kid. But the best part of this corner of the park, on Fifth Avenue and 58th Street, was that he could sit amidst the trees and look out at the city — his city — the city he had always fought to protect. It wasn't that Bergdorf Goodman's was the most beautiful store or even had the most beautiful clothes, but it was *her* favorite store, or that the Sherry Netherland was the most elegant of hotels in a city known for elegant hotels, but it was home to Cipriani's, *her* favorite place to meet him for lunch. He missed Maria so much.

He had always wanted a daughter who would look just like her, but time had slipped away so quickly. He had always thought there would be more time.

He looked out at a group of children playing in the grass and thought of the children he would probably never have. Not because at 53 he was too old to be a father, but because children didn't seem to be a priority anymore. He couldn't envision himself with a woman so young that her desire for children would be his motivation. He couldn't envision himself with anyone, ever again. He knew the thought was ridiculous; there were plenty of eligible women in Manhattan and he was still handsome, when he didn't have big bags under his eyes. He was a successful partner in a security firm and still famous from his days as Chief of Police. He knew he needed to stop drinking and he fully intended to do that someday. He knew he wasn't supposed to mix alcohol with his medication, but somehow he couldn't help himself. That was also something he was working on. After all, it wasn't like he was drunk all the time. In fact, most of the time he couldn't even tell the difference until he tried to stand up.

The security business had been good to him. There was always a terrorist threatening all that Americans held sacred, a new computer virus to shut down an industry, or a billionaire who needed protecting. He missed being in the thick of things, but he was proud to be the spokesperson for his firm and was frequently called upon by the media to discuss security issues. And he never drank *before* a public appearance — at least not much.

Still, with all he had to be happy about, he couldn't stop the negative thoughts. That's what the medication was supposed to do. So, why didn't it work?

He closed his eyes to rerun the security plan for the upcoming United Nations conclave. It would have to run flawlessly. He knew he could have devised a better plan if Lockhart had consulted him earlier. But he hadn't. So Robert worked the angles in his head, looking for any critical flaw that might bring the whole thing down.

He could hear children laughing around him, and before he knew it he was drifting off to sleep, re-entering a dream that had plagued him for weeks.

It all started out innocently enough. He was working a security plan for the city, going over details with his colleagues, when all of a sudden a giant dragon appeared, moving through the streets of the city like Godzilla in an old movie. Only the dragon didn't hurt the buildings or the shops, it just devoured the people. They screamed to Robert for help, one after another, as they were chomped in half and thrown, some into the East River and the others into a huge fire. There were legs and arms that had been bitten off and strewn around the streets, and there was nothing Robert could do about it. He stood powerlessly watching the beast as it consumed all human life. He knew he was next.

He woke with a start as a child's ball bounced off his park bench.

The children laughed and jumped as they kicked and chased after the bright orange ball. One little girl always kept herself apart from the group. She looked to be about six or seven. Her beautiful blond curls were blowing in the warm air but never seemed to get mussed. The curls bounced as she leapt up and down, and her perfectly pressed pink jumper revealed a lacy underskirt as she turned to look at him. The ball rolled his way again and she came toward him. He tossed it back, right to her, thinking at least she'd have her chance at the ball. But she let it roll past her feet and just kept walking closer to him.

"He's coming," she said with a laugh. "I promise you, he's coming."

"Who's coming?" he asked.

"You know," she said and she just kept walking, right past him. He followed her with his eyes until he lost her in the rush of Fifth Avenue foot traffic.

5

Manhattan was the greatest city on earth, Justin's mom always said. He paused in the middle of the sidewalk to look at a white bird swooping up the side of a skyscraper. He squinted as the sun peaked over the rooftop and lost sight of the bird. His mom loved it here. He loved it too.

Of course, Justin didn't know anyplace else, except for when he hung out with his dad in Los Angeles. Mom said that was no comparison. There was a whole other country out there that had nothing to do with either coast. Besides, she said, LA was just a suburb of Manhattan anyway.

Everything was extreme here, by design. The buildings were taller, the restaurants better, the people faster, and the atmosphere more intense. Only the best and brightest survived well here. The rich were richer and the poor were poorer. Money was a prime motivator, because without an abundance of it, it was almost impossible to live a decent life. There wasn't much of a middle class in New York, at least not the kind his mother talked about from her childhood; she had grown up in the Midwest.

Maybe that's why the more successful his mother became the more afraid she was to lose her success — she didn't want to be middle-anything. She was nothing like Grams. Grams paid no attention to status and was never afraid. He hoped she wasn't afraid now.

The minute he turned into Manhattan Mercy Hospital the granite and marble lobby brought a chill to his bones.

He loved Grams more than anyone he had ever known. She was always ready to laugh and play. She craved fun and excitement and to learn new things. His mother only learned new things for a living.

He walked through the second floor, glancing in the rooms of sick people lying there in those awful gowns, mouths open and drooling with wrinkled skin and fear in their eyes, a step away from a ventilator or worse.

The graying walls made him nauseous as if the color had coated the lining of his stomach. And that *smell*, he hated the smell. He prayed Grams wouldn't go that way.

He peeked around the corner of the door, hiding flowers behind his back. "I have a special delivery," he announced, affecting a British accent, "for the most beautiful old lady on the floor."

"Well, young man, I suppose that would be me," she said, clicking the remote to mute the volume on the TV.

He pulled the roses out from behind his back.

"Oh my, lavender roses," Claire said, holding her breath for a moment so as not to endure the pain of coughing.

"Purple," he corrected.

"Purple would be darker. These are lavender. Either way, not a color found in nature, at least not on roses. So much more fun, I think. Thank you, my love."

"They were the brightest, most beautiful flowers at the Korean deli," he announced as he leaned over her bedside and kissed her on the cheek. Suddenly Natasha, a small red dachshund, poked her head out from the backpack over his shoulder.

"Oh my God, you smuggled her in! Don't let anyone see her, they'll have a fit," Claire said.

"I won't. I stopped home and she wouldn't let me out of the door without crying. She just really wanted to see you."

"Oh, put her down here," Claire said excitedly, nodding toward her bedside. She began to caress Natasha's head.

"What are you watching, Grams? Channel 142? You're watching kids play Battle Ultimo?"

"I thought maybe I'd see you playing. I watched you play yesterday, but you lost. I guess that's why your mom said you were in a bad mood last night."

"I've never been a particularly good loser, have I?"

"So, just resolve never to lose. That's what I'm doing, and so help me, I'm gonna beat this thing." Tears suddenly welled up in her eyes.

"If anybody can do it, you can, Grams."

"Do me a favor, Justin. Go over to my suitcase and bring it back here for me."

Justin walked over to the small closet, door ajar, where Grams' overnight bag rested on the floor. He wheeled it to her bed, laid it on its side, and unzipped it.

"There's a book at the bottom," Claire said. "Will you get it out for me, please?"

He rummaged around, pushing aside her makeup bag and a few tee-shirts and sweat pants neatly folded and stored in plastic Ziploc bags.

It was an old book, leather bound and worn, dark brown almost black, with tissue-thin pages.

"This, Grams?"

"That's it," she said extending her hand for it. "This is a very special book." She took it with her right hand and caressed it with her left, pushing away imaginary dust. It was well-worn, yet pristine. It had been carried many places, but never read.

"It's a bible, my bible, my only bible for that matter. It was given to me many years ago when I went on a spiritual retreat upstate. You see, there was this very handsome young man, and I fell very much in love." Tears came to her eyes and she stopped speaking for a moment, covering her mouth with her hand. "He was so handsome and we were so in love and so young and everything was so intense and glorious and miserable all at the same time." She smiled through her tears. "I'm sorry, sweetie, I don't mean to cry. Memories bring out funny things in me lately. Anyway, I want you to have this."

"Me?"

"Of course, you," she said. "Who else would I give it to, your atheist mother?"

"An agnostic, Grams. She's an agnostic."

"Whatever you say. Anyway, you're the only one who has the sense to read it, or the brains to understand it. Lord knows, I don't. I tried reading it once, but it never made much sense to me, all those 'thees' and 'thous.' It was so confusing. *He* loved it though. He read it all day and all night sometimes. He got so much meaning from it, so much comfort. I wish I could get that from a book, but I never understood."

"So, what happened to you guys?"

"The usual, I guess. We were young, we hadn't found ourselves. I certainly hadn't, and he wanted to be a priest. It seemed like a stupid thought — considering we were in love, unconsummated mind you, but still in love. I told him if God had wanted him to be a priest he wouldn't have fallen in love with me."

"What did he say?"

"'The devil goes after those he fears the most, and he uses your greatest weakness.' I'll never forget that. He meant *me*. I was incensed. I was also flattered, I suppose. *I* was his great weakness, and he believed the devil was using *me* to keep him from his God. And I have no idea why he thought the devil feared him so much.

"Nonetheless, it was pointless after that, very romantic, but pointless. It was pretty amazing though, to be viewed as someone's great, but forbidden temptation. Very *Casablanca*. So, I went back to Michigan and fell in love with your grandfather." She laughed. "That was a helluva choice."

"Wow," Justin said. "You've had some life, Grams. So what happened to him?"

"He became a priest — Father David," she said wistfully. "We kept in touch for a while, but I got sick of him trying to convert me. Anyway, he was a good man. He found something very special inside this book. Maybe you'll find it too. He always wanted me to read it. He said, 'A particular religion is not as important as finding your own personal relationship with God,' and this is where he found that relationship. Personally, I prefer meditation, but you'll let me know if there's anything important in there, won't you Justin?"

"Of course I will, Grams. You know I'd do anything for you."

"I know. You can read about Armageddon."

"You mean like in Battle Ultimo — Armageddon the Ultimate Battle? Is that real?"

"It's in there somewhere towards the end."

"Cool. But you don't mind if I leave this here for now, do you? I've got a game at a friend's house and I don't think...."

"Of course," she said as the phone rang. "I wouldn't expect you to walk in somebody's house with a *bible*. And leave the backpack. Your mother is on her way over. She can take Natasha home."

"Great. Thanks Grams. Oh, don't tell mom about the game...I mean, she thinks I'm studying."

The phone rang and she picked the receiver off the nightstand. Justin placed the bible next to the base of the phone.

"Hello." Her eyes immediately lit up. "Of course, of course. Tell me." There was excitement in her voice. "When? Tomorrow? I'll be here. Thank you. Thank you so much." She hung up the phone breathlessly. Justin could see her heart pounding in her frail chest.

Just then, Helene walked in the room. She rolled her eyes and shook her head in disbelief at the sight of Natasha's little head sticking out of the backpack. Before she could scold Justin for bringing the dog to the hospital, Claire hung up the phone.

"I have the most incredible news," she announced.

6

"Are you sure you don't want to come?" Evelyn Claiborne said as she fastened the clip of a diamond earring to her right ear.

"I'm sure, dear."

Archibald Claiborne was grateful to have some time alone in his apartment, when he would be left to the machinations of his mind and heart to make the most important decision of his life. It was a decision he made theoretically many years ago, never imaging he would actually have to choose in real life. But now the time had come, and he prayed he would be up to the challenge.

He watched adoringly as his wife of forty years moved gracefully through the bedroom in her long black gown. Soon she would be off honoring a long-since-planned commitment to a charity gala. It was one of the most important events of the year for the medical community; all the prominent physicians would be there, but not Archibald.

"What are you going to do?" she called out from the bathroom where she was putting the finishing touches on her hair.

"Read, relax. Maybe watch TV."

"Are you sure you're okay, dear?" she said kissing him on the cheek. "You really haven't been yourself lately."

"I'm fine dear. You go and have a good time."

Archibald walked his wife to the front door. She turned to blow him a kiss as the elevator arrived.

She knew nothing of his dilemma. He had kept it from her out of love, at first. He didn't want her fragile psyche to struggle with the inevitable. Later, he kept it from her out of the hope that she would never *need* to know. She was a worrier by nature and worry would not alleviate the situation at hand. Now, he would have to tell the story — all he had learned — the dark secret he harbored, that would change so many things.

He hoped for a moment that he was wrong, that he could find some divine guidance to pull him through this phase, but he only felt forsaken. There was no where to turn.

He walked to his office and stood in front of the bookshelves filled with antique medical books. As he gazed at them, seeking the pleasure these possessions always offered him, he raised his right hand to his collarbone.

14

He felt the thin gold chain around his neck. *Nothing* was right anymore. He had never grown accustomed to wearing a necklace. It might as well have been a shackle. He tugged on it, and when it broke, he hurled it to the floor. He glanced at his feet, but he didn't see where it had fallen. It didn't much matter. Nothing mattered anymore.

He was startled when the doorbell rang, although he half expected it. There were two imposing figures in black trench coats with hoods pulled over their heads; the kind you would find in a coven of witches. Archibald couldn't stifle a brief chuckle at the theatrics.

He surprised even himself when he calmly led them into the library. It was his favorite room in the house, with its oak paneled bookshelves and fancy moldings that announced to all who entered that he had done very well in life. Behind his desk was a very valuable, framed copy of the Hippocratic Oath, not the modern one, rewritten in 1964, but the original version, in Latin, as written by Hippocrates, the father of medicine. On it was the Staff of Asclepius; a single serpent entwined around a knotty tree limb, the staff of the ancient Greek physician deified as the god of medicine. It was the traditional symbol of the medical arts.

To first of all do no harm, he thought. Despite popular perception, that line had never been part of the Hippocratic Oath. For the first time he found himself wondering why not.

He took his seat behind his desk. Without a word, the smaller of the two men took a seat in one of the chairs across from him, while the larger leaned against Archibald's wall of precious medical books. Archibald glanced over as the man pushed back his sleeves to reveal his massive forearms tattooed with skull and cross bones.

"I can't go through with this," Archibald said. The flame from the fireplace glowed with a reassuring warmth. "I just want things to go back the way they were."

"Think of what you're saying, Archibald," the smaller man said. "You're not being rational. You're not thinking clearly. Give it some time. You'll see, everything is going to be fine. You worry too much. Don't make a hasty decision when so much is at stake for all of us."

"I don't care. This is an unexpected development, and I cannot continue."

Archibald watched as the larger man pressed against his books. The man adjusted his arm and a rare volume sitting on the edge of the shelf fell to the ground with a thud. The man kicked it to the side.

15

"Are you contemplating suicide?" the man in front of him said.

Archibald looked back at him but didn't answer.

"You were greedy. You wanted it all," the man said. "There's nothing wrong with that. Everyone does. But you can wind up with nothing if you're not willing to pay the price."

7

Justin was happy to be home. He quickly climbed into bed. He snuggled deep into his pillow with a content smile on his face and went to sleep thinking about his win and what he would do with the three, twenty dollar bills he picked up beating the guys at Battle Ultimo.

Somewhere in the darkness, he woke up to the sound of his own screams.

Helene called to him from the other room.

He wasn't sure where he was. He couldn't get his bearings. Then he saw the outline of his sixth grade tennis trophy on his dresser.

"I'm fine mom. Go back to sleep. I just had a nightmare."

"Are you sure?" she asked. She was next to his bed.

"Leave me alone, mom," he said, annoyed that she had come in.

He was shaken, but he couldn't remember why. He lay quietly while Natasha cried and pawed at the side of his bed. He slipped her under the covers and she crawled to his feet.

The gleam of glass, his grandmother, and something breaking. Then he remembered — Grams was calling out to him. She was reaching for him asking for help — begging — but he couldn't reach her. He flicked the crystal ball on the kitchen chandelier and it crashed to the ground and broke into a million pieces. Grams watched, and then, as if she were a fragile Christmas ornament, she fell to the ground and shattered into tiny pieces of glass. The dream was gone, but the darkness in it lingered.

He tried to push it out of his mind and fall back to sleep. As he began to doze a brightness grew. He opened his eyes to focus on the light. He tried to move, but he was frozen. Fear gripped his paralyzed body. Was it another dream?

The image of a man began to take shape. The light hurt his eyes at first. A cool wind passed over his right foot as Natasha stuck her head out from under the covers.

"Who are you?" he whispered.

"You are being called, Justin."

"Called to what?"

"All those who are called will answer," the man said. His face and robed body were barely visible through a cloudy mass of white light. "'Do not be

17

afraid of them. There is nothing concealed that will not be disclosed, nothing hidden that will not be made known. What I tell you in the dark, speak in the daylight; what is whispered in your ear, proclaim from the rooftops. Do not be afraid of those who kill the body but cannot kill the soul. Rather be afraid of the One who can destroy both soul and body in hell.'"

Justin trembled.

"Do not be afraid of me Justin. I am with you always."

He couldn't make sense of it, but he suddenly felt completely at ease.

There was something familiar about this man, something reassuring. A barrage of images and sensations whirled through Justin's mind. He tried to grasp one, to hold it and analyze it, but it was gone in an instant.

"I think I know you," Justin said. "I remember you...from when I was little kid, don't I?"

"I've known you much longer than that," the man said with a smile, as he dissolved into the light, then the darkness of Justin's room.

Helene stood at the side of his bed, quietly watching and listening to her son. She tried to get his attention by leaning over him and looking directly into his open eyes, but he didn't notice her. With a quiet sigh, he closed his eyes.

8

The cordless phone was lying next to Robert Morgan's pillow exactly where he had left it in a drunken stupor the night before. He remembered how he had held the phone in his hand, ready to call Maria. He must have passed out before he had the chance. He wondered now what number he would have dialed. For a moment last night, it was as if she weren't gone, as if a simple phone call could have brought her back into his life. Now he wanted to hold on to that feeling for a moment, but the damn phone kept ringing and the sound was pounding in his brain.

Who was bothering him at this indecent hour? He glanced at the clock and realized it wasn't indecent at all. It was late morning. He picked up the phone and was immediately put on hold for the Chief of Police.

"I've got a high profile murder," Chief Lario said when he came on the line. The Chief was a bright young Latino who, unlike his predecessor, was not intimidated by Robert's star power in the field of law enforcement. "It's about to be all over the news and we don't have a clue how it happened. This is going to be a political hot potato, and I want to make sure we don't miss anything."

Robert had to cough and clear his throat before he could speak. "Well, you know, Chief, Assurance Security is always ready to help out. I'm sure I can get John Lockhart on the phone. He'll be delighted to send a security crew out to the scene."

"No crews, Robert. No Lockhart. I'm looking for you."

"Chief, I love ya, but I'm a little under the weather these days, and Lockhart is my partner; he's kind of running things for both of us."

"You've been under the weather for a year now, Robert. When are you going to get back into the game? Shit happens, and there's nothing you can do about it. It's not all your fault."

"Well, that may be. Look, I appreciate the vote of confidence and all, Chief, but I'm really not taking on any new assignments right now. Consider Lockhart. He's the brains of the organization."

"I'll be happy to do that. But it just so happens I'm not looking for brains on this one. I'm looking for instincts. I've never seen anyone with better instincts than you."

"Well, like I said, my instincts are a little fucked up these days."

Robert walked to the refrigerator and poured a Diet Coke into an empty jelly jar. He took a long gulp, finishing the glass, and brought it down with a hard clink on the black granite countertop.

"I'd still like you to give it a try," the Chief said.

"Who's the victim?"

"Maybe you know him, Dr. Archibald Claiborne?"

Robert's heart sank. Archibald had been the top dog at the Association of American Medical Professionals when Robert was the top dog in law enforcement. Of course he knew him. He considered it his job to know him and all the other top people who could either cut through red tape when necessary or be the likely targets of criminals.

"Yes, I knew him, Chief, not well, but I liked him. He was a good guy. His wife must be devastated. They were very close."

"Why don't you get over here, and let's talk this through. I'm on Park Avenue, at the scene. I could use the help."

"All right, Chief. I'll take a look, but that's all. Lockhart is really the man you want; I'll let him know what I pick up."

Robert had been one of the most effective police chiefs the city of New York ever had. He reduced violent crime by fifty percent with old fashioned beat cops and determined investigators. He shook the cobwebs of futility out of a department overrun with bureaucracy. He gave law enforcement officers the tools they needed to do their jobs and the motivation to get things done. He cut paperwork and gave officers ownership over their cases. When a job was well done, he was the first to parade his people in front of the community for kudos. Of course, it didn't hurt that he took the reins during a time of heightened fears over terrorism, when everyone knew the city could not afford lax security.

Robert had been a shoo-in for mayor. He was carrying all five boroughs, even Staten Island, where he had his smallest lead, but was still a strong front runner. He was a liberal Republican, running against a conservative Democrat who was more Republican than he was.

Robert thought of those times often, almost incessantly. The leaves of Central Park had changed to amber and red when an early frost unexpectedly hit the city, bringing out the winter coats. The roasting nuts on the street corners made it smell like the holidays. Runners in shorts and tee-shirts were meeting at the crack of dawn in anticipation of the New York City Marathon, oblivious to the chill. New Yorkers big and small were rooting for the Mets as spectacular pitching inched them closer to the World Series.

Broadway was buzzing with four new hits. The Metropolitan Museum of Art was boasting record attendance. Manhattan was already gearing up for the all important Christmas tourist season. All was well with the world.

The November election was still weeks away when on Yom Kippur, the Holiest of Holy days for Jews worldwide, his life changed.

Robert always believed life didn't change in a year or a month or a week; life changed in a day and a second. It changed in the split second a kid made a decision to get into a car with a drunk driver, or someone chose to walk down that dangerous street at the wrong hour. It changed the second someone pulled the trigger or said 'I do' to the situation or person they should have said 'I don't' to. But Maria never listened.

"Don't go to the city today," he begged, but she wanted to stop at Bergdorf's, never believing *that* could be a terrorist target. But that's where he was, a suicide bomber disguised in a traditional prayer shawl. He nonchalantly walked down Fifth Avenue and exploded. He killed himself and a couple of dozen others.

Out of eight million people in three hundred and nine square miles, the bomber picked the half block section where Maria was shopping.

As far as Robert was concerned, the Book of Life was closed on him a year ago, on Yom Kippur.

The next day he dropped out of the race — the political race, the rat race, and in many ways the human race.

He decided that Absolut vodka was his most dependable companion; the name itself evoked the kind of certainty he was looking for in life. Now he kept completely to himself, reading stories about vintage police work, as he liked to call it, and made thrice weekly trips to the office to go over security plans that someone else had drawn up. His visits were mostly a formality. He was a fifty-fifty partner and his name was the company's main draw. Sure, he'd been written up in the New York tabloids for occasionally drinking to excess, but since he did most of his drinking in private it wasn't a major concern. His responsibilities were down to being a talking head for the company and he still did that quite well. The term was 'functional drunk,' and as far as he was concerned, as long as he was functioning he was going to be drunk.

With the previous night's anxieties showered off, Robert mixed himself a vodka and grapefruit juice and headed to Claiborne's Park Avenue address. Despite his resistance, he couldn't help but feel a little proud about having been pressured to look into an important case. Maybe this was a diversion that would take his mind off his own life.

A handful of officers stood outside the building, some puffing away on smokes in the cool afternoon breeze. A couple of the officers smiled and nodded to him in recognition. He nodded back. Just being there made him feel like he was part of something bigger than himself.

When Robert got inside he could see the chief in the distance, standing, hands on his belt, in awe of a brutal and baffling situation. News of the murder was out, and the media was all over the details. Robert knew the chief was faced with the sticky task of preserving the privacy of the influential family as best he could with the mayor looking over his shoulder every step of the way.

The chief couldn't afford any mistakes. Any slips he made would immediately become public.

Robert surveyed the crime scene. The body had been taken to the morgue and a white chalk outline delineated where Claiborne's head and upper torso had come to rest on the desk.

The dried blood mixed so perfectly with the red leather of the desk top that at first it appeared to be only a dull stain on a shiny surface, but as Robert drew closer he could see the texture of a massive amount of congealed blood.

"Pretty messy," Robert said.

"He was decapitated," the chief said. "An up close and personal killing, as intimate as you get. Now, who does that?"

"A wife, a jilted lover, an angry family member," Robert answered. "Someone who's been wronged and couldn't carry the anger any longer."

"The wife was at a charity gala, though she could have hired someone. As far as we can tell he didn't have a lover, and neither did she."

"I think he liked his wife," Robert said, "but you never really know what goes on in people's lives until you're in them. How were his finances?"

"Judging by this apartment, I'd say rich."

"Never count other people's money till you've got all the numbers. What does the bank say?"

"We're getting the records now, but there's no major debt we're aware of."

Robert took a deep breath; this one wasn't going to be any fun at all. The alarm systems were off; there was no sign of forced entry; the doorman said no one came by to see the victim all evening; and everyone who entered the building was accounted for. The service entrance to the building remained locked, suggesting an inside job. Everyone with access to the keys was being questioned.

"Where was the head?" Robert said.

"Pinned to the desk. The wife came home and found him. The axe was sticking out of his neck."

Robert walked to the corner of the room and picked up the large plastic bag containing the axe. Through the plastic he examined the blood and hair on the blade, looking for anything out of the ordinary, but there was nothing he could see.

"Heavy," he said, raising and lowering the bag. "What about the struggle? What angle was he facing? It doesn't look like much in the room was disturbed."

"That's the crazy part. There doesn't seem to have been a struggle. There's no blood or skin under his nails that we could find, and his head was pinned straight down, like he never even looked at his killer. No cuts or bruises either. We'll see what the coroner says."

"How does someone get you from behind with a big ol' mother fucking axe and you don't even turn around? It's like a medieval execution," Robert said.

"Maybe there was someone in front of him, distracting him," the chief said, "or maybe someone held his head down. But who lets that happen without a struggle?"

"Do you think he just gave up?" Robert asked.

"I don't know. No signs of a struggle, no evidence of breaking in — it's like he just let some madman with an axe in and said, 'Chop my fucking head off.' It makes no sense. There were panic buttons all through the house, and as far as we can tell, none of them were touched."

"This is as angry as it gets, maybe just plain crazy. What was taken?"

"Nothing. The wife has a couple hundred thousand in jewelry sitting in the bedroom right next door."

"Was it hidden?"

"It was in a drawer."

"What do we know about him?" Robert asked, pacing the room, staring at the bookshelves.

"The wife is being interviewed in the other room right now, but so far we're hearing he was one of the straightest guys on the planet. He was a good father, loyal husband — all that kind of stuff. He played golf on weekends in the Hamptons and went to church with his wife on Sundays. Sometimes he even went during the week."

Robert's instincts were telling him nothing. His old friend and mentor, Yitzhak Barrouck would say: *Pull back the curtains of assumption from your eyes so you can see now, what will become obvious only after it's discovered.*

"How about drugs, or a gay lover? Was he prone to bringing charity cases home?"

"Negative," the Chief said. "And it looks like the perpetrators never entered the bedroom. No, this was a vendetta, an up close and personal vendetta. They got what they wanted when they killed him. Then they left."

"Was the axe in the house?"

"No. It was brought in from the outside. We're tracking it now."

Robert moved past an officer dusting the woodwork for fingerprints. Something caught his eye in the shaded recess of the library cabinets.

He knelt down to the floor and called an officer over. "Can I have an evidence bag?" he said, as he pulled a pair of rubber gloves from his inside breast pocket and put them on.

The officer handed him a bag and Robert pulled a small gold medallion on a chain from under the overhang of the cabinet. A loop of the chain had been pulled open, so it looked as if the necklace fell or was pulled off. Robert placed it in the bag and examined it. It was the medical symbol, the caduceus; a single rod with two entwined serpents and a pair of wings at the top. The serpent's eyes were diamonds.

Mrs. Claiborne, her eyes puffy and bloodshot from crying, entered the room with an officer. Robert rose to his feet.

"Mrs. Claiborne," he said, walking toward her and extending his hand. "I'm Robert Morgan, and I am so sorry about the death of your husband."

She sniffled back some tears. "I know who you are Mr. Morgan," she said softly. "We've met before."

"I didn't know if you'd remember under the circumstances."

She used a soggy tissue to wipe an endless flow of tears from her eyes.

"May I ask why your husband wasn't with you at the charity event?"

"He hadn't been feeling well lately. He wanted to stay home and rest."

"Was he seriously ill?"

"No, only a little under the weather. I think he just didn't want to go to another charity gala, and I didn't mind. We did that sometimes."

"You're a pretty understanding wife."

"He was a very understanding husband."

"I found this charm on the floor," Robert said, handing her the plastic bag. "I assume it belonged to your husband?"

She took the bag and looked at it. "Yes. It was his. He had been wearing it recently."

"It looks like he collected a lot of medical artifacts."

"He did. Now, I'm going to have to figure out what to do with his collection of antique medical books."

"Are they very valuable?"

"Their sale could finance a few retirements, but Archibald always wanted them donated to a place where the world could enjoy them. I'm certain I'll have no lack of calls from curators as word spreads."

9

"I seek only your truth, Lord," Father David Consolo said as he made the sign of the cross. He stood in front of what had become a shrine on the steps of an undistinguished Harlem brownstone. Candles illuminated the mounds of cut flowers, photographs of loved ones, handwritten prayers, and words of thanks that were strewn across the steps.

Two elderly women, one white and one black, in traditional nun's habits, stood as sentries at the front door.

"Welcome Father."

"Where is she?" he asked softly.

"Inside."

A voice in Father David's head said "Come, see the miracle, but this is not for *you*, David."

He didn't understand the words, but he felt a familiar rush of emotion as he made his way up the steps. That was always a good sign.

As soon as he reached the door, he could see the statue. It was barely a foot high, placed on a card table covered with a lace tablecloth. It was his beloved Mary, made of white ceramic, yellowed by the years, wearing light blue robes. There was a small candle lit in front of the Virgin and a woman motionless on her knees in prayer before her.

"How long has she been like this?"

"The woman? This time, five hours," one of the nuns said. "The statue will start to cry about the time she comes out of the trance."

Father David stood beside the kneeling woman. Her dark skin was heavily wrinkled. Her head was tilted slightly toward the heavens, her eyes wide open, yet never blinking.

He passed his hand in front of her eyes but there was no reaction.

He looked down at the cold, hard tile pressing her bony knees.

"How old is she?"

"Seventy," one of the nuns said.

He bent down, holding his own tired frame, and got close to her face. Her breath was imperceptible. He blew directly into her eye — again no reaction.

Father David reached into his jacket pocket and pulled out a safety pin. His arthritic hands opened it and bent the pin straight.

He stuck the old woman in the forearm. She didn't flinch.

He stuck her in the center of her hand clasped in prayer and then deeply in the side of her cheek. Still nothing, not even a mark.

"What is she saying?" he said to the nuns. "That the antichrist is here? That he will have his reign? I've heard all these things before. It seems the Lord has sent more signs and prophets this year than hurricanes and earthquakes. I am weary, sisters. What am I to do?"

"She has spoken of the rapture," one of the nuns said.

"Tell me more," he said hopefully. "Speak to me of multitudes in white robes washed clean in the blood of the Lamb."

Father David had always thought the rapture was a curious concept in Christianity. The bible didn't actually use the word rapture, but it spoke of believers being taken up into the heavens during the antichrist's reign in the final days of the earth. Jesus said that when he returned to earth he would gather his elect. In Corinthians, the Apostle Paul said believers would not all die, but would be changed in the twinkling of an eye. Many Christians, including Catholics, didn't believe in the rapture. Of those who did, there was disagreement as to whether this would happen before, during, or after the period of the Great Tribulation. And there was no consensus as to whether the elect would be taken in secret or in public view.

To complicate matters further, Revelations spoke of multitudes coming out of the Tribulation, but then talked about only a meager 144,000 of the purest souls being redeemed from the earth with God's name written on their foreheads. The rest of God's people would presumably be left to suffer until the appointed time.

"Actually Father, she's spoken only of the one-hundred-forty-four-thousand, quoting scriptures."

"What does she say?"

"There are one-hundred-forty-four-thousand from the twelve tribes of Israel who have the Lord's name and his Father's name written on their foreheads. They have remained pure. They will be redeemed from the earth, purchased from among men and offered as first fruits to God."

Only two of the original twelve tribes were still known to be in existence. The other ten separated themselves after a Jewish civil war and were eventually defeated by the Assyrians in 722 B.C. Some believed their remnants would be found some day, scattered throughout the world.

"Are there so few, dear Lord, who have found favor in your eyes? So few you will spare this dreadful time to come? Tell me sisters, did she speak in Latin, in Aramaic…"

"In English."

"Arghh," he said suddenly. "You know I can't take that back to the Vatican…"

"And then," the nun said, "she turned to me in Aramaic and said the Lord did not send her to speak to the church, but to the Lord's people here in Harlem."

Father David's eyes flooded with tears, and he dropped to his knees because he knew these words were true.

As the tears streamed down his face, the statue wept.

10

Yitzhak Barrouck exhaled deeply as his body slowly sank into the comfortable leather chair across the desk from his old friend. The seriousness of the moment weighed heavily on both men. Barrouck could see desperation in his friend's eyes.

"Thank you for coming to Tel Aviv," the Prime Minister said. He leaned forward at his desk and took a small sip of Turkish coffee from a demitasse cup. "There's been another death threat against you, Yitzhak."

"I know."

"You should be taking this very seriously."

"I take them all seriously. I just don't let them alter my life. Is that why you called me here?"

"No. I had to see you in person. I need you to look me in the eye and tell me you absolutely believe this is the right thing to do — the right thing for Israel."

"What choice do we have? Without it, all our people will be at war."

"Where have you been, my friend? We *are* at war. We have been at war from the beginning of time and probably will be until the end of time."

"I want peace for our children, Prime Minister. I want them to run in the streets and play without fear of a sniper's bullet. I want them to board a bus without being afraid to take the window seat, because the person sitting there is most likely to be blown to bits. I believe the Palestinians want peace for their children too."

"Suicide bombers don't have the same reverence for life that you and I do."

"They are desperate. We are all desperate. People face their desperation in different ways. We were at peace with them once and we can be again."

Barrouck was referring to a time centuries ago, when Islam was a young religion. In those times Islam and Jewish culture flourished in peace together.

"You are the same idealistic child who used to eat his lunch by the Dome of the Rock, waiting for the Messiah to come. I am a pragmatist. We are five million Jews in the middle of the desert, surrounded by those who despise us. There will never be a lasting peace. I see hatred in the eyes of their young people as I drive through their neighborhoods."

29

"Young people do what their parents tell them, until they are taught to see a better way. I am a Jew with or without this land we call Israel. Israel is in my heart and soul and God has promised to reside with us one day in it. So I, my friend, could give all this land, without giving an inch of Israel. But I am suggesting we give only a small piece."

Barrouck could feel the strength of the Prime Minister's gaze penetrate to the core of his being. Kabbalah teaches that the eyes lead directly to the soul and there is power in the gaze. Barrouck could feel the Prime Minister's power and the sadness of the abandoned dream that lay behind it.

"It is difficult for you to dream," Barrouck said, "because your shoulders are heavy with responsibility. Mine are light. If you permit me, I will hold a portion of your burden in the peace talks, if you will take a portion of my hope."

"You have a heavy enough burden, though you seem intent on ignoring it. There are those who don't want peace, and your life is a small price to pay for their dream."

"God will protect me as long as I am of use to Him here, and when I'm not, He will take me. If it pleases Him to receive me by the hands of His enemies, as He has done to so many before us, then so be it. Their threats will not dictate my life."

"We will go forward with your plan," the Prime Minister said.

"Thank you," Barrouck said, rising to his feet. "I will do my best." He extended his hand, but the Prime Minister ignored the gesture as he approached and embraced him. For a moment, the hope of the world was in their hug.

After a time, the Prime Minister patted Barrouck on the back and Barrouck moved to the door. As he placed his hand on the doorknob the Prime Minister called out, "I will take a portion of your hope, my friend. Be well and keep yourself safe, so we may both live to see your dream.

"But Yitzhak...."

"Yes?" Barrouck said.

"The Messiah's not coming today."

11

"Mister Cummings, are you with us?" Mr. Zelasco said in a mocking tone. Justin perked up from his daydream.

"Yeah, sure, sorry," Justin replied. "I mean of course I am."

"Good. Then you'll summarize for the class what a Smith Integer is."

"A what?" Justin asked, provoking the obligatory giggles from the class.

"A Smith Integer," the teacher repeated.

"Uh, I know it's a number," Justin replied, prompting more giggles.

"No shit, Sherlock," the guy next to him whispered.

"Miss Quinonez, can you please tell the class what a Smith Integer is?"

Madeline Quinonez was exotic and beautiful and ridiculously smart. If anyone knew the answer, she would.

"It's a number where the sum of the digits equals the sum of the digits of the prime divisors," she stated.

"Tell me more," the teacher said.

"A mathematician named Albert Wilansky noticed that his brother-in-law's phone number had that property, so he named the concept after his brother-in-law — Smith."

"How did you know that?" Justin whispered, but Madeline just smiled and continued.

"Some people question whether this is serious math or just recreational math, because it has to do with decimal digits, and that's not considered serious by all mathematicians."

She was kidding, right? Recreational math? That was certainly an oxymoron. Justin could listen to Madeline speak all day; it didn't even matter what she was saying. He watched her lips move and thought about what it would feel like to kiss them.

"Can you give me an example, Miss Quinonez?"

"Sure," she continued. "There are a lot of Smith numbers. 85 is a Smith number because 8 + 5 equals 13, and the integers of its prime factors total 13. The factors are 17 and 5, so 1 + 7 + 5 = 13.

"Very good, Madeline," the teacher replied. "Now, who can tell me what a Rhoda number is?"

"So, do you know *my* number?" Justin whispered to Madeline.

"I had *your* number a long time ago."

31

"Will you come to Rebecca's party with me?" he asked.

"Mister Cummings, is there something you would like to share with the class?" the teacher said.

"No, sir." Justin slid down in his chair.

"Call me," Madeline whispered. "That is, *if* you can remember ten consecutive digits. On second thought, I'll write it down."

12

"There *are* second chances in life, and this is mine. I will take it and I will run with it. It will work. There *are* second chances. I *know* there are second chances. What do these doctors know anyway? They all think they're God. I won't accept their death sentence. I simply will not accept it."

Claire was jumping inside, speaking out loud to herself, with clenched fists, tethered to her hospital bed by a tube running through her ribs into her lung. Yesterday she could barely move. Today she was ready to jump out of bed and run out of the building, if only someone would take this damn tube out.

Tears streamed down her cheeks as she struggled with a breath. Her chest hurt, her body ached, but she was trying to believe in the power of something other than herself to redeem her from her plight, to vanquish the inevitable and commute this death sentence that had been so unfairly handed down. She would strike any deal and pay any price for the chance to do it all again.

All the things she had tried to do right — exercise, meditation, yoga, no smoking, no sugar — in the end it all meant nothing. And worst of all, what if she was wrong about everything — reincarnation, heaven, a hereafter of any sort — what if none of it was real and the buck stopped here? What if Helene had been right all along? Birth, life, death, oblivion.

"But maybe this is not it," she whispered. "Maybe this is not my end. It doesn't feel over." Her white knight would ride up on his white horse and save her. Could it be true? Why not? Life was filled with surprises; medical science made huge strides every day. Perhaps she could turn the corner and put this whole mess behind her like a bad flu. She needed strength and faith. Suddenly, she was all fight and no surrender.

When Helene walked in she immediately commented on her mother's state of agitation.

"This isn't agitation," Claire said. "It's exhilaration. Don't you see what's happening here? I'm going to be a part of history. I *have* to believe that. You of all people, my daughter, the hotshot TV personality, should understand, this is big news. I may be the first person in the United States medically proven to be cured of incurable cancer!"

33

"Mom, I love you and I want this for you more than anything in the world, but you can't get so worked up about it. He could be a quack or a charlatan. Who knows what he wants from you."

"I shouldn't be so optimistic, is that what you're saying? I already told you, he wants nothing. He's taking no money. He just wants to save the world from this despicable disease."

"Why you, mom?"

"Well, if you're thinking it's because of you, Helene, forget it. He doesn't want the publicity. This all has to be a big secret. In fact, when I told him who you were he almost backed out. He said he's not in this for the glory. And absolutely no one can know."

"Then why? There must be thousands of people dying of cancer right now. Why you?"

"Because I'm open minded, and the cure requires an open mind. That's what he said."

"I don't like this whole thing. You get a call from one of your new age psychic friends. She claims to know someone who can cure cancer. The next thing you know, without even getting a moment to think, some mysterious doctor is on his way from China and we're all supposed to just say, 'Thank you, thank you, thank you.' You're not allowed to talk to your own doctor who's known you for twenty years. This doesn't feel right. I just want you to think."

Claire struggled to take a deep and painful breath. She felt almost peaceful.

"Helene, what's there to think about? I'm a dead person. My doctor for twenty years is offering me nothing, not even a pain-free way to die. This man is offering me life. What choice do I have?"

"But what about the risk?"

"Losing a couple of months? You call that a risk? Besides, that's why I don't want to do anything without you and Justin being here."

13

Justin's head spun. Had he really just scored a date with the woman of his dreams? Other parts of his body were even more excited. Justin had been in love with Madeline for as long as he could remember. When she moved away a couple of years ago he thought he'd never see her again. Now, here she was and she was *his* date.

"Hey, Just Man," a boy down the hall yelled, "bring your GamePad to the party. We're gonna play Battle Ultimo. And bring some cash, because you're going down, mother fucker."

"Yeah, yeah, sure, Sean," Justin said. "You're all talk and no action. Anyway, don't count on me."

"What do you mean, don't count on you? You owe me money. How am I gonna get it back if you don't play me?"

"Not this time, buddy. I've got a date."

"A date? Oh, man. Samantha?"

"Madeline."

"Forget it," Sean said. "You are not getting laid. Just be there with your GamePad. It's a lot less frustrating."

"Ha ha," Justin said as he strolled down the hallway and out the door onto East 23rd Street.

"Hey you, buddy," a voice beckoned from between the buildings.

"Me?" Justin asked.

"Yeah, come here," the voice called.

No savvy Manhattan kid would walk into the shadows for a beckoning stranger, especially a shady looking figure lurking outside one of the city's most exclusive preparatory schools dressed in baggy jeans and a leather jacket. Two kids from the school had been mugged recently and the students had been advised to be careful. Despite that, Justin had heard a skilled Battle Ultimo player had been coming around after school and when he recognized the guy standing next to the stranger as a fellow student, he felt safe.

"What do you want?"

"Hey man, want to score something for the party? I got whatever you need."

"No thanks, man."

35

"I got crank, crack, coke, or just a little smoke for your buzzing pleasure."

"No, I'm cool, thanks," Justin said. It was pathetic that someone from his school was hanging out with this low life. He walked away, but he could still hear the dealer and the student talking.

"No. You're definitely not cool," the dealer said under his breath.

"Spider," the student said to the dealer, "they say he's great at Battle Ultimo."

"You and your stupid ass friends," Spider snarled. "You wouldn't know a great player if he bit you in the ass."

Justin turned to face them. Spider couldn't have been more than seventeen years old, but there was a darkness about him that Justin had never seen in a teenager. Spider stared Justin down as he handed the kid a baggie with something white in it.

"Then why are you so interested in him?" the boy asked.

"I want to get to know my enemy before I play him."

14

There was a slight spring to Robert's step as he walked out of Claiborne's building. He felt stronger and more like himself with a crime on his mind to solve. His pace was quick and his mind raced as he logged block after block without slowing a step.

He turned the corner in his walking daydream and was startled by the sight of the blond curls from the park. It was the same little girl, walking right in front of him. What was she doing here? Where were her parents? She turned to face him and started laughing. "Have any good dreams lately?"

"Who are you?"

She laughed a sinister laugh as a drop of blood formed in her tear duct.

His heart pounded. He turned into the nearest doorway and ordered a double vodka on the rocks.

There he sat, the big brave Robert Morgan, downing his fears in a seedy bar with a flashing neon martini in the window. Yet somehow he liked this place. It was comforting, like a worn out blanket or an old pair of jeans that hadn't been washed in a very long time.

As he ordered his third double vodka, a well dressed man in his late thirties walked into the otherwise empty bar. Robert sized him up: an investment banker stopping to take a little pressure off the day. He ordered a virgin strawberry daiquiri.

"Wuss," Robert mumbled under his breath.

"Excuse me," the man said. "Did you say something to me?"

"No, sorry. I was just finding myself amusing."

Robert watched for awhile as the man sipped his drink and finally he said, "Let me ask you a question. Why do you come to a bar and not drink?"

"This used to be my favorite place," the man said, as he took a long last gulp. "I like to stop in every now and then. It reminds me of where I've been." He put his glass down and headed for the door. Just before he walked through, he turned to face Robert.

"You got to fight the demon, man. You got to fight the demon, any way you can."

15

"Mother, if you're absolutely sure you want to go through with this," Helene said in a disapproving tone, "then let's at least let Dr. Cohen in on it."

The sound of her voice made Claire bristle.

"I already told you. This is very experimental, and he's not licensed to practice in this country. Someone will come after him."

Claire stared out the window, into the bleak afternoon. Ominous looking clouds were gathering overhead as a few rain drops splattered on her window sill. She was wondering if Justin was stuck in the rain somewhere, unable to get a cab, when something made her look over at the door of her room.

From the moment she turned, perhaps even before, she knew it was Dr. Smith Viviee. He was exactly as Claire had pictured him: tall, stately, and larger than life. A dense lock of dark brown hair fell over one side of his forehead. He was haloed, as she looked up from her bed, by the overhead fluorescent lighting. She realized she couldn't be sure what color his eyes were. They seemed soft and kind, yet there was great depth in them, as if they might probe directly to her soul. He was familiar in a way she couldn't place. Perhaps she had dreamt of him.

Claire felt his energy before he even touched her. It was like a wave of electricity that made her shudder and surrender. Her white knight had arrived and she believed in him.

He took her hand and gently caressed it between his palms. "It's going to be all right," he said. "I've come to wipe all your tears away."

"Oh, Dr. Viviee, I'm so happy to see you," Claire said, bursting into sobs.

Her breath seemed to leave her for a moment.

His words were soothing and hypnotic. "It's going to be okay, Claire. It's all going to be okay."

As he held her with his left hand, he removed his right hand and opened the drawer to the nightstand. He picked up the bible sitting on top of it, placed it in the drawer, and closed it.

16

There were tears in Helene's eyes. Watching her mother die was the most difficult thing that could have happened to her. Sure, they had had their differences over the years — they still did. But her love for this woman was the only pure love she had ever felt, other than for Justin. She felt as if the life was being squeezed out of her. There were so many things she wanted to say, but she could only cry silently, watching the tears in her mother's eyes.

She had quickly regained her composure when the doctor walked in. She stood silently behind him. After a time, he turned to her, as if he had just sensed her presence.

"Your mother is going to be fine," he said. "I know you're apprehensive, but there's no need to worry. She's going to be fine. I'm going to explain to you how this works, and I want you to feel free to ask me any questions you would like to ask."

"I thought you were Chinese," Helene blurted out, but his Anglo appearance and accent were just a part of her surprise. He looked more like an artist than a doctor. His gentleness didn't quite fit with his swarthy look. He was unkempt in a way that indicated he was too busy to worry about appearances, yet he was well dressed, in a traditional black silk jacquard Chinese jacket with a mandarin collar and dragon motif. Bits of the red silk lining were visible when he moved, or when he pushed his jacket back to place his hands on his hips in a gesture of evaluation. He wasn't classically handsome, but for a moment Helene thought he was very appealing — seductive in power, real or imagined — the power of life itself.

He said, "I bring you life and you're so concerned with appearances."

"I'm just surprised," Helene said.

"I know. You've seen it all. You categorize quickly. I'm sure that serves you well in your business, but one must always be mindful of the unexpected."

"So, you're not Chinese? You're what, American?"

"My father was American, of European dissent. I have many bloods in me. He was a noted physician who chose to do his research in China. I was raised there, in English, French, and Italian schools." He walked to the foot of the bed. "Which is why, as you're about to ask, I have no accent.

"Now, let me explain to you how the process works."

39

He looked intently down at Claire. "I will give you a simple injection," he said. "You will sleep off and on for the remainder of the day and night. If anyone disturbs you, you must tell them you just want to rest. No one should be suspicious of that. While you rest, your body will begin to heal itself. I understand you are scheduled to go home tomorrow. Is that correct?"

"Yes, tomorrow afternoon."

"You'll be fine to go home. In fact, I prefer it. When you are there, I want you to rest as much as possible. By tomorrow evening you'll have a bit more energy and, again, get a good night's sleep. The body repairs itself best during sleep. I want you to sleep as much as you can for at least a week, maybe two. These pills will help you with that." He handed her a small plastic bottle. "Once you've been treated, sleeping is the most important thing you can do."

"Yes, I've heard that. Do I have to *do* anything?"

"Nothing special. But remember what I told you on the phone, Claire. Don't fight it. Work with it. The technology needs your help — to help you heal yourself."

"Technology?" Helene said.

"Yes. It *is* technology. I don't use pharmaceuticals."

"As in what, computers?" she asked, suddenly noticing the legal sized briefcase he had placed at the end of the bed.

"Specifically, nanotechnology. A very small computer chip. It will work with Claire's body to root out the cancerous cells and destroy them; then it will impel the body's healthy reproduction of new cells."

"It sounds so simple when you put it that way, doctor," Helene said.

"The process *is* simple. It's the technology that's complicated. My father spent his lifetime and I am spending mine creating this miracle of modern science. We've reduced it all to a size so small that I can inject the computer chip into your spinal fluid and just let it do its job. I monitor your progress with a small computer, and within no time, Claire, you'll be feeling like yourself again."

"You're telling me that's it?" Helene said abruptly. "It can't be *that* simple."

"You can choose to believe whatever you want, Ms. Cummings. Success is not always achieved by fighting. In this case, it's achieved by surrender."

"That's exactly what I was thinking after we spoke," Claire said. "But I want to do more. I want to help."

"The most important thing for you to do is rest and relax into it. Let the technology do its job. There's a natural tendency for the body and mind to fight anything foreign that's introduced." He took a step back from the bed and gave Claire's hand a quick squeeze. *"Don't fight it,"* he said emphatically. "Shall we get started? I don't have much time."

"No," Helene said suddenly. "We need to wait for my son." She felt out of control in the presence of this authoritative man. "What if there's a problem? There are problems sometimes, aren't there? And how will we find you if there are?"

"You will have a number where you can find me 24 hours a day, no matter where I am," he said. He pulled a business card from the side pocket of his pants and handed it smoothly to Helene.

"What are the risks?" Helene asked. "The side effects? There must be risks. There are always side effects."

"Such little faith," he said in a tone that indicated he was beginning to lose his patience. "The risks are almost nonexistent, but nothing comes completely without them. There is a small minority of people who reject the technology. We believe it is a *very* small minority and we don't know why it happens."

"And what happens?" Claire asked.

"It's only happened once, but within a few days of getting the injection, the patient's body absorbed the chip and she died."

"It killed the patient?" Helene said. Here was the fly in the ointment. She knew there had to be one.

"No. The cancer killed the patient. The technology may have sped up the process. We simply don't know." Viviee took a breath, paused for a moment, and then softened. "They should have explained this to you on the phone, Claire. Perhaps it's best if you wait. I had been led to believe you were ready, but perhaps you need to spend more time thinking this over and talking it over with your family." He took Claire's hand again. "Please, I only want what's best for you," he said.

"Bring it on," Claire said. "Don't mind my daughter. She's a journalist. It's her way of doing things. Can we just wait until my grandson gets here?"

"When is he due?"

"He should have been here a half hour ago. I'm sure he's stuck in traffic, with the rain and all. You can never get a cab in New York in the rain."

"Let me get things set up and we'll see if he comes in time. I have an appointment downtown in 45 minutes. It's urgent I be there on time."

Helene didn't believe him.

17

A yellow taxi pulled up to the curb on First Avenue just as the rain drops turned to a significant downpour, but it was obvious traffic was going nowhere. There were protestors at the United Nations and 50th Street was closed down to shuttle dignitaries from the Waldorf to the UN. If the president was leaving now, Justin was screwed. His only chance to make it to the hospital on time, was on foot.

Justin ran for thirty long blocks in the rain. In the process he shed his tie and blazer and stuffed them into his backpack. What remained on his body was soaking wet. His shirt tails flapped against his hips as he ran into the hospital entrance.

"I've got to get to Grams right away," he said, as the security guard waved him through.

"Slow down," the guard yelled. "No running allowed."

Justin abruptly took his pace down to a brisk walk through the corridor and onto the stairway. He knew the hospital well by now and didn't even bother to check for the deadly slow elevator. He ran two steps at a time to the fourth floor and flung the door open. Drops of water flew off him.

Grams' room was in his line of sight when he took a hard turn. He felt the water sloshing in his rain soaked shoe as he skidded down to his knees in a small puddle of his own creation. He struggled to stand up, but the wet rubber of his sole wouldn't grip the polished floor. He lost his footing and slipped back down hard. He could hear a gurney rapidly rolling toward him. The attendant was running.

"Code blue!" the man yelled.

Justin wriggled and pushed but he couldn't muster the ability to move out of the way.

The bottom shelf of the gurney rattled and clanged until the thin steel shelf fell partially to the floor, skidding and bouncing as a spark flew in the air. Still, the attendant ran, shouting "code blue, code blue," as the sharp steel edge honed even sharper dragging along the floor — like a three foot long razor. It headed directly for Justin.

"Stop!" he screamed, but he was inaudible over the clanging metal.

Suddenly a bare foot appeared between him and the gurney. Before he could look to see whom it belonged to, the foot was gone, the shelf dropped off and the gurney slammed into his left shin.

He cried out in pain, grasping his leg as he fell flat on his back.

18

"What was that?" Claire said. "There was some kind of commotion out in the hall."

"This is the cancer ward," Dr. Viviee said. He walked over and shut the door to her room. "I think we best get started."

"Can't we just wait a little longer," Claire pleaded.

"I'm sorry," Dr. Viviee said. "I don't want to rush you, but I'm going to have to go. If you're not ready yet, you should take all the time you need to talk this over with your grandson and your daughter. Call me when you're ready, and I can see you on my next trip."

"Your next trip? What about tomorrow?"

"I have another patient waiting in Switzerland. If I'm not treating you I'll be treating him. But I'll be back in a few months and we can talk further then."

"A few months? I may not be alive in a few months."

"That's true," Dr. Viviee said. "Once I start treating someone I have to stay to monitor their progress. You wouldn't want me to just jet off to some far corner of the world after giving you the injection, now would you? So, I'm sorry, Claire. My nanochip is in very great demand. I want to help you, I truly do. There is so little time for so many people, and I need to move forward with this technology in a way that will establish this cure beyond a doubt, so we can save the world from this horrible disease."

19

Two orderlies put Justin on a gurney and wheeled him in the opposite direction from where he wanted to go.

"It's hospital policy," Nurse Johnson — according to her name tag — said firmly. "I can't let you move from here. We've got to make sure there are no broken bones. We don't want a lawsuit on our hands."

Justin was angered by his own stupidity. Why hadn't he slowed down? If he had worn his sneakers this wouldn't have happened.

"You're one lucky guy," an orderly said. "I don't want to think of what would have happened if that shelf hadn't fallen off at the last second."

"Where's the guy with the bare feet?" Justin said, glancing down at the footwear of the orderlies.

"There better not be anyone walking around this hospital with bare feet," Nurse Johnson said. "That's totally against policy. What did he look like?"

"I don't know. I didn't see him." The nurse walked alongside as they headed toward the emergency room.

"Will you please go tell my grandmother and my mother what happened? They're right down the hall in 420. They're waiting for me. Just let them know I'm here. It's important."

"Of course, I will," said Nurse Johnson. "Does your mom have your insurance information?"

45

20

Dr. Viviee unlocked the top two combination locks on his black briefcase, flipped open the latch, and used a key he kept in his pocket to open a third interior lock.

"Don't you need her to sign papers?" Helene asked.

"That won't be necessary. All our research information is kept right in here." He pulled out a small black computer that looked like an ordinary laptop and walked with it under his arm to the side of Claire's bed. He placed it on the nightstand and typed in a few commands.

"But aren't you afraid of being sued?"

"No, I am not. I know you don't understand such things in this country, but I am a healer. I have come to give life where it is fading away. It is my destiny and I will not run from it. Whatever happens, happens. There's no need to protect yourself when you are doing the good work. Can you see that?"

Sure, if anything goes wrong you'll just head back to China. "I suppose," she said.

"Please try. Now, Claire, if you are ready, I would like to ask Helene to wait outside the room. This won't take more than a minute."

"I'd like to stay here," Helene said.

"I need someone to make sure no one else enters the room. Please, Ms. Cummings, I'll call you in a moment."

"Well, what am I supposed to tell them, if someone comes?"

"Just that she's speaking privately with an old friend. You'll see. It will be fine."

Helene hesitated but Claire's eyes burned.

"I'm fine Helene. I trust him completely. Please do it."

Helene stepped outside the door. Tears once again began to flow. This was the one person she had known longer than any other — she felt a strange, powerful connection to the woman who had given her life, and now it might all be over. She had thought about her mother's death many times in the past several weeks, even fantasized about how she would handle it and what kind of tribute she would give, but the reality was so much harsher than even the most dire prophecy. She wanted to scream and run back in and hug her and tell her how much she loved her. Her heart raced. She almost said a prayer. Then she saw a nurse fast approaching.

"Oh, shit! Just what I need." But before she could even begin to put the words for her lie together, a doctor stepped forward from the nurse's station and placed his arms around the nurse. "Just the person I've been looking for," he said, and the two disappeared into a room.

21

The injection stung for a moment, then became an intense burn that moved up from the base of her spinal column. Claire thought about the last time she had a needle there, the only time. It was for the epidural when she was giving birth. How appropriate that both times would be so intricately entwined with new life.

The injection of the nanochip didn't affect the hospital medical equipment she was hooked up to in any noticeable way. But she felt a distinct and almost uncontrollable urge to push it out, like when she stood on the edge of a balcony and feared she would jump. Then she heard Viviee's voice.

"Just relax," he said softly. "Just relax into it. Everything is going to be fine."

"But I'm feeling…" She began to hyperventilate.

"I know. It's okay. Just look into my eyes and concentrate on relaxing. Think about all the things you will now be alive to do. And sleep. Think about sleeping."

She became peaceful and her eyes slowly closed. He gently ran his hand from the top of her forehead, over her nose and her lips, down between her breasts and lower, past her belly button. She felt that with a motion of his hand he had removed everything that had been stored within her long ago.

He put away the hypodermic needle and the computer and opened the door.

"She'll need her rest now," Claire could hear him say. "I'll be around to see her soon. If there are any problems, call me. You can reach me any time. Trust me," he said. "She's going to be fine."

22

The moment Robert walked through the lobby of the Manhattan Medical Center he wanted to turn around and leave, but the doctor promised to have Robert in and out of the office quickly, so Robert promised to show up. He had little patience for physicians and even less for his own physical weaknesses. But Dr. Jerry Brandt was among the most respected cardiologists in Manhattan, as well as a social friend. Though Robert believed taking drugs for depression was for the weak-minded, he had let Brandt convince him to give it a try. It seemed the whole world was using them, and Brandt's penchant for prescribing a particular brand that also killed the appetite had made him the elite's preferred doctor. Robert hated being so common.

Robert didn't have a psychiatrist; he didn't need one. But there was a deep feeling of fear growing in the core of his being, and he had to find a way to stop it before it got out of control.

"Robert," Dr. Brandt said, entering the examination room, "Tell me what's going on." He moved Robert's open shirt to the side and placed the cold stethoscope on his bare chest.

"Hey doc, a little more foreplay is in order."

Brandt just laughed. "Breathe deep."

"I have this recurring dream about a dragon with a bunch of heads eating people. I always wake up before it eats me. I had the dream one day in the park and when I woke up this little blond girl was there. Then I was coming out of a crime scene today..."

"Yes, one of the nurses said she saw you on the news," the doctor interrupted.

"....and I see the girl again. First she says 'He's coming.'"

"Who's coming?"

"How the hell am I supposed to know? But it didn't sound like anyone you'd want to meet. And then she asks me if I had any good dreams."

"Your heart rate is fine — a little agitated, but fine." He tapped twice on Robert's chest. "The same kid?" he asked.

"Yes."

"So, she lives in the neighborhood?"

"She was too young to be walking around alone."

"How old?"

"Six, seven, eight. I don't know."

"First of all, Robert," Brandt said, taking a seat in his desk chair, "you're not responsible for her parents' neglect. Secondly, everybody has nightmares and sometimes they're recurrent. You've been through a lot. Bad dreams are to be expected. Think of the dragon as the enemy. He devours whatever he can. Pretty common imagery, actually. Is that all that's bothering you?"

Robert imagined the dream again. There was the dragon. It went for a bite of an old lady. There was a flash of black and the scene momentarily froze, like a glitch on a video tape. It grabbed her in its mouth and chopped down hard, sending blood gushing through the streets.

"It's really more about the girl. Something isn't right. I feel like I'm ready for the loony bin."

"You think you're being stalked by an eight year old? Are you taking the medication?"

"No."

"No? Why didn't you tell me?"

"Because you would have told me to keep taking it."

"When did you stop?"

"A couple days ago."

"You're not self-medicating are you?"

"What's that supposed to mean?"

"Are you drinking?"

Robert hemmed and hawed a bit. Then he said, "Not much."

"Why did you stop the antidepressant?"

"I was tired, out of it, and had no interest in sex. Do you need more reasons? The whole thing sucked."

"So, you just stopped cold turkey? Robert, I told you, you can't do that."

"When I've had enough, I've had enough."

"Well, that's your problem," the doctor said.

"Damn right that's my problem."

"No, I mean coming off it so quickly, that's the problem. Anti-depressants aren't made to be withdrawn all at once. They take time to build up in your system and they take time to come out. Doing what you did can cause all kinds of problems, including hallucinations in a small number of people. As the serotonin levels change in your brain it can also cause nightmares. Why don't you just relax here overnight, so I can keep an eye on you?"

"In the hospital? Not a chance."

"We're just going to observe you."

"There isn't a hospital built that can just observe you. When you're around they find shit to do to you." He buttoned up his shirt.

"You're leaving against my advice."

"That's a first," he said sarcastically.

"Can you go straight home and rest?"

"Sure," Robert said, trying to appear sincere.

"And no drinking, for God's sake. Give your liver a rest too."

"Done."

"Call me immediately if anything seems strange," Brandt said. "You have my cell."

"What could possibly seem strange in Manhattan?"

23

Nurse Johnson arrived at Claire's room disheveled and brushing her hair back. She informed Helene that her son had been in a minor accident with a gurney. Claire was sound asleep, tossing and turning. She moaned softly, as if having a nightmare. Helene thought about waking her but decided against it. Instead, she ran to see Justin.

He looked to be in pain, but not agony.

"He's going to be fine," Dr. Jane Flemming said. She placed four x-rays of Justin's right ankle, one after another, onto the lighted board. "There's no fracture, just a bad sprain with some soft tissue swelling. We can do an MRI if you have the time — they're pretty backed up in there right now. Either way, the treatment's the same."

"What's the treatment?" Helene said.

"Think RICE, rest, ice, compression and elevation. Keep your leg up tonight," she said turning to Justin, "with some ice on the ankle. I'll give you a prescription for an anti-inflammatory and you should be fine. You're going to need to take it easy for a couple of days; no running, playing sports, or anything like that."

Justin reluctantly nodded.

"It's only for a few days," the doctor said. "We don't want it to get worse."

A nurse pushed Justin down the hall in a wheelchair, in accordance with hospital policy.

"I want to see Grams," he said to Helene.

"She's sleeping and isn't supposed to be disturbed."

"What do you mean? What's going on?"

"I'll explain it to you on the way home."

As they headed to the exit, Helene recognized Robert Morgan's unmistakable baritone chastising a nurse. It was a voice she hadn't heard in person, in years.

"Come this way," she said, moving in the direction of the voice.

"I'm just fine, nurse," Robert was saying. "It's a pleasure to do business in this haven of medical miracles, as always, but I'm quite capable of getting myself into a cab."

Through a half open doorway, she caught the smallest glimpse of his profile.

"Robert?" she called out. "Robert, is that you?"

He turned. "Helene Cummings," he said in a surprised tone. "Well, I'll be damned," he said walking toward her.

They had known each other from when Helene was anchoring the local news and Robert was the Chief of Police. In addition to the professional association she considered him a social friend.

"What are you doing here?" She walked closer, checking out his every detail. His shoulders were wide and strong; his stomach was trim for a man his age; and his face was the face of a weathered young boy. His appearance was improved by the extra gray lately added to his thick hair.

They met in the middle of the hall. He seemed embarrassed.

"I had a doctor's appointment — routine stuff. I can see what you're doing here," he said referring to Justin. He reached over, took Helene by the shoulders and kissed her cheek. "You look beautiful, as always. You haven't changed a bit."

"Thanks." Helene felt a spark of attraction. "Meet my son, Justin. Actually we're here visiting my mother. Justin just happened to get hurt along the way."

Robert reached out and they shook hands.

"What happened?" Robert said.

"I slipped. It's just a sprain," Justin said.

Robert addressed a smile to Helene that seemed boyish, as if he wanted her approval. She felt a pleasant chill run up her spine.

"So, you're seeing Dr. Brandt, are you?" Helene said knowingly.

"We go way back."

"He's quite popular now."

"And so are you," Robert said. "I see you on TV all the time."

"And you — aren't you handling security for the UN talks?"

"My company's handling special security for the city for the duration of the meetings. We've been working with police and Homeland Security for about a year now."

"Why don't you come on my show and tell us about it?"

"I can't talk about an operation in progress," he said.

Helene smiled. "No, but you can talk around it. We need to know what to do in case of an attack. How much plastic and duct tape should I keep in the house?"

Robert laughed. "You're still the 'can't take 'no' for an answer' journalist you always were. I suppose I could do that anytime."

"Good. How's tomorrow?"

24

At 6:00 a.m. light streamed in the side window of the Harlem brownstone; it hit Father David like a beacon from God. He opened his eyes to see his body shrouded in sunlight, particles of dust glimmering in the air.

Holy Hazel, as she'd come to be called, was six feet away in the shadows, still kneeling before her precious Madonna, right where he'd left her the night before. He wanted to hold the old woman in his arms and take the pressure off her feeble knees, but he knew the comfort she was receiving at that moment was much greater than any he could offer.

He got down on his knees next to Hazel in front of the statue. He noticed the glimmer of a tear on her cheek. He quickly looked to the Virgin; a single droplet hit the cloth beneath the statue. He wanted to run to collect the fluid, but before he could move, the statue began to weep. He raised his hands in prayer and closed his eyes. After a few moments he felt a hand on his shoulder and when he looked up, Holy Hazel was standing over him smiling.

It was the first time he had seen her out of her trance. There was a peace in her eyes that belied the years of wear on her skin. Her body was old but her spirit was youthful — mature, but fresh and full of life.

"Thank you for coming, Father David."

"You know my name?"

"The Lord knows the number of hairs on your head and he loves them all."

She threw her head back and laughed.

Father David was struck by her joyfulness.

"What's the matter?" Hazel said. "Are you surprised that I would come from the presence of the Lord and be happy?"

"It's just that…the message, the message you bring is a warning of great danger."

"The danger has been with each of us from the very beginning. And each of us must make a choice from the beginning, what master we will serve. Where your treasure is so is your heart."

"But everyone doesn't come to the Lord from the beginning. Some come to know him much later."

"Don't worry David, those who know the Lord cannot forget him for long."

"So that's it? The end is here? We must take this message to the church."

"The church has messages of its own. My message is for God's people — that the Lord stands ready to make himself known.

"*Your* message, David, is that some things can only be cured with faith and prayer. You must tell God's children that some things can only be cured by prayer. Those who wish to see will understand what is about to happen. Those who cannot bear the choice will be sucked into the devil's deception and go about their lives as it was in the days before the great flood of Noah — in confident ignorance — and then the Lord will come to judge the inhabitants of earth."

And so, Father David began to tell the visitors to Holy Hazel's home, the biblical story of the Apostles trying unsuccessfully to drive a demon from a young boy. Jesus had to personally heal the boy. When they asked him why they could not do it, Jesus told them this kind could only come out by prayer.

Hazel smiled when she heard the story.

"So the end is imminent," Father David said to her.

"What does that mean — imminent? To God a thousand years is like a day and a day like a thousand years."

25

Claire awoke but kept her eyes closed; she was afraid to open them, unsure of where she would find herself or in what condition. So much of what had happened had the quality of a bad dream, yet there was hope in her heart and she wanted to hang onto it.

By the time she opened her eyes it was afternoon. She could hear the muffled sounds of hurried New Yorkers rushing about on their lunch hour and horns blaring on the streets below.

The tube had been removed from her chest. She felt rested and able to move around. She tried slowly to gather her things into her bag.

Helene would be coming to pick her up soon, and she wanted to be ready so she could leave this hell hole as quickly as possible. As she started to make her way to the bathroom, Dr. Steven Cohen paused at her door. He watched quietly for a moment, looking like a beaten man.

"Hi, Steve, come on in," Claire said almost cheerfully, climbing back into bed.

"You sound like you're feeling pretty good today."

"Well, you know, doc, I *am* feeling pretty good today. In fact, I'm breathing a lot better." She took a deep breath to demonstrate. "The pain is almost completely gone."

"There are going to be days like that," he said. "We took a lot of fluid out of your lungs. I'm glad it helped. I'm going to send you home with a prescription for Percocet. You can take two every four to six hours or as you need it, for pain." As he spoke, he slowly reached under her gown.

She braced herself for the familiar chill of the metal stethoscope making contact with her skin, but it never came. In fact, except for the anticipation, she felt nothing at all.

"Yes, I'd say you're breathing much better," he commented, as if *she* didn't know how she *really* felt.

He sat down on the edge of the bed and held her hand, "You've been my patient for many years, Claire. You can still change your mind on the chemo. Just let me know, but I believe you're doing the right thing. Go home and be with your family now. You need each other. I'll stop in and see you as often as I can. I'm in the neighborhood. That's if you don't mind?"

"Of course I don't."

"And I expect you to call me with any problems." He stood up and headed for the door. "You always know where to find me," he added.

"Steve," Claire said. "Do you believe in miracles?"

Dr. Cohen paused for just a moment, his white doctor's coat illuminated by the light from the hallway. "Well, I've never seen one," he said.

Then I guess I'll have to show you one, Claire thought, as she got up from her bed and headed to the bathroom. She lingered at the mirror staring at the face that had betrayed her. She had once been very beautiful, but now dark gray lines had proliferated there, as if someone had taken a number two pencil and cruelly drawn them in.

At first, when she started to lose weight, everyone commented on how great she looked. Finally, those last ten, ugly pounds were gone. But then the weight just kept coming off. She was left with sagging jowls and eyes that had lost their glimmer, like an old dog relegated to a sleepy corner. She splashed water on her face. If she came out of this, she would surely schedule a face lift.

She grabbed a bite of a leftover sandwich from her lingering lunch tray. The coffee was cold, but the juice was drinkable. Suddenly she felt very hungry.

She cleared magazines from the night stand and opened the drawer that was filled with old newspapers and the bible.

Claire paused to look at the small mark that was forming on her right hand. It was almost unnoticeable, if you didn't know to look for it. It was a small circle. Like a fingerprint, it would be unique to her, Dr. Viviee had said. It was so delicate and beautiful, she thought, like a flower blooming, just beginning to open and show its magic.

"The cure," she said to herself softly. "It really is the cure."

She pulled out the drawer and emptied the entire contents into the waste basket. She dumped the cold coffee on top. She went to the bathroom and removed the plastic garbage liner from the basket and proceeded to clear the room of magazines, books, get well cards and flowers. She wanted a fresh start.

26

Helene stood patiently as the audio man attached a wireless microphone to the back of her skirt and ran the wire around the front of her jacket to clip it on her lapel. She had the sensation of a nervous teenager, thinking about seeing Robert again. He had been quite handsome last night, more than she remembered.

"Testing, one, two, three," she said. "Testing, testing, testing."

She walked from her backstage dressing room into the packed studio where she recorded her daily show. Kyle walked briskly beside her jotting notes on a clipboard. Helene didn't think she was walking fast until she noticed Kyle struggling to keep up.

"So where are our tough, edgy shows today?" she said refocusing her thoughts.

Kyle riffled the papers on his clipboard. "Morgan's running late, so we're taping the Apocalyptic Youth show first — you saw the Village Voice article on them. It ties in with the crying Madonna statue in Harlem. Viewers love this metaphysical stuff."

"Why aren't we doing the crying Madonna story?"

"Everybody has the house staked out. The woman's not talking to anyone."

"And the rest of the week?"

"I've pretty much blown up the rest of the week, so there'll be a lot of late adds. I did *salvage,* no pun intended, a segment on some treasure hunters. They picked up the biggest find in the past twenty years off the coast of Bermuda."

"What are they bringing?"

"A lot of coins, some jewelry, stuff like that."

"Think out of the box, Kyle."

Helene sat down in her large round yellow chair. The makeup artist pressed a powder puff to the shine on her forehead and lightly combed the back of her hair.

The stage manager brought her guests on to the stage and seated them across from Helene. She smiled and looked into the faces of people she knew she didn't understand.

Two of them, a man and a woman, looked just like her; sophisticated and well-dressed, albeit a bit younger. The third was different. He was the youngest, an artist dressed all in black. He had long curly brown hair.

"Three, two…" the stage manager cued her from behind a camera.

"They are being called the leaders of the 'Apocalyptic Youth,' a small but noticeable group of young people from the East Village in New York. They believe the end of the world is near.

"These are not the sandwich-board-toting homeless guys on the Bowery. They are polished, savvy New Yorkers — well educated professionals who say the world is full of signs that people are ignoring.

"They join us today to explain their ideas — they hope people will pay attention. John Turner, you're an investment banker on Wall Street. I'm sure a lot of your clients and colleagues are surprised to learn about your views…."

"Some of them may be," John said with a smile. In a navy pinstripe suit and tie, he was the oldest and most conservatively dressed of the group. "But as long as I make everybody money, no one seems to mind."

"Okay. So, what signs are we talking about?"

"We're experiencing devastating earthquakes, catastrophic hurricanes, mudslides, freak snow storms, flooding and tsunamis. There's biological warfare and pandemics. Global warming may already be beyond our ability to stop it. We're told it's a matter of time before some terrorist detonates a nuclear explosive in a populated area. Yet no one seems to see these things as signs we were told to watch out for thousands of years ago."

"And they call us irrational!" the pretty woman next to him said. She was Katrina, a midtown attorney.

"But scientists tell us natural disasters are cyclical," Helene said, "and we just happen to be in the period of increased activity right now."

"The bottom line," the young artist, said, "is that science doesn't know that much."

"Ezra," Helene said, anxiously tapping her Manolo Blahnik-ed foot, "some say science is all we've got."

"Einstein said, 'Science without religion is lame. Religion without science is blind.' Scientists only have theories. That's why we also have the word of God."

"He's rambling," Kyle said in Helene's ear.

"Science has breached the territory of the gods," Katrina said, "and where has it gotten us? We've mapped the human genome. We have cloning, stem cells and smart drugs. Science fiction has become science fact, but the world is more uncertain than ever because science has outpaced the ethical and moral maturity of the scientists."

"Because the priests are all pedophiles," Kyle said.

"Some would say that's because religion, that great moral compass, isn't so moral anymore," Helene said. "Priests are accused of pedophilia, rabbis of blessing contaminated food as kosher; some Islamic clerics are telling people it's okay to kill people with different viewpoints in the name of Allah. There's the televangelist and the prostitute, and the healer who paid people to feign miracles."

"Maybe that's why God seems to be by-passing organized religions," John said. "He's speaking directly to the people through the miracles we see all around us these days."

"But some of the things people take as miracles are questionable," Helene said. "A lot of people are saying, 'Seek and ye shall find'. If you want to see the Virgin Mary in a moldy grilled cheese sandwich or the water stains of a dank underpass, you will. What do you say to them?"

"Look at the crying statute of the Virgin Mary in Harlem," Katrina said.

"Is it crying?" Helene said. She tugged at her short red Chanel jacket and stood to approach the audience. "What do you think?" she said to a man in his forties sitting in the front row.

"I don't know — it might be crying," he said. "It could be a miracle. I believe miracles are possible."

"We have repeatedly invited the woman to bring her statue on this show, and she has repeatedly declined. If this statue is crying real tears, why not come on and let us put the statue in a controlled environment and see if it still cries?"

An elderly woman in the back row stood up. "I've seen it cry," she said, "and they've analyzed the tears — they're real."

"Actually, it's been analyzed as a saline solution similar in composition to human tears," Helene said. "The statue is plaster, right?"

"Ceramic," someone in the audience yelled out.

"De-bunkers of things like this want to remind us that ceramic is a porous material. You have to glaze ceramic to make it impermeable. So, if you scratch off the glaze at the eyes and then fill it with a salty liquid, guess where it will leak?

"But let's talk more about the signs," Helene continued. "You believe the antichrist is, or is about to be, among us, correct?"

"Yes, basically," Katrina said.

"So what about the 666?"

"The 666 is the mark of the beast," John said. "It's also the number of the antichrist's name. He sets himself up to be worshipped and he forces everyone to get his mark."

"And what or who is the 666?"

"There are some theories," John said, "but we don't believe the antichrist has made himself known yet. There are many signs and symbols that have meanings beyond what is commonly known.

"The Rx we use to denote prescriptions comes from the Egyptian Eye of Horus. The gesture with the forefinger and the pinky we commonly see used by music stars symbolizes the devil's horns, but to most kids it's just a cool thing to do. Italians used it to ward off the evil eye. Versions of crosses, the Star of David, a lot of things that mean one thing to us, have other meanings for people involved in the occult.

"So, the 666 could turn out to be anything. It all depends on how you look at it," he said.

"Cut to the chase," Kyle said into her earpiece.

"Some would say everything we're talking about is just a matter of viewpoint, including God," Helene said. "They want to know; are we God's creation or is he ours?

"It's been suggested that most of us are just too vain to ever think we will simply cease to exist, so our brains are hard-wired to look for God in the hopes that through God we can live forever. Some people believe if we ever figure out how to live forever on our own, we won't need to look for God anymore.

"In other words, man is on an eternal quest for immortality and when he finds it, the search for God becomes irrelevant."

As Helene spoke her closing line to throw to a commercial, Ezra interrupted. "Maybe you're right. The bible says, in the end days men will seek death, but death will elude them. So, maybe we'll find immortality after all."

27

Robert sat motionless at his computer screen staring at the images from the security camera in Claiborne's building, but he was thinking about Helene. There were four camera shots on the screen with two views each of the front and back entrances to the building. He refocused his thoughts. For some reason, he wanted to work today. He had fast forwarded through the images so many times he knew the shots by heart, but on the last pass through something caught his eye. There was a flash. It was fast, but he was sure it was there. He rewound the image and advanced it frame by frame.

"Aha! There it is," he yelled, banging his hand down on the desk. "I knew it. Damn it, I knew it!" A frame of black covered the camera to the back door at exactly 8:58 p.m. It was only a millisecond long, but it was there. In real time it appeared as an almost unnoticeable flash of black on the screen. He checked the time code on the bottom of the frame. It went from 8:58:05 to 8:58:20. Fifteen seconds were unaccounted for. The camera was off for 15 seconds.

He rang the Chief.

"Are you sure about this?" the Chief said. "We know there was a power surge about that time, but the security company assured us the battery backup on the camera was on.

"I'm sure they did, but it didn't go on," Robert said. "The question is why."

"My men checked the battery backup on the cameras this afternoon, and everything was working fine. Five seconds longer would have triggered an alarm."

"So, that means whoever turned them off knew exactly when to turn them back on."

"Shit!" the Chief yelled. "Anyone could have gotten in unnoticed."

"Yeah, but not everyone could have known how to turn that camera off."

"I had someone check the tape," the Chief said. "What made you check the tape *that* closely?"

"It reminded me of a dream," Robert said.

"Sure, buddy," the Chief said with a laugh. "You and your fucking instincts."

28

Justin had sat through English Lit, Chem, and Psychology without hearing a single word. He took meticulous notes on nothing, in the form of doodles and swirls. He anxiously awaited Math.

He couldn't wait to see Madeline. She was all he thought about. It took his mind off the dull pain in his ankle. It was as if he had never hurt it at all. When he did see Madeline he felt a rush of emotion somewhere between exhilaration and fear. Even the mundane navy blazer and plaid school skirt looked beautiful on her. Now all he had to do was be cool.

"Hey, Madeline," Justin said with a nod as he walked past her seat. "We're on for the party tonight, right?"

"Sure. How's your Grams?"

"She's coming home tonight. I really want to see her. Would you have dinner with us at my house before the party?"

"Good afternoon class," the teacher said. "Please open your books to page 217."

Justin did exactly as he was told with no clowning around, jokes or horseplay. He listened intently the entire class, exchanging an occasional smile with Madeline, but being sure to grasp the magnitude of the academics being put forth that day. This was no longer a class he could afford to blow off. Maybe it was competition with the smartest girl in school or maybe he had just found someone whose opinion he really valued. In any event, he didn't want Madeline to think he wasn't bright enough for her. He would try harder at math.

Their assignment was to write a paper about an imaginary universe as seen through quantum physics and string theory. *Oh, great,* he thought. This was way out of his league. Quantum physics was some ethereal mathematical bullshit that even Einstein didn't truly understand. And string theory was just a theory — no one understood it and no one could prove it. Some guy just invented it to make sense of other stuff that didn't make sense. He was doomed! And judging by the groans coming from the class, he wasn't the only one.

"All right, class," Mr. Zelasco said, "this has the potential to be a fun assignment."

"Fun? I'd rather have brain surgery!" Jimmy yelled.

64

"Would it help if we went over some of the basics?" Mr. Zelasco asked.

"Yes!" was the resounding response.

"Okay, let's start with why this stuff is important. In the universe, we have rules that explain how big things, like planets and galaxies and stars, behave. That's Albert Einstein's general relativity — gravity, velocity, all that kind of stuff. We can prove it works." He grabbed an apple from his desk and tossed it into the air. "How do we know?"

"Isaac Newton got hit with the apple so we know gravity exits," Janice in the front row said.

"Good. We also have a rule for really small things like molecules and atoms, and the even smaller things; the subatomic particles like electrons and quarks and gluons. That's called quantum physics — it is, very simply, the science of the incredibly small.

"This quantum world is very strange. When we try to watch it, it changes. Simply *observing* it makes it act differently. This world is filled with organized chaos and quantum probabilities where anything can happen. We use this to explain black holes. We don't necessarily know why, but we know it's all true mathematically.

"The problem is, these two rules — general relatively and quantum physics — don't work together. So, either the world has two very different rules running things — one for big and one for small — or the rules are wrong on some level. Einstein spent much of his life trying to figure out how to make these two sets of rules work together, but he couldn't.

Mr. Zelasco set the apple down on Madeline's desk, walked to the smart board, and started squiggling circles with his finger.

"The best theory we have today for unifying the universe — the closest thing to a unified field theory — is string theory, or M theory as it's called sometimes. It says, very simply, that the world at its smallest level is made up of vibrating strings, like tiny rubber bands. They are microscopically tiny loops that dance and move and resonate like the strings on a violin. In a universe of vibrating strings, relativity and quantum physics work together. Hence, it is sometimes called the Theory of Everything."

Grams believed that everything had a good or bad vibration, even things like cell phones, movies, and different kinds of music. Justin didn't know if that was the same thing.

"Now here's where it all gets interesting," the teacher said. "If string theory is correct, the mathematical equations that are used require — let me repeat that: *require* — multiple dimensions — no less than ten.

"Now, what did I just say?"

Madeline raised her hand.

"Yes, Madeline."

"You said that everything is made up of tiny vibrating strings that operate in at least ten dimensions."

"Good," Mr. Zelasco said. "Now, how many dimensions are we aware of?"

"Three," Madeline responded.

"Correct."

"Give me an example of something that's two dimensional."

"A square."

"And three dimensional?"

"A cube."

"Give me an example of something that's four-dimensional?"

The class was quiet.

"Having trouble?" Mr. Zelaso said. "Of course you are. Our brains are not equipped to think in four dimensions. Some people believe we can only see what we're taught to see. Those other dimensions are right in front of us, but our brains are not capable of seeing them.

"What I'm asking you to do is write a paper describing life in a world that consists of at least one other dimension."

"So it's a world that exists on a vibrational level?" Janice asked.

"Perhaps all worlds exist on a vibrational level," Mr. Zelasco replied.

"It sounds like science fiction," Tom said.

"Exactly. I want you to write a fictionalized version of this particular science. In quantum physics, if I bump into this smart board long enough, I will eventually move through it. Now, it may take me more tries than I have in a lifetime, but mathematically I will move through it. I want you to make the mental move through this smart board and bring me back a new dimension. And the best part is — he touched the apple on Madeline's desk — "you get to pick a partner to work with." He tossed the apple to Justin, who reflexively snatched it in his right hand.

29

"We're two minutes away, Helene," the stage manager said, as Kyle walked off the set and into the control room.

Helene took her seat across from Robert Morgan. She settled in with a comfortable smile.

"Excuse me, Mr. Morgan," the audio man said. "Let me just run this wire behind your jacket and I'll clip the microphone right here on your tie."

Robert moved to accommodate him.

"What's the latest on the Claiborne murder investigation?" Helene said.

"You know I can't talk about that. It's a secret," he said with smile.

"There are no secrets in this city, Robert. So, who do you think did it?"

"Off the record?" he asked.

"Of course," she replied.

"Whoever did it must have had help inside the building."

"Wait, hold the thought," Helene said. She adjusted herself in the chair, crossed her legs, and gave a little tug at her jacket.

"Helene," Kyle said abruptly into her earpiece, "the network just called and said there's a shit load of cops *and* Homeland Security at the North Shore water treatment plant. They're desperate to get a hold of Morgan."

"How do you want to handle this?"

"Let's go as scripted for now, but keep in mind the show airs in a couple of hours. We may need to do it again, live. See if Morgan can stay."

She turned to Robert. "What are you doing tonight?"

"Are you asking me to dinner?" He smiled.

"There may be a terrorist threat at one of the water treatment plants. It's happening right now."

Robert seemed genuinely surprised and disappointed. "How much time do we have?"

"One minute to air," the stage manager said.

Robert moved into action like a tiger ready to strike his prey. His motions were quick and decisive. With barely a greeting to the person on the other end of his cell phone, he was collecting information.

He was confident and strong, like when he was Chief. And he was very, very handsome.

Helene loved the adrenaline kick of breaking news; perhaps that's what made him seem so sexy. The lines around his eyes were deeper now, the tan still there, and it looked like his hair had gone gray overnight. He was rugged in a Western hero sort of way, yet completely comfortable all dressed up in a suit and tie.

"Out in ten, nine, eight..." the stage manager said.

"I'm getting ready to go on the air, can I go with that?" Robert said into the phone. He gave a smile and an affirmative nod to Helene.

Her eyes widened. He was teasing her. She took a deep breathe to collect her thoughts.

"I'm efforting more info," Kyle said in her ear.

"I'll ad-lib," she said into the microphone.

"...four, three, two..." the stage manager said. He waved his right arm in a whooshing motion beneath the camera to indicate they were on.

"Hello, everyone. As we host one of the most important meetings of the United Nations in years, Americans everywhere are on heightened alert for a terrorist strike. Already today we've heard of a possible attempt at one of the largest water treatment plants serving New York.

"One man is under arrest," Kyle said in her ear.

"A suspect is in custody and authorities are trying to sort out exactly what happened.

"The Department of Homeland Security has been developing the plan to keep the city safe during these meetings for close to a year now, and it has been doing so with the help of the New York City Police Department and a private firm, Assurance Security. We are fortunate to have the head of Assurance, and the former New York City Chief of Police, Robert Morgan, with us today" she said.

30

The sound of the applause was louder than Robert had anticipated. He watched Helene speak with poise and authority. He knew the suspense was killing her.

"Is this our worst nightmare? Is our drinking supply in danger?"

"In this instance we're not worried about contamination of the drinking supply," Robert said with great confidence. "North Shore is primarily a waste water treatment plant. The real concern is how this man, who had no business being in the plant, gained access, and what his intentions were. That's going to take some time to ascertain and security at all the water treatment facilities in the area is being beefed up as we speak."

"They're putting the plant on lockdown," Kyle said to Helene.

"Why are they putting North Shore on lockdown?" Helene asked.

"That's routine under the current security threat. We don't want to take any chances."

"How scared should we be?"

"Well, Helene, you're asking the question as if fear were a necessary component of our daily lives…."

He noticed his cell phone vibrating on the table. Helene saw it too. She began to talk about various safety precautions the average person could take, as the director put up a full screen listing safety supplies: bottled water, duct tape, plastic, first aid kits, etc. Robert took the cue and quickly read a text message. He taunted Helene with a raised eyebrow.

"Terrorism is psychological warfare as much as it is anything physical," he said.

She looked disappointed, as if she had expected him to offer at least a veiled clue as to the message on his phone. The stage manager held up a sign indicating there were two minutes left in the segment, but Helene cut it short and threw to a commercial break.

"Well?" she said.

Robert laughed. "You have no patience, do you?"

"No, I don't. Now what's going on?"

"Everything is back to normal. There was never a serious threat and we won't be hearing about the suspect for some time, so we can go with the rest of the show."

69

"Did you hear that, Kyle?" she said.

"Got it. Thanks. We're way ahead of everybody on this one," he said.

Robert watched Helene's face and body relax as if she had just been relieved of some great burden. They continued with the show, demonstrating how to properly seal off a window on a roll-away wall.

As they wrapped up the segment she extended her hand and reached over to kiss him on the cheek.

"Now how about dinner?" he whispered in her ear.

"Nice team work," Kyle said into her IFB. "And he's cute."

"Actually my mother is coming home from the hospital tonight and I really need to be with her."

"Oh," Robert said looking down.

"But why don't you come for dinner at my house? I'd love to see you. Besides, they're having some security issues at my son's school…."

"I've heard."

"You have?"

"There are no secrets in this town, Helene."

31

Justin walked into the marble lobby of his apartment building filled, as usual, with a lavish display of fresh cut flowers that changed weekly. Orchids, roses, Birds of Paradise; the best and the most expensive, probably flown in from distant corners of the world.

"Welcome home, sir," the doorman called out from behind his rostrum. "I have a delivery for your mom in the back. Do you want to take it up with you?"

"Sure," Justin said.

He watched Max pull a key ring from a pants pocket out of sight beneath the overhang of his belly. He picked out a key and unlocked the delivery room door. Max was an average sized man with an oversized gut. He had a cheerful smile and large round eyes that on some days perfectly matched the gray in his uniform. A lock of thinning gray hair fell in his eyes as he bent forward, trying to find the slot where he could slip the keys back into his pocket. He missed, and they dropped to the ground.

Justin reached for the keys and handed them to Max in exchange for his mother's dry cleaning.

"Wow, that's an awfully nice ring to carry on your key chain, Max."

"Thanks, Justin. It's been there so long I can't bring myself to take it off. It was my wife's wedding ring. She asked me to put it with my keys so it wouldn't get lost when she went into the hospital for surgery."

"Is she okay?"

"I like to think so. She died at the hospital."

"Oh. I'm sorry Max. I didn't mean…"

"It's not a problem, Justin. I keep the ring there to remember her by. Not that I'd ever forget her. It's just sentimental. Stupid I guess."

"I don't think it's stupid. My mom would say it's sweet."

Justin smiled. It was nice to learn something new about a man he'd known his whole life, but never really knew. He waited for the elevator that took him to the private entrance of his eleventh floor apartment.

With four bedrooms, a den, and a maid's room, it was small by lavish New York standards, huge by the standards of the average New Yorker. The living room was expansive and too fancy for Justin's liking. He didn't spend much time on the pastel Persian carpet or the pink silk sofas and chairs decorated with tassels and fringe.

Natasha sat at the elevator waiting for him, as she always did. As soon as Natasha saw him, she leapt to her short little legs and furiously wagged her tail, waiting for his greeting. He walked over, picked her up, and held her tight while she squirmed and wriggled and tried to lick his face.

"Natasha, guess who's coming home? Grams! I know that will make you happy."

Natasha followed him into the kitchen. A freshly prepared BLT on a toasted bagel was waiting for him on a white plate, with a white linen, monogrammed napkin, on the white marble countertop of the island. He removed an errant piece of bacon from the sandwich and tossed it to the dog, who snapped it up long before it hit the chocolate brown wood floor. Everything else in the room was white and stainless steel.

Justin tossed the napkin to the sink, grabbed a paper towel from the rack, held the sandwich in his mouth, and spun the crystal ball on the overhead chandelier like a disco ball, as was his custom.

He foraged the Tiffany crystal bowl beneath the chandelier as Natasha tugged at the leg of his pants, looking amidst the keys and loose change for any extra cash his mother might have left there. He removed a 'twenty' and three 'ones'.

He walked down the hall to his bedroom with Natasha tucked under his arm. Justin could hear the housekeeper, Erbie, vacuuming in his room.

He threw off his backpack, tie and blazer, gray pants and oxford shirt and tossed them on the bed as he stood in his boxers rummaging through his drawers for his favorite Levi's and a black tee-shirt.

"You know, that dog of yours sheds, Mr. Justin," Erbie yelled above the noise from the vacuum cleaner. "You need to give her a bath or comb her or something."

"She's a short-haired dachshund, Erbie. They don't shed."

"Oh yes they do. What do you call this?" She picked a few stray hairs off the carpet.

"All right, she sheds a little."

Justin dressed and pulled a sales receipt from his dresser. He wrote "DEDUCTION" across it in big bold letters. "Can you throw this in my mom's tax drawer, please Erbie? I ordered some upgrades to the cable and she always forgets that's a tax deduction."

"Sure thing," Erbie said. She stuffed the receipt in the pocket of the same perfectly pressed white uniform she wore day after day. "But you know your mother hires people to pay attention to stuff like that."

"Yeah, but they're idiots. They never remember."

Erbie smiled.

"Hey, I just want to make sure she takes the deductions she's entitled to," he said, "she's in the business."

Erbie turned off the vacuum cleaner and pulled a dust rag from her apron. Justin found himself wondering how old she was. Maybe she was 60. She moved his dresser to wipe the floorboards behind it. It didn't faze her to lift couches, move dressers, or do whatever it took to get the apartment clean — except for where the windows were concerned. Erbie didn't go near the windows. She had a bad case of vertigo and the height of the apartment made her dizzy. Sometimes when she looked out she would lose her balance. Justin used his dirty shirt to wipe the window ledge as he walked by.

Erbie was a born and raised New York African-American. She had been a proud resident of Harlem her entire life and had what his mother referred to as a Midwestern work ethic. Erbie maintained it was part of her faith to put her whole heart into her work. She attended church every single evening when she wasn't working and loved to tell Justin stories of young men giving up a life of crime or drugs because they had found the Lord.

He wanted to visit her church one day. It was a conversation they had often had over the years, though he never took enough interest to actually do it. Her church sounded so much more interesting than the typical Catholic and Protestant churches that filled the Upper East Side. At Erbie's church people danced and sang out loud and did whatever the Spirit moved them to do.

"Leave that there, Erbie," he said, when she touched the study papers on his dresser.

"Don't worry. I'm not moving 'em; I'm just cleaning under 'em."

"You don't have to clean my room today. I'm just going to make it messy again."

"My job is to clean this house every day, not clean the house excluding your room."

"But I'm telling you, you don't have to clean it today."

"And I'm telling you it's my job. Do you think your mother would go out there and not ask the important questions today because some lame audience member told her she didn't have to work so hard?"

"Oh, now I'm a lame audience member?"

"Well, I certainly thought you'd be lame, but you look like you're walking just fine," Erbie said.

"It was just a little sprain."

"That's not what your mother said. Anyway, you know, I take pride in my work. Lazy hands make a body poor in more ways than one. The good Lord wants us to work with joy and be good at what we do."

"That you are, Erbie. No one can argue that."

Erbie knew the bible so well. Now that Grams had asked him to read her bible, probably as her last request, he needed to learn more about religion.

"So, what's going on at church these days? Anything interesting?" Justin asked, half facetiously.

"Everybody is talking about that lady that has a statue of the Blessed Virgin that cries real tears. She's right in my neighborhood."

"Do you believe that?"

"I sure do," she said. "One of the men in my church has been speaking in tongues and he says the Virgin's crying is a warning."

"About what?"

"He says the devil's work is going on and then this old man just passes out straight away. Every day it's the same thing. Good thing, so now they catch him when he falls."

"What does that mean — speaking in tongues?"

"It's a gift of the Spirit. It means the Holy Ghost is speaking directly to God, through you. The Holy Ghost knows what to pray for even when we don't."

"So can I speak in tongues?"

"Well, you have to ask. Although sometimes I think you already have a gift, but maybe it's a different one."

"What do you mean?"

"Oh, it's just a sense I have about you. I've had it ever since you were in diapers. You used to lay there on the changing table looking up at the ceiling, laughing and laughing just like someone was playing with you. Sometimes you'd be sitting in your playpen, singing and talking gibberish like your mom or I was right there with you. I never could figure out what caught your attention. I just assumed you had an angel at your side."

"An angel?"

"The bible says God gives everybody angels. But the angels of children are special, because they see the face of God every day. So who knows, maybe you've always been blessed with the Spirit."

"What other kinds of gifts are there?"

"Well, let me see, there are healers…"

"You mean people can actually be healed?" he asked.

"Of course. Don't you know Jesus laid hands on people and he healed them and now the Holy Ghost works through other believers to heal people? They do it in my church. When someone is sick we pray for them and lay hands on them. You know, we don't all have health insurance, and hospitals aren't a good place to be when you don't have health insurance…. I suppose they aren't a good place to be even *with* health insurance."

32

"Hi, mom. Sorry I'm late. I got stuck at the studio." Helene was trying to be cheerful. "How are you feeling?"

"Pretty damn good actually."

"Great. I guess you're ready to go." She took the last sip of a coffee she'd bought at the corner. She tossed it into the almost overflowing wastebasket.

As the remnants seeped through the newspaper, Helene could see the leather edge of the bible peaking out from the trash.

She pulled it out from under the refuse with her thumb and index finger. She walked to the bathroom and wiped off the dripping book with a paper towel. Apparently only the well-worn cover had been soiled. As she checked the pages she paused to read an inscription in faded blue ink:

For my beautiful Claire;

There are many kinds of love: the love of God, the love of family, the love of self, and the love of a woman. I believe my love for you is second only to my love for God, because through you I have come to love myself and God more and to learn what He intended for most, but not for me.

May His angels take charge of you and keep you in all His ways.

My love always,

David

And then beneath it, a new inscription:

To My Dearest Justin;

I was once told there is great meaning in this book. May you have the wisdom to find it and the grace to understand it.

My love always,

Grams

Helene held the book out to Claire. "Mom, isn't this the bible you gave to Justin?"

"I guess it is. Someone must have thrown it into the trash by mistake."

Helene tossed the bible into her red Hermes Birkin bag. "You know, he has such a sense of your spirituality. I'm sure this will mean a lot to Justin. I know I make fun of religion and all, but this is an important remembrance of you for him."

"Maybe I'm not planning on going anywhere soon."

"That's not what I meant."

"I know exactly what you meant. Now, let's get out of here before I pick up some new disease."

33

Barrouck was happy to be in his modest but comfortable home in Jerusalem, where he could quietly ponder the details of his peace plan. His slow and gentle movements belied the endless excitement he felt in his belly. The Prime Minister had approved his plan and now he could finally move forward with his dream. Was it really possible he could live to see peace in Israel? It felt like a miracle even to imagine the possibility.

The knock at the door startled him. He wasn't expecting any visitors, and it was extremely rare for anyone to come calling unannounced. He hesitated. Had someone come to fulfill a threat? Was the faceless enemy poised at the door?

There was another knock.

A polite executioner? That seemed ridiculous. He approached the door. Slowly he peered out the window, taking care not to be seen. He could only make out the hand of a man, holding a long, dark object. There was cause for fear.

"Yitzhak, Yitzhak," a voice called out. "It's me, Ben. Benjamin Meir. Open the door."

"Benjamin? Is everything all right?"

"Completely. Please open. I'm sorry to bother you but it's urgent."

Barrouck breathed a sigh of relief.

"For God's sake, Benjamin, what are you doing here at this hour?"

The dark air brought a chill into the house when Barrouck opened the door.

"I was just getting ready for bed."

"Never mind that. This couldn't wait."

Meir spoke in a breathless whisper. He delicately swirled the three foot long black leather tube as if it were a magic wand.

"You will thank me for disturbing you. I came right over as soon as I got the okay from the Prime Minister."

"I just saw the Prime Minister," Barrouck said.

"I know. This is different."

Barrouck cleared off the dining room table, and Meir gently laid the tube down. It was evident from the delicacy of Meir's gestures that this was precious cargo.

"It's like the Scrolls," Meir whispered. "I had to bring it to you right away. This is the first."

Barrouck knew he was referring to the Dead Sea Scrolls. They had been placed in jars, where they remained undisturbed for centuries. The first fragments were discovered in 1947 by Bedouin shepherds searching for a stray goat in the Judean desert. It took nearly a decade for thousands of fragments to be discovered in eleven caves.

The scrolls dated from a time when Jesus of Nazareth walked the earth. They were almost a thousand years older than any other biblical manuscript.

The Israeli Antiquities Authority granted only a few scholars access to all the scroll fragments. Barrouck and Meir were two of these. In their studies of the scrolls they had been granted a stunning new understanding of two of the world's great religions.

The Dead Sea scrolls described a time of change for the people of Israel, a time when Judaism evolved from the Judaism of the bible to the Judaism of the rabbis as defined by the Mishnah, a book of Jewish laws and customs written in the third century.

They were written on papyrus and animal skin.

As Mier gently slid the contents out of the black leather tube, Barrouck could see that this too was a piece of animal skin.

"And you carry such precious cargo through the streets?" Barrouck said.

"There are soldiers outside. I don't dare call attention to myself. This is old, Yitzhak, very old. Older than the Dead Sea Scrolls."

34

Justin looked out the window of his bedroom and was only half surprised to see Samantha sitting in the coffee shop across the street talking on her cell phone. She had called up to the apartment to see Justin, but at Justin's request, Erbie said he wasn't there. He knew Erbie was happy to do it. She didn't like Samantha. Justin hoped she would just go away.

Samantha was new to the school this year. She came from Texas. Her father was in the oil business. She was by far the most well-developed of all the girls her age, and she didn't hesitate to flaunt it with push-up bras and low-cut blouses. That didn't make her very popular with the other girls. They considered her slutty, but Samantha didn't seem to mind the sneers and whispers as she walked down the halls. She had the attention of every boy, but she was interested in Justin. He was flattered. His friends said he was crazy for not going out with her, but he was only interested in Madeline.

Justin peaked into Claire's room and inhaled a deep lavender breath. When Erbie wanted to do something really special, she ironed the sheets with lavender water. It was something she hadn't done since Claire first got sick. He knew it would make Grams sleep well. Grams always said the scent of lavender had a calming effect. Justin laughed at how she could always smell it the moment she walked off the elevator. Grams had an incredible sense of smell.

Pale pink peonies were scattered throughout the house, and although they didn't seem to carry the strong scent Grams always talked about remembering as a kid, she would be happy to see them.

He couldn't wait for Grams to get home. He wanted to talk to her about so many things. He wanted to hear her side of the story on this new treatment.

The doorman rang up to announce a visitor.

"Send her up," Justin said cheerfully as he placed himself down on the bed and hit the TV remote "on" button. He flipped right past some breaking news and stopped at a cartoon. He could hear the elevator open down the hall.

"Hello," Madeline yelled.

The phone rang. The caller ID showed it was Samantha. He didn't pick it up.

80

"You look beautiful," Justin said. No, she looked absolutely gorgeous — straight, black, shoulder length hair; dark, almond-shaped eyes; and fine features. She was exotic; a mixture of Japanese, Venezuelan and Italian ancestry. Her long lanky legs were barely covered by a short red skirt; a giant pink grosgrain ribbon was tied around her waist. She wore thick black tights and low red suede Peter Pan boots. Fortunately they had flat heels; Justin wouldn't have to stand on his toes to try and reach her shiny lips.

"Justin!" She gave him a soft punch on the arm as he slid over to make room for her to sit on the bed. The softness of her white angora sweater tickled his arm as she touched him.

"Is it okay for us to sit here?" he said. Justin had no idea whether it was proper to have Madeline in his bedroom. He frequently had friends in his room, but now that Madeline had agreed to go to a party as his date, it seemed strange for her to be there.

"It's fine," she said, sitting on the edge of the bed. "I've been thinking about this math project. Do you want to talk it out?"

"Sure."

"Some scientists say space and time are like a fabric surrounding us. We could pass through it if the weave were big enough or we were small enough."

"So we need a shrinking machine? It sounds pretty ridiculous to me."

"Everything in physics sounded ridiculous at one time." Madeline said.

Natasha started barking before the elevator arrived.

"It's Grams," Justin said excitedly. He was grateful to get out of the conversation. He quickly stood and learned a painful lesson about his ankle.

"Ow!" he screamed.

"Are you okay?" Madeline said.

"Yeah, I just — oh shit! That really hurt."

He moved a little slower.

"Welcome home, Miss Claire," Erbie was saying at the front door. "It's so good to have you back." She took the overnight bag from Helene's hand.

"I've made your favorite for whenever you're hungry — miso soup and brown rice with vegetables," she said. "How about a nice hot cup of green tea?"

Justin could see Natasha pawing at Claire's feet, but Claire just shook her off.

"Cut the crap," Claire snapped. "All this organic shit hasn't gotten me anywhere. Call the deli and get me pastrami on an onion roll with heavy mustard."

Erbie choked back a laugh. "It's about time," she mumbled.

"Mom," Helene said, "that might be a little hard on your stomach. You haven't eaten anything like that in years. Maybe you should start out a little easier?"

"If not now, when?" Claire said, already on her way to her room.

"Grams!" Justin called out. He wanted to give her a hug, but she walked right past him.

She muttered a brief, "Hi Justin."

"Grams!" he repeated.

"Oh, sorry Justin," she said, stopping. "I'm just tired. I'm not feeling like myself. I have to sleep a lot." Before she could go to her room Justin wrapped his arms around her and gave her a hug.

"I missed having you here," he whispered.

"Good to be back," she said and walked into her room.

Natasha followed close behind, but Claire shut the door before Natasha could get in.

"Don't mind her," Helene said. "She's supposed to sleep all the time. It's part of the treatment. She's just out of it. Let's give her some space."

"What do you want me to do about the deli?" Erbie asked.

"Get her what she wants," Helene said.

Justin and Madeline went back to Justin's room.

Madeline took Natasha in her arms. "Don't worry sweetie, I'm sure she didn't see you," she said. "It must be really tough getting chemotherapy."

"She's not getting chemo. She's on some new experimental treatment that no one outside of the family is supposed to know about. It's a huge secret, so you can't tell anybody."

35

Helene walked into Justin's room.
"So, how's your ankle?"

"It's fine."

"I'm not so sure you should go out tonight. Maybe you should stay in and rest," she said.

"Mom, I'm fine. We're going to a party after dinner."

"Can't you just stay home and watch a movie with your foot up? I hear you ordered every channel known to mankind."

"Come on," he whined. "We've been working so hard. We need a break."

She turned to Madeline. "What are you two working on?"

"We're partnering on a big math project," Madeline said.

"How nice. Has anyone seen the news today?" Helene said, reaching for the remote on Justin's dresser. Justin shook his head 'no'. Helene flipped through the channels till she found what she wanted.

The anchor was grim faced. In the box over his shoulder was a photo of a distinguished gray-haired gentleman with the words "Prescription for Murder" written in bold red letters at the bottom. The anchor was saying, "We've learned that while authorities are still perplexed as to just how the killer or killers got into Claiborne's apartment, they are focusing on people who worked in and around the building that day." The picture switched to file video of police activity outside the victim's Park Avenue apartment building.

"That's right down the street from here, isn't it?" Madeline asked.

Helene turned the volume down. "Yes, it is," she said. "And see that guy right there, going into the building?" She pointed to the television screen. "He's going to be here for dinner tonight."

"Is he a police officer?" Madeline said.

"He used to be. Now he's a security expert."

"Do you think there's a serial killer on the loose or something?" Madeline said.

"I hope not. It's pretty creepy though, having a murder like that right down the street. And apparently they have no idea what the motive is. Not to be paranoid, but let's make sure the doorman gets you right into a cab when you leave here tonight. And make sure you take cabs directly home from the party. You know, killers do tend to return to their crime scenes; we can't be too careful."

"For sure. And my mom and dad left for France tonight, so I'm stuck home with the nanny. Yuck. She's useless."

"You're staying alone with a nanny?" Justin asked.

"Yeah. They're probably at the airport now. They're going to a wedding in Paris."

"Well, that doesn't sound like very much fun for you," Helene said. "Would you like me to ask your mother if you can stay here with us till they get back? I think I'd feel more comfortable, and I bet you your mother would too, with all that's going on."

Madeline looked to Justin for a clue.

"Sure, Madeline, that would be great," Justin said.

Helene said, "I think you're a very good influence on Justin and, well, you're practically family." She wanted to make the point that they should think of each other as brother and sister.

"Sure, that would be great," Madeline said.

"I'll see if I can catch your mom on the cell phone," Helene said. "Oh, here, Justin. I almost forgot." She pulled the bible out of her handbag and handed it to him. "Is this the bible Grams gave you?"

"Thanks, mom." A flush came to Justin's cheeks.

"Cool. It looks really old," Madeline said.

"My grandmother's old boyfriend gave it to her. She wants me to read it."

"Yes, and that's fine," Helene said, "but you can read American History first."

"Excuse me, mother," Justin said with an attitude. "I can read anything I want."

"Sure, like you're going to give up Battle Ultimo to read the bible. That'll be the day."

36

Justin groaned. "She pisses me of when she does that."

"She's your mother, she's supposed to piss you off," Madeline replied.

"Where does she get off thinking she knows what I'm going to do better than I do?"

"Well, she's probably right, Justin. Do you really intend to read it? I hardly even read it anymore."

"You've read the bible?" Justin asked.

"Yeah, sure. My aunt gave me one when I was little, and I still have it. I read it once in a while. There are some good stories."

"Like what?"

"I don't know — Jesus healing people and hanging out with kids. I mean I always thought it was cool when I was a kid that he was a baby once like I was."

"Do you believe in this stuff?"

"It usually works when I pray. I always got the toys I prayed for when I was a kid."

"But it never worked with anything big, right?"

"It worked when my parents were getting a divorce."

"You're kidding."

"I prayed about it every day. It was when we were living in Boston. Then my mom got a call from an old girlfriend she hadn't spoken to since college and she told her to see this psychologist.

"At first, they weren't going to go, but I told God this was totally not fair and that a divorce would ruin my life. They went and decided to stay together."

"Wow," Justin said.

"My mom always talks about how the shrink saved their marriage," Madeline said with a laugh. "She has no clue what really happened."

"Do you believe in angels?" Justin asked, but just then Helene boldly entered the room.

"Well, guess what!" she said. "You're going to be staying here for the next several days, Madeline, till your mother and father get back in town."

"Really?" Justin said. This was too good to be true.

"Really," Helene said. "We'll all sleep better. You can take the guest room right next to Grams."

As soon as Helene left the room the kids looked at each other and screamed, "Can you believe it?"

37

Erbie greeted Robert at the elevator. He had a bottle of premium vodka in one hand and a bottle of wine in the other.

"Ms. Cummings went to powder her nose. She'll be out in a moment," Erbie said. "Would you like a drink? I see you brought your own."

"Point me to the bar and I'll help myself, if that's all right?"

Erbie took Robert to the pink marble bar off the living room. As he looked around, he tried to remember what it felt like to live in a real home rather than an apartment that was almost entirely neglected except for its sleeping facilities.

The antique white-finished, glassed-in cabinets, were filled with Baccarat crystal glasses — no jelly jars. Robert poured the vodka into a silver martini shaker sitting on the bar. He scooped ice from the icemaker, put the cubes into two simple martini glasses, and added the olives Erbie had found for him in the small refrigerator.

By the time Helene made her entrance Robert was halfway through his drink. He had a chilled one waiting for her.

"I don't mean to be presumptuous, but I thought you might like to have a martini with me."

"Perfect," she said as they clinked glasses.

After taking a sip, she put her drink down on the bar. "My son has a friend who's joining us for dinner tonight. They go to the same school. From what I understand, two kids were mugged after school this year. Both times it happened off school property. The headmaster says it has nothing to do with the school. Justin won't tell me anything. Maybe you can find something out."

"I'd be happy to," Robert said, as Helene ushered him into the dining room and called the kids to come to dinner.

The long rectangular dining room table was set with four white dishes in a blue Provençal pattern. The tablecloth was white, and there was a blue and white print underskirt that skimmed the floor with thick white fringe. The blue was a beautiful shade.

"What a lovely dining room," Robert said. "What color would you call this — periwinkle?"

"I'd call it 'Fra Angelico blue,'" Helene said.

"Oh." That was disappointing; he'd been certain it was periwinkle.

The four sat widely spaced at the table that normally seated twelve. Helene and Robert were on one long side and Justin and Madeline were on the other.

As Robert looked at the two teenagers in front of him he was struck by how beautiful Madeline looked against the blue wall with its shiny moldings. She seemed to be framed in a portrait from long ago — from the Renaissance perhaps. It was a unique image — something meaningful, it seemed — but he couldn't quite place it. Even so, it made him smile.

On the table, candles burned in two silver candelabras. Two small silver cups were each filled with four pink peonies

"Everything is so beautiful, Ms. Cummings," Madeline said.

Erbie placed shrimp cocktails at each place, as Robert refilled the martini glasses from the silver shaker.

"So, what's the latest on the murder investigation?" Helene said.

"The guy was slaughtered." Robert responded, almost off-handedly.

"You know, kids, Robert has been called in on the big murder down the street, because the police are having trouble figuring out what to do."

"Cool," Justin said. "We saw you on TV going into the building."

"Was it a robbery?" Madeline said.

"No. I think it was a vendetta."

"Maybe it was a former patient," Madeline said, "someone he harmed somehow, or maybe it was a family member wanting retribution for a patient who died."

"That's not a bad thought, except he hasn't practiced medicine for at least a decade."

"Why were you at the apartment?" Justin asked.

"I wanted another look around. You never know what gets overlooked at a crime scene."

"Did you find anything?" Helene asked.

"Not really. There are a lot of creeps out there. Look at what's been going on at your school. I heard there've been some muggings."

"No way!" Justin said. "You heard about that?"

"Well, I *am* in the security business. There's some question as to whether the incidents are connected to something that's going on at your school. What do you two think?"

"Nah," Justin said.

"Oh, you just say that because you play that stupid game," Madeline responded.

"What game?" Robert said.

"Battle Ultimo. You know, they made a TV show out of it."

"Battle Ultimo Primetime" Helene said. "The network has high hopes for it."

"All the guys play it, including the two guys who were mugged," Madeline said. "Now there's some weird guy named Spider who comes around challenging everyone all the time."

"Who's that?" Helene demanded.

Robert was now pouring his third martini.

Erbie removed dishes from the table and brought in steaks, cottage fries and creamed spinach from The Palm.

"I don't really know, but they say he's good," Justin said. "He's friends with some of the guys. He plays them for money and he wins. He didn't mug anybody."

"Do you play BU with him?" Helene said, picking at a salad.

"Mother, you obviously don't understand, thousands of people play on channel 142. I don't know everybody I play."

"Actually, I do understand. I was talking about playing in person. And for future reference, I happen to know a lot about Battle Ultimo, especially BU Primetime."

"Like what?" Justin challenged.

"First of all, only the top 50 players from channel 142 are invited to compete live, in-studio on BU Primetime."

"Everyone knows that."

"Then there is the Entrance Challenge to BU Primetime, just before the show goes on the air. The qualifiers get to compete from home against the In-Studio Player for cash and prizes.

"Eighty percent of the players are eliminated in the first five levels, within the first five minutes. Only about a hundred to a hundred and fifty people get to compete live, but statistically the top three are the only ones to watch. The rest are usually eliminated by level ten of the live show."

"They can't predict that," Justin protested.

"Of course they can. They use a series of tricks to get people to make mistakes."

"Like what?"

"Oh, I don't know. It looks like you're supposed to do one thing when really you're supposed to do something else."

"How do you know this?" Justin said.

"I'm in television, honey. That's why you can't play in the Entrance Challenge. I know too much."

"They give away a lot of money on that show," Robert said.

"Actually, no one has ever won the five mil," Justin said, "but a lot of at-home players have won six figures."

"Not as many as you'd think," Helene said. "You have to be eighteen to play, but many of the good players are only pretending to be eighteen, so they end up getting disqualified and have to forfeit the money. Believe me, the network knew that ahead of time."

Erbie removed some plates from the table. "I'm going to go sit with Miss Claire now," she said.

Helene turned to Robert. "So, Robert, what did you think of *our* show today?"

"I think I'm glad I saw you," he said raising his glass.

38

Claire was sleeping peacefully when Erbie entered her room and sat down in the corner chair. She pulled the red toile ottoman closer and put her feet up for the first time all day. She took a deep breath and inhaled the scent of lavender she had sprayed on Claire's sheets. The relaxing aroma was balm to her tired mind. She wondered why Claire hadn't commented. She hoped she noticed, after all the trouble she went through.

Erbie had gotten up at six that morning, to catch a bus to be at work on time. Now though exhausted, she was grateful to have her arms and legs free of arthritis. She was satisfied that she had done a decent day's work. She closed her eyes and quickly drifted off to sleep.

39

"I did the craziest show today," Helene said. "All these young Christian people think the world is coming to an end. It was really quite shocking. Have you kids heard anything about that? They're called Apocalyptic Youth."

"Not really," Justin said.

"They say they're part of a new movement. It sounds like a cult or something. I hope these kids don't end up pulling a Jim Jones."

"Who's that?" Madeline said.

"Some crazy guy who convinced his followers he was God. One day they all killed themselves," Robert said.

"With Kool-Aid, they killed themselves with Kool-Aid. Imagine that." Helene shook her head. "You never know what people are going to do when they get obsessed with religion."

"You're so prejudiced, mother."

"I am not. See for yourself. Next week's shows are all on my desk. I'll put the DVD in your room. People get very carried away sometimes. Wait till you hear these people and they're supposed to be on the forefront of a new movement."

"My mother doesn't believe in God," Justin said to Madeline.

"What I believe, is that God was invented by man to give him hope," Helene said. "It's all about not wanting to die. It's about wanting to live forever. Think about the Egyptians. All their rituals were about meeting their gods in the afterlife. No one wants to die. Look at my mother!"

"But what if God is more than that?" Madeline said.

"It's possible, but it doesn't change the fact that every major war has been fought in the name of religion," Helene said. "More people have been tortured and killed in the name of God than for any other reason or excuse."

"Except maybe money," Robert said.

"It would certainly be close," Helene conceded. "From the Crusades to the Holocaust, it's all about my God versus yours. Millions of people have been exterminated in the name of God. What kind of God is that?"

"You're not going to talk me out of reading Grams' bible," Justin said.

"I'm not trying to talk you out of it. I just prefer you read something a bit more useful to your academic life, like U.S. History, which you are only barely passing."

"I'm getting a 'C' mother; that's not barely passing."

"Well, 'C's' won't get you into Harvard. But we can discuss it later."

Robert found her stridency charming. "You know, I have an incredible friend if you like this sort of thing. His name is Yitzhak Barrouck and he is *the* expert on Judeo-Christian traditions. He's been studying religion his entire life and he has the answer to any question you can come up with."

"The name sounds familiar," Helene said.

"He won a Nobel Prize about ten years ago. He's a philosopher and a writer. We studied Kabbalah together in college."

"You studied Kabbalah?" Helene said.

"What's that?" Justin blurted out.

"It's Jewish mysticism," Robert said.

"You mean like religious psychics?" Justin said.

"Sort of. It talks about using numbers to predict things and reincarnation and other stuff like that."

"Oh yeah," Madeline said. "I've read about it. A bunch of celebrities are studying it now, but it used to be only for old men."

Robert laughed. "Well, middle aged men anyway, but that's right. Kabbalah teaches that nothing is as it seems. Everything is really under the surface and we have to find it."

"So it's like solving a murder," Madeline said.

"Exactly. In Kabbalah words are special. The mystics teach that God created the world with words. In Hebrew there are no numbers; all the letters are also numbers. So each word and number of the Hebrew bible has a hidden meaning. Kabbalah teaches how to figure out the meaning.

"Where does Barrouck live?" Justin asked.

"He moved to Israel about fifteen years ago."

"So he's Jewish, Justin," Helene said, "and you're not."

"He's a devout Jew, but he studies both the Old and the New Testaments," Robert said. "He's enamored with the whole thing. He never married and he has no kids. He's basically dedicated his entire life to the pursuit of God."

Helene was surprised to learn of Robert's interest in religion, but she liked him anyway. The kids left for their party and Helene and Robert turned to less controversial subject matter.

40

Justin was feeling lighter than he had in some time. He took a long swig off a can of beer and attempted to smile nonchalantly at Madeline. There was a right way to maneuver a kiss, if he could only figure out what it was. The music was loud, too loud for conversation. He was grateful for that. His life was a constant battle between his mother's forcing incessant conversation and his wanting to wander alone through a dream landscape of girls and Battle Ultimo.

His mother didn't understand that when she asked him what he was thinking and he said nothing, he meant it. He really was thinking of nothing. His mother always talked about the importance of being in the here and now, but when he was there she wanted to know what he was planning. It made no sense to Justin, but he knew it also made no sense to his mother that he wasn't desperate to divulge every detail of his life like some poor schmuck on her talk show. He was too young to have regrets. He was grateful to be out of the interrogator's jurisdiction, for the time being.

The townhouse was packed with lecherous young boys and girls with lithe bodies, developing breasts, and lip gloss. It was easier for the girls to transition. All they had to do was wear makeup and high heels, and most could easily pass for sixteen.

The boys, on the other hand, were an ungainly assortment, trying desperately to feel comfortable in their new, sprouting bodies; it helped if they were lucky enough to have had their growth spurt already.

Most had minimal or no facial hair, but there were a few with full grown beards. Justin was somewhere in the middle. He was beginning to *feel* the effects of puberty rather than see them, and like every other boy in the room, he was hoping to make a connection for the night or longer on somebody's mother's down filled, antique sofa.

The room glowed dimly in candlelight. He could barely see what people were doing ten feet away. That was the point. The kids could get lost here. Everyone was trying to let off steam from long days of being boiled in the rigorous classrooms of the competitive Manhattan prep schools they all attended. The beer helped.

Beneath the worries about college entrance exam scores and determinations of "Ivy League or die" ran a current of raw adolescent rebellion. For all the things their parents' money could buy, it couldn't buy the obedience of children blossoming into adults.

It couldn't keep them from questioning their parent's values, morals, politics, and fashion. They were wealthy, influential and on top of every trend. Here was a generation of teenagers looking to rebel against a generation of parents that had done it all — not an easy task.

For Justin, trying to keep up with the brainiest girl in school wasn't easy. He was pretty smart himself, but as his mom always said, he was sorely lacking in the motivation department. That was where school was concerned, not where Madeline was concerned.

Justin slipped his arm around her shoulder. She looked at him and smiled, and for a moment, none of the fifty or so friends were even there, crowded into the bottom floor of their classmate's townhouse.

This was the first year he had noticed her small, round breasts and the beginning of cleavage in her tight sweater that exposed a hint of belly button. She was hot, there was no doubt about it, and tonight she was with him.

"Do you want to dance?" she yelled over the pounding drumbeat.

"Sure, if you want to." He lied. He only wanted to be all over her.

As they stepped to the center of the room, the song was over and a slow dance came through the speakers. This was his lucky day. He placed his arm on her waist and pulled her tight. He took a deep breath. His mom had told him a thousand times to watch out for his raging hormones, and now he knew exactly what she meant. "I don't know what I'd do if you got some girl pregnant," she'd said. "Your life would be over and so would hers." *Ugh!*, he thought, trying to shake it off. How could he possibly be hearing his mother's voice at a time like this?

"What's the matter?" Madeline asked.

"Oh, nothing," he said, realizing he had literally tried to shake it off. "I just had a crazy thought."

"About what?"

He held her tight. She felt so good to him. Her hair in his face, her cologne, the feel of her body — he inhaled her with every fiber of his being.

"Do you remember the first time we met?" he asked.

"Of course I do. We were at Cotillion. We were seven. I asked you to dance."

"I thought I asked you to dance," he protested.

"You didn't have the nerve. I remember. So I asked you. You didn't even want to dance with me at first. Your mother had to come over and insist."

"Yeah, she was afraid I'd hurt your feelings. I was just shy. I really had a crush on you."

"You did?"

"I think I still do." As she looked at him, he saw his moment. He slowly, gently kissed her, like he had seen in the movies and like he had dreamt of so many times in class. She pulled away.

"I'm sorry," he said. "Is something wrong? Oh, God, my breath, I must smell like beer."

"No," she said. "There's nothing wrong with your breath. Look over in the corner. There's that Spider creep. What is *he* doing here?"

"Looks like they're playing Battle Ultimo."

"Is it really that much fun?" Madeline asked.

The guys were motioning to him from the corner.

"Do you want me to teach you how to play?"

"You can't play with that creep."

"I'm sure he's harmless. Besides, what's he going to do? He's outnumbered here."

41

"The Just Man, my man!" Sean shouted, jumping up and giving Justin an enthusiastic slap on the back. "Take a seat, baby, and prepare to do battle!" He turned to Spider and another guy from school named Whiley. "I knew he couldn't stay away." He looked back at Justin. "We've already warmed up. Hurry up or they're going to shut down the show."

"You know I can't play on TV," Justin said. "The network airs my mom's show."

"Oh yeah, it's like payola or something," Sean said.

"No, idiot. It's a conflict of interest or something. Anyway it doesn't matter, I can't play on the TV show."

"Dude, you really think your sorry ass can make it to the TV show?" Spider said. "I've got a hundred bucks that says I'll get closer than you. I think you're just scared to play me."

"Fine, I'm in," Justin said, pulling his GamePad Pro Player out of his back pocket.

He knew Spider was right. What harm would it do if he played? The Entrance Challenge was the simplest part of the game.

The top players would become Home Players and stood to win up to $500,000, while the In-Studio Player battled for up to $5,000,000. But like his mom said, the odds of that happening were clearly nil.

The show had been on for a few months and no one had cleared all 20 levels of the game. There had been only one million dollar winner, a wheelchair bound farm kid from Beverly, Nebraska.

Justin powered up his game, selected the Purple King, and linked up to the Entrance Challenge just as the last players were allowed in.

He placed his thumbs and fingers on the controls and hit the start button.

1,536,258 people around the country were now linked to the show, a respectable number for a new game show. They each had ten minutes to clear ten levels.

This was Justin's moment to shine in front of Madeline, and he didn't want to blow it. Spider couldn't be that good. He could see him out of the corner of his eye. Spider was calm and motionless.

Justin didn't feel calm at all. He fidgeted in his seat as he watched 3, 2, 1, 0 on the screen.

Kings all across the country appeared in flowing robes and crowns, in the middle of a mountainous region facing a Challenger made entirely of rock.

Justin's King kicked it in the head. It was unfazed. He kicked its arm and a hand fell off, but when Rock Challenger placed his stump on the rocky ground it was restored.

He repeatedly threw RC against the wall. Finally, a boulder loosened and smashed RC. KILL flashed on the screen. Justin's King advanced to the next level.

He breathed a quiet sigh of relief, but he knew the toughest Challengers lay ahead. By the time he completed Level 5 he felt a renewed sense of confidence.

Within five minutes, Sean and Whiley were eliminated from the game, just like his mother would have predicted. Spider let out a loud "Yesssssss!" A bead of sweat formed on Justin's forehead.

42

Madeline's attention was diverted from Justin's screen to the flicker of a shadow in a far corner of the room. Suddenly, she saw Samantha approaching. Her smile was bigger than life; so were her breasts. Madeline knew full well Samantha was coming to see Justin in a tight black dress that showed off the curves only she had.

"You know, I can explain the game to you if you like," Samantha whispered to Madeline, bending over to show off her ample bosom. She stood and placed her hand just above Justin's shoulder, as if to touch him, but then changed her mind. "I was his good luck charm last time he played."

A knot formed in Madeline's stomach. She felt Justin's breathing intensify.

"But I guess you'll have to suffice this time," Samantha said as she turned to pick up a can of beer from a side table.

Madeline watched as Justin's King, now clad in a Medieval Knight's armor was placed atop a horse, facing a Jousting Challenger. Justin quickly made the Kill and moved to the Fencing Challenger.

Samantha finished her beer and went for another.

Justin's King moved swiftly through a Venetian garden, defending his life with an epee; he cleared the field just in time to beat the clock. Next up was Level 7 — a Sailing Ship off an island. Madeline had heard the guys talk about how much they hated this level — it perplexed them. The King was on the ship as Native Challengers attacked with bows and arrows. There was a cannon and a rifle for sending the Natives to Oblivion. Justin was moving for the cannon to inflict the greatest number of casualties when a Native's arrow delivered a fatal wound.

LOSER flashed on the screen. Justin's shoulders sank, otherwise he didn't move. Spider was still playing. He was eventually defeated at Level 9 by the Brainiac Challenger, hurling Mensa level problems to solve, but not before the entire party had gathered around and seen that Spider had handily defeated Justin and almost made it to the live show.

Madeline jumped and Justin bristled as Spider stood victorious, raising his fists and pumping them in the air. Several of the guys came to pat him on the back; Spider laughed and luxuriated in the glory. Justin counted out five twenty dollar bills from his wallet. The host of the Battle Ultimo Primetime Version came on the flat screen in the corner.

"Good Evening and welcome to the ultimate game show, where you, the viewer, can compete for thousands of dollars in cash and prizes! But the man in the studio seat is going to do his best to stop you, so he can go for five million big ones!

"Jimmy in Roanoke, West Virginia, Charlotte in Toledo, Ohio, and the K-Man from Los Angeles, California are the top three contenders; they will play our reigning champion of Digital Games, Mickey Vitale from Englewood, New Jersey!

"Mickey, how are you feeling?" the host said.

"Pretty good, Mitch, uh, pretty good."

"Are you ready?"

"Yes," he said with a nod of his head.

"Then let the games begin!"

43

"See, I told you I was your lucky charm," Samantha giggled. Justin was leaning against the wall — waiting in line for the bathroom. "You shouldn't have let me leave. Maybe if I'd have stayed you wouldn't have been so publicly humiliated."

"Yeah, well, you win some you lose some."

"I've been thinking, maybe you can still score tonight," Samantha said.

"What's that supposed to mean?"

"I want you to be my first. That is, if you can tear yourself away from your new girlfriend for long enough."

"No can do, Samantha."

"She's a child," Samantha said, sounding much more serious. "Do you think she loves you like I love you?"

"What do you mean, Sam? We're teenagers. This isn't serious stuff."

"Well maybe it isn't for you, but it is for me. I love you Justin, and I want to be with you forever."

"Sam, we're fourteen. Fourteen year olds don't fall in love forever."

"Some of them do, and I'm one of them. I want you Justin." She placed her arms against the wall, pinning him back and pressing into his body. He had nowhere to go as she straddled his leg, pushing harder. She leaned forward to kiss him.

It was like a scene out of one of Grams' soap operas. Was she really willing to have sex with him? And was he really turning her down? Her breath was hot, it tickled his ear.

"Come on, Sam. This is crazy." He pushed her away. "I'm not going to do this."

"I want you. Drop your girlfriend off and meet me at my house."

"What about your parents?"

"They're not home."

"What time?"

"An hour?"

"I don't know, Sam. It's not right."

"What are you, a virgin?"

He took a deep breath and closed his eyes as she rubbed against his groin. He thought about where he could buy condoms. When he opened his eyes he spotted Madeline in the distance; he watched just long enough to see her run out the door.

"I've got to go," he said.

The evening had brought a bold chill to the air that smacked Justin's face as he ran out the door of the townhouse. His injured ankle throbbed as it pounded against the pavement, but he had to keep up.

Madeline was halfway down the block when he caught up with her. She was shivering under her short brown leather motorcycle-style jacket. He took his jacket off and placed it around her shoulders. Mom's rule for getting the babes: If you have an opportunity to be gallant — be it. Mom's other rule: The faster you apologize the easier everything is.

"I'm really sorry. That wasn't really what it looked like."

Madeline just kept walking. He could see the hurt in her eyes. Mom's rule #3: Take responsibility.

"Okay, it was what it looked like, sort of. I promise I didn't start it and I have no intention of being with her again. Do you believe me?"

"No."

"Please Madeline. I'm really sorry you had to see that."

"But not sorry you did it? What, was she offering to sleep with you? Because I'm not offering you that, Justin."

He stopped talking; he had to quicken his pace to keep up with her.

"Look, I think you should just go back with her," Madeline said. "You obviously had a close relationship. It's not that big of a deal."

"Madeline, I...I don't know what to say. I would never do that to you."

"Don't worry," she said sharply. "I'll get over you. And I'm perfectly fine staying with my nanny."

"I didn't mean it that way. So, if I promise to not get within a hundred feet of her, can we just pretend this didn't happen? I really don't want to see her."

"I'm not going to sleep with you!"

"I know you're not going to sleep with me! Everything is not about sex. Geez, can't we just be together?"

He had apparently said precisely the right words, because Madeline smiled at him and slowed her gait.

"Do you mean that?"

"I really mean that."

She noticed he was limping badly. They hopped in a cab and went home. They could still hear his mother and Robert talking and giggling in the living room. Justin didn't want his mother to see him limping. He showed Madeline to the guest room and quietly went to his room and slid himself into bed.

44

Erbie squirmed with an uncomfortable sensation and woke to a feeling of being suffocated. She opened her eyes to find Claire standing over her.

"Get out," Claire said.

"Ms. Claire, you should be…"

"Get out, I said." Claire spoke softly but sternly.

"Let me help you get back in bed," Erbie said. She started to stand up, but before she could get out of the chair, Claire was already back in bed and sleeping soundly.

"Dear God, she must have been sleep walking," Erbie mumbled to herself. She tucked Claire in, pulling the covers neatly up to her shoulders and placed her hands on the outside of the sheets. As she was gently stroking the hands she noticed the small mark that had formed on the right one. She said a prayer and went to the bathroom to throw some water on her face. With her head in the basin and the water running, she was overcome with dizziness. A wave of distress engulfed her body and she vomited into the sink. She was flooded with sickness and couldn't control her body. She finally managed to stagger to the night table and grab the bell she had left for Claire.

She rang it and rang it and rang it, until in desperation she banged against the wall three times and collapsed to the floor.

45

When Helene and Robert heard the ringing and felt the thud of something falling in Claire's room, they leaped up from the sofa. They found Erbie lying face down on the carpet with the bell still in her hand. There was a smell of vomit coming from the bathroom.

Robert turned her over; she had a pulse. Helene called 911 as Justin and Madeline rushed into the room. Robert was preparing to do CPR when Erbie abruptly awoke.

"I fainted, I think," she said.

Robert carried her to the chair and put her feet up on the ottoman. She stayed there until the paramedics arrived and took her to the hospital.

Claire slept through the entire ruckus, apparently unaware of the arrival of the paramedics in her room. One of them even stopped to check her breathing and heart rate. Helene told them she was on medication and was prone to being a heavy sleeper. It was the simplest of explanations, if not entirely truthful.

The kids went back to bed and Robert stayed with Helene into the early morning hours. They talked about everything.

Robert couldn't believe he was still capable of feeling the way he did about Helene — or anyone. There was comfort in the promise of new love — it didn't replace old love, but it brought back into his barren heart everything and everyone he had ever loved before.

46

Everyone was sleeping when Claire awoke thirsty just before dawn. Her bedside bottle of water, usually filled for her by Erbie, was missing. Claire was so annoyed by the prospect of walking on the cold wooden floor all the way to the kitchen that she neglected to put on her slippers.

The floors weren't cold at all and she made it to the kitchen with great ease. She noticed her reflection in the refrigerator door and paused to fix her hair. She removed a bottle of water and picked at a piece of chocolate cake with her fingers. On second thought, she decided to have a piece and sat down on a bar chair at the island. She felt voracious and ate more than she had in some time.

As she walked back through the living room to her bedroom, she felt the need to stop and smell the peonies in a crystal Lalique angel vase that stood on top of an ochre marble pedestal. She couldn't smell them. As she moved in for a closer whiff, the vase began to move. Claire hadn't meant to disturb anything — in fact she didn't even realize she'd touched it — but suddenly Helene's favorite vase was tumbling in slow motion to the floor.

Claire watched it hit the ground with a thud. It cracked in two. She looked around to see if anyone had woken up, but everything was quiet. She walked back to the kitchen and pulled a garbage bag and a mop from the cabinet. She placed the two large pieces of the broken vase in the bag and mopped up the water on the floor, taking the small pieces of glass too. She returned the mop to the cabinet, walked back to her room with the bag of crystal in her hand, opened the window, and dumped the bag down the side of the building. It plunged eleven floors to the deserted Park Avenue sidewalk below.

47

Justin awoke writhing in pain. He grabbed for his medication and noticed his ankle was now swollen to twice its size. He was also ravenous. Maybe some food would take his mind off the pain.

Without Erbie to cook for him, he was at a loss about what he could find to eat in the house. Madeline was taking advantage of some teacher work days to take a dance clinic and Helene was at work. Only he and Grams were home. He hopped on one leg and fumbled through the kitchen drawer looking for take-out menus.

"So what should we order, Grams?" he yelled, standing on one foot, while he balanced with the other against the counter top. "Do you want deli, Chinese, or Italian?"

"Chinese," she yelled back, "and last night's desert."

Justin smiled. He pulled the cake out of the refrigerator and spun the crystal ball on the chandelier on his way to the island. This time he spun it just hard enough to fling it off its tiny metal hook. As it fell he instinctively reached for it, lost his balance, and stumbled to the floor just as the crystal hit the marble counter top and broke in two. He sat on the floor, unable to respond to the ringing that meant the doorman was signaling the arrival of a visitor.

By the time he pulled himself off the floor, Grams had already answered the call and was waiting at the elevator. He was amazed at his grandmother's progress.

Justin immediately knew who the visitor was. Dr. Viviee's presence was strong and unmistakable; his black Chinese shirt was crisp, like a well pressed suit. He seemed too young and slightly too radical to be someone who could cure cancer — not at all the stodgy old doctor with glasses, or the scientist in a white lab coat. Besides, Viviee made house calls. Justin watched the doctor touch his grandmother on the cheek and put his arm around her as they turned to walk to her room.

"Oh, Dr. Viviee," Claire was saying. "I am so happy you've come."

The doctor just smiled.

"Hi, I'm Justin," he said extending his hand to Dr. Viviee. But as Justin hopped closer to the doctor, his good ankle gave out and he lost his balance.

He caught himself before he fell and regained his stability. Viviee watched silently. Justin had a moment of déjà vu.

After what seemed like an extremely long time, Dr. Viviee said, "Hello, Justin. I'm Dr. Viviee, and I'm taking care of your grandmother now."

"It's pretty amazing," Justin exclaimed. "I can't believe her progress. She looks great today. Is it possible this is real progress? I'm mean, look at her — she's up and walking around like nothing ever happened. I haven't heard her cough once since she's been home."

"Let's not get too excited just yet. Her progress is not complete. But she does seem to be doing very well. Meantime, let's have a look at your ankle there. You seem to have injured it."

"It's nothing," Justin said. "I twisted it the other day and then I ran on it a little last night and it's just sore now."

"Have a seat," Viviee said, leading Justin to an empty chair. He took the chair next to him and examined his leg.

"Does this hurt?" he said pushing at the swollen flesh.

"No, ouch, yes, yes, that hurts."

"You've got a bad sprain and you're going to have to be off this for awhile, I'm afraid. You'll be fine in a week or two," Dr. Viviee said. "It's either a grade 2 or 3 sprain with some soft tissue swelling. You need to elevate it and ice it and stay in bed — no more walking around for at least a week, probably two."

"I can't stay in bed for two weeks!"

"That's what happens when you reinjure yourself. Eventually you'll be able to put weight on it, as tolerated."

"I can't miss school! I've got a killer math paper coming up!"

"You'll have to do it in bed with your foot up and you'll need crutches for walking around the house."

"The crutches are in the closet," Justin said looking down, "from the last time I hurt my leg."

"I'll call your mother," Viviee said as he pulled a roll of bandages out of his bag and wrapped Justin's ankle.

"How do you…."

"How do I know how to treat a sprain?" Viviee said. "In China you learn how to treat everything."

Natasha was pawing at Claire's feet. Claire ignored her, but the dog persisted. Claire swept her away with her foot.

When they were finished Justin dug out his old crutches and quietly followed Dr. Viviee as he led Claire to her room.

Justin was trying not to be obtrusive. He watched as Claire lay down on her bed. Dr. Viviee pulled a chair to the bedside, unlocked his attaché case, and pulled out his laptop computer. After logging on, he placed the computer on Claire's bed and her right hand on the mouse pad. He tapped in a code, and a real-time scan of her spinal cord, organs, nerves, and arteries appeared on the screen. A small flashing light moved very slowly down one of the pathways. As it passed over an area, the color changed from red to blue. A large section of blue covered much of her lungs. Claire lay motionless.

Dr. Viviee stood over her, slowly and gently unbuttoning her dressing gown. As he pulled it away from her chest, Justin turned away. He was embarrassed at the sight of his grandmother's breasts. But he didn't avert his gaze for long. He watched as Viviee gently massaged Claire's sagging breasts in an almost seductive way. Then, with his back to Justin and while still looking at Claire, Viviee said, "If you're curious, just come in, Justin. There's no need to stand in the hallway."

Justin shuffled closer to the bed.

"Don't be ashamed," Viviee said. "A gentle massage brings warmth to the area and activates the neurons. That attracts the nanochip to work in that area."

"Her breasts?" Justin blurted.

"Yes, Justin. It's very common for cancer to spread to a woman's breasts."

"Oh, right." Justin felt like an idiot. As if Grams was going to let some doctor stand there and feel her up.

"What you're seeing on the screen here, Justin, is the nanochip moving through the spinal fluid. Think of the brain as the computer. The spinal cord is the cable. The nerves are the wires to every organ. The chip moves through the spinal fluid and sends signals to turn off the bad cells — the cancer cells — and turn on or reactivate the good cells. The areas you see in blue are the new healthy cells, and the red cells are ones that still have to be worked on."

"But there are red cells all over her body."

"Precisely. That's why she was diagnosed as terminal." He continued massaging Claire's chest, in large slow circles. "Do you see the red area? That's the cancer. When the technology moves through, the surrounding tissue turns completely blue. You can see her lungs have a lot of blue in them now. When I first saw her, they were all red. That's why she's breathing so much better."

"Is this really making her better?"

"You see it happening before your eyes. How can you doubt it? Do you not believe what you see? Can you still doubt?"

"Yes, I mean no. I don't doubt you at all. This is just so incredible. You're going to make a fortune on this! It's a dream come true."

"This is not about money. This is about saving the world, one Claire Cummings at a time." Dr. Viviee smiled and removed Claire's hand from the computer.

"Wait, can I see that again?"

"No, it's not good to keep her hooked up for too long."

Justin watched as the computer screen went blank and Viviee's logo appeared as a screensaver. It was a small circle with three curved spokes coming out at noon, four, and eight o'clock. It rotated like a propeller.

Claire seemed to come out of a daze.

"You're well on your way," Dr. Viviee said. "Don't fight it. If you feel a little unusual or find yourself doing some strange things, don't worry; all that will all go away. It's just the nanochip incorporating into your body. Sometimes it can turn on strange cravings or impulses when cells that haven't been used in a long time get tweaked."

"I don't understand," Justin said. "Why are you keeping this a secret? This is huge!"

Claire stood up.

"No one will believe it," Viviee said. "They're not ready yet. Not everyone can see and understand this. It is special."

Natasha nipped at Claire's heels. Claire kicked her away, but she refused to stop jumping and snapping as if she'd been electrified.

"Justin, will you please get this dog out of here?" she grumbled.

"Aw, Grams, but Natasha loves you." He hobbled over, and scooped the dachshund up in his arms. "She just bugs you because you're not paying attention to her. If you'd play with her once in awhile like you used to, she'd leave you alone."

Natasha settled quickly into Justin's arms; she stretched up to lick his face.

"You see," he said, "she just wants attention."

"Well, I'm allergic," Claire said. "So, I would appreciate it if you would keep her away."

"Allergic!"

"That's right. But I'm sure it won't last for long. Right, Dr. Viviee?"

"Since when are you allergic to Natasha?"

"Your grandmother has been through a lot, Justin," Dr. Viviee said. "Her body is making a huge adjustment. A healing of this magnitude takes effort on the part of every system in the body. That's why she needs to sleep so much, so the body can conserve its energy to do what it needs to do most — get rid of the cancer and keep it gone."

"But she was never allergic to Natasha," Justin insisted.

"She may have just been sensitive before, and you never noticed it. Now that her body is concentrating on more important things, the sensitivity is more acute."

Justin watched as Claire walked Dr. Viviee to the door. Natasha followed. Dr. Viviee turned to Justin. "You know Justin, I think you do understand this," he said.

Justin returned to his room, flattered and feeling very proud of himself to be complimented by such a great man. Then he heard Natasha let out a yelp.

"Is everything okay, Grams?"

"Of course. I stepped on her tail by accident."

48

"Hey, Robert," Lockhart said. "Good to see you at this hour."

"Nice to be here," Robert said, walking directly to his office.

He fumbled through the papers scattered across his desk and found the Claiborne autopsy report. The obvious had been confirmed. The axe had killed him by separating his head from his body. There were no other wounds and no indications of a struggle.

One of the assistants stuck her head into his office. "Would you like some coffee?" she said.

"Sure." He was embarrassed he didn't know her name.

He phoned the company that handled security for Claiborne's building and compiled the names of five people who had knowledge of the building's security details. Within an hour it was clear that none of them was anywhere near the building at the time of the murder.

People in the office kept bringing Robert coffee. Finally he asked for an orange juice. When he was all alone with the door shut, he opened his bottom drawer and removed a bottle of vodka. He poured a bit into the juice and took a long sip.

He studied the building's employment records. He called the building manager and questioned him, trying to identify anyone who had done maintenance on the back cameras or who had sufficient knowledge of the system to turn the cameras off.

One person stood out, a handyman who had been in Claiborne's apartment earlier that day and was still working in the building that evening.

Robert called the Chief.

"I'm right there with you," Lario said. "We're bringing him in for questioning."

Robert sat back in his chair, swiveling left and right. He had a feeling of satisfaction he hadn't felt in a long time. It had been simple enough, almost embarrassingly so, to come up with the same suspect the detectives had spotted. It was even easier than he remembered. He took another sip of his juice.

He started thinking of Helene. He wanted to call her, but he resisted the urge. *She'll think I'm a stalker. No, she won't. She'll be angry if I don't call.* He hadn't had thoughts like these in a very long time.

He positioned himself at his keyboard to send an email.

Dear Yitzhak:

How are you? Have you solved the world's problems yet? If you have, please get in touch. I have a few I'd like you to tackle.

Robert chuckled to himself. Imagine asking Yitzhak for advice on his love life — he'd get a bible quote.

I was speaking of you at dinner the other night — to a young man who is the son of a friend. He reminded me of you; he seemed to be searching for God. We talked about Kabbalah, and there was so much I couldn't remember. If you have a moment, drop me a note about Kabbalah, so I can impress the kid.

Perhaps I'll put you in touch directly. Do you have room in your life for a pen pal?

Robert

He dialed the phone and was somewhat startled when Helene answered.

"I don't want to bother you," he said. "I thought I was going to leave you a message."

"I'm in between shows. It's no bother. How are you?"

"Very well. Thank you for last night. I want you to know I sent an email to my friend Barrouck about Justin. If he has time, I'll put them in touch so Justin can satisfy some of his curiosity about religion."

"Oh, that's nice."

"You don't mind, do you?"

"No, of course not. I'm thrilled to have my son talk to a Nobel Prize winner about anything."

"I'm not saying he has time, I just wanted you to know I followed up so you can tell Justin. I'm also following up on the incidents at school, but nothing to report yet."

"That's terrific, Robert. Thank you. I really appreciate it."

He could hear some noise in the background.

"Uh, they're calling me for the next show," she said.

"Of course, go ahead. Uh, wait a minute. How about dinner some time soon?"

49

Justin layed in bed, his foot propped up, with Natasha by his side. He put down his study materials; his eyes were weary from reading. He flipped through all the television channels twice. When he still couldn't find anything to watch, he turned on the DVD player that was loaded with several of his mother's shows.

The words "Apocalyptic Youth" immediately caught his eye. This was the show his mother had talked about at dinner.

He had heard people talk about the world ending because of a nuclear war or out-of-control global warming. He had even seen movies about that, but he had never before heard that ancient prophecies foretold a time when earth as he knew it would disappear, to be replaced by a new heaven and a new earth where God would dwell with his people.

It sounded like a fantasy-adventure movie inhabited by hobbits and gnomes. Above all, he couldn't imagine a stranger show topic for his mother — even crazier than the transsexual man who became a woman to marry a guy.

His mother was questioning one of her young studio guests.

"How does your church feel about other religions?" she asked.

"Well, for one thing, we're not a church," the guest said. Written beneath him on the screen was the name John Turner.

"Then what are you?"

"We're a study group. We believe the bible is the inspired word of God, so we get together to discuss it and learn, preparing for the end, so to speak. We think we're just typical young New Yorkers, but I guess we're a novelty."

"Maybe mom's right," Justin said to Natasha, curled in his arms. "Maybe they are crazy."

"Tell me, then," Helene said. "How do you novel New Yorkers feel about other religions? You clearly believe you have to believe in Jesus to be saved. So, political correctness aside, do Jewish people go to heaven?"

Katrina continued, "Clearly the Jews are God's chosen people — always were, always will be. Maybe Jesus didn't come to save the Jews right now. I don't know. You make of that what you will."

"That sounds blasphemous to me," Helene said.

"For me, it's hard to not draw parallels between the coming of the Messiah and the second coming of Jesus," Ezra said. "Let's not forget, the early Christians were all Jews, but many Jews expected the Messiah to come as God, not as a man. When Jesus comes back to earth he tells us he will come on the clouds in full glory and everyone will get what they expected."

Justin quickly flipped to the back of Grams' bible and started looking things up.

In Hebrew the word Messiah meant "the anointed one." It came from the word *mashiach*, which in Greek translated to Christos or Christ in English.

Helene was saying, "People who don't believe in Jesus as the Christ say if he was really God he should have taken himself off the cross."

The phone rang. Justin answered without checking the caller ID. He cringed at the sound of Samantha's voice.

"Are you avoiding me?" she said.

"Of course not. I just haven't been feeling well."

"Walk to your window."

"Think of it this way," Ezra said. "Maybe God had to send His son to come as a man and experience first hand the pain, suffering, joy, and temptations we go through so He could more fully understand how free will allows us so easily to turn away from Him."

"Surely an all-knowing God would understand that already," Helene said.

"I'm in bed, Sam," Justin said.

"Good. I'm on my way up."

"No, wait," he said, pushing himself out of bed and hopping on one foot to the window. His foot throbbed from the sudden movement. He looked out and saw Samantha standing on the corner. She was waving at him.

"I want to come up and make you feel better," Samantha said.

"This isn't a good time, Sam. Grams isn't feeling well, and I really need to stay with her."

"I'll just come up for a few minutes."

"'The spirit is willing but the body is weak,'" Ezra said. "Maybe God didn't realize just how weak it was before Jesus told him."

"Really, no," Justin said in a stern voice.

"Please?"

"I can't, Sam, really I can't. I've got to go. My foot is killing me."

Justin clicked the phone off and leaned against the wall. He blew a long breath out through his lips.

"Let's assume for a moment you're correct about all this, Ezra. Why do you think God would choose you to be the one He reveals his big plan to?"

"I think he's revealing it to a lot of believers right now."

Justin stared at the TV screen. For a moment he stopped breathing.

"God said, 'In the end days I will pour out my Spirit upon the nations. Your sons and daughters will prophesize. Your young men will see visions and your old men will dream dreams.'"

The words reverberated in Justin's head.

"Perhaps they're a little embarrassed to talk about it openly yet," Ezra said, "but they know in their hearts what's coming."

"Your young men will see visions," Justin repeated.

"Where are you?" he called out to *his* vision, but nothing happened. "If you're real I need to speak with you."

He fell back on his bed and picked up the bible. He turned randomly to a section and began to read:

"Some men came, bringing him a paralytic, carried by four of them. Since they could not get him to Jesus because of the crowd, they made an opening in the roof above Jesus and, after digging through it, lowered the mat the paralyzed man was lying on." Jesus told the man to "...get up. Take your mat and go home," and that's exactly what the man did.

Justin turned to another page. "Blessed are your eyes because they see." He closed the book and held it close to his chest. He closed his eyes.

"I need to speak with you," he said softly.

Soon he could feel the light forming outside his closed eyelids. He opened his eyes to find his friend in the midst of the light.

"Do you have a name?" Justin asked.

"Everything on earth and in the heavens has a name. Mine is Fouick."

"Fooweek," Justin repeatedly softly. "I know, it's French."

"It is."

"What am I being called to do?"

Fouick smiled.

"You have to tell me," Justin said. "Am I supposed to help Dr. Viviee? Is that it?"

"You'll know what to do when the time is right," Fouick said. "When was the last time you played the piano?"

"When I was six."

"You should play again. Music is good for the body and soul."

50

Wind whipped around buildings and buffeted busy New York pedestrians. Dark storm clouds hung low around skyscraper tops with a palpable weight. Robert was delighted, even as the wind flew up under his coat. It flash chilled his chest and his legs and everything in between. He took this as a harbinger that God was on his side.

Today was the riskiest day of talks at the United Nations — the day of maximum risk for a terrorist strike. All the top dignitaries were in town, and decisions of global importance would be announced.

NYPD, Homeland Security, and Robert's security team were positioned at key locations throughout the city. Every conceivable precaution that could be taken in a free society had been implemented. The city was all but locked down.

Four important security tactics were being employed. Accurate and timely intelligence was being collected on an ongoing basis. All known suspicious persons had been rounded up and were being held on some basis or other. Effective radiation and toxin sensors were deployed throughout the city that would, at least in theory, detect any weapons grade substance entering the perimeter. And teams of trained personnel were poised for rapid deployment, rigorous follow up, and assessment of any scene in the event of a strike.

We don't choose our enemies, Robert thought. *They choose us — and there is not a damn thing we can do about it.* There would always be loopholes; if the enemy exploited them, it could spell disaster. But Robert knew that a chemical weapon or dirty bomb deployed on a rainy, windy day would not yield the maximum bang for the buck the terrorists were looking for.

With a little luck, today's big crime news would come not from the United Nations, but from police headquarters, where a man was now being questioned in the death of Archibald Claiborne.

Robert found himself staring through the one-way mirror at a scrawny, sorry looking excuse for a suspect. This handyman who worked in Claiborne's building — a petty thief — was being questioned in a gruesome killing that seemed beyond his reach. Robert searched his eyes for some trace of evil, for some sign on his body or in his gestures that he was capable of the kind of rage this murder had required.

Patrick Seafore's long, dirty blond hair hung down over his face. The interrogators circled his chair, peppering him with questions; regularly they banged on the worn metal table at which the suspect sat. He looked small, almost dainty in the presence of the two bulky officers. The suspect propped his elbows on the table, his forehead on his hands; he was weeping. One of the officers yelled, "We know you did it! Why don't you just tell us why?"

"Leave me alone," the man cried. "I didn't do it. I swear I've never killed anyone."

The police were anxious to put an end to the investigation and neatly wrap up the murder. Robert's fear was that it was just a little too neat.

He watched Seafore's body language, the fear, the meekness, and his repeated denials.

Chief Lario stood next to Robert. He was under a lot of political pressure to bring this ugly chapter to a close.

"He doesn't look like the kind of guy who could pull this off," Robert said.

"They never do. Don't worry. His prints are all over the place. And get this — he used to work as a handyman in Vermont; he chopped a lot of wood, very handy with an axe. He claims he was working late in 9F the entire evening. He left the building around 11p.m., which would have given him plenty of time."

"And where were the owners of 9F?"

"They were out of town. The doorman let him up. The doorman also says he let him into Claiborne's apartment to check on a leaky faucet, but no one was in the apartment at the time and the doorman stayed with him the whole time."

Robert watched the interrogators work on their woeful suspect. They were skillful, alternating threat with sympathy, menace with promises of relief, if the man would only acknowledge the truth they already were certain they knew. One of the officers offered him coffee; he sniffled back tears.

"So, what are you thinking?" Robert asked Lario. "Why would he turn the cameras off if he was already in the building?"

"To bring in the axe. He couldn't walk through the door with it. He must have hid it somewhere near by and then went to retrieve it when he killed the power.

"He knew the layout of the apartment, probably knocked on the door, said he was the handyman who had checked on the broken faucet earlier, and Claiborne let him in. I'm getting a warrant to search his apartment now.

"I'm hoping for a confession before the five o'clock news."

51

Helene laughed and talked with the treasure hunter as the closing credits of the show ran to her theme music. Behind the smiles, she was worried.

Were the current topics strong enough to keep her numbers up? Had she engaged her guests well enough? Were the discussions presented in a provocative way?

These were strong nights for the competition, and it was important they didn't make any headway in the ratings.

The audience had taken to the relationship segment more than she thought they would. They were brimming with thoughtful questions and seemed genuinely to like the author.

There had been excitement in the studio during the segment with the treasure hunters. They passed around a velvet pouch that contained small items pulled from the sunken wreckage of an old Spanish galleon. One by one people dipped their hands into the bag, hoping for a barnacle covered piece of jewelry or a gold coin. One woman pulled out a silver ring adorned with sapphire chips.

Now, with the camera still on her, Helene dramatically covered her eyes with her left hand and dipped her right hand into the bag.

The director faded to black and Helene got up from her chair. She tossed her selection in her jacket pocket and extended her hand to the treasure hunter.

"Great show," she said. "Thank you so much for coming on."

As the treasure hunter packed his loot into a set of plain black suitcases, Helene walked to the audience for the final time that day. She stopped to shake hands and sign autographs for anyone who was interested.

"Thank you for coming," she said with a smile. "I hope you enjoyed the program today."

"Oh, I did," an elderly woman said.

"This was fun," another said.

She reached out to a smiling teenage girl. "Did you enjoy the show?"

"Being here is so cool."

"You're welcome any time," Helene said. She eyed the teen carefully. "Come back soon and bring your friends."

Kyle approached.

"Kyle, why don't you give this young woman your card so if she ever wants to come back with some friends we can make sure she gets tickets." Helene turned back to the girl. "And send us an email. I'd love to hear about some show topics you'd be interested in seeing."

"Sure," said the teenager. "That would be great."

Kyle handed the girl his card. As he walked Helene back toward her dressing room, he said, "Can you stick around for a bit? I might have some good news."

"What's up?"

"I just got word from one of my sources in Rome that the Vatican sent its chief miracle examiner over to see Holy Hazel."

"Are you sure?"

"I sent one of the producers over there to confirm it. We should get word shortly. If it's confirmed, I want to go live at the top of tonight's show with the info. It'll be our 'exclusive.' I'm having the show edited with a two, four, and five minute hole at the top. We'll just go with the flow and drop in the rest of the show after you throw to break." He handed her a packet of papers and photos — research on the crying Madonna statue.

"Oh man, I would love to get lucky tonight," she said. "How do you want to do this?"

"You'll open the show, say we have some late breaking developments on the weeping Madonna. We'll pull up a live shot and then some video tape of the statue. You can debrief Susan on the air."

"You want to put Susan on the air? Don't you think she'll get nervous?"

"She says she can handle it. She was a reporter in Flint, Michigan once. I think she'll be fine. No one's going to expect her to be polished."

52

Madeline went home immediately after the dance clinic to collect some of her things to take to the Cummings house. She was excited and giddy. She couldn't wait to kiss Justin. She just wanted to be close to him. He made her feel so good. She supposed this was what it felt like to fall in love, or at least infatuation. She wanted to feel this way forever.

She passed by school and was startled when Spider abruptly stepped out from a doorway.

"Hey, Madeline, where's your friend? I hear he hurt his foot."

"Home, I guess," she responded.

"Aw, poor little boy," Spider said mockingly. Now the two of them were walking together. "Where are you going with that bag? Looks like you're spending the night somewhere."

"What's it to you?"

"I just want you to give your boyfriend a message for me. I want him to accept a Battle Ultimo challenge, one on one, for cash, as soon as his little footsy wootsy gets better."

"You already won. Why do you care so much about that stupid game?"

"Because your idiot boyfriend told one of the boys he only lost because he had too much to drink. My reputation is at stake."

Madeline quickly picked up the pace, and Spider fell behind; she occasionally looked over her shoulder to see if he was following her. He was gone. By the time she got to Justin's condo she had broken into a sweat.

53

"Going live in three, two…" the stage manager said as he cued Helene into the camera.

"Good evening, everyone. I'm Helene Cummings, and we have a great show tonight, beginning with a story you will only see here.

"It is a story that has captivated our community. Some call it an indication of God's love while others fear it is little more than trickery. Whatever it is, it continues to draw thousands a day to a small brownstone in Harlem where it's reported that tears are flowing from a ceramic statue of the Virgin Mary. The owner of the statue, a woman who's come to be known as Holy Hazel, is said by observers to go into trances for hours at a time while the faithful gather for a glimpse of what they believe is a miracle.

"We have now learned exclusively that the Vatican wants to evaluate this phenomenon and has sent a member of the clergy to verify whether the weeping Madonna is a miracle or a hoax.

"Kyle, please, can you take us live out to the house in Harlem."

The camera cut to a wide shot of the brownstone. What appeared to be hundreds of men, women, and children lined the sidewalk, their hands clasped in prayer.

"We sent one of our producers out to the scene to see what she could learn. Susan, what is the mood out there? Have the visitors reacted to reports that a 'miracle finder' from the Vatican is in the house?"

"People are just jubilant, Helene. They believe this is real, and they are anxious to have that confirmed by someone they accept as an authority on miracles. His name is Father David, although I'm told he's actually much higher up in the church than merely a priest. He travels around the world for the Vatican, debunking acts of fraud and confirming miracles."

The director cut to a video in which some of the believers explained how they were hoping for their own personal miracles and would wait as long as it took to see the statue and Holy Hazel. The tape abruptly stopped in the middle.

"Susan," Helene said, "I'm sorry to interrupt your piece, but there seems to be some sort of a commotion behind you. Can you tell us what's going on there?"

"I'm seeing this just as you are, Helene, but it looks like someone is coming out of the house and people are running up to him."

"Susan, my guess is that's Father David. Can you move in and see if you can get him to speak with us?"

"Father David, Father David," Susan yelled. "You're live on the Helene Cummings show. What can you tell us? Is this a real miracle?"

Father David looked shell shocked as the camera lights shone in his eyes.

"Father David, is this a miracle?" Susan repeated.

"Miss, I've only just recently arrived. I haven't been able yet to conduct all the tests necessary to validate a miracle. The Vatican is very strict about matters such as this, and my investigation will take some time. Thank you."

"No father, wait. Can you tell us what's going on in there right now?"

"Right now Holy Hazel is going to have some food. She hasn't eaten for some time, and she needs her rest, so I am going to ask everyone to please go home for the night and let her be. You will all be welcomed back tomorrow morning."

Helene spoke into Susan's earpiece. "Ask him if the statue is crying. Is he analyzing the fluid? What exactly is he doing to determine if this is really a miracle? What are the criteria and when will he have an answer?"

Susan yelled out some questions, but Father David returned to the brownstone.

54

"You're an idiot!" Madeline said to Justin as he sat on the bed playing Battle Ultimo.

"What?" Justin said.

"You told the guys you only lost to Spider because you were drunk? Now he wants to play you again."

Justin let out an exasperated sigh as LOSER flashed on the screen.

"No biggie. I can kick his ass anyway." He put the game down and changed the channel on the TV.

"You weren't drunk, Justin, and you told your mother you wouldn't play the guy!"

"So I won't play him. Don't get all worked up. What's he going to do, make me?"

"I guess you're right," she said, plopping a backpack full of homework on the bed. She took a seat on the edge. He took her hand, pulled her close and kissed her neck.

"Justin," she said, between giggles, "someone is going to see us."

"No, they aren't. Grams is sleeping, as usual."

Madeline kicked her shoes off and cuddled up with Justin on the bed. Natasha tried to nuzzle between them, but they wouldn't stop kissing. They kissed and kissed, sometimes softly and sometimes with great urgency, but always the way people do when they first realize the joy of communicating in a way that only a short time ago they thought was disgusting.

"So, how's Grams?" Madeline said, coming up for air.

"You can't even believe it," Justin said excitedly. "I met the guy today. I saw how the nano works and everything. This guy is not just a doctor. He's a healer."

Grams walked past Justin's room in a beautiful dressing gown, with her hair fixed and a little make up on.

"Hi, Mrs. Cummings," Madeline said. "You look beautiful."

Natasha dug in deeper next to Justin, pushing under the covers and snuggling next to his leg.

Claire mumbled hello but didn't stop to chat.

"Grams, come on in," Justin said. "We're not doing anything you can't see."

124

"I'll pass," she said, never missing a step on her way to the kitchen.

"Your grandmother looks different."

"Yeah, a little. She acts different too. It's pretty strange. But I guess we'd all be different if we thought we were going to die and then all of a sudden we're alive again." He pulled her close. "Enough talking," he said.

"Did you hear that loud crash last night?"

"What crash?"

"Outside my window. It woke me up. I got kind of scared, so I didn't look out. It sounded like glass breaking."

He tried to kiss her again.

"Wait a minute, Justin." Madeline pushed him aside. "Look at the TV. It's the murder. Turn up the volume."

"Our Investigative Unit has learned exclusively that a suspect is under arrest in the decapitation death of prominent retired physician Archibald Claiborne, who was brutally slain in his Park Avenue condo. Sources tell us a black hooded sweatshirt has been retrieved from a dumpster in Queens, with DNA reportedly matching Claiborne's. The dumpster is immediately behind the apartment of the suspect. We'll have full details coming up on the news at 6 o'clock. Join us."

"That's a relief," Madeline said as she leaned in to kiss Justin.

55

"Look, Seafore, I'm with you," Robert said. "I don't think you did it. Call me crazy, but I've been a cop for a long time, and you don't strike me as the kind of guy who could walk into an apartment and chop some guy's head off."

Seafore nodded urgently.

Robert was playing good cop to the detectives' bad cop, but there was truth in his words, despite the mounting evidence.

"I don't think you realize what kind of trouble you're in, buddy. There's a sweatshirt with a dead man's blood on it. It was found in a dumpster behind your apartment."

"It's not mine," Seafore said nervously.

"Then how did it get there?"

"I don't know. It's not mine. I swear it's not mine. I didn't kill him." His body trembled with fear as he spoke. "I don't know, I don't know, I don't know," he kept repeating. It was like every cell in his body was in a panic.

"Maybe that's true, but whoever killed Claiborne knows you. He's trying to set you up. You're going to take the fall for this if you don't come clean."

Robert watched the man squirm. He hadn't seen someone this scared since the Colombian drug lords were taking buzz saws to snitches.

"Tell me about this group you belong to."

Seafore went pale. "No, no, no. We're just some guys who get together and talk. That's all."

"What do you talk about?"

"UFOs, aliens, shit like that."

"So you're Trekkies?"

"No, we talk about the real stuff, not the shit on TV."

"What's the real stuff?"

"The stuff the government hides. Visitors that come from other planets. Stuff the pilots see."

"Gotcha. So were any of your space friends at Claiborne's building the other night?"

"No. I don't know anything about what happened over there."

He was still repeating those words over and over as Robert walked out of the room.

"You're wasting your time," Chief Lario said. "This is the guy. One of his hairs was on the sweatshirt. What more do you want?"

"A guy wears a sweatshirt and there's one hair on it?"

"Look, this kid's a wack job. You heard him. He's chasing space aliens in his spare time."

Robert looked back through the one-way glass where the detectives were again questioning Seafore.

"Let me know if he has any visitors," Robert said to the chief.

"There's nothing worse than what's going to happen to you when you become fully acquainted with the New York State Department of Correctional Services," a detective was saying.

Seafore looked straight in Robert's direction. Robert knew the man couldn't see him through the glass, but the blank desperation in his eyes was a message.

56

A dimmed chandelier illuminated the white marble of the otherwise dark kitchen as Helene walked in the door. She turned the lights up, threw her keys in the crystal bowl beneath the chandelier, and emptied her pockets of all loose change.

"Justin, are you back here?" she yelled.

"Where else would I be, mom?" he yelled. "Remember — I can't walk."

"Oh shut up," she said playfully as she walked into his room. "Well, look at you two. Doing your homework?"

"Right here," Madeline said, holding up a stack of papers. "We're kind of stuck on this string theory paper. If you could create a new dimension, what would it be like, Ms. Cummings?"

"We're all limited by our own perspective. The key to a new dimension is probably just to see more. It's like when you cover a disaster for TV news, the people caught in the middle of it have no idea what's going on. They have no electricity and limited, if any, phone communication, but the people in Montana are watching it all happen from helicopter shots on TV. Wouldn't it be great to always have access to the big picture?

"Anyway, I've got to get ready for dinner. Did you see they arrested someone for the murder?"

"We just heard it." Justin said.

The doorbell rang.

"We can ask Robert about it at dinner tonight," Helene said, heading for the front door.

She smiled as she heard Justin say, "Wow! She never sees anyone two nights in a row."

"Surprise!" Robert said as Helene greeted him, his arms full of take out bags. "I hope everyone likes Italian, because I've got enough to feed the island of Sicily."

"Who doesn't like Italian?" Helene giggled. "I just walked in the door myself. What a day!" She led him back to the kitchen. "And I have Italian wine."

"Oh, no you don't," Robert said, following behind. "I have a special bottle just for you. One of my old friends in Italy sent it to me. It's supposed to be the finest wine his dirty feet have ever stomped the grapes of."

"You make it sound so appetizing."

"In Italy that's half the fun. That's why Italian guests always examine the feet of their host."

"Oh, they do not. Now let's see what you've got here." She reached into the bag and started pulling out containers.

"You may know a lot, but you don't know my friends," Robert said. "You've never been to a tasting where the wine had the smell of old socks?"

"Ew!" Justin said as he swung into the kitchen on his crutches. Madeline was right behind him. "Now I know why I don't drink."

"Oh, and here I thought it was because you're not old enough," Helene said. "Silly me."

57

Robert knew he and Helene were acting like a couple of teenagers. Still he couldn't wipe the smile off his face. He had gone an entire day without thinking of Maria, and the furrow in his forehead was beginning to ease.

They sat down to dinner still laughing. He couldn't remember the last time he'd laughed so hard.

"How did your day go, Helene?" he asked. He wanted to be as attentive as possible.

"Not so well, actually. Between Justin getting laid up for a while and some stuff going on at the office, it was a mess. One of the studios just picked up a new talk show for syndication next fall. It's hosted by a bunch of twenty-somethings. It's supposed to be the young, hip version of my show."

"Is that a problem for you?" Robert asked.

"It's demoralizing to my staff. We'll be competing for the same time slot in most markets. So, if my ratings weaken at all and buyers find the new show appealing, we could be in a lot of trouble. And my bosses have made me acutely aware of that. I need really strong numbers right now so we don't have people thinking we're losing momentum."

"You're great and your show is great," Madeline said. "I can't imagine how anyone could replace you."

"Sure, I'm good, but I'm getting older while the audience gets younger. And the more demoralized my staff gets, the more they'll be worried about finding new jobs and the less time they'll be spending on making us winners. It's a vicious circle."

"So, make it look like you know you're going to win," Justin said. "And make them think the honchos are all behind you."

"How do you propose I do that?"

"Do what you always do when you win — buy them presents."

"You know, that's not a bad idea. It would show them I appreciate how hard they're working, and it would also show them that the inside track says we're in good shape. After all, I wouldn't be buying expensive presents if I thought we were going down the tubes."

Robert nodded.

"But what do I buy them? I know this great piece of jewelry I could get all the women. They'll absolutely love it. But what do I get Kyle and the other men? I never know what to get the men."

"Why don't you get them the same thing?" Robert said.

Helene looked at him like he was from a different planet.

"I don't mean the exact same thing."

"Robert, men don't wear jewelry. Do you wear jewelry?"

"I wear a watch."

"That's right and I've given them watches before. Men wear watches and wedding rings. Unless they're urban musicians — and none of my staff are — they don't wear jewelry."

"How about a necklace?" Robert said.

"When was the last time you wore a necklace? When John Travolta was dancing in white suits?"

"Claiborne wore a necklace."

"Archibald Claiborne? The ultraconservative establishment pillar? A pair of cufflinks, maybe even a stud set, but not a necklace."

"It was the medical symbol — the caduceus."

"A professional symbol, but how would that translate to television — wireless microphones? I suppose I could just do cufflinks."

"I bet they'd rather have a gadget," Justin said. "You can get a laptop with a phone in it."

"You can?"

"Don't worry, mom. You always think of something." Justin propped himself on the table to stand up. "We need to do some homework, Madeline."

"By all means, go," Helene said.

Robert helped her clear the table and put the dirty dishes in the kitchen.

"At last we're alone, he said. He waited for her to put down what was left of the chicken parmesan before leaning toward her and kissing her on the lips. There was a hint of garlic and the fresh taste of wine. "When am I going to get you out for a real date, so I can woo you properly?"

"When Erbie comes back I'll get her to stay," Helene said. "I don't want to leave mom and the kids alone. I'm sorry. I'd like to be alone with you too."

He kissed her again in front of the sink, then at the bar, on the sofa, and in the hallway. They chatted in between kisses. Eventually they settled into the privacy of a small sitting room outside her bedroom.

"I don't mean to rush you," he said, "It's been a very long time since I felt this way about someone."

"Fifteen years isn't exactly a rush."

Robert woke up in Helene's bed at 3:11 a.m. He was in a cold sweat. He was being chased by a dragon with many heads and it was going for his throat. The little girl with the blond curls was standing off to the side laughing.

He softly kissed Helene on the cheek, dressed, and headed out into the cold night air.

58

Justin woke up in the middle of the night, missing Grams. He felt desperately out of touch with her. She'd been acting like a different person ever since coming home from the hospital. He understood her need for space to heal and recover, but she'd never needed to be so distant from him before. He wanted so much to feel their closeness again.

Justin thought of himself as a grown-up, yet sometimes he just wanted to feel secure, like a child. He wanted to crawl into bed with Grams and have her hold him like she used to, safe and warm next to her body. She would rub his back and sing him songs. It made him feel loved.

He could hear the TV was on in her room, so he decided to go check on her.

"Grams?"

"Oh hi, Justin," she said nonchalantly. "Do you ever watch this show?"

On the screen were a group of naked men and women fondling one another.

"Not really."

"It's interesting," she said. "All these people screwing each other." She paused to look at Justin. "Oh, I see. You haven't had sex yet, have you? Well, she's right down the hallway, honey."

"Grams!" Justin said, feeling a flush come across his face. "Hey, I really don't want to watch this stuff with my grandmother!"

"Sorry," she said, changing the channel. She stopped at a teen slasher movie. "You're no angel, so don't look at me like I've done something wrong. I just want to keep up with the times. You should too. You don't want to be the last virgin in your class now, do you?"

"I'm so glad you're feeling good again, Grams," he said. He sat down next to her and gave her a hug. "Even though you are a little weird."

"I'm not weird, I'm just ready to live again. I have faith in Dr. Viviee. This is going to work for me."

"Are you still doing your meditations and stuff?"

"No."

"Why not?"

"Too much of a bother. I tried the other day and I couldn't get into it. I can't seem to get to that place at all anymore."

There was a scream from the TV.

"I didn't know you liked movies like that, Grams. That one's pretty cool. Watch out for the football player."

"Don't spoil it for me."

He took a deep breath. "Mmmm, smells good in here."

"I hadn't noticed."

"Erbie's been putting lavender on your sheets again."

"I don't smell anything," she said.

He placed his crutches on the end of her bed and hopped over to her window.

"Your window isn't shut properly. Someone must have left it open. I don't think it's good for you to be breathing all the pollution from outside." He snapped the latch tight. "Maybe that's why you don't smell the lavender."

"Thanks."

"You know, Grams, Erbie says they have a lot of healings at her church. I've always wanted to go check it out. I was thinking maybe you and I could go there one day. You know, like extra insurance."

"I've already found my healing, Justin. Can't you see that?"

"There are a lot of healings in the bible. I've been reading it like you asked me to. Should I tell you about it?"

"You need to have more faith in the process I'm going through."

"Yeah, okay. I'll leave you to the movie. This is the good part." As he was leaving the room Justin paused for a moment to look back at his grandmother watching TV.

The room grew dark. He felt faint, but he didn't move. For a moment he saw Claire reach out to him, as if she were begging for help. Then, just like in an old zombie movie, her flesh rotted and shrunk from her bones. She crumbled to a pile of dust. He squeezed his eyes shut and shook his head.

Everything was back as it should be.

59

Somewhere between wakefulness and sleep Justin's eyes became fixated on a glaring light that seemed to suck him into its center. A deafening silence echoed in his ears. Fouick was in the center of it.

"Who are you, Fouick?" Justin asked, but Fouick smiled and said nothing.

Justin was not afraid of his vision. There was warmth to his light — not hot, just soothing — and there was great peace in his eyes. He tried to capture what Fouick looked like, to describe it in his mind so he could remember later, but he couldn't put the words together. Fouick's image was strong and clear, but when he was gone the details of his likeness faded. Justin didn't know how long he had been staring into the light when Fouick began to speak.

"Take care, Justin. The dragon has been loosed and many will die. 'They did not love their lives so much as to shrink from death. Therefore rejoice, you heavens and you who dwell in them. But woe to the earth and sea because the devil has gone down to you. He is filled with fury, because he knows that his time is short.'"

A chill ran up Justin's spine. As quickly as he had been sucked in, he was pushed out to the feeling of his bed shaking. Then it was his whole body. Unexpectedly his mother came into focus, pushing and shoving at his shoulder.

"What's the matter?" He sat up.

"What's the matter with *you?*" his mother said. "You're lying there like you're in a trance. I've been trying to wake you. What's going on?"

"I was sleeping," he stammered.

Helene's tone was angry and fearful, bordering on hysteria. Justin didn't know what to make of it.

"With your eyes open?" she asked.

"Yes," he responded curtly.

"Are you doing drugs?" his mother yelled.

"Drugs? No. I am not doing drugs."

"Well, why didn't you wake up when I shook you? Since when are you such a heavy sleeper?"

"I don't know. Will you get out of here please and leave me alone. I was just sleeping."

"If you're doing drugs," his mother said in a much quieter, somber tone, "you will kill me, your grandmother and yourself and everything we've all worked so hard for all these years."

"I am not doing drugs. Now please leave."

As she left, Justin could see that Grams had been standing in the doorway listening to every word. He expected her to come in and ask him what had happened, to take his side and tell him his mother was out of line and not to worry about it, but she didn't. She just walked away.

60

Father David sat quietly in the corner watching Holy Hazel on her knees. She had come out of her trance for a brief time to speak to some of her neighbors and drink some broth the nuns had prepared. They were at her side praying now. He had been up all night watching her. As he stared in her direction his eyes began to blur, casting a soft glow around the woman. He closed his eyes and began to sleep, but his dreams were restless and fearful, and then suddenly he was awakened by the sound of Holy Hazel's voice.

"'Do not harm the land or the sea or the trees until we put a seal on the foreheads of the servants of our God.' They were told not to harm the grass of the earth or any plant or tree, but only those people who did not have the seal of God on their foreheads. They were not given power to kill them, but only to torture them....'"

The woman collapsed. Father David rushed to her side. He tried to lift her but could not raise the full weight of her body from the floor.

"Help me," he cried out to the nuns.

They came. Each took a portion of her body and together the three of them carried her to the rollout bed next to the statue.

The statue was weeping; Father David fell to his knees.

"Dear Mary, Mother of God, pray for us sinners, now and at the hour of our death. Guide me, Blessed Mother. What am I to do?"

"The devil is at work," Hazel whispered, "and you will find him in the eyes of your love."

61

With great care and deliberation Yitzhak Barrouck brushed the dust first from his right palm, then from his left. Finally he brought his hands into prayer position.

His forefingers were rough against the softness of his lips, and the smell of preservatives was on his nails. As he sat in silent prayer and meditation, a tear made its way down his right cheek onto his right index finger. He licked it off the fingertip.

He glanced across the room to the air tight tube that contained the rolled up sheepskin.

Jerusalem was cool this time of year. The wind blew in between the cracks of the old window frame. The shutter on the window clanged against the stucco façade of the house. The rhythmic banging helped him to pray.

It was cool inside, not cold, but Barrouck pulled his sweater tight across his chest. The chill that ran down his spine was not caused by the desert wind.

Barrouck considered himself a peacemaker. A man of God first, a religious historian, but always a peacemaker. He had worked for peace his whole life. He had come to be respected even by the Palestinians for his fairness and generosity of spirit. Yet with the most important peace talks in years just days away, something even more important confronted him. The document was so amazing it was difficult to sit four feet from it.

He had been unable to resist the urge to rub his fingertips along what he believed might prove to be sacred material. He had photographed the sheepskin and quickly returned it to the safety of its container.

He found it amusing that the most knowledgeable experts in ancient artifacts had seen fit to transfer the document from the sealed pot where it had been safely preserved for centuries to this modern airtight tube. It must have been guarded by the angels themselves to have survived in such condition, and now it was entrusted to Barrouck. The report in front of him detailed the tests already conducted on the sheepskin. He longed to hold it in his arms and raise the skin to his cheek.

What he sought was linguistic evidence that would corroborate the carbon dating that placed this sheepskin around the time some scholars believed the Book of Daniel was written.

He called it sheepskin but he knew that by tradition it could have been made from the specially prepared skin of any kosher animal.

He thought back to Daniel's many prophecies and in particular to the often debated section on the coming of the Anointed One. "The Anointed One will be cut off and will have nothing." Christians believed this was Daniel's prophecy of Jesus's crucifixion.

What concerned him most was the rest of the passage. It referred to the "ruler who will come," destroy the city and the sanctuary, and set up the "abomination that causes desolation." Both Daniel and Jesus spoke of this character, who Christians believed was the antichrist of the last days.

According to Daniel, the ruler would establish a seven year covenant with the Jews but would violate the covenant half way through. "The end will come like a flood," Daniel said. "War will continue until the end, and desolations have been decreed."

Barrouck stared at the container, attempting to look into his own heart. If the document was what he suspected, *his* peace plan could be *the* peace plan that would mark the end of an age. Was it possible? How could he think such a thing? Many plans had been tried, and many had failed to bring a lasting peace over the centuries. If his was approved it would be the accomplishment of a lifetime. Yet now Barrouck no longer feared that his dreams of peace were never to be. He feared that his plan *would* be approved and *would* work for exactly three and a half years.

62

Justin yawned at the breakfast table, where homework papers were spread out next to juice and a half eaten bagel with cream cheese. Madeline yawned back and gave him a flirtatious glance.

Morning sun was streaming in from behind him, casting a peculiar shadow on the wall — two errant sections of hair standing straight up and making his head look like an alien's. He pushed at the hair, but it wouldn't stay down. He wanted to look presentable at breakfast. He wondered if husbands worried about what they looked like to their wives in the morning. Justin couldn't remember any time when his father had breakfast with his mother. No, but that was stupid. Husbands didn't care what they looked like after they got married. But maybe guys did, after having their girlfriend spend the night, which was the situation he was in.

"You might as well give it up," Madeline said between bites of Rice Krispies and fresh strawberries. "Your hair is not going to stay down unless you wet it and put some gel on it. It looks fine." She was typing THE SEVENTH DIMENSION, BY MADELINE QUINONEZ AND JUSTIN CUMMINGS into her laptop computer.

He was busted. "I don't care what it looks like," he said. "It's just bugging me."

"You've been fooling around with your hair for the last ten minutes. Don't worry about it. It looks cute."

"It does?"

"Everyone has a cowlick somewhere. Yours just happen to make you look like you've got antennae sticking out of the back of your head." She appraised him carefully and added, "You probably just slept funny."

"I'm not sure if I slept at all." He yawned again.

"How come?"

"I saw this guy," Justin whispered, not sure if anyone else was in earshot. "It was sort of a vision — a guy with like a back light behind him."

"You mean like a spirit guide?" Madeline said quietly. "What did he do?"

He told her everything.

"What kind of dragon was he talking about?" Madeline asked.

"A flying one… a fire breathing one, I guess. I don't know." It all seemed so distant and muddled.

Grams walked into the kitchen.

"Hi, Grams," Justin said forcefully, as a hint to Madeline to change the subject.

Grams nodded hello.

"What are we going to do with this stupid math paper?" Justin asked.

"Oh, I forgot to tell you what I figured out," Madeline said. "It has extra credit written all over it. Everyone is going to be writing about these dimensions, right? Well, I figured out how to get to one of the dimensions."

"You did?"

"Yeah, listen," she said, logging onto the laptop computer. "Now," she continued, "do you remember when we were studying black holes?"

"Oh yeah." Justin perked up. "I know everything about black holes. It's all in Star Trek."

"Do you remember how they're formed?" she asked.

"Yeah. Gravity is always trying to squeeze the gas from the star inward, and the heat from the star is pushing from the inside out, so it's all balanced."

"That's called hydrostatic equilibrium."

"Whatever. Then something gets out of whack because the core starts to cool or something, and when it gets out of balance the pressure from the outside starts making it cave in on itself. The velocity you need to escape the pull is greater than the speed of light, which is 186 thousand miles a second" — he grinned smugly — "so, even the light gets sucked in. Ergo, a black hole!" Standing on one foot, he took a grand bow.

"I'm very impressed," Madeline said.

"Yeah, sure. But Madeline, every sci-fi film has somebody traveling to a different dimension through a black hole. It's been done a zillion times."

Grams returned to her room without a word.

"Take a look at this," Madeline said, turning the laptop screen so Justin could see it. "This is a college website where they're talking about a field that only feels gravity and its own pressure.

"They say that at a certain strength the field can't decide if it should evaporate or collapse to form a black hole. So, instead it just moves back and forth faster and faster."

Justin looked up from the screen to Madeline. "You mean like vibrating strings?"

"That's right," Madeline said. "But look. If the field goes one way it forms a black hole, the other way it doesn't. But get this, the initial strength differs by only a miniscule amount, in the fifteenth decimal place. Think .000000000000001. One point the other way and it's a black hole that has the power to suck up the universe. The other way — it's nothing."

"So you evaporate into a new dimension? Oh, wait a minute.... I get it. You're suggesting that the opposite of a black hole only appears to be evaporation. What it really is, is movement to a different dimension."

"Exactly, because the particles are now small enough. Think of boiling water. It doesn't disappear, it turns to vapor and becomes small enough to move to another dimension."

"But how do you get it to make the move?"

"We need something to move it. To propel it forward."

"Like what?" he asked.

"Justin, if we could figure that out we wouldn't have to worry about getting into an Ivy League college. We'd be teaching at one."

63

Dr. Cohen tugged at his raincoat to keep the chill out. He was waiting in the lobby of Claire's building for the doorman to tell him he could see her. He'd stopped on his way to the office; she only lived a few blocks away; he hadn't been able to keep her out of his mind. She'd been his patient since he was a young doctor first hanging out his shingle. She had brought her daughter and grandchild to him and had proved a friend through his divorce and when his second wife died. He had expected Claire to put on a good face through her illness, but he didn't expect that she would mind his lack of advance notice. He was wrong.

"What are *you* doing here?" was her first reaction as Justin ushered him into her room.

She was dressed in tight black stretch pants and a black tee-shirt, and was twisted like a pretzel into a yoga pose called "eagle."

"Claire?" Dr. Cohen said. For a split second he felt as if he might have gotten her confused with another patient.

She took a long deep breath, raised her hands over her head, and folded her body in half to grab the back of her calves with her face tucked into her shins. What shocked him most was not her incredible agility but the way she filled out the clothes. This was not the emaciated body he had released from the hospital.

"What are you doing?" he asked.

"Yoga. Can't you tell?" she said. "Oh, what's the use. I hate yoga anyway."

"No, I don't mean the yoga. I mean you look like you've put on five pounds. Are you swollen? Are you bloated?" He picked up an empty Snickers wrapper from her night table and glanced into the waste basket. There were two Twinkie wrappers there.

"No, I'm not bloated. I'm just trying to put back some of the weight I lost eating that crap hospital food."

Dr. Cohen knew full well that cancer cells multiplied ten times faster than normal cells and they did so by eating all the available energy. If you could starve the cancer cells without starving the body you could conceivably win the battle, but it never worked that way. The cancer cells robbed the body of nutrients, leaving the victim with nothing to live on. Yet here was a patient gaining weight.

"Is this how you're doing it?" he asked, holding up the Snickers wrapper.

"I'm feeling great," Claire said.

Was this a sugar high?

"Well, if you're going to stay, come on — I'll make you breakfast," Claire said, grabbing a small white-on-white monogrammed hand towel from the chair and wiping the sweat from her face. He followed her silently to the kitchen. He wasn't hungry but he couldn't miss this. A cancer patient cooking at this stage of the game was a complete contradiction. It just didn't happen. It had never happened in his forty years of practice.

"That damn housekeeper is still off, and I have to make my own eggs," Claire said, grabbing a frying pan from beneath the counter. "Hand me some butter, will you?"

Justin and Madeline sat silently at the island. Dr. Cohen couldn't take his eyes off Claire. He didn't say anything. He just reached into the refrigerator to find the butter and handed it to her.

"What are you taking, Claire?" he asked.

"Nothing."

"Is it shark cartilage, vitamins, herbs? I know you're doing something. Sea cucumber... is it sea cucumber?"

"No, nothing like that," she said.

"Well, I have to be honest with you, Claire. All cancer patients have good days, but you're doing a heck of a lot better than most patients."

He watched her flip a fried egg onto a plate with the skill of a short order cook. She handed it to him.

"No thanks, I have patients this morning. I just wanted to stop by and check in on you, and I'm glad I did. Can you come by the office today?"

"Today? No. I'm going to go shopping today."

This was unreal.

"It's important, Claire. I need to run some tests. I have to make sure everything is okay. This really isn't normal." He picked up his cell phone to call the office.

"It's Dr. Cohen. I need to make some time to see Claire Cummings today. When can we fit her in? That's okay, clear some time. How about eleven? Good, make it happen. He'll just have to wait. Better yet, cancel him." He turned to Claire. "I'll expect you in an hour. You can shop after. The power of the mind is an amazing thing, Claire, and you're sure showing me just how powerful it can be."

"I hate to tell you this, doc, but I'm cured."

"I'll admit, I can't explain why you're breathing so well, or why you have so much energy, but don't get your hopes up. I don't want you to be disappointed. I've seen your chest x-rays and your CAT scans, and cancer like that doesn't disappear. But whatever you're doing, just keep doing it. I'll see you in an hour."

Walking uptown, Dr. Cohen got his head nurse on the cell phone. "I want you to call all our cancer patients and ask them about their sugar intake — in particular Snickers and Twinkies."

64

Robert scanned the front door of Claiborne's apartment, wondering if he might be able to see something there that all the others had missed. The cops, the detectives, CSI had all been over the entire apartment like ants on honey, but still — sometimes it took a fresh eye to spot something that would seem to have been obvious only after it was discovered. Maybe they had failed to recognize some tiny indication of a forced entry. He studied every surface and every edge of the door, carefully examined the lock and the area around it, and looked at the floor over which the door would swing. He could detect nothing unusual, so finally he knocked.

The maid answered the door and ushered him into the living room.

"Mrs. Claiborne is expecting you," she said. "Can I get you some tea?"

"No, thank you."

He ignored her offer to sit and instead paced the room, examining the ceiling, walls, and floor.

"So you don't believe it, do you Mr. Morgan?" Mrs. Claiborne had just walked into room.

"Believe what?"

"That this man killed my husband. The police say it's all wrapped up, but you don't believe them, do you?"

"The evidence is quite convincing. I just don't like to leave any stone unturned."

"And what stone is that?"

He pulled a plastic bag from his jacket. "This necklace."

"They think he killed my husband for money and then got scared and left before he could take anything."

"Yes," Robert said. "As I understand it, one of your TVs was on a timer, and they think the sudden noise might have scared him away."

Mrs. Claiborne stared at him. "Mr. Morgan, do you think a man with an axe scares that easily?"

"I don't know. When I saw you last, I asked you if this necklace belonged to your husband, and you said he had recently started wearing it. Did he often wear jewelry?"

"No, Mr. Morgan. My husband never wore a piece of jewelry in his life other than a watch and a wedding band. I don't know why he started wearing that. He came back from a trip, a medical conference, and he had it on. I asked him about it, and he just said he wanted to wear it for awhile."

"You found that odd."

"I just assumed it was one of those things the doctors decided to do, like a fraternity. He did collect medical symbols. Though, I must say, rarely if ever did I see him collect the caduceus. He was always much more fond of the Staff of Asclepius."

"Do you mind if I take one more look around his study?"

"Of course not."

Robert walked the perimeter of the room, skimming the wood of the moldings with a soft handkerchief.

"What are you doing?"

"Just looking for any nicks that might have been caused by the axe."

"I think my housekeeper would have found any if there were. She's quite thorough."

He noticed a book on medical symbols.

"Would you mind if I borrowed this?"

"Please, go ahead. I'll be putting them all into storage shortly."

"I'll take very good care of it."

As Robert was climbing into a cab on Park Avenue, his cell phone notified him of new email.

Dear Robert:

What a pleasant surprise. I apologize for the delay but I am overwhelmed. I cannot afford the luxury of a pen pal right now, but tell your young friend I said the answers to all questions of God and Man are hidden in plain sight.

Yitzhak

Who would lift the veil that obscured the details of Claiborne's murder? Surely they too, must be in plain sight, Robert told himself, as his cab came to a complete stop in traffic.

He sat back and opened Claiborne's book.

The caduceus was a rod with two snakes entwined around it and a pair of wings at the top. This was the Caduceus of Hermes or Mercury, depending on whether you were thinking in terms of Greek or Roman mythology. Mercury was the messenger of the gods and the inventor of magical incantations.

Asclepius was a doctor in Greek mythology — a mortal who was later deified. No wonder doctors thought of themselves as gods. The Staff of Asclepius — a single serpent entwined around a pole — was also a medical symbol; snakes were often used in medical rituals.

In the seventh century, alchemists, who claimed to turn base metal into gold and prepared elixirs for longevity, called themselves Hermeticists — practitioners of the hermetic arts — because they used the incantations associated with Hermes. By the sixteenth century, the hermetic arts included medicine, pharmacy, and chemistry, and as the nineteenth and twentieth centuries approached, the caduceus was adopted as their symbol, alongside the Staff of Asclepius.

It was the caduceus, not the Staff of Asclepius, that became the official insignia of the Medical Department of the US Army in 1902, and then became the more common symbol of medicine in the United States. Meanwhile it retained its occult symbolism; the Caduceus Power Wand was sold in occult stores, which claimed it was ideal for magic spells.

The serpents represented positive and negative kundalini energy that moved through the body's chakras and around the spine. The spine was represented by the staff. The kundalini moved into the head, where it communicated with the mind, represented by Mercury's wings.

The driver hit a mammoth pothole, sending Robert's head into the roof of the cab. Reading in cabs always gave him a stomach ache, and now his head was hurting too. He closed the book and pressed his fingers against the outer edge of the pages.

"Ouch!" He looked down to see a drop of blood form from a paper cut. He put his finger to his mouth and stared out the window at all the rushing Manhattanites. The cab turned a corner, and he saw the back of a little girl with blond curls. She was wearing a woolen coat. She turned to face him. Her eyes locked on his, and as the cab pulled away, a drop of blood fell from her mouth.

65

Justin eyed the black baby grand piano in the living room, trying to remember what it was like to play it. When he was little, there had been a bear skin rug underneath it that he loved to roll around on, but his dad took it during the divorce. His mother had replaced it with a silk Persian rug. He slowly made his way to the bench and began to pick at the keys with the first finger of his right hand.

He was amazed he still remembered Chopsticks. He played it faster and faster, adding in more fingers.

He thought back to Mlle. Ponseau. She was his piano teacher, and even as a little boy, he knew she was a babe. She had gorgeous, long, red hair, and she always wore tight sweaters and giant scarves she called *foulards* thrown across her shoulders. She was *tres Francaise*; she would pucker up and kiss his cheek with her glossy pink lips.

"*Mon cher* Justin," she would say, and then, as he would play, one finger at a time, she would sing a song without lyrics. Fouick. Fouick, fouick, fouick, fouick. It was such a strange word but so beautiful — it floated from her mouth like opalescent soap bubbles. Justin could see the air move through the space in her teeth — "Foo-week, foo-week" — as she smiled.

Now he had a feeling, an allusion, a palpable thought he couldn't quite grasp. It was real — he could feel it — but he couldn't hold on to it.

He remembered a place made of ink blue and white, and then it all came rushing back to him.

There was a stream that flowed into a cave, and inside there was a large chair carved out of darkened stone. On it sat a man with long hair and a beard. He was thin and had beautiful eyes. Next to him stood a very tall person, perhaps eight or ten feet high, in long robes. Justin expected to be greeted warmly by the man on the throne, but instead he was rejected. Justin grabbed at the thin man's legs, but he only said, "You don't belong here."

Justin begged to stay. "I don't want to go back," he said.

But the man told him sternly, "No."

"Then let me take him with me," Justin said, referring to the large man who stood beside the man on the throne.

"He belongs with me. He has been with me from the beginning. You have your own angel."

The tall man scooped Justin up in his arms and carried him to a small wooden boat at the mouth of the cave. He laid him down in the boat, and another man standing in the boat used the single paddle he held in his hand to launch them into the river.

"Don't be afraid," the man in the boat said. "There is still much to do. I'll take care of you."

"May I call you Fouick?" Justin asked.

The man just smiled.

"It's the sound a piano makes when I hit it just right."

Justin remembered opening his eyes to find his mother standing over him crying.

"My baby!" she screamed. "I thought you stopped breathing!"

He wanted to tell her what had happened, but he was much too young to explain.

66

Dr. Cohen's waiting room was filled with coughing and sniffling patients talking on cell phones and flipping though the pages of magazines. Claire was disgusted by the atmosphere, and she didn't feel much like reading. But Dr. Viviee had told her to keep the appointment, so she sat quietly for a few minutes, expecting that soon she would be ushered out of the main room to the small waiting room Dr. Cohen kept for his high-profile patients or personal friends. Instead, when the head nurse saw she had arrived, she was taken directly to x-ray.

"Dr. Cohen wants us to start with a chest x-ray," the nurse said. "If you'll just take your top and bra off, and your necklace, and put this gown on, I'll be back in a minute."

Claire obliged, giving no thought to the significance of this visit. She slipped off her white blouse and bra and removed her necklace and earrings and placed them delicately in the side zipper pocket of her beige handbag. She put on the paper dressing gown with the opening in front.

She stood in front of the glass and metal box, facing the wall. She held her breath on cue and marveled at the depth to which she could inhale.

"Okay, you can breathe," the nurse said.

"How much radiation am I getting?" Claire asked as the nurse repositioned her.

"They say a lot less than flying to California. Now breathe in, and hold your breath."

"That's why *you* have to stand behind a lead wall, because it's such an insignificant amount of radiation."

"Mrs. Cummings, I do this all day."

Claire didn't care. She felt powerful. Her lungs were so full she felt she might float over mountains.

"Okay, you can breathe. The doctor wants one more view and that's it." The nurse repositioned Claire's body.

Claire felt like someone's guinea pig. She couldn't wait to see Dr. Cohen's face. Doctors always thought they knew everything. For years she had been touting the benefits of alternative medicine, and they had all laughed at her. None of her doctors wanted to hear about different ways of approaching a problem; they were satisfied with their drugs and their hospitals. They all

151

told her chemotherapy was her only hope, but now they would all know how wrong they had been.

The nurse took Claire to an empty examination room, commented on how good her blood pressure was, and pulled out a rubber tube to tie around her right arm.

"The vein is better on the left," Claire pointed out, as the needle punctured the swollen vein.

For the first time in her life, Claire watched closely as the blood slowly filled the vials. When the needle withdrew, it left a miniscule hole. The nurse put a cotton ball over it, but Claire wanted to stare at her perforated flesh; she was anxious to see how long it would take to heal. She wondered if the nanochip was rushing to the site of the tiny puncture and telling the cells how to heal quickly. The nurse put a bandage over the spot and left the room.

Claire lay back on the examination table and closed her eyes.

67

D r. Cohen leaned back in his chair. The lighted boxes contained two
sets of Claire's x-rays, one set from six months ago and the other from
today. He stared at them for several minutes. He called the nurse back into
his office.

"I think you brought me the wrong x-rays," he said.

"Those are Claire Cummings's. Isn't that who you wanted?"

"Yes, I do want Claire's x-rays, but these can't be hers."

"They certainly are. I took them myself not more than ten minutes
ago."

"Do you know who Claire Cummings is?" Dr. Cohen asked the nurse.

"Of course I do. She's wearing black pants and a white blouse. She's in
room three."

"And you took *this* x-ray?" He put the tip of his right index finger directly
on the image of today's x-ray on the screen.

"Sure did."

"Well, what would you say," he said, pointing at the box with the older
film, "if I told you these were her x-rays six months ago?"

"I'd say somebody screwed up on those x-rays," the nurse said confidently, "because these are her x-rays today."

"And I'd agree with you, except they were backed up by a CAT scan and
a PET scan."

"Then you should run, don't walk, in there, and tell her the good news,"
the nurse said.

Dr. Cohen sat on the edge of his desk. The contrast in the two sets of
films was impossible.

"Get Dr. Geiger on the phone and see if he can squeeze Mrs. Cummings
in for a scan this afternoon. Tell him it's important. And get those bloods
analyzed immediately."

He walked down the hall to the examining room where Claire was
waiting. He had no idea what to say to her.

"Claire," he began, "remission simply means a cancer is too small for us
to detect."

153

68

Madeline helped Justin into the elevator as he struggled with the rubber tip of one of his crutches on the elevator floor. He was frustrated and on the verge of tears. He and Madeline had made only a brief trip across the street to the deli, but it felt like he had walked ten miles. He was exhausted and his ankle throbbed despite the anti-inflammatory. Having Madeline with him kept him from complaining, but by the time he made it to the coat closet of his apartment he practically collapsed.

"Here, let me have your coat," Madeline said as he struggled to pull it off his shoulders.

She reached over and kissed him on the cheek.

"What was that for?"

"You just look like you're having such a tough time." She took his jacket and blindly reached for a hanger as Justin rested his tired arms on her shoulders and kissed her.

Natasha ran up, wagging her tail and looking for affection. She rubbed up against Justin's good leg. As Madeline pulled a hanger off the rack, a coat that was next to it dropped to the floor.

Justin heard a clink.

"I think you dropped something," he said.

Madeline scoured the closet floor with her hand. She inhaled a whiff of a mink coat that tickled her nose and started her sneezing. She backed out of the closet.

"There's nothing there," she said, handing Justin his grandmother's coat to hold while she put his coat on a hanger and placed it in the closet.

As Madeline was shutting the door Natasha pushed past and nuzzled something shiny on the floor.

"Wait," Justin said. He walked one hand down the wall until he could reach the other over to what Natasha had found in the closet.

When he stood up again he was holding a small platinum band with five small diamonds in a row.

"Whoa! Look at this," he said, inspecting it. He recognized it.

"That's not mine," Madeline said. "It must have fallen out of the other coat."

"Grams' coat?"

"I guess. Do you want me to go give it to her? I'm sure she didn't mean to leave it in her coat."

"No, I'll take it. This belongs to Max's wife." He slipped it into his pocket.

Madeline walked to her room, with Justin hopping behind. She clicked on the TV.

Justin sat on the bed, put his hands on her hips, and stared at her standing before him in the mirror. He placed his head in the small of her back and gently kissed it. He tugged at her skirt to get her to sit down.

He forgot all about the ring in his pocket and the pain in his ankle.

69

The sound of Helene and Robert's voice in the kitchen brought Justin back to reality. He couldn't help but think how happy she sounded. He suddenly realized how lonely his mother must have been all these years.

"I'd better get ready for dinner," Madeline said ushering him toward his own room.

He sat on his bed and fired up Battle Ultimo, but he was distracted by the memories of Madeline's kisses swooping around in his mind like a flock of doves. Then suddenly with a shout he sprang up. The birds scattered. "Yessssssss!" he said, hopping on one foot.

Madeline ran into his room. "Are you okay?"

"I just figured out a major strategy! I may have to play that Spider dude after all."

"Ugh! Battle Ultimo." Madeline shook her head and walked out. Eventually he followed her into the dining room, pausing to take a rest at the piano along the way.

His mother and Robert were unloading containers of take out food. She seemed happy working as part of a two person team. Justin felt a twang of jealousy.

"Mom, what happened that time when I was little and the paramedics came?"

Helene looked surprised. "What are you talking about?"

"I remember it was in the park. Something happened."

"Geez, I can't believe you remember that. You were so little. We had a new nanny." She opened a container and spooned Thai food onto a plate.

"We had just come out of the Central Park Zoo and we stopped at the kids' playground. I went to say hello to a friend. The nanny was supposed to be watching you. You fell off the swing and hit your head."

"Was I knocked out?"

"Yes. I was frantic. Somebody called the paramedics right away."

"Did I stop breathing?"

Helene let out a curious laugh. She shook her head. "Well, I thought you did. I didn't see you breathing and I couldn't feel your pulse, but then all of a sudden you just woke up. I was crying and you were making some noise you used to make."

"Fouick?"

"Yes, that was it." She laughed at the memory. "Such a strange word, though I must admit it was cute when you said it. That French girl used to say it all the time. 'Foo-week, Foo-week.'"

"How old was I?"

"Maybe around three. It was right when your father and I were getting a divorce. You were very sad about him leaving."

Helene handed Justin his plate.

"You were such an adorable kid," she said wistfully. She placed her arm around him and hugged him to her body. She kissed his forehead. "I miss holding you in my arms."

Robert poured some wine, and everyone sat down at the table.

"Thank God they caught that killer," Madeline said. "It's all anybody's talking about."

Robert just smiled.

"I don't think Robert's convinced," Helene said.

"He's not evil enough to be the killer."

"Oh come on," Helene said. "Great psychopaths never appear evil or they would never get away with all the crap they do. If you're really going to be bad you have to look good or you'll never get any victims. The really bad ones are the regular guys who fly under the radar."

"You're right," Robert conceded. "There is no obvious face of evil, but in this case I was expecting more of a Charles Manson type — someone consumed with his evil. The only thing this guy is consumed with is fear.

"My gut says he would rob you and steal your car, but he wouldn't kill someone and leave behind all the valuables."

"A psychopath doesn't have a conscience," Helene said. "That's why they can lie so convincingly — there's no sense of guilt or remorse. Maybe your guy's not really scared at all; maybe he's just acting that way to fool you."

Claire marched into the room. "I'm hungry," she announced loudly, and then she sat down.

"Mom, I've been dying to talk to you," Helene said. "What did Dr. Cohen say today?"

"He's an asshole."

"Mother! That kind of language isn't necessary."

"Helene, the kids hear worse than that every day. Besides, it's a most descriptive word."

There was silence as Claire indelicately gobbled a forkful of cheese-cake.

"Well, are you going to tell us what he said?"

"He said he couldn't find the cancer on the x-ray, so he sent me for another scan. He's waiting for the results. He said the chest x-ray looked pretty good, but he didn't want me to get my hopes up because remission just means the cancer is too small to detect, and he's sure the scan will show something different. Either way, I'm better than he expected."

"That's great news, Grams!" Justin said.

"Pisses me off he refused to admit I'm cured. Fucking doctors. If they can't take credit for it they don't want to hear about it, just like Dr. Viviee said."

"He's just being cautious, Mother. Dr. Cohen is a wonderful man. He doesn't want you to get your hopes up and then be disappointed. Let's wait and see what the scan says."

"You don't get it, Helene. I'm cured. You can choose to believe it or not."

Robert looked confused, but he didn't ask any questions.

Madeline quietly nudged Justin, "The ring," she whispered. "Show her the ring you found in the closet."

"Oh, yeah," Justin said. He braced himself on the table to stand and reach into his pants pocket. He pulled the ring out and held it out to Claire. "Where did you find Max's ring?" he said. "He's going to be so excited. He must be going crazy right now."

"What are you talking about?" she said.

"This fell out of your coat pocket. It belongs to Max, the doorman. It really means a lot to him because it reminds him of his wife. She died, and the ring used to be hers. You found it, right?"

Justin was still holding the ring out in front of Claire. She never reached for it and barely even looked at it.

"I don't know what you're talking about," she said. "I'm still hungry."

"I have some fresh fruit in the kitchen," Helene said.

"I don't want fruit," Claire complained. "Don't we have anything decent to eat in this house? Where's the chocolate?"

"Grams," Justin said, still holding out the ring. He was thoroughly con-fused by Claire's response to it. "We found this ring in your coat pocket. You really don't know how much this is going to mean to him." There was still no reaction from Grams. "He's going to be so grateful to you. I can't wait to give it to him tomorrow."

"Since when do you eat so much processed sugar?" Helene asked.

"Since I became immortal," Claire said sarcastically. She got up from the table and returned to her room.

70

D r. Cohen was torn between hopes for a miracle and disbelief that such a thing was possible. He didn't know why Claire looked and felt so good, but the rapidity with which her "recovery" was taking place contradicted everything he had experienced in his practice of medicine. A complete cure of her devastating cancer was in the realm of sheer fantasy. Long after the departure of his last patient, he was still sitting in his office, trying to figure out what in the name of God was going on.

The blood work had come back remarkably good. There was no evidence of circulating tumor cells or even antibodies to cancer cells. So where had these cells gone? Had they suddenly become suicidal? Wouldn't that be nice?

He had heard of cases of spontaneous recovery in kidney cancer, even in melanoma and low grade lymphoma. He had even located obscure reports of recovery in lung metastases from a primary uterine cancer, but never when it had spread to the liver, never when it was as aggressive as Claire's. There was a medical paper that associated cancer recovery with a high fever or even coma, but nothing like that applied to Claire. The usual thinking on cases like this was that there had been a primary misdiagnosis or that the cure was attributable to previous treatment. Nothing like that could possibly explain Claire's case.

Having cancer was playing the odds; the patient was entering a world of survival statistics, risk factors, odds ratios, and prognostications. Even if Claire had a ninety-nine percent chance of dying from her disease within four months, the proficient gambler would know there was a one percent chance she would be alive. Sure. But it wasn't a good enough answer.

Cohen called the radiologist, Dr. Geiger, at home. His wife said he was just about to sit down to dinner, but Cohen pressed her urgently to put him on the line.

"Hi, Al," Cohen said. "I'm sorry to bother you at dinnertime, but late today I sent a woman by for a PET scan. Her name is Claire Cummings."

"Sure, I remember. She's the mother of that TV woman. We just did her a few weeks ago, didn't we?"

"Yes, you did. Did you get to check today's scan."

Geiger took the phone to his desk and looked up the results on the computer.

After about a minute Geiger said, "Isn't this lady supposed to be critically ill?"

"Yes."

There was another long period of silence as Geiger reviewed the slides again.

"I'd say you have a healthy patient on your hands."

"Three weeks ago your office ran a scan that showed inoperable cancer," Cohen said. "A chest and abdomen scan showed a lot of nodes in the chest and multiple tumors in the liver. I have it right in front of me."

"I have all her records in front of me, Steve. It must be a mix up. Last month this was a dead person walking. What does the pathologist say?"

Cohen knew that Al was searching his patient records, comparing the names, addresses, birth dates and social security numbers of the patients in the two sets of test results. There had to be two people by the name of Claire Cummings.

"He says the same thing as you. So what's the likelihood of error on something like this?"

"Error? You mean in the machine? No. I'm looking at these slides, pal, and there's no mistake."

"Have you ever heard about anything like this before?" Cohen asked.

"In this kind of cancer? No way. I mean we've all heard of spontaneous remissions."

"Yeah, but have you ever actually seen one?"

"Sure, but not like this and never this fast."

Cohen was actually feeling his heart pumping hard in his chest.

"So, have you asked her what she's been taking?" Geiger said.

"She won't tell me."

"Well, you better jump on that. And you certainly have to write this up for the medical journals. But I think I'd call my broker first. No one's going to believe you anyway."

161

71

"I believe you are in complete remission," Dr. Cohen had said in measured tones.

Claire heard the words over and over in her head — the complete sentence — as if he had shouted it from an Alpine peak and it was echoing down the valleys and across the fields. She already knew she was clear of the massive brown globules that had been destroying her life. She knew it from the core of her being. She wondered what more the tiny nanochip could do.

As she stared at her face in the bathroom mirror, it was different in a vaguely familiar way. The dark pallor had left her skin. She examined the whites of her once bloodshot eyes and noticed a clarity she hadn't seen in years, maybe decades. The lines were smoother, the texture softer, as she pulled and tugged at her skin. Perhaps she didn't need another facelift after all. It was the cancer that had ravaged her, and now that it was gone, her glow was coming back. Odd for a woman pushing seventy to think of a glow, but there it was, along with the beginnings of a slight blush in her cheeks. She was positively giddy at the realization. She dipped two fingers into a jar of lush, scented body crème and began to smooth it on her chest.

Her heart raced with excitement at the thought of seeing the man who had saved her life. She couldn't wait for Dr. Viviee to arrive so she could thank him in person.

She wriggled into a flattering pair of snug black trousers and slipped her feet into black embroidered mules with three inch heels. She hadn't worn them in years. They covered her toes, which had grown slightly crooked and arthritic over the years. She refused to be one of those older women who wouldn't wear heels.

Her insides were jumping, but she maintained a trance-like facial expression. She sat down on her bed and called her salon. The receptionist was surprised to hear from her and offered to send someone out to do her hair and nails, but Claire said she preferred to come in for her appointment. She buttoned up a black cashmere cardigan.

She made a mental list of all the things she would do now. Have her gray hair dyed back to warm chestnut brown, with some blonde highlights to lighten her up. A manicure with natural white polish and a pedicure with a bright melon color. She would get a facial, buy a new outfit and wear it to lunch at '21'. She would find a new husband, or at the very least have sex. She missed having sex.

She would keep her mental check list; she would add new items for all the days of her life. As long as she kept the list, she would live — because she knew that, from now on, as long as she felt alive, she would keep adding to the list. She would reinvent her previous self in a younger, more vibrant, and less needy version. This would be her life. All the things she didn't do before, because she was always doing things for someone else, she would now be doing for herself. It sounded deliciously selfish and she loved it.

But there was one thing she wanted to do for someone else. Just exactly how do you thank a man who saved your life? Do you buy him a gift? Of course you do. But what kind of gift? Do you hug and kiss him? Would he like that or think it foolish? Do you grovel at his feet, sing his praises, tell the world of his greatness? You do all that, she supposed, except she had been forbidden from doing the latter. It made no sense. The world refused to admit that what had already been done was even possible, but the world had to learn about this kind and humble man who sought no recognition for himself, only a cure for her and the millions of others like her.

72

Helene walked in the door, tossed her keys into the crystal bowl beneath the chandelier, and draped her coat over the kitchen chair. She proceeded methodically to wipe the island counter clean, over and over again. She was stunned at the news of her mother's recovery; the rote motions helped her focus on the possibilities.

As much as Helene had seen Claire improve, a complete recovery still seemed too far fetched for her to fathom. She had seen people — and heard reports of many others — living out their last days with renewed enthusiasm and even hyperactivity, but all that was no more than a signal of death's proximity. This was more like a healing — a true and valid cure. The ramifications were immense.

This was big. It was beyond big. It was momentous; it was huge; it was earth shattering. It was exactly the sort of thing that could resuscitate her show and vault her to the front of the television pack. This story would be unbeatable; she would have an exclusive to end all exclusives. The powers that be could never cancel her after this.

And it was *her* mother! She was swimming in a genetic pool of astonishingly good fortune.

THE BODY INDOMINATABLE. She could see the headline on the front page of the New York Times with a picture of her standing at Claire's side, her hand lovingly placed on her mother's shoulder. *The indomitable spirit. It runs in the family.* CUMMING'S SHOW REVEALS CANCER CURE, the Daily News would announce; HE'S CUMMINGS TO CURE YOU would be the headline in the Post, followed by CUMMINGS UP IN THE WORLD, as her show moved to #1. Her time had come. Now all she had to do was convince Dr. Viviee that his time had come as well.

73

"No, Justin," Madeline said, pushing his hand down and away from her underarm.

"Aw, come on" he said, leaning forward to lock lips with the real life woman of his dreams. "I'm crazy about you, Madeline. I can't stop thinking about you. All I ever do is sit around thinking about you and waiting for you to come home."

"Justin, we need to get you out more," she said. She was smiling ear to ear as she pushed him away, stood up, and walked around the room. He knew his charms were working.

"What am I going to do when your parents come home and you go back to your apartment? If we were older, I'd ask you to move in with me."

"You're totally crazy."

"No. I'm just crazy about you. And you can't stand me." He flopped dramatically back on his doubled up pillows, arms outstretched — an invitation.

"Oh, stop it, you jerk. You know I'm crazy about you too."

"Then why don't you show me?"

"I do show you," she said, now slightly irritated. "I just don't want you getting carried away."

"Okay, I won't touch your breasts," he said. "Ever." He paused for a moment, then whined, "I just want you to feel good. Is that such a crime?"

"Give it up, Justin. It ain't happening today."

"Oh, thank God," he said, his hands raised in prayer. "There's hope for tomorrow."

She giggled, and he knew it was just a matter of time.

"If you can get your mind to focus on something more important for a moment here — do you realize, we're part of history?"

It took a moment for Justin to catch up. "You mean Grams?"

"No, I mean your not getting laid, you idiot. Of course I mean Grams. We are all a part of this. You and I are witnesses to the ultimate breakthrough in medical science. People have been trying to cure cancer ever since they figured out it existed, and now it's done. This is beyond amazing. This can't be a secret forever."

"But you can't tell my mother or Grams that you know about Dr. Viviee. They'll kill me. I wasn't supposed to tell anyone."

"Don't worry, I won't tell anyone. But I'm not so sure about your mother. After all, she *is* a journalist."

74

Dr. Viviee kept Claire waiting long enough for her to become concerned and then agitated. She was worried about his well being.

"Maybe we should call the emergency number," she said to Helene, who was making a pot of herbal tea.

"It's not an emergency, mom. He'll be here."

"He's over an hour late. What if something happened to him? What if he got hit by a car? Or mugged! What if he got mugged on the way over here? I'll never forgive myself."

"Don't say that, mother. Nothing can happen to him. Not now. He did not get mugged. I'm sure he's fine. He probably just got held up in traffic. Or caught up on some business. He's a busy man."

"That's true," Claire said, calming down. "He's out saving the world, and I'm complaining he's an hour late. How ridiculous of me. I've got to get a grip. I've got to be patient."

It was easy for Helene to be calm; she didn't have her whole life riding on the man. If anything happened to Dr. Viviee, no one else would have a clue about how to handle the nanochip. Claire knew that without him all her hopes would be down the drain. She also knew that she needed to get everything about the cure to the public as soon as possible. Then the entire scientific community could get to work figuring out how to use the chip. But how would she ever get Dr. Viviee to reveal his secrets?

Helene poured Claire a cup of tea. Claire pushed it away. Helene poured one for herself.

"You know, mother, he really can't continue to deprive the world of what he's created. We need to convince him of that."

"I agree completely."

"My show can help. We need to explain to him how my show can help."

Helene reached across the kitchen table and grasped Claire's hand with a hopeful squeeze. Just then the doorman rang up.

Claire took a deep breath. She felt blood tingling through her body, coursing to tiny capillaries that hadn't felt life in years.

"Thank goodness!" Helene exclaimed. "He's finally here."

They were on him like a couple of rock band groupies the moment he came through the door.

"There is nothing in the world I will ever be able to do to thank you, Dr. Viviee," Claire said breathlessly.

"That goes for me too," Helene said.

"Tell us, please, what we can do for you?"

"Your good health is my reward, Claire. That is thanks enough for me."

"But there must be something I can do for you — something I can give you in return for what you've done for me?"

"I need only to continue my research."

"Then let us help you," Helene said. "Television is very powerful in this country. I can get you research grants, and a lab, a place to do your work. You shouldn't be running around sneaking into hospitals. When I'm through with you you'll have the finest research facility on the East Coast, the finest in the country. No, make that the world."

"And how will you do that, Helene?"

"I'll put you on TV and tell the world of your genius. I have a lot of powerful friends."

"No, I'm afraid I can't do that."

"You must do it," Claire said. "The world needs you!"

"I shall get to the world in due time."

"With all due respect Dr. Viviee," Helene said. "People are dying of cancer every day."

"I'm well aware of that."

"But you can save them. Think of the children, the parents, the grand-parents. You — only you — can save babies from being orphans. You can change the world single handedly. You'll win the Nobel Prize!"

"I can see how much that means to *you*, but it means nothing to me."

"But what if something happens to you, Dr. Viviee?" Claire cried out. "Who will carry on your work?"

"Are you concerned for mankind or for yourself?" he asked.

Claire waited for a moment. "I am concerned for everyone, doctor. You hold the key to hope for millions."

"And what would you propose I do?"

"Go on Helene's show. I'll go with you. Let's tell the world what you've done. When they know what you offer, the whole country will act to see that you achieve your goals."

"Ah, but those in power do not want a cure for cancer. The Association of American Medical Professionals is a very powerful organization. The current treatments bring in billions of dollars a year. The pharmaceutical companies would lose billions. They will fight this every step of the way. They will call me a charlatan and do anything they can to discredit me."

"But, Dr. Viviee," Helene said, "that's exactly why you need me. And why you need my show. The world needs to see you in person. They need to hear you tell them what this is and why you created it and what it can do for so many people who need it. The world will stand behind you, and no special interests can fight the whole world."

"I have treated you without a license to practice medicine in this country, Claire."

"They won't dare touch you!" Claire said.

"You underestimate the power of money. I have only the desire to cure."

"Then we'll get you money," Helene said excitedly. "We'll get you as much money as you could ever want. I will find every billionaire on the planet who has cancer or has a family member with cancer, and you will have all the money you need in a matter of weeks. That I know I can deliver — if you will just do my show."

"Oh, Claire, Helene, you're so dear and I know you mean well, but you have to understand I have sacrificed my life for this cure over and over. I will sacrifice it again when the time is right — but it has to be right. What makes you think people are willing to accept this now?"

"Now you have me," Helene stated emphatically.

He smiled. "Do I have you, Helene?"

"You have my heart and soul in this."

"Your heart and soul in what?" Justin asked. Claire hadn't seen him come into the living room. He kicked the tassels on the bottom of the sofa and plopped down.

Natasha was nipping at Claire's heels. Claire kicked her away.

Justin picked Natasha up in his arms. "She's not getting any better," Justin said to Viviee.

Helene looked at Justin abruptly.

"Grams is still allergic," he said disdainfully, "and she's mean to her."

"I told you, it's important to keep the dog away from her, so her body doesn't have to fight off any more toxins than it needs to," Viviee said.

"Surely you can understand how your grandmother would get angry at something that threatens her like that."

"Now Natasha's a toxin? Yeah, sure." He shook his head in disapproval. "You're different Grams." A tear formed in his eye and slid slowly down his cheek. Justin turned to leave the room, but Dr. Viviee asked him to stop.

"Wait a minute, Justin. That's actually extremely perceptive of you. I didn't realize you were such an acutely aware young man. If I had, I would have mentioned this to you sooner."

"What?"

"It's very common. When people are going through such important changes in their bodies they can seem to be, well, for lack of a better word, different. Sometimes they can be downright forgetful. It may seem like they're not paying attention to details. They may seem angry or argumentative. Have you noticed anything like that?"

"Well, yeah," he said. "Sort of."

"These are all symptoms of sleep deprivation. While you probably think your grandmother is sleeping a lot, an enormous amount of sleep is essential for the healing process. For what she's going through, her body is not sleeping enough. Now, why don't you tell me what you've noticed?"

Justin shrugged his shoulders. "I don't know."

"You can tell me," Dr. Viviee prodded.

"I can't think of anything specific."

"Are you sure?"

"I'm sure," Justin said.

"Good," Dr. Viviee said. "Then don't worry. This is just a temporary adjustment. Soon your grandmother will be back to normal. Just be patient. It can take some time."

Justin took Natasha to his bedroom.

Helene watched him go. "Don't mind him," she said. "He's just missing the time he usually spends with his grandmother."

Claire watched as Helene walked to the other end of the room, turned around, and headed back. She stopped next to a marble column; it seemed as if she was contemplating something. She stared at the floor for a moment, and when she looked up there was a quizzical look on her face. She said "Where's my Lalique vase? Wasn't my Lalique vase here — the one with the angels on it?"

Dr. Viviee turned to Claire.

"Oh, it's probably that stupid housekeeper of yours," she said. "She's so careless. You know I heard a bang the other day when she was here. I bet that was it."

"Mom, Erbie would tell me if she broke something that important."

"She doesn't want to pay for it," Claire said. "You should fire her and take it out of her pay."

"I'm sorry, Dr. Viviee," Helene said. "You don't need to hear this. Let me refresh your drink."

"I'm fine, but I must tell you, Claire, you're not the only person who's been cured."

"Who else is there?" Helene said.

"My nanny. He's been with me since I was a child. He was my first cure."

"Oh, my. Well, that's a very significant fact, doctor. It's also an additional boost for your credibility."

"I understand that. But, Helene, this is all I ask. You must promise me the show will be conducted in the most professional way and not pander to the lowest common denominator."

75

Justin couldn't sleep all night. He lay across his bed, his hands behind his head, staring at the ceiling and thinking about the events of the day. A warmth spread throughout his body. A vision began to appear.

For the first time, Justin saw Fouick's entire body, from his head to his feet, emerging from the bright light, stronger and more vivid than ever.

"You must be real," Justin whispered.

"Bring light to what is shrouded in darkness, and you will provide a beacon to the world," Fouick said. He reached out to Justin and placed a small object on his chest. "Take this gift, so you will know this is real."

Justin was unable to move.

"Wait," he said. He was staring at Fouick's feet. They were unusually soft and smooth looking, with the skin of a small child. "Your feet," he said. "That was you in the hospital. Why didn't you stop the gurney?"

"I did," Fouick said, "or it would have severed your bone."

Fouick disappeared and Justin was fast asleep.

76

Robert went home from the office feeling tired and sluggish. He had spent his day reading the latest research on terrorism and the effects of various bombs on the human body. But it was difficult to concentrate. He was still troubled by the Claiborne case.

His head sunk deep into the down pillow, freshly covered with a new pillowcase. The housekeeper had changed the sheets that morning. He could tell from the smell of fabric softener she used. The sheets were cool and crisp; he pulled his legs up to his chest to get warm under the comforter. His bed linens were stark white, hotel style, but he felt himself enveloped in a warm reddish glow as he closed his eyes.

He was still and peaceful for a time; he hadn't felt that way in quite a long time. His entire atmosphere was one of calmness. Helene made him believe in possibilities again.

As he drifted into sleep he found himself by a riverbank, seated on a park bench surrounded by freshly mowed grass and small flowers. He noticed the dryness in his throat; the arid breeze tickled his cracked lips. He was wondering whether it was safe to drink from the river, when the little blonde girl approached him. She was smiling. She poured him a glass of water from a silver pitcher, dripping with condensation. He struggled to bring the glass to his lips, but he couldn't make his arm move; it was stiff and recalcitrant. He tried harder and harder; the little girl began to laugh. At last he was able to touch his lips to the glass, but the fluid burned his chapped lips; it was something strong and acrid. It burned as it traveled down his throat and stung his belly. It was a familiar taste that he couldn't place. The little girl tapped him on the shoulder, and the entire park bench fell backward. As he tried to thrust himself forward, the odor of vodka burned in his nostrils. He was on his back, surrounded by darkness with only the image of the girl in his sight.

"He's coming, and don't even think of trying to stop him," she said. "Or you know what will happen." She shook her right finger at him; her left arm was bent, her left fist on her waist. "The dragon is coming and he's going to eat you alive!"

Robert awoke trembling, in a cold sweat.

77

Justin awoke pondering the events of the night before. What a strange dream, he thought as he struggled to recall the words. Then he remembered the object that had been placed on his chest. It was small and dark, smaller than a dime. A circle of some sort, but not a perfect one. It had rough edges and was light as a feather. He was anxious to open his eyes to see if his dream had really happened. At the same time he was afraid. Perhaps it had been real. And if there were something on his chest, what on earth would he do? What did it all mean? For certain, it would scare the hell out of him.

He remained still a few minutes longer, debating what to do. He shifted his weight a couple of times to see if he could feel something drop off his chest. He felt nothing. He began to move his right hand, slowly at first, across his chest and then his neck and stomach. There was nothing there. He opened his eyes and jumped out of bed, stumbling to the floor. He had put too much weight on his foot too quickly. It didn't matter.

"Whew!" It was only a dream.

Justin put on the same clothes he had worn the day before. He barely checked the swelling of his ankle; he already knew from the throbbing that if it wasn't still swollen it soon would be.

He grabbed his crutches and reached for a jacket; he was anxious to get some fresh air and bring back some fresh bagels. He quietly slipped into the kitchen. In the darkness he fumbled through the lose change in the bowl on the island. He found a set of keys and then slipped out the front door.

Max was outside sweeping up the sidewalk. Justin gave him a wave.

"Hey Justin," Max said. "That girl has it bad for you."

"Madeline?"

"No, that Samantha girl. She hangs around here all the time. I see her across the street at the coffee shop. I don't mean to eavesdrop, but I even heard her talking on the phone to one of her girlfriends the other day. She was complaining about you."

"What did she say?"

"Oh, she was mad. She said, 'How the hell am I supposed to get anywhere? He won't even see me.' Then she said something about how she didn't think there was much more she could do."

"That's strange."

"Nah, she's just got it bad for you."

"No, I mean, because I didn't think she had any friends." When he turned around he noticed some fragments of distinctive frosted glass pushed against the building. He knelt down to pick up a piece.

"Does that look familiar?" Max said. "Looks like someone dropped it out the window. It was a huge piece. I cleaned it up. I guess I missed some. It could have killed someone."

"When did it happen?" Justin asked.

"I found it the day before yesterday. It must have happened during the night. Is it yours? The manager's gonna have a fit if he finds out who did it."

Justin looked up, squinting to protect his eyes from the dull glare of the sun behind the building. He tried to balance on one crutch and then as he focused, he could see he was standing directly under his grandmother's bedroom window.

"Nah. I think my mom used to have something like this, but I haven't seen it for a long time. Catch you later."

Justin hobbled, his head down, to the deli. He bought some sesame bagels and cream cheese, and as he reached into his pocket to pay for the items he retrieved the diamond ring.

"Oh, God," he said. "I completely forget."

"What?" the cashier said.

"No, nothing." Justin handed him some cash but left before he could collect his change.

"Hey, Max," Justin said, moving as quickly as he could and trying to be cheerful. "You're not going to believe what I found."

"What's that?"

Justin pulled the ring from his pocket and handed it to Max. The doorman stood stock still next to the elevator; he appeared dumbfounded.

"Well, here, take it," Justin motioned.

Max reached for the ring. He looked at it for a moment and looked back at Justin.

"What's the matter?" Justin said. "Aren't you happy I found it?"

"Of all the people," Max said, "not *you*, Justin. I can't believe you...."

"Hey wait a minute. I didn't take it, if that's what you're thinking. I found it in my...." Justin stopped abruptly. "How did you lose it?" he asked.

"I didn't lose it, Justin. Somebody took it. I left my key ring on the counter and the phone rang. I had to go check for a package in the backroom, and when I came back the ring was gone."

"Well, why would you think I took it?"

"I watched the elevator go to your floor."

78

"Two pink dots right here, and it will look like you slept all night." The makeup artist dabbed globs of thick pink concealer into the gray circles under Helene's eyes.

"I didn't really sleep that badly," Helene said. "I was doing a lot of thinking, that's all."

"Hasn't anyone ever told you thinking is the enemy of sleep?" the makeup artist asked. "Now, just take a couple of deep breaths and close your eyes." She put down the makeup brush and began to rub Helene's temples.

"Mmmmmm," Helene purred. "You are the best, Margie. I don't know what I'd do without you."

"No talking, just relax," Margie said. She reached for pressure points on Helene's chin and the bridge of her nose, then circled out toward the corners of her eye sockets. After thirty seconds she said, "There, that's better." She picked up an extra large fluffy brush, dipped it in loose power, and shook it off.

Helene watched the particles of powder fall onto the paper-towel-covered counter, like grains in a snow globe. When she looked back into the mirror, she saw Kyle's reflection and he didn't look happy.

"What's up?" she said, turning to him.

"I don't even know how to say this, it pisses me off so much. But it might work to our advantage," he said, his arms folded in front of him. "The network canceled that loser of a 4p.m. pseudo-news show they put on to save money. They've decimated the numbers, there's nothing worth watching on anywhere in that time slot, and now they want to put us there, in addition to our regular slot."

"So? We'll put a rerun there."

"We'll, that's just it. I think they want to try us out there. They want us to put the new show at four and then rerun it at seven."

"What?! That's crazy. They can't do that. That will ruin our evening numbers. Tell them no!"

"I can't really tell them no, Helene. Their point is that there are two completely different audiences in the late afternoon and evening, so it doesn't matter if we run the shows back to back. It's all new to the audience."

"This is just…just…insulting! How soon do they want to do it?"

"As soon as possible."

Helene stared into Kyle's eyes. She could hear her own angry breathing.

"But, we can make it work for us," he said. "I'm going to suggest we start today — with a live broadcast at four."

"What?! You're nuts."

"Why? Think about it. It's ratings. We've got your cancer-cure guy coming in. That's perfect for the housewives and for people sitting around in their offices watching TV. I've got a couple of friends at the financial channels and I think I can buy some time to promo it today. That'll put all the business people on notice. I know the network will give us lots of promo time all day. We could get very lucky."

"Do you really believe people watching the markets are going to turn away from the price of gold to watch a talk show?"

"No, but they might turn away from the price of SBDH-Co Pharmaceuticals. Of course they will, if we promo it right. Everybody's impacted by cancer."

Helene thought back to her early days in the business, when people told her she was crazy to think she could ever get a job on TV — it was too competitive and she had the wrong degree. She didn't know anyone who even knew anyone who was on TV. But she did know how to fight for what she wanted, and she had learned that it was easier to guide the flow in her direction than to swim upstream. There was no sense in fighting the network brass on this one. What she needed to do was make *their* decision work for *her*!

"Do it. We go live today at four with Dr. Smith Viviee."

79

The room was illuminated by a small lamp and the moon shining in from the window. The moonlight cast a curious glow on the black leather cylinder in the corner. Barrouck had not moved it from that spot since he had placed it there — afraid that at any moment it might turn to dust.

He rubbed his face with a sweeping motion of his right hand as he went over photographs of the sheepskin on his computer, but nothing could clear away the realizations that were flooding his brain. On the screen was a meaningless series of lines and circles. He wiped a tear from his eye as he prepared to read, not from the computer, but from the bible that sat at his side. He put on his reading glasses and turned to the Book of Daniel.

"But you, Daniel, close up and seal the words of the scroll until the time of the end."

He spoke the words softly to himself and then continued.

"The man clothed in linen, who was above the waters of the river, lifted his right hand and his left hand toward heaven, and I heard him swear by him who lives forever, saying, 'It will be for a time, times and a half a time. When the power of the holy people has been finally broken, all these things will be completed.'"

He could feel his breath quicken.

"…So, I asked, 'My lord, what will the outcome of all this be?'

"He replied, 'Go your way, Daniel, because the words are closed up and sealed until the time of the end. Many will be purified, made spotless and refined, but the wicked will continue to be wicked. None of the wicked will understand, but those who are wise will understand.'"

"Close up and seal the words of the scroll until the time of the end," Barrouck said. He stared at the cylindrical container.

"As for you, go your way till the end. You will rest, and then at the end of days you will rise to receive your allotted inheritance."

What was this here before him on the screen and in the black container in the corner? Could it be the sealed scroll of Daniel? No, it was not the scroll itself, but a key — a miraculous key beyond the scope of any mortal. Would this ancient sheepskin decode Daniel's scroll? And where was that scroll? Was it the Book of Daniel itself?

Sir Issac Newton had spent half his lifetime searching for a key to open the sealed books he believed were in the bible. Barrouck turned to the Revelation of John in the New Testament.

"Then I saw in the right hand of him who sat on the throne a scroll with writing on both sides and sealed with seven seals."

The opening of the seals would launch a series of disasters — war, famine, plague, earthquake, and the rise of the antichrist. Then the worst suffering would come. "During those days men will seek death, but will not find it; they will long to die, but death will elude them."

Barrouck could not imagine a worse fate.

He knew little about the sheepskin in the corner, only that it had been found in the depths of a mountain cave that had been exposed after an earthquake in the surrounding area. It had been smuggled out of Damascus on the back of donkey and carried across the desert by an American CIA agent. The agent was looking for a terrorist hideout in the mountains when he stumbled across the sheepskin, rolled in a pot wedged between two boulders. He had no idea what he had found, but he knew it was important, so he carried it across the border to Jerusalem, whence Benjamin had brought it to Barrouck to authenticate and decipher.

Kabbalah had taught him that in the bible there were coded messages predicting the future. Barrouck had even once known an Israeli mathematician who believed he found a code buried in the Torah — Genesis, Exodus, Leviticus, Numbers, and Deuteronomy.

The mathematician had taken the scrolls of the five books of the Torah, just as they were dictated to Moses by God. He removed the spaces between the sacred words to come up with a letter sequence 304,805 letters long.

By running a simple skip sequence on a computer, he revealed a startling series of intersecting words, which he claimed were predictions of modern day events, embedded in the Torah thousands of years ago. Future names, dates, and locations were revealed vertically, horizontally and diagonally, like a giant word search of God.

The odds of those words randomly appearing in the bible, in formation, were hundreds of thousands, even millions, to one. The find was mathematically significant within the most stringent margin of error.

Was it possible a computer had decoded what had been hidden — in plain sight — for thousands of years among the words of the bible?

Barrouck searched the internet — site after site claimed to have deciphered hidden codes in both the Old and New Testaments. He even found a site that claimed to have found hidden pictures. Each had its own formula and accompanying software that anyone could purchase and download.

Barrouck lifted his eyes from the computer screen and stared at the container housing the ancient relic.

His sheepskin was different. This was not some formula figured out by mere mortals. This was a message dictated by God — a key that would unlock a secret foretold long ago, that would reveal the end of an age. The ramifications were literally earth shattering.

The sheepskin had been carbon dated from around 530 B.C., shortly after Cyrus captured Babylon and around the time the Book of Daniel was believed to have been written.

Daniel was an exiled Jew and a powerful ruler in Babylon. He was known for his courage in the den of lions, his faith in God, and his talent as a dream interpreter.

For millennia the lines and circles on the skin, like ancient doodles, would have meant absolutely nothing. But on this day, Barrouck recognized them as a basis for a simple computer program, written like all computer codes, in a series of zeros and ones.

80

Helene was on a roll, taping promo after promo. Kyle had canceled everything else for the day so the two of them could devote all their energy to making the live broadcast at four perfect. He had managed to get last minute commercial spots on the major financial channels and cable outlets as well as on every important network show. He inundated the radio and the internet with spots and called in every favor he had in the media world. It cost a small fortune, but they both agreed they had to give it their best shot.

There were no strong shows — network or cable — in the 4pm time slot; while that would certainly work to their advantage, the problem was that viewers had long since turned away from *their* network at that hour, because of the dismal performance of the previous occupant of the time slot. It had been a sinking ship for a long time and instead of pulling the plug and putting in something fresh while they still had viewers, the network chose to save money. They didn't produce or buy a new show, but let the ratings dwindle virtually to zero. Now Helene could be the victim of that decision, or she could be a hero. It was "do or die" time.

Trying to stay calm while keeping her energy level up, she settled into the makeup chair. Margie began the process of freshening her up.

"You're going to kick ass. I just know it," she said. "That'll show the assholes. They can't mess with Helene Cummings."

"Thanks, Margie." Helene wasn't so sure, but she knew she had to believe. More important, she had to concentrate.

"Hey, the numbers can only go up," Margie said.

Helene didn't hear her.

The mirror was surrounded by lights; it covered the full length of a ten foot long wall. In it, Helene could see the clear reflection of her mother, who was sitting quietly against the wall behind them. Helene closed her eyes, and Margie delicately flicked the soft brush over her face. The tickling sensation made Helene smile.

"You look soooo good, Mrs. Cummings," Margie said to Claire's reflection. "I don't know what you've been doing, but whatever it is, keep doing it."

Claire smiled amiably, preoccupied with watching her daughter get ready for the show.

"Oh, come on," Margie prodded. "You're not going to tell me your secret?"

"I don't really have a secret," Claire said.

Margie couldn't let it go. "You look like you had a really good facelift or something. You can tell me. Makeup artists know everything. We don't tell."

"I did not have a facelift."

"Then I really do have to take up yoga. The people who look the best always seem to do yoga or meditate or something. It's really amazing. It's like Botox. It relaxes the facial muscles."

An intern poked her head into the dressing room. "Your guests are here," she said to Helene.

"Oh, send them in," Helene said, sitting up in the salon chair. She pulled off the headband that held the hair off her face while her makeup was being applied.

She paused for a moment to examine her face in the mirror. She noticed all the makeup spread out on the counter in front of her — so many colors and textures, all calculated to make her look as if she had very little makeup on. Helene knew that cosmetics, lots of them, were a necessity on television, but today she wondered when the thick, professional foundation had started to sink into the lines and crevasses of her face. She ran her ring fingers under her eyes to smooth out any uneven patches and applied a quick coat of lipstick. Satisfied that all that could be done had been done, she removed the apron that covered her clothes and stood to greet Dr. Viviee.

His black-silk Chinese jacket flowed, flamboyantly exposing flashes of its red satin lining as he walked, it seemed to Helene, triumphantly. She admired his confidence at a time when most guests would be trying to coddle frayed nerves. After all, no one knew what lay ahead; this was live television.

Beneath the jacket, he wore dark gray flannel pants and conservative black Ferragamo lace-up shoes. His hair was too long to be conservative; it draped over one eye in a manner Helene could only think of as seductive. She was so focused on Dr. Viviee she barely noticed the man who walked in beside him.

He was petite, no more than 5'6, and he appeared frail. He walked slowly, hunched over, with a cane; he looked to be riddled with osteoporosis. His long gray beard almost touched his knees. He wore a traditional black Chinese cap and loose shirt and pants. Margie led him to a chair and helped him sit down. He took a deep breath, then reached under his shirt and released two hooks of a shoulder harness. Slowly he began to straighten his spine, until finally, he sat completely erect.

"May I present Teng Hao Li," Dr. Viviee said dramatically. "My nanny."

"Oh," Helene said. "Does he speak English?"

"Yes, Ma'am," Teng said. He rose to his feet, clasped his hands in prayer position, and bowed from the waist.

"Oh, my!" Helene said. Now the man was standing perfectly straight — without the use of his cane.

Helene felt her pulse quicken.

"Forgive my deception," Teng said, "but it is a necessary evil to get through customs."

The performance was just beginning. The old man began to pull off the long gray beard; it had been held in place by spirit gum. He removed his small dark glasses to expose piercing, vibrant eyes and pulled off two unsightly skin prostheses that had deepened the folds around his nose and mouth. He pulled a white handkerchief from his pant pocket and wiped his face, leaving a grayish residue on the white cotton fabric.

Claire watched intently from the makeup chair.

Finally, he removed his cap, exposing a thick head of black and gray hair. Within moments, the fragile old man had turned into a lively middle-aged Chinese guy.

"I'm confused," Helene said, unable to mask her annoyance. "I thought you were bringing your childhood nanny."

"That is Mr. Teng," Dr. Viviee said matter of factly.

"Explain," Helene said curtly. "In this country nannies take care of babies, not men."

"Mr. Teng, please tell Ms. Cummings how old you are."

"Madam, I am ninety-five years old."

This couldn't be happening. "Oh, don't be ridiculous," Helene snapped. "Do you both take me for a fool? I can't put this man on the air. This is a sham. What kind of show do you think I have?"

"Calm down, Helene, and let me explain," Dr. Viviee said.

"Explain what? That he's a space alien? This is absurd. No one is going to believe that this — your nanny — is a ninety-five year old man." She was on the verge of panic.

"Let him talk," Claire said. "Let him talk, Helene."

"Fine, go ahead."

"Mr. Teng has been my nanny since I was born. He was with my father before that. After my father died, he stayed on with me. Now he is the only family I have. About ten years ago we learned he had lung cancer. Mr. Teng smoked his whole life, and eventually it caught up with him. There was no appropriate medical care in China, so although my work was still at a very rudimentary stage, we decided to take the risk. That is how Teng Hao Li became the first person to receive this treatment. It took a bit longer for the cure to take effect in those days; we've added a few upgrades since." He smiled, almost shyly, and nodded toward Teng. "What's happened over time is that not only are cancer cells repaired, but all cells are rejuvenated. People seem to grow younger. This effect seems to stop in middle age, depending on the age of the patient when the nanochip is administered, but you can see the promise it holds.

"Your nanochip not only cures cancer but it's the fountain of youth?" Helene said. "Is that what you're telling me?"

"That's exactly what I'm telling you. If all else remains the same, your mother will outlive you."

"Dr. Viviee, this is just too much!"

81

There was a thundering crash; an explosion rocked the virtual city.

"Yes!" Justin shouted, even as the word "LOSER" appeared on the TV screen and on his GamePad Pro Player. For the first time, Justin had advanced to Level 15 out of 20 on the Battle Ultimo digital channel, making him one of the top 100 ranked players. He relished his victory; it was spoiled only by the fact that Madeline wasn't there to see it. She was at school, while Justin milked the last few holidays out of his injured ankle.

There was still some swelling and pain when he walked around too much, so, technically he was still on bed rest — on the condition that he was studying. If his mother found him playing Battle Ultimo he'd be cooked, but he had been studying all day, and a guy needs a little diversion every now and then.

Justin was fairly comfortable walking around and had started practicing with a cane so he wouldn't have to go back to school on crutches. He reached for his study papers again, but then decided on Battle Ultimo instead. The game provided a distraction from the troubling feelings he couldn't shake.

He was hearing conflicting voices in his head, and he didn't know how to reconcile them. He felt viscerally that his visions had been real, but he understood that his certainty was absurd. Now he was beginning to question his sanity. He considered telling his mother he wanted to speak to someone about "teenage issues." She would love that! Her son reaching out, saying he wanted to air his feelings with a professional, would put his mother in a state of bliss. It would validate all she had worked for; it would confirm she was a great mother who raised her son to be an open, sensitive young man in touch with his feelings. "Oh, brother," he said to himself. "There's no way I'm going there. She'll tell the world and I'll never live it down." Besides, he was never really sure whether those psychologist types kept their confidentiality promises to teenagers.

There was always Madeline. He wondered if he could tell her. It felt sort of safe, but also sort of too weird to share. In the old days he would have talked to Grams, but *she* was too weird these days. He needed comfort, and the best thing he could think of at this point was a good pizza. He checked his pockets for cash but came up a couple bucks short for delivery. So he limped to the kitchen to raid his mom's change bowl. He propped himself on the barstool at the island and spun the ball on the chandelier — but the replacement ball didn't spin well. The coins, keys and whatever else was in the crystal bowl made a loud clanging sound as he dumped everything onto the white marble counter top. He was disappointed to find only a single bill in the pile; usually his mom liked to keep at least a spare twenty in there.

He thumbed through the change, pulling out quarters until he ran across a blackened penny. Wait a minute; this coin was too small and rough around the edges to be a penny. He held his breath as he brought it into the light of the chandelier. His heart began to pound, and his breathing grew rapid and shallow. It was the object from his dream, or perhaps it hadn't been a dream at all. He could feel the outline of something as he moved the little disc between his fingers, but it was so black from tarnish he couldn't make out what it was.

Justin jumped from the barstool and started rummaging the kitchen for a cleaning solution that would work; in a top cabinet, above the brooms, he found where Erbie kept the silver cleaner. He read the directions on the bottle, poured some of the clear liquid into a cup, and dropped the coin in. In an instant, just as the label promised, the tarnish began to disappear, and Justin could discern the outline of a face. He removed the coin from the cup, rinsed it in water, and wiped it with a dishrag. The face was in profile on one side of the coin; on the other side were some letters and a human figure with one arm raised. He wrapped the object in a paper napkin and hurriedly limped for his cane and a jacket.

82

"The photo looks like one of those age progression pictures," Kyle said, examining Teng Hao Li's passport. "We did a show on it. This looks exactly like him, only with wrinkles and saggy skin. It's amazing."

An off-duty detective was pressing the fingers of Teng's right hand against the glass of a mobile fingerprinting station. Helene stared at the small mark on the back of the hand — it looked like a tattoo — a small circle with three curved spokes coming out of it.

"It *is* amazing," she said. "Except we're not passport experts. How do we know this isn't a phony?"

"I doubt it's a phony," the detective said, "It doesn't look doctored; everything about it is in order. The prints are a match."

"What else can we do?" Helene asked.

"To insure this man is the same man on that passport? Nothing really, unless you go for a DNA match. But you don't have anything to compare it to, and even if you did that couldn't happen before you go on the air."

"Now you can see the need for the disguise," Dr. Viviee said. "A phony passport would be easier, but I want to preserve integrity in everything I do. The photo is almost ten years old. In order to get him into the country we had to cosmetically age him — make him look the way he looked ten years ago — or no one would believe it's him. I have no other way to prove to you what we've done — only my word and his."

"What do you think?" Helene said to Kyle.

"I think we have to get out there *now*. We've been promo-ing this all day. We can't back down."

"Really?" Helene asked, suddenly unsure of her own judgment. "We have no way of knowing if anyone is even going to tune in at four. Maybe we could put on something else and no one would even notice."

"Hey, you wanted to take more chances. What's the down side?"

"I'll end up on the front page of *The Post* for the next week under the headline 'Biggest Idiot in Town.'"

"People don't read that stuff anyway. They'll just remember seeing your face. You believe in this, right?"

"Yes."

"If you want to take more risks, I'd say now is the time. You can handle this, Helene. I've seen you take dead air and turn it into compelling TV. This is already compelling, you just need to keep it honest. No one does that better than you." He smiled. "Trust me, Helene. No one knows that better than me."

"Thanks, Kyle." She reached over to give him a hug. He blushed. "Okay, let's go," Helene said. She overheard Dr. Viviee talking to Claire.

"This mark looks very good," he was saying. "We have the circle and two spokes. Ultimately we want three. This means the cure is almost complete. For all intents and purposes the cancer is gone. You're in the final stage of the nanochip integrating into your body. We know that, because the mark is changing very slowly."

"We need to move, people," the stage manager said, ushering everyone into the main studio.

83

"Hello, everyone. I'm Helene Cummings. We have a truly amazing program for you today, and it's one that's very personal to me." She spoke with the utmost sincerity, pausing for effect after almost every word.

"What would you say if I introduced you to a mysterious physician, an American who's been living and working in the Far East, who now claims to have discovered the cure for cancer?"

Some audience members snickered.

"But wait. He's also discovered the fountain of youth."

"Yeah, right," someone in the audience yelled.

"That's okay. We've all heard incredible claims from charlatans and quacks. But this is different."

A hush came over the crowd.

"What would you say if I told you someone was diagnosed with terminal cancer, given only months to live, and then, after treatment from this mysterious doctor, in a matter of days... I repeat, *days*, not months, or years... was given a clean bill of health?

"Does it sound too good to be true? Don't worry, I wouldn't have believed it myself if it hadn't happened to me. But it did. You see, that cancer patient is my mother, and I have all the tests to prove she's been cured."

The crowd let out a collective gasp.

"Let me begin the story by showing you a brief clip of one of Manhattan's most noted oncologists, and a frequent guest on this program, Dr. Harvey Galipeau."

Helene motioned to a large screen monitor that descended from the ceiling. The studio lights dimmed and a digital picture of Dr. Galipeau appeared on the screen. He was studying the results of a PET scan on a computer screen, flashing through section after section. "You can see this patient's lung is riddled with cancer," the doctor said, pointing to slices of the three dimensional image. "But when we move to this picture here, we see the lung is completely clean." He pointed to another image.

Helene's voice was heard off camera, "What would you say if I told you this is the same patient, a short time later?"

The doctor didn't speak for a moment. "Well, I don't like to talk in terms of miracles...." He laughed. "So I'd have to say that's not possible."

The screen faded to black and the studio lights came up.

"The doctor was examining PET scan results of my mother's lung a few months ago and a few days ago. Please welcome my mother, Ms. Claire Cummings. Mother, will you come up here please?"

Claire got up to a rigorous round of applause and took a seat in the middle of the stage.

"Hello, Helene," she said.

"Mother, will you please tell your story to the audience."

The audience was silent. Helene was in a state of intense joy — she was, as athletes called it, in the groove. If luck was with her, viewers all over the country were now under her spell; they were pausing in their work, reading, or meals; whatever they were doing, to listen to Claire. People watching the show were calling friends to tell them to watch, because *this* was compelling TV. That's how it's done. For all the consultants, research and focus groups, nothing could beat giving the viewer something that *affects their life*.

Claire explained how she had been hopeless, how she had been told to wait for death. Then she had met Dr. Viviee. She smiled demurely at him in the audience, and the camera cut to his humble but appreciative reaction as he modestly smiled and bowed his head. For a moment, Helene was just a viewer, wanting to hear from the woman who beat the odds.

As Claire completed her story, she explained that Dr. Viviee was coming forward at great personal risk to himself and was only doing so out of a deep concern for the well being of others. "He can no longer stand by and see people die needlessly when he knows they can be healed — just as I have been. He's here to bring hope where there was none."

To thunderous applause, Dr. Viviee rose from his seat and walked to the stage.

He was even more striking and powerful on television than in person. The studio lighting cast an aura around his head, and his vivid eyes seemed violet against the cobalt blue walls of the studio. His voice danced with rhythm as he spoke. His enthusiasm was contagious.

Around the country people were glued to their sets, mesmerized by his deep voice and unwavering confidence. Helene could feel it. Viviee was slow to accept praise.

"Dr. Viviee," Helene said, "this is such an incredible story that if I had not experienced it in such a personal way, frankly I would never have believed it. You are truly an amazing man."

"But, Helene, this creation is my father's work as well as mine. I was given a tremendous foundation to build upon. He was the genius. I just continued his work. And frankly, I would like everyone to view this discovery with a healthy dose of skepticism until it can be shown to be true beyond a shadow of a doubt. But I also hope this will be viewed with a sense of wonderment at the possibilities. We are truly limitless creatures, and we can see this clearly now that what seemed for so long to be a limitation has been removed. I bring hope where there was none. Surely that can't be a crime."

It was time to move back from soft sentiment to the hard facts news. "Let's focus on the technology for a moment, Dr. Viviee," Helene said. "Can you tell us exactly how it works?"

"Of course," he said with a smile. "Cancer cells are essentially cells that go crazy and wreak havoc on the body. We can kill them by cutting off their food supply, which is blood. But if we do that, we kill the affected organ as well.

"We can kill them with chemotherapy, but that also kills healthy cells.

"Stem cells are attracted to damaged areas of the body and in many cases will repair those areas. But using blood from umbilical cords or stem cells is very controversial; hence most of the important research in that area is being conducted off shore.

"My father set out to create a nanochip that would work much like a stem cell, only better. It moves through the spinal fluid, locates damaged areas and out-of-control cells, and repairs the genetic blueprints that turn the cells on and off. In this way it turns off destructive cells and turns back on healthy, therapeutic cells — it's a genetic light switch, if you will."

"Why the spinal fluid?"

"Think of the brain as the computer that runs the body and the spinal cord as its cable. The nerves are wired to every organ — heart, lungs, kidneys, etcetera.

"The nanochip travels through the spinal fluid and sends signals to the nerves. The signals indicate which cells to turn off and which ones to turn on. The end result is not only healing, but rejuvenating. We have, in effect, created smart cells. It's really very simple."

"Dr. Viviee, if this is all as easy as you say, why hasn't someone else come up with it, or at least explored the possibilities?"

"Ah," he said, staring pensively into Helene's eyes. "Therein lies the billion dollar question. I've been trying to answer that same question for years. And the answer is the reason I have conducted my research in China."

"Many would say you conducted your research in China because here you would have been subjected to the scrutiny of the Food and Drug Administration and a variety of other agencies assigned to protect the American public from dangerous medical techniques, crackpot remedies, and medications with serious side effects."

"And they would be right. The government agencies, the pharmaceutical companies and a few other significant interests would never let me or anyone else cure cancer."

Everything in the studio seemed to stop for a moment.

"Dr. Viviee, really…" Helene began.

"Can you tell me how it is that billions of dollars have been spent to cure cancer, yet there is no cure? You're a smart woman, Helene. Your audience is smart. Hundreds of billions of dollars have been spent to cure cancer, yet you, and the members of your audience, are more likely to get cancer today than at any other time in history."

"Perhaps that's because there are more people around to get cancer."

"Then why is the percentage of those who die today the same as it was fifty years ago? Americans spend five trillion dollars a year on health care. How much would they spend if they were healthy? I have conducted my research in China because I would never have been allowed to achieve what I have achieved if I had worked in this country."

"That's an extreme charge you're making doctor. It's very difficult to believe."

"Have you ever noticed how fundraising escalates at the promise of a cure — whether it's for muscular dystrophy, paralysis, heart disease or cancer — yet there is never a cure?"

"But there have been many advances in medical technology," Helene said.

"True, there are thousands of advances. They are called pharmaceuticals, and they are very useful. Mainly they're useful in creating a need for more pharmaceuticals to address the problems they cause. That's what keeps the machine running."

"And you're suggesting…?"

"Here I am, a lone doctor working in the worst conditions in China, and I figure out how to cure cancer. Now either I'm some sort of a super-genius, or I'm the only one really trying. My money says I'm the only one really trying."

"There are thousands of medical researchers around the world who would say they are trying with all their heart and soul to rid the world of disease."

"And I'm sure they believe that, but big business won't let them. Do you know there are cures for cancers and various other diseases right now, sitting on the shelves of pharmaceutical companies, and they will never be made available to the public? It's true. They are considered unmarketable because they can't make enough money on them to make them worth their while. They can't make enough of a profit, so they just shelve them and let innocent people die. They're called 'orphan drugs'.

"Oh, it's not obvious. That's the insidious nature of big business. It's subtle. In many cases the researchers never even know the full value of the discoveries they've made."

"How is that possible?"

"Do you realize who funds all this research into health care? The health care industry. If they can't make money on it, they won't fund it. Frankly that's a conflict of interest if I've ever heard of one."

Dr. Viviee had captivated the audience. Some looked skeptical, but there wasn't a soul who wasn't paying attention. It was as if an invisible wand had passed over the room, bringing everyone under the spell of a single deep voice.

A man stood up in the audience. Instantly an usher dashed over to him and stuck a microphone under his chin. "I work for a major pharmaceutical company," the man said, "and in no way do I believe that anyone is intentionally manipulating the process to keep people sick. That's absurd. However, some of what you're saying about the research process is true. What people forget is that all these drugs we produce cost a lot of money in research and development — millions of dollars. How do you expect us to study things we can't make money on? Are we supposed to just put out tens of millions of dollars on something we can never recoup the investment for? We're not a charity. We are a business, and we have an obligation to our stockholders to make money."

"That's exactly right. You have an obligation to your stockholders," Dr. Viviee said. "And for all the money your company and those like it spend on research and development of new medicines, they spend more money on marketing the products they come up with. People acknowledge this. But what people are not so aware of, is that the watchdog groups are funded by the companies they are supposed to be watching.

"According to the law, the FDA is not supposed to hire people who have conflicts of interest, yet they constantly hire from inside the pharmaceutical companies and wave the restrictions. No one knows how often, because it's a secret. I stand before you with a revolutionary medical development that threatens to cripple the health care industry as we know it. Do you think I'm not afraid that they will try and ruin me or worse? I am. But, I am willing to sacrifice myself rather than let the current system continue."

"What exactly do you think is going to happen to you?" Helene said.

"I have no idea. My father was offered tens of millions of dollars by a pharmaceutical company not to continue his research into this life saving device. It is why he moved to China and why I continued my work there."

"Do you have evidence that confirms what you're saying? We'd like to see it."

"In time I will share all the evidence with you. Right now it is time to bring this life giving discovery to the world."

A stage crew member was holding up a large sign next to Camera #1. Helene got the message. "We are going to take a break right here," she said directly into the camera. "There is still so much to talk about, and I'm going to introduce you to another unbelievable person in just a moment. Don't go away because you will not want to miss this for sure!"

When the tally light turned off she turned to Dr. Viviee, "Nice job! Excellent."

He smiled as she paced the floor assessing audience reaction.

"What do you think?" she said to no one in particular.

"I believe it," one audience member shouted.

"Boy, are they going to go after him," another said.

"Follow the money," still another said. "That will take you to the heart of everything."

Helene went for a drink of water. Her mind raced. Where should she go next? Should she bring in the old guy right away or wait for an opportune moment. She spotted Kyle, walking toward her from the control room. "What do you think?" she said to him.

"I think the phones are lighting up like a Christmas tree. The lines are jammed. What else do you need to know?"

"It's good TV, huh?"

"It's great TV. You picked a winner. Is he single? You could be a good match."

"Ten seconds to air," the stage manager said.

84

On top of the world in midtown Manhattan, Lars Studor sat in his penthouse office. Despite the magnificent view, he never glanced out the floor to ceiling windows.

He had been there so long, won so many battles, thwarted so many takeovers, and made so many breakthroughs; his stock was as strong as the company's. In fact, the two were inextricably linked. As long as SBDH-CO's stock was strong, Lars Studor was untouchable as chairman and CEO of one of the world's largest and most progressive pharmaceutical companies. He had a reputation for knowing precisely what drugs to develop, how to get them quickly through the FDA screening process, and when to bring them to market.

He had worked the system for over 40 years; no one had ever known how to do it better than Lars. He could always be counted on for a generous research grant when the FDA or Association of American Medical Professionals needed something studied. Under his tenure the company courted doctors and politicians at unprecedented levels in an industry already known for extravagance.

In return, he didn't expect much, just occasional consideration for his knowledge and experience, and a level of trust. So, when one of his VP's came into his office ranting about some lunatic on television trashing the drug industry, he knew exactly what to do.

"I'm going to need to talk to Dr. Schultz, over at the AAMP," he said to his assistant through the speakerphone. "But first, get me Charlie Block at the FDA."

"I already have him on the line, sir," his assistant said.

"Hi, Charlie, how are you?" Lars said, betraying no genuine concern.

"I'm good, Lars. What can I do for you?"

"Do you happen to be near a television?"

"No."

"Well, you need to get to one. Apparently there is some charlatan on television claiming to cure cancer."

"Not another one."

"And he's practicing medicine without a license. I think you better get the boys on it right away. He's on… what show is that?"

"Helene Cummings show," the VP responded. "It's on right now."

"Did you get that, Charlie?" Lars asked.

"Sure did. I'll get right on it."

"And Charlie...."

"Yes, Lars?"

"I suspect this one could pose a very serious threat to the well being of our sick population."

85

"Welcome back, everyone. I'm Helene Cummings, and in case you're just joining us, this could be the most important show I've ever done.

"I'm going to introduce you now to someone who, like my mother, seems out of the realm of possibility. He defies all logic and reason, so much so that I almost cancelled today's show. But I decided to let you judge for yourself.

"Please welcome Mr. Teng Hao Li."

The audience was quiet as Teng walked onto the stage and took his seat.

Helene shifted in her chair to face him. "Mr. Teng, you too have received Dr. Viviee's nanochip. Is that correct?"

"Yes. Ten years ago I was dying of cancer, and everyone had given up hope — everyone except Dr. Viviee. He cured me."

"But, Mr. Teng, you say he did more than cure you."

"That's right. It seems I have been completely rejuvenated by the nanochip."

"Rejuvenated? How so?"

"I look and feel younger and stronger now than I have for decades."

"You've worked for Dr. Viviee for a long time. What do you do for him? What has your job been?"

"I started as his nanny."

Helene paused to let the words sink in. The audience was confused.

"In this country nannies take care of babies."

"In my country as well. I have taken care of Dr. Viviee since he was born."

"But you look like you are only slightly older than he is."

"Thank you," Teng said. He bent his body forward from the waist and dipped his head forward. "You are most kind."

"How old are you?"

"Ninety-five."

The audience was totally silent.

"You sure do look good for ninety-five." Helene laughed. So did the audience.

"Dr. Viviee, can you explain this to us?"

Dr. Viviee nodded. "It is simply the result of cells being reactivated, cells that have slowed down with age and even become dormant. It takes some time, but we have seen that people do grow younger. But I must emphasize, this is only a side benefit. The purpose of the nanochip is to save lives."

"How many times have you tried this technology?"

"Ten people with terminal cancer have received the nanochip."

"And what has been your cure rate?"

"One hundred percent."

"One hundred percent?"

"Yes."

Helene was confused. Hadn't Dr. Viviee told her about a person who fought the technology and died? Had she misunderstood? She didn't think so, but she didn't want to make a fool out of him now. The audience loved him, and at this point she couldn't afford to alienate them — or him.

"And, Doctor, can you tell me about the mark Mr. Teng has on his hand?"

"It's called a dry eruption. It is an immune system response as the body assimilates the chip — essentially an allergic reaction. Technically it can show up anywhere but usually it shows up on the hand."

"But this is actually something you look for, right? You actually want this mark to occur?"

"Yes. It shows the technology is working."

"Is it permanent?"

"Yes. It changes as the body assimilates the nanochip, but eventually, once the process is completed, the mark looks pretty much the same on everyone, as you can see on Mr. Teng. In truth there are very subtle differences between people; no two people will have exactly the same mark. In that way it's very much like a finger print."

"So, if someone is sick and they come to you to get this nanochip, what do they have to do?"

"It's a simple injection of a not-so-simple chip. The only thing we ask is that the patient doesn't fight the technology. In the East we are very familiar with the mind-body connection in the healing process. This is an area that standard medicine has been sorely lacking in for years."

"And if you do fight it?"

"You're back to square one, and you will die of the disease."

"Is the nanochip ever removed?"

"No. In order to do what it does, it lodges itself at the base of the brain; it becomes a control center if you will. It will keep the cancer from coming back, or any other disease for that matter."

A man in the audience stood up. "I'm listening to all of this, but really it's just crazy."

"So was electricity, once," Viviee said. "So was landing on the moon."

Helene got up and moved into the audience. Next to her an elderly woman spoke. "What did you say?" Helene said, extending her microphone and holding it at the woman's chin.

"I just can't believe this is an old man. I mean it's amazing, miraculous, if it's true."

Helene turned back toward the stage. "But, Teng Hao Li, you insist you are in fact approaching one hundred years old!"

"I have been with Dr. Viviee since he was an infant. I worked for his father and have cared for him since the day he was born. When we learned I was dying of cancer, Dr. Viviee decided his cure was ready and I was a most willing subject. Together we took the gamble, and as you can see, it paid off handsomely. You've seen my passport and you've had it examined for fraud."

"Yes, we have," Helene said. "I believe I understand how the nanochip can cure cancer, but I'm not sure I understand how it can make a 95 year old look like a 45 year old."

"With the nanochip, cells are simply reprogrammed to rejuvenate," Dr. Viviee said. "In older people, that's likely to take them back to an optimal time, which is interesting because as you can see, he's not a twenty-year-old. If I had to come up with a chronological age for him, I would say he's a fit, healthy forty-year-old."

"Might he get younger?"

"It's possible but not likely. He has been this way for five years now with absolutely no degeneration."

"No degeneration? How long do you think he will live?"

"I see no reason why he won't live a healthy hundred and fifty to two hundred years."

There was another gasp from the audience.

"Two hundred years!" Helene said, emphasizing the hundred.

"Maybe longer, we simply don't know."

"What do you mean, maybe longer?"

"Provided the nanochip is properly maintained I can't say when or even how he will die."

"Immortality. Are you talking about immortality?"

"In the year 2000 scientists discovered how to make some cells immortal. I've just put the whole picture together. Short of a gun shot to the brain or a dramatic accident, I can't figure out how Mr. Teng will ever die."

86

The show was over, but the story was just beginning. Everyone wanted more. Kyle had immediately ushered Helene and Viviee back to Helene's dressing room.

"We are going to hang out here for a bit, Dr. Viviee," Kyle said.

"What's up, Kyle?" Helene said.

"I think you might want to wait a bit before you leave. There are some people out there."

"Are the cops here to arrest Dr. Viviee?" Helene said.

"It's hard to tell. There are too many people."

"What do you mean?"

"Come on," Kyle said. "Why don't you see for yourself?" He walked them quickly down the hall and into the control room. It was a large room with five ascending rows of counter tops. During the show the producers, directors, and technical people sat behind these counters working their control panels and computers. The room was illuminated only by the light from twelve inch monitors that covered the front wall of the room. They showed the images captured by eight studio cameras, and also various television programs, network feeds, satellite intakes, and security camera scans. Kyle walked down the ramp to six security monitors in two rows of three; they were on the bottom right corner of the monitor wall.

What they saw was unbelievable. Helene was amazed. "I knew this was going to be big," she said, "but I never expected anything like this."

The crowd outside the studio was at least twenty people deep. It filled the entire block and stopped traffic as it spilled onto Seventh Avenue. There were old people and young people, people with chemotherapy bald heads and some so sick they had to be propped up by friends and family. There were parents with small children. Some carried infants. A man in a wheelchair spun in circles in the traffic, while another with cerebral palsy yelled incoherently into the crowd. The crowd was increasingly loud. All decorum was broken when a bald and painfully frail young man climbed to the top of another's shoulders and with fists raised to the heavens screamed, "We want Viviee!"

Helene looked to Kyle in awe. They could practically see the wave of excitement overcome the crowd as first the back row began chanting, then the middle and front rows: "We want Viviee! We want Viviee!"

NYPD stood the perimeter. Any pushing and shoving among these clearly sick people could result in serious injuries. Officers scanned the crowd looking for agitators — passersby who might join the crowd just to cause trouble. A few bums were quickly ejected, but there seemed to be little the police could do without creating an even bigger scene.

Television cameras were arriving from all the networks, many of whose studios were within walking distance. A huge traffic jam had formed from midtown into the twenties on Seventh Avenue; cars and buses in a thirty square block area were utterly immobilized.

Photographers vied for the best shot of the door. Reporters rushed, microphones in hand, to anyone they could get to speak on camera.

"Excuse me, ma'am," one young female reporter said to a bald woman, "why are you here?"

"To get the cure!" the woman yelled above the noise of the crowd. "To get the cure and meet this incredible man!"

A small group formed around the microphone.

"We want to make sure this cure makes it to the public!" one man yelled.

"I'm dying," a woman shouted. "I don't need government approval to die, and I don't need it to live. I want this nanochip!"

"I left work just to see this man," a forty-ish man in a business suit said. "I think he's amazing."

"We all deserve a chance," another woman screamed. "Give us life, Dr. Viviee!"

"No one could have predicted this," Kyle said, staring into the monitors. "This is just beyond anything…"

"These are rational, sane people so moved by a television show they dropped whatever they were doing, left their offices and homes, and came here to meet the man who would save them," Helene said. "It's the fear of death — and the promise of mortality — that binds us all."

What if it was really true, she wondered. What if Viviee really was offering immortality? The implications were enormous, not just for the medical industry but for population control, the food supply, drinking water, everything.

"I have to get out there," Dr. Viviee said, breaking the spell that had glued Helene and Kyle to the monitors. "I need to speak to them." He walked away.

Kyle shoved Helene in his direction.

"You're not going alone," she said. "I'm coming with you."

87

Navigating down Fifth Avenue during rush hour was akin to almost drowning in a sea of people, smoke-breathing buses, and flashing "Don't Walk" signs, but Justin knew it would be faster than taking a taxi. Even for rush hour, foot traffic and street traffic was exceptionally bad.

In the thickening throng of rushing humans at Rockefeller Center, he felt like a suit flattened in one of those steamy professional pressers. He glanced up at the spire of St. Patrick's. The Cathedral in all its glory was an oasis of calm, empty except for the tourists, gathered on the steps like pigeons at the base of a gothic statue.

He was almost there. In three blocks he would be at 47th Street — a solid block of separate jewelry booths, hundreds of them in twenty-five different groups — the Diamond Exchange. These people knew everything there possibly was to know about anything of value, and Justin was sure he had something of value.

He walked into one of the exchanges, up an aisle below the neon lights, and into a randomly selected booth.

"Hi, excuse me," Justin said to a woman reading the New York Post behind a counter of gold wedding bands. "Do you know anything about old coins?"

"Coins? No, honey, but there's a guy down there at the end to the right that sells a lot of coin jewelry."

"Okay, thanks," he said. He headed down the aisle, past booth after booth handling the range from glittering hip-hop jewels to old-fashioned estate pieces, until he came to a vendor with a display cabinet filled with black and gold coins made into necklaces and rings with diamonds around them.

"Excuse me, sir?"

"What can I do for you, young man?"

"Do you know anything about old coins?"

"Does it look like I know anything about old coins?" the man said, shrugging his shoulders with his hands facing the heavens. "Come on kid. What you need, I got. Who's this for, your mom?"

"Actually, I don't need anything... to buy, that is. I need to know about a coin I have."

"Then take it to a coin dealer."

Funny, the thought had never occurred to him. "Yeah, I'm sorry. I guess you're right. I just found this coin, and I didn't know what to do. I thought someone who deals in jewelry might be able to appreciate its significance."

"What makes you think it's significant?" the jeweler said.

"Someone told me it could be very important, and I just…."

"Well, then, let's see it."

Justin pulled the crumpled napkin from his pocket and began to unfold it. The jeweler looked on with the eager anticipation of a small child around the Christmas tree.

"Well, what do we have here," he said, gently taking the coin from Justin's palm. "Looks like silver."

"I put some silver cleaner on it."

"Hmmm," the jeweler said, putting a loop to his eye. He pulled a pencil from behind his ear and began to scratch some letters on a pad. T-I C-A-E-S-A-R D-I-V-I A-V-G-V-S-T-V-S.

He flipped the coin over. On that side, a figure seated on a chair was raising his right arm up in the air, and there was another inscription. Again he began to write. P-O-N-T. He paused, moved his hand across the paper to leave a gap, then wrote M-A-X-I-M.

"Rebecca!" he yelled.

"I'm busy, Saul."

"Get me that book on Roman coins."

"What book?"

"The one on the shelf back there."

"We've got three thousand books on the shelf, and that's the best description you can give me?" A middle aged woman with dark hair and harlequin glasses, parted the back curtain and handed Saul a large book.

"No, this isn't it," he said irritably.

"Yes, it is," Rebecca responded.

Saul licked his thumb and began flipping pages.

"Ceasar, Ceasar, let's see…." he said intently. "Ah, here's something." He scanned the page with his finger, then flipped a few more pages over. "Okay. It looks like it's a silver *denarius*, from sometime around 14 to 37 AD." He looked up at Justin. "Wow, that's an old one. We've got Tiberius on the front and a female figure holding an olive branch on the back." He flipped the coin from front to back and back again, like a magician. "The inscription on the front is TI CEASAR DIVI AVG F AVGVSTVS, whatever that means. And on the back it should be… there it is, PONTIF MAXIM. Yep, that's it."

"How do I find out what it means?" Justin asked.

"Do you know anyone who understands Latin?"

"No," Justin said with his head down.

"Hey, don't be so glum," Saul said. "You did pretty good here, kid. It looks like it's worth a couple hundred bucks. Not too shabby a find. I guess it's also called a Tribute Penny." Saul turned the book for Justin to read.

TIBERIUS "Tribute Penny"

TIBERIUS was the Roman Emperor from 14-37 AD also known as TIBERIUS CEASAR AUGUSTUS, or TIBERIUS JULIUS CEASAR AUGUSTUS. His original name was TIBERIUS CLAUDIUS NERO. He was the adopted son of Augustus and he sought to preserve the imperial boundaries.

"Thanks," Justin said. "I really appreciate this." He took the coin and left the counter.

"Hang on, kid," Saul said, turning the page. "Want an interesting footnote?"

But Justin had already disappeared into the crowd.

"Well look at that," Saul said quietly. "This coin's been in the bible."

88

Helene watched Dr. Viviee walk the halls like the master of his domain. The studio had become his domain. He hit the horizontal bar on the large metal door with enough force to fling the door open and stepped into a beam of cool sunlight to meet his adoring crowd.

He waited as a hush came over the people, then waited a moment longer. He raised his arms just slightly off his sides, turned his palms toward the crowd, and smiled. Everyone cheered.

Helene resisted the urge to take control. She stopped several steps behind Dr. Viviee. There was nothing she could offer that would satisfy the life-seekers. This was his moment.

A young woman raised her hand. In black magic marker she had drawn a large circle with three curved spokes. "I want the cure, Dr. Viviee. Please use me. I need the cure."

Others in the crowd grabbed pens and markers and drew circles on their hands; they looked to one another for the exact design, like students copying answers on an exam, then one by one they held their arms to the sky.

Teng and Claire walked up behind Helene and stood next to her on the platform at the top of the staircase. They all watched the desperate people beseeching the man who was their only hope.

Then, from the back of the crowd, six armed officers cleared a path to the front. They climbed the stairs to meet Viviee where he stood apart from the others, smiling and watching.

"Dr. Smith Viviee?" the officer said.

"Yes. I am Dr. Viviee."

"You're under arrest for practicing medicine without a license. Now if you please...." but Dr. Viviee had already offered his hands. Another officer began to place the handcuffs on his sinewy wrists. Two officers took him, one by each arm, as two others led the way and the final two — the one who had spoken and the one who had cuffed him — followed behind.

Dr. Viviee stopped for a moment as they descended the stairs.

"I will not let you down," he yelled to the crowd. "Don't worry. I will not let you down."

As the words came out of his mouth, a young woman, lying flat on a makeshift stretcher that looked to be an old Southwestern blanket, was lifted

207

above the crowd. She couldn't have been more than nineteen or twenty years old.

"Help my daughter, Dr. Viviee," a man pleaded. Helene could see the television cameras zooming in to catch his tears. "I know you can help her. Please, I beg of you. You're her only hope."

A photographer climbed on top of a pile of broken furniture in a dumpster and extended his camera over his head. He pointed it down into the young woman's grimacing face; her pale flesh tones contrasted sharply with the dark blues and reds of the old blanket. The light caught the tear in her eye at just the right angle, and Helene imagined it glistening on television screens all across New York City as local stations broke in to regular programming, one after another, to cover the commotion.

"This is not the end," Helene shouted. "This is the beginning. We are hiring the best lawyer in town to get this man out of jail immediately. I will not stand by for this injustice. This man does not deserve to be in handcuffs. My mother is living proof of that." The crowd roared. "We will find out exactly where he is being taken. If you'll all just sit tight we'll have the answer in a few minutes. We can all head there together." She raised her fist defiantly. "I'll see you on the court house steps!"

The crowd became almost preternaturally silent. Now they would wait. They sat down on the curbs, on the sidewalk, anywhere they could find to sit, awaiting their deliverance.

Back inside the studio, Helene was out of breath. "Dear God," she said. "Kyle, who's the biggest publicity hound lawyer we know?"

"You have to ask?" Kyle laughed. "I put a call through to Jeff Stone before the show just in case."

"You're good, Kyle. But Jeff Stone? I thought he was in L.A. on a case."

"He *was* in L.A. He just had a facelift. He's back now and ready for his coming out party."

"You're brilliant!"

Before he could even say thank you, Kyle's cell phone rang. It was Jeff Stone. Kyle activated the speaker. Jeff Stone had seen everything on television. He had already called the District Attorney and asked for an agreement on bond. The DA had refused.

"Get everybody to meet at the courthouse downtown," he said. Helene could hear the excitement in his voice, even through the distortion of the speaker phone. "We'll force an immediate bond hearing. Keep the crowd outside until I get there."

89

All the New York stations had broken into programming with wall to wall coverage of a story that quickly captivated the city.

Thousands of people arrived at the courthouse steps. It was an amazing sight. These people weren't just gawkers or the curious; they were patients accompanied by their loved ones.

Their bald heads shone in the sunshine and in the glare of the enormous lights the camera crews aimed from flatbed trucks on the colorful mass gathering. The cameras captured individual faces riddled with pain and exhaustion. But their eyes gleamed with the hope of a miracle.

Tears streamed down faces; the remotest possibility of a cure was enough to bring them to an emotional peak. These were battered, broken people who refused to be defeated. They knew that if they could win this battle, then what they had prepared for — their imminent death — could be a fading memory in a matter of days. It seemed too good to be true, but there was no shortage of hope for the hopeless.

The silence of the crowd expressed its fortitude and steadfastness in its mission. These people would not move at the urging of the NYPD or anyone else. When police tried to physically remove one frail patient who was blocking the courthouse steps, he moaned in pain as the officer took him by the arm and the camera crew caught it all on live TV. Calls immediately flooded the police station, and Chief Lario, who had also seen the coverage, immediately called the field patrol and instructed them to hang back and keep their hands off everyone, unless someone was actively creating a serious problem.

Inside, the courtroom was packed with the sickest of the protesters — Jeff Stone had even seen to that. He was brash, loud and larger than life; the crowd was mesmerized as, smiling confidently, he assured them that their voices would be heard.

He spoke quietly to an assistant, but his grand gestures gave away his intentions. The assistant promptly rearranged the audience to put the most sickly and tearful in the front row; anyone who seemed prone to hysterics was placed in the back.

Jeff Stone was six feet tall; his too-long gray hair curled up at the base of his expensive shirt collar as if he hadn't had time for a haircut. His perfectly tailored gray pinstripe suit and Hermes tie indicated his concern for appearances. The vintage 1964 Rolex he wore looked appropriately common, though he had actually paid a fortune for the limited edition at auction.

Appearances were everything. Stone, with his entourage of assistants, was infinitely more polished and successful looking than the overworked, underpaid assistant D.A., Tim O'Neil, who sat slumped in his disheveled navy suit, button down collar, and nondescript tie, waiting for the judge to arrive. Stone had the look of a lion, a warrior for the underdog. O'Neil looked more like something an alley cat had dragged into the courtroom.

Judge Harvey Jones must have been alerted to the commotion, but he still looked surprised to see his seats filled with sallow faces that seemed only barely alive.

He sat down in his chair, averting his eyes from the misery that silently cried out to him.

"Mr. O'Neil, would you like to begin?"

"Yes, Your Honor. Smith Viviee is not a licensed physician in the state of New York, yet he has, by his own admission, practiced medicine. By doing so he is preying on the hopes and fears of all the helpless people you see here today. He is a danger to the community. This nanochip, the results of which he flaunts, has not been studied by any reputable authority. In fact it hasn't been studied by anyone; we don't even know for sure if it exists. Viviee has failed to provide any evidence that even remotely demonstrates he might have a cure of such magnitude. It's all smoke and mirrors, Your Honor. Mr. Viviee resides in China, Your Honor; he has no ties to this community and is a significant flight risk. There is no condition or combination of conditions that could assure Smith Viviee's appearance for trial. We ask that he be held without bond."

"Mr. Stone?" the judge said.

"Thank you, Your Honor. Smoke and mirrors? That's an interesting phrase. It's used to suggest that some feat of magic has been performed. Your Honor, I would say that truly revolutionary scientific advances have always been viewed as impossible — feats of magic, if you will. Magic is nothing more than forces we've yet to discover.

"Dr. Viviee...."

"I object, Your Honor," O'Neil interrupted, "to the defense counsel referring to the defendant as 'doctor.' I remind you that this man is not licensed to practice medicine in New York State; as a matter of fact, we have no way of knowing if he is licensed to practice anywhere."

"Oh, come on," Stone responded. "This is ridiculous. Here is a copy of Dr. Viviee's diploma from the UCLA medical school. He is a product of the American educational system, but he chose to practice in China."

"Let me see that," O'Neil said. "But it doesn't matter, Your Honor. While the defendant may have graduated from medical school, he is still not licensed to practice anywhere in this country, and certainly not here."

"Overruled," the judge said. "You may refer to your client as doctor."

"As I was saying, Your Honor," Stone continued, "Dr. Viviee is not a charlatan or a quack. He is a genius who has brought hope to millions. What in that requires that he be held in jail without bond? Is saving a life now a felony? This woman here, Claire Cummings, was at the door of death just a matter of days ago. She doesn't look like she's dying now, does she? Because she's not. Because Dr. Viviee cured her. He has no profit motive and has accepted no money. He did not have to go public. He did so because he can't keep this secret any longer. We ask that he be released on his own recognizance."

"Mr. Stone," Judge Jones said, "is Helene Cummings here?"

"Yes, Your Honor." Stone looked to the back of the audience and found Helene standing against the wall. He waved for her to come forward.

Helene walked through the small wooden gate separating the spectators from the proceeding. She stopped and stood next to Jeff Stone.

"Ms. Cummings, I understand it was your show that brought this matter to light."

"Yes, Your Honor."

"And you have hired Jeff Stone to represent Smith Viviee?"

"Yes, Your Honor."

"Why is that?"

"Because this man may be the greatest genius of our time. I couldn't stand by and let his healing powers remain a secret any more than I can stand by and see this innocent man prosecuted for trying to save lives."

"It sounds like you have a lot of faith in Smith Viviee's abilities."

"I do."

"And his character?"

"He is a man of great character and I would stake my reputation on it."

"Good. I'm going to give you the chance."

"Smith Viviee," Judge Jones said.

Viviee rose to his feet, standing on the other side of Stone.

"You're being charged with one count of practicing medicine without a license. That's a Class E Felony in the state of New York, punishable by up to four years in prison. I'm going to grant a corporate surety bond of fifty thousand dollars and I'm going to hold Helene Cummings responsible under penalty of contempt, for your showing up for court. You are not to leave this city. Understood Mr. Viviee?"

"Your Honor," the DA said, rising from his seat, "the people move to have Mr. Viviee enjoined from practicing medicine in any form until this matter is resolved."

"Yes, of course, Mr. O'Neil. Do you understand that, Mr. Viviee? You are not to practice medicine in any form. No one else should get this nanochip until this matter is resolved."

"Yes, Your Honor, I understand. I don't have any more of the nanochips, so I couldn't implant another one even if I wanted to. Claire Cummings received my last one."

"All rise," the bailiff said, and those who could do so promptly did. The judge did not wait for the others who struggled and flailed desperately to lift their bodies from the seats. He quickly left the courtroom.

90

Stone attended to the matter of his client's bail, while Helene and Claire waited in the hallway. Helene nervously paced up and down. The stakes had been raised. Viviee was now her responsibility. How did it happen? She couldn't believe it. She had already staked her reputation on the man. She had never intended to stake her freedom on him.

"Oh, calm down," Claire said. "You can count on Dr. Viviee. He's not going to skip town."

"You better be right, mother. They throw people in jail for contempt. What if he runs off to China?"

"You've got to trust him, Helene. He's a great man."

"Yeah, well this better be worth it."

"How can you say that? Look at all the people out there and the press."

Helene knew the press would not leave, no matter how long it took until she would emerge, triumphant, with Dr. Viviee, her mother, and Stone. They would stop at the microphones and each would give a brief statement. Helene was well aware that now Viviee would be referred to as the doctor whose legal defense was financed by the Helene Cummings Show and whose character was guaranteed by hers.

Stone was now by her side.

"If we stop and talk to the press we run the risk of antagonizing the judge," he said.

"Oh, Jeff, don't be ridiculous. You and I both know we're not in this to avoid publicity. We have a desperate crowd out there that has been waiting patiently to see this man. We are certainly not going to just keep walking."

"No, of course not," Stone said with a smile. "Just checking to see where your head was at."

"Kyle told the media to set up for a news conference right out front."

"Good. Do you think Viviee is going to want to talk?" Stone said.

"Didn't you see him basking in the warm glow of the television lights?"

"True. I'll go get him."

Stone returned with Dr. Viviee. He was looking none the worse for wear.

Stone and Helene flanked Viviee and Claire. They strode down the hall almost in lockstep.

"There's going to be a lot of people out there," Helene said to Viviee, "and they're going to mob you when they see you. That can be very intimidating."

"These people need help. I have no reason to be intimidated."

"I was talking about the press," she said. "We told them to set up for a brief statement so they wouldn't come running after you like lunatics. Hopefully they'll be right out front. A few photographers will be running around shooting us as we walk down the stairs. Take your time and ignore the cameras. If we just talk amongst ourselves, we'll look as normal as possible."

"Normal? One of the officers told me there are at least five thousand people standing around out there. Yes, I'll try to appear normal."

It happened exactly as Helene predicted. The moment they walked into the sunlight on the courthouse steps, the mob began to cheer. Most of the press waited at the bottom of the steps, where a podium had been set up. The trip from top to bottom would provide the media its chance to capture cover video to the story — the triumphant descent from the palace of the law. Viviee's hair blew in the breeze like the mane of a dark stallion eager for battle.

Jeff Stone stepped to the podium first.

"Good afternoon. We are thrilled that the judge has released this brilliant man on bail. We realize there are important interests that legitimately question the validity of his amazing technology, and we hope to use the opportunity these questions will provide to prove to the world that this is a man whose only desire is to help the people of the world. There is no profit motive and no malice in his heart. He wants to help, and we hope and pray he will have that opportunity in the near future."

"Dr. Viviee, Dr. Viviee," a reporter yelled. "Can you really cure cancer?"

Without hesitation, Viviee stepped to the podium. "Of course I can," he said. "Is that not what brought me here today? Look at this beautiful woman." He swept his arm toward Claire. "Is she not full of life? When I found her, she was literally on her death bed. Now, she shows no signs of the disease. Eventually someone will say she was misdiagnosed, but you have seen the evidence. You have seen her tests. We have made them public. Don't be fooled by those who aim to deceive you." He looked directly into the eyes of all the desperate and infirm, all those upon whom the death sentence had long since been pronounced. "The day will come, fifty years from now, when we will all stand here again, together. I can feel it!"

The crowd cheered wildly, and the photographers quickly swung their cameras around to catch the action. Viviee stepped back from the podium.

Helene quickly stepped forward. "My mother was a guinea pig!" she shouted. "Her recovery proves that dreams can come true and miracles really do happen!"

"How does it feel to be personally responsible for Viviee showing up in court?" a reporter yelled.

"I have complete faith in Dr. Smith Viviee. I will stand by this man till this fight is done and we have conquered this disease! Justice must be done!"

The fervor of her own words surprised her. She sounded like a revivalist preacher. The road she had chosen stretched out before her.

91

Robert sat in his office going over security plans for the United Nations. He wanted to be sure that every "t" was crossed and every "i" dotted. The plan was as solid as it could get, but Robert knew that might not be solid enough. He worried there could be a breach, but he didn't know what to do about it. A drink would help him to think more clearly, so he pulled a bottle of vodka from his bottom drawer and poured a few sips into a glass. He fired off an e-mail detailing an additional security measure.

He checked his incoming mail and found one from the NYPD informing him Seafore had had a male visitor, John Dorey, aka Bull Dorey whose criminal record included a few assorted petty crimes.

The phone rang.

"Yeah," Robert said, taking a swallow from his glass.

"Robert? It's Jim Schultz... Dr. Schultz."

"Sure, Jim. How are you? Good to hear from you."

"Well, I'm not good, Robert. I don't know if you know this, but I sit on the board of trustees for the Association of American Medical Professionals, and I am very troubled by what's going on with the Helene Cummings Show."

"Really? What's that?"

"You're not watching?"

"No."

"Well, everyone else is. Are you near a TV?"

"Sure." Robert fumbled under some papers, found the remote, and turned on the first in a row of four small television sets. On the screen Dr. Viviee was addressing the crowd. Robert recognized the location as the foot of the courthouse steps in Foley Square. He clicked from one channel to another; they all carried the same picture. He increased the volume and listened, while Dr. Schultz remained holding on the line. For several minutes Robert watched the coverage and listened. He downed the remainder of his drink and poured some more.

"I'll be honest with you, Robert," Jim Shultz said at last. "We want him out. He's a threat to the community and to sick people everywhere. The anguish he will put these families through is just unconscionable. Now, I know you're close to Cummings, but this is ridiculous, and her show's sponsorship of this man is really wrong. I'm not a journalist, but I can tell you there are those who believe this is really outside the bounds of good journalistic ethics. Her show's involvement with this quack will do nothing but serve to keep him in the news, and when the truth comes out that he's a liar and maybe just plain crazy, she's going to look bad — very bad. I like Helene. I've met her in the past and she seems to be a lovely and talented woman. I would hate to see her go down because of this... this wacko."

"You have me at a loss, Jim. This is the first I'm hearing of this." He took a deep breath and another drink.

"Oh. Well, let me also say that we need to find out more about who this guy is and what his angle is. I would like to hire you to look into his past — personally."

"Why me, Jim? You know I'm pretty much retired."

"Who's better than you? You're the best and I don't want to fool around with this."

"I'll get back to you tomorrow," Robert said.

"By the way, I see they caught the guy who killed Archibald."

"Yeah, it looks that way."

"Poor sucker. Well, he probably did him a favor taking him out quickly."

"What do you mean?" Robert said.

"He was dying of cancer," Schultz said. "I was his doctor. He only had a couple months left."

"But his wife never said..."

"He didn't want her to know — didn't want her to worry. He thought he was going to beat it. Crazy bastard. Anyway, I'd really appreciate it if you could help us out on this Viviee matter. We don't want it to ruin Helene. You couldn't save Maria, no one could have. But you can certainly help Helene."

92

"Oh, my God!" Madeline screamed." This is amazing, Justin!" She made a flying dive onto his bed. "Your mother is huge! Everybody in the world must be watching!"

"Man," he said. "This is going to put her over the top. I can't even answer the phone. It hasn't stopped ringing."

"Your mother looks soooo great. And look at your grandmother. She looks phenomenal." She pointed at the TV. "That crème colored suit is the perfect thing to wear. She looks so... so... above it all."

"Ugh," Justin said. "Only a girl would notice that."

"Dressing appropriately for an occasion makes a big difference."

"You sound just like my mother."

The phone rang. Madeline checked the caller ID.

"Speak of the devil. It's your mom's cell," she said as she picked up. "Ms. Cummings, you are soooo cool. This is so amazing, and you look fabulous. Everyone is watching. The phone has been ringing off the hook."

After a moment, she said, "Sure. Hang on," and handed the phone to Justin.

Justin was fixated on the screen. The station was replaying the video of Dr. Viviee being arrested as the young girl was raised up to him on a blanket. Justin recalled the story of the sick person brought to Jesus on a stretcher.

Just then, an instantaneous black curtain flashed over Viviee's face. He turned directly to Justin and hissed with a serpent's tongue.

"Justin, are you there? Justin!" his mother said loudly.

And he heard Fouick's voice: "They will perform great signs to fool even the elect, if that were possible."

"Justin, what's wrong with you? I hear you breathing."

"Oh mom, I'm sorry, I was watching the TV." He felt over-the-top excitement, but at the same time he felt strangely calm. "They're replaying the arrest. You were great, mom."

"Thanks, honey. Have I gotten a lot of calls at home?"

"Are you kidding? About twenty of them. Your agent, the head of the network guy, everybody's called."

"Great. Listen, tonight I'm exhausted, but tomorrow we celebrate, so don't make any plans. Okay?"

"Sure, mom."

"All right, I'll see you later. Can you order Chinese? Robert's coming, and Dr. Viviee, so order enough. Make it expensive Chinese. I want to keep Dr. Viviee *very* happy."

93

Max watched Samantha pass by the building as if she just happened to be in the neighborhood. She stopped to make small talk, but the topic quickly turned.

"Why don't you call up to him, Max? I know he's up there."

"I'd love to do that for you, Miss, but I was told no visitors today. He's not feeling well with his foot and all."

"That girl is up there, isn't she? I know she's up there."

"I don't know who you're talking about."

"Oh, come on. Are you telling me she's not up there?"

"I have no idea who's up there. I know it's tough when you have a crush and all, but he'll be back in school soon. Why don't you just wait?"

"This is not a crush," she said. She turned on her heel and walked away. She took out her cell phone and dialed.

Max stepped into the street. He heard her say, "This kid is really starting to get on my nerves. I'm not sure what else I can do."

94

A quiet uneasiness settled over the usually vocal group when Lars Studor walked into the conference room. Worried faces seated around a long oval table looked to him for reassurance, but they found none.

As the head of the largest pharmaceutical company, Studor had offered to host the top secret meeting in his offices. Executives from all the major drug companies were there, along with Dr. Schultz, representing the board of the Association of American Medical Professionals; Charlie Block from the FDA; the CEOs of two medical equipment manufacturing companies; the heads of the nation's largest hospital chains; a state senator; and a congressman. They had flown in from all over the country.

"Gentlemen, and ladies," Studor said, nodding to the two women present. "I appreciate your all coming on such short notice and with such secrecy, but this may be the single most important meeting in the history of the healthcare industry. You have all heard about Smith Viviee. Today I've asked Dr. Steve Cohen, the treating physician for Claire Cummings, to brief us on what he knows.

Studor motioned to a young man standing by the double doors that led to a lobby area. The young man opened the doors and asked Dr. Cohen to join them.

Cohen looked startled by the sight of so many well dressed, somber individuals staring intently at him.

"Can you please tell everyone what you told me about Claire Cummings?" Studor said.

"Of course. My patient of twenty some odd years came to me complaining about a persistent cough and cold. We ran some tests and determined she had lung cancer that had spread to the liver with multiple nodes. I gave her an honest prognosis of six months. Two months later I admitted her to the hospital to have her lung drained. She took it well, refused chemo, and was sent home to live out the remainder of her life.

"A few days later it seemed she had made remarkable progress, so I retested her. There is zero evidence of any cancer at this point. I asked her what she had done and she told me nothing. Then she went on her daughter's talk show."

"I don't mean to question your effectiveness as a physician," Studor said, "but is it possible this was a misdiagnosis?"

"No."

"You sound so sure," Studor persisted, "yet time after time, that's exactly what these cases turn out to be."

"Not this case."

"Surely the records could have gotten mixed up?" Block said.

"Gentlemen, I have a small office. It would be next to impossible for records to get mixed up."

"But it's *possible*," Studor insisted. "You can't say anything with absolute certainty, now can you, Dr. Cohen? For all you know, there could be a third variable at work here; something else that prompted the result. Perhaps one of the treatments *you* gave her was responsible."

"I didn't give her any treatments."

"Nothing?"

"She's very holistic. She refused everything."

"Perhaps she took some herbal remedy we should be looking into," John Davis, a pharmaceutical executive said. "We need to be very careful what we attribute this result to, if indeed the result is reliable."

"The nanochip is the only plausible explanation," Dr. Cohen said.

Studor shook his head in disapproval. "Can we count on you to keep that opinion to yourself for the time being?"

"Yes, for the time being," Dr. Cohen said.

"So we can count on you not to submit any journal write-ups?" Schultz said.

"I suspect I would have trouble getting them published anyway, judging by the political climate in this room."

"We've spoken to our finest researchers," Davis said, "and they all say it's impossible. We're not anywhere near that kind of technology. How can it be, that some man from China develops a nanochip that our own people can not conceive of?"

"I don't know," Dr. Cohen replied.

"Thank you, doctor," Studor said.

But before Dr. Cohen could leave the room, Congressman Andrew Reggio from New York stopped him. "Dr. Cohen, I was wondering; if you found out that you or a member of your family had cancer, would you rely on the knowledge your profession has afforded you all these years, or would you seek out Dr. Viviee?"

"I would, without a doubt, seek our Dr. Viviee."

"And Dr. Cohen," Peter Franklin, from the top medical equipment manufacturing company said, "would getting this nanochip require repeated annual tests such as CAT scans to assure the cancer remain in remission?"

"Yes. I believe it would."

Dr. Cohen left the room.

"Look," Davis said, "cases of spontaneous remission occur. They are never properly documented and eventually they go away. This will go away just like all the rest of them. Pick anything you want; shark cartilage, sea cucumber, apricot pits; and someone will claim to be cured by it. Hell, I heard of a woman who said she was cured by swimming with dolphins." He laughed.

"None of them have ever been so good, or so fast," Nancy Feins Cooper said sternly. "I need to remind this group that we care for the sick and the needy, but hospitals are very expensive places to run. Something like this, if it took away our cancer patients and chemotherapy, well, I don't know how we'd stay in business."

"So, not only cancer patients are at risk here," Studor said.

"Charlie, it seems to me the FDA cannot give him an opportunity to demonstrate his nanochip again. At least not until it has been thoroughly and completely studied," Feins Cooper said.

Block nodded his head silently.

"How long would it take to get federal approval for something like this?" the State Senator said.

"Years," Block replied. "Definitely years."

"What about the old guy?" Studor said.

"The Chinese don't keep good records and he could be anyone. How are they going to prove how old he is? The whole notion is crazy," Congressman Reggio said.

"We've got the best lawyers in the business working with the DA right now to stop this man," Block said. "The FDA is on it."

"Viviee claims he doesn't have anymore of the chips and he says everything is in China," Studor said.

"Are we doing anything about China?" the Congressman asked.

"We have no jurisdiction there," Block said.

"Will the Chinese cooperate?" Studor asked.

"Not so far," Block responded.

"We must be diligent and give this matter our top priority," Studor said. "The proper care and treatment of our nation rests in our hands. If this man is allowed to continue he will bring false hope and hardships to people everywhere. And I don't need to remind you what he'll do to us."

95

Robert poured over the Claiborne autopsy. There was no mention of cancer, terminal or otherwise.

He placed a call to the Chief of Police.

"Just the man I was looking for," Lario said. "I've got some news. Our handyman just gave us a confession."

Robert didn't speak right away. Then, "What was the motive?"

"Exactly what we thought. He worked in Claiborne's apartment in the afternoon. He saw all the valuables they had and decided to rob them. He turned off the security camera so he could get the axe out of the back of his truck in the alley; he was thinking he might need it to get the door open. When he got to the back door he knocked as a precaution, and Archibald answered. Archibald caught him snooping around and said he was going to his office to call security. The kid got nervous. He followed him in and killed him."

"Then why no signs of a struggle?"

"He said he caught him by surprise."

"And you buy it?"

"It fits with our theory."

"That it does."

"Now, what's your news?"

"Did you know Claiborne had terminal cancer?" Robert said.

"No I didn't."

"Apparently he didn't want anyone to know. Don't you find it curious that it's not in the autopsy?"

"If it weren't for the confession, I'd be outraged at the coroner's incompetence. But it doesn't much matter now, does it?" Chief Lario said.

96

Justin tried to immerse himself in a game of Battle Ultimo, but he couldn't get the vision of Dr. Viviee out of his head. Without warning, all that he had come to believe was unraveling before his eyes. If helping Dr. Viviee was not his destiny, then what was? If Viviee was not a healer, then what was he? Where could he turn for the answers? Despite his repeated prayers, Fouick was silent.

And the coin. What was he to make of the coin? He turned to his computer and ran a search on Tribute Penny. At the first site on the list he found this biblical story, which Matthew told in his Gospel:

In the days when Jesus was preaching, some men tried to trick him into saying something against Roman law, so they could have him thrown in jail. They asked him if it was proper to pay taxes, knowing it was against the law not to.

Jesus asked to see a coin and he asked whose face they saw. They said Caesar's face was on the coin. Jesus said "Render to Caesar the things that are Caesar's and to God the things that are God's."

This coin became known as the Tribute Penny; the picture on the web site showed it was just like the one Justin held in his hand.

He reached for the phone to call his mother's office. He spoke with one of the bookers of the show and asked for a contact number for Ezra. She gave him the number and informed him the show on Apocalyptic Youth would likely air tomorrow.

Ezra picked up the phone on the first ring.

Justin introduced himself only by his first name and explained that he had gotten Ezra's number from people he knew who worked at the Helene Cummings Show.

"I'm wondering if you're taking any new members into your group?"

"Anybody is welcome to join our discussions," Ezra told him. "We meet at the Little Church in the Village every week."

Justin was grateful Ezra didn't ask too many questions. It was comforting just speaking to him. Justin jotted down the location and time of the meetings and said he would probably see Ezra there. Ezra said that would be fine.

97

Madeline helped Helene set the table and unpack the Chinese take-out they'd ordered for dinner.

"I'm so glad we're all going to be here together tonight," Madeline said. "I really want to hear the details of your day."

"I'd love to talk to you while we're alone for a moment," Helene said.

"Sure."

"What's going on with Justin? His behavior is very peculiar lately. Is he doing drugs?"

"No way, Ms. Cummings. Justin is definitely not doing drugs."

"Then what's going on? Something is going on. I know my son, Madeline."

"Well, what do you mean exactly?"

"What do I mean? I talk to him sometimes, and it's as if he doesn't hear me. And that's a sign of someone who's doing drugs."

"Honest, Ms. Cummings, Justin is not doing drugs."

"Don't tell me he's just daydreaming. People do not go into a trance when they daydream."

"He's just... well he's having some weird things going on right now," Madeline said.

"Weird? Like what exactly?"

"He's sort of seeing someone. Or someone is talking to him. I don't know exactly."

"That sounds pretty nutty, Madeline. What are you talking about?"

"It's like a spirit."

"You mean a ghost? Does he think this apartment is haunted?"

"Not exactly. Well, I don't know really, but it might be more of an angel."

"An angel?" Helene was dumbfounded. "Do you realize how crazy this is?" Of all the theories she had come up with to explain Justin's strange behavior, seeing an angel was not one of them. A learning disorder was a possibility: those video games eating away at his brain were a likely culprit. Drinking and even drug use she was prepared to face, but an angel? What on earth could that mean other than that he was completely out of touch with reality? She hoped for a moment he *was* doing drugs and Madeline either

227

didn't know about it or wouldn't say. At least there were treatment centers for things like that.

"It's really not so crazy," Madeline said. "He even left him something, this angel. It's an old coin."

"An old coin," Helene repeated. She thought for a moment. "You're not talking about that coin I brought home from my show, are you?"

"I don't know. I just know this angel said he was leaving something, and then he found a coin."

Helene quickly rummaged through the crystal bowl.

"It's not here. Whew! You had me worried for a bit there. *I* brought home an old coin. I did a show on some treasure hunters. I brought it home for Justin. That's all it was."

She turned around at the sound of Justin's arrival in the room. He was doing an odd jig on leg and cane.

"Hi, Mom," he said, planting a big kiss on her cheek. "That's all what was?"

"The coin. Justin, did you take my coin out of this bowl? It was a really old coin, all jagged around the edges."

"That was yours?"

"Yes. That was mine. Actually, I brought it for you. I did a show with some guys who dug up a treasure off the coast of Bermuda, and they brought some of their treasure along." Life for Helene was wonderful when there was an explanation for things. "The guy had a big bag of really old coins and stuff, and he told me to take one. It's as simple as that. So you see, there's nothing more to it."

Justin looked at Madeline.

"I had to tell her about the angel, Justin. She was worried about you. She thought you were doing drugs!"

"Madeline, how could you?" Justin said.

"Justin, I made her tell," Helene said. "Listen, I know this guy who talks to dead people. If you really think you're seeing a ghost or something, I'll call John Edward. I don't really believe in that sort of thing, but everyone says he's really brilliant. I've done shows with him, and he blows everyone away. His waiting list is forever, but I'm sure I can get an appointment."

"I don't need to talk to someone who talks to dead people, mother. I'm alive, in case you haven't noticed. A regular old living psychiatrist will do."

98

Justin opened the door for Robert, who looked about as happy as Justin felt.

He had no idea which was more devastating — that his angel's gift was a figment of his imagination or that his relationship with Madeline was not as special as he'd thought. He had believed Madeline understood about the angel and the grand plan that was forming for his life, but now he knew that she really thought he was just a kid with a good imagination. And maybe she was right.

Even if there were spirits, why on earth would they be contacting him? He was just a kid. The coin was just another of mom's souvenirs.

"Is everything okay?" Robert said.

"Sometimes it really sucks being the only guy in this place."

"I know what you mean." Robert patted him on the back as they headed toward the kitchen. "Glad to see your ankle is improving."

"It's still swollen, but I'm trying to put weight on it. The doctor said it's okay for short periods of time," he said, trying to get into the rhythm of walking with a cane.

Robert kissed Helene on the cheek. "I hear you had a hell of a show and since when are you on in the afternoon?"

"Oh, it's a long story. I'll explain it to you later. The important part is, the show was amazing," Helene said gleefully. "Our numbers are going to be through the roof!"

"Were you ever going to tell me?" He went to the cabinet and took out the fixings for martinis.

Robert's angry tone of voice was a surprise to Justin. He tried to keep his attention focused on the task at hand — emptying containers onto various plates.

"Tell you what?" Helene said.

"About this cancer cure."

"Hey," Helene said. "I made a promise I wouldn't tell anyone about this."

"Yeah, well, you know I got some calls about it this afternoon, and I sounded like an idiot not knowing what was going on. There are those who think you're taking a very serious risk here."

"No kidding. Like maybe some people from the drug industry? Really, Robert, I know you're savvier than that. We smashed the whole industry to pieces today. Of course they're upset."

"There are legitimate concerns."

"My concerns are that I need to keep competitive, and this just put me over the top — if saving the world from cancer isn't enough for you! We've had calls from everyone — all the newspapers, the magazines. Every network was on this all day long."

"I just want you to be cautious. How much do you really know about this man? What if he's a fraud? Are you ready to go to jail if he skips town?"

"Look, I'll admit I'm not crazy about what the judge did today, but what was I supposed to do? I had no idea he was going to release him on *my word*." Helene paused and took a breath. "Why don't you find out who he is?"

"I intend to."

"Good. You can start tonight. He's coming for dinner."

Justin wasn't about to jump into the long silence that ensued, but Madeline did.

"So, Robert," she said. "Ms. Cummings knows this guy who talks to dead people. Maybe you should use him to solve that murder."

Robert let out a laugh. "Yeah, that would go over big with the Chief."

"He's worked with cops before," Helene said. "He's not a joke."

When Robert spoke again he had regained a softer tone. "It doesn't matter now. The handyman just confessed."

"Really?" Helene said.

"So I guess my gut was wrong on this one. Where did the subject of talking to dead people come from anyway?"

"Justin thought he saw a ghost," Helene said.

"Oh great, now the world has to know you have a psychotic son!" This was too much.

Robert looked at him intensely. "I have experience with psychotics, and you are definitely not psychotic. What happened?"

"I just had a crazy dream and I, I, I…"

"Thought that it was real?" Robert said.

Justin nodded his head.

"That's not exactly unusual. I've had dreams so vivid that when I woke up I couldn't tell if they had actually happened or not. I'm sure it happens to everyone."

"I'm sure that *is* what happened," Justin said. To his mother he added, "So I won't need to talk to your medium friend."

"It's just like quantum physics," Madeline said. "Dead people exist in a different dimension."

"Why seek the dead in matters of the living?" Justin said.

Madeline gave a perplexed look. "My grandmother used to say that. It's in the bible."

Justin had no idea where it came from.

"All right, that's it," his mother said. "Are you in a cult?"

99

Helene leaned against the counter as Robert walked to the Subzero and grabbed his bottle of vodka from the freezer. The kids were in the dining room waiting for the others.

"You know, Helene, some parents would love for their kid to read the bible," he said as he freshened their drinks.

"Well, I'm not one of those parents," Helene said.

"Maybe that's why he does it."

Helene took a sip and a deep breath. She knew he was right. "He's always been a rebel. I'm sure it's just a phase."

Robert kissed her. She liked his lips.

"So, how about if I make a reservation at '21' tomorrow night and we celebrate you not having to worry about your show anymore."

"That's sounds nice," Helene said. "Let's do it."

The doorman rang up to announce Viviee's arrival but Claire had already answered by the time Helene picked up. She could hear Claire speaking in the hallway.

"Oh, that must be the good doctor," she said. She took Robert by the hand and led him into the living room.

Viviee was seated next to Claire on the pale pink silk sofa. His dark image cut a bold picture against the softness of the background.

He stood to greet Helene.

"Smith, can I make you a martini?"

"Just water, please."

"Pelligrino?"

"Perfect."

"Meet my friend, Robert Morgan."

"Hello, Robert," Dr. Viviee said, extending his hand and grasping Robert's. Robert grimaced. "Is something wrong?" Dr. Viviee said.

"Just an old tennis injury."

"So, how do you feel after all the craziness today?" Helene asked.

"I feel I've done the right thing and the rest is inevitable," Viviee said. "Truth will prevail. Do you believe in your American justice system?"

"Of course I do. It's the best in the world."

"Then I have nothing to fear."

"Well, that's not to say it doesn't have its flaws," she said.

"*Nothing* in the universe is perfect," Viviee said as they walked to the dining room.

"I ordered Chinese," Helene said, "I thought you might be missing a bit of home."

"That was very thoughtful," Viviee said. He took a seat across from Justin.

"I hear you two have the medical community in an uproar," Robert said.

"That was to be expected," Dr. Viviee said.

"Yes, I guess it was. Have you had much contact with the American medical community?"

"No, not really."

"I had a doctor friend who also believed cancer could be cured. His name was Dr. Archibald Claiborne. Did you ever meet him?" Robert said.

"No, I don't believe I ever did," Viviee said.

"Claiborne?" Helene said. "Robert, why on earth would you ask about him?"

"I heard he also believed in a cure. Too bad he's dead. In any event, Dr. Viviee, you might find yourself with some pretty formidable enemies."

"Thank you for the warning."

Helene thought Robert's tone was bordering on rude. She quickly tried to change the subject.

"So, Dr. Viviee," she said, "before you arrived we were having a rather interesting discussion about religion. What is your position?"

"My position?" He paused for a moment and without the slightest hint of irony said, "Downward Facing Dog."

Claire immediately began to laugh.

Justin just stared.

"Oh right, you're from the East," Helene said. "So of course you must do yoga. Are you a yogi? Is that even a religion?"

"Actually, I have always believed that religion is for the masses. It's a talisman to bring hope to those who have neither the skills nor the good fortune to attain joy in this life," Dr. Viviee said.

"You mean like poor people?" Justin said.

"Exactly. The weakest economically always have the strongest faith. Religious commitment is directly correlated to desperation."

"And religions have been used to excuse the slaughter of millions of innocent people throughout the centuries," Helene said.

"Indeed," Viviee said. "I prefer to rely on the god within me. There is so much untapped human potential."

Helene nodded her head in agreement, but her brain had already turned to the ringing telephone. Everything was happening so quickly. There was excitement at every turn, but she couldn't rid herself of the nagging feeling that Viviee now held a power over her greater than she held over him. She liked when he was in her sightline she thought, as she left the table to answer the phone. At least it wouldn't be Stone calling to say Viviee had disappeared.

By the time she returned to the table, all concerns were behind her. She was filled with enthusiasm as she announced another day that would bring her and Dr. Viviee together.

"Everyone wants us on the air in the morning," she said. "Every network morning show wants all of us — Dr. Viviee, me, mom, and Stone. I think they're afraid to touch Teng with a ten foot pole. Limos will be waiting for us at 6:15 a.m. for our first hit at 7:04. Kyle is working on the schedule now. I certainly hope your schedule is clear tomorrow, Dr. Viviee."

"Of course."

"What about *your* show?" Robert asked.

"We're going to rerun today's. We've had a zillion calls."

Dr. Viviee got up from the table and started clearing away his dishes.

"Please, doctor, there's no need for that," Claire said.

"I need to complete some work before the morning, so the time has come for me to say goodnight."

"Perhaps you should stay here," Helene said.

She could feel Robert's penetrating glare.

Dr. Viviee smiled. "I think you have a houseful already."

"We can make room."

"I'm not going to leave town, if that's what you're worried about, Helene. I have no intention of going anywhere until I have seen this matter through to its fruition."

Dr. Viviee walked, plates in hand, to the kitchen. Helene followed him.

He placed his dishes on the counter and abruptly turned to face her. He had intensity in his eyes she hadn't seen before. He stared at her with such force that she was unable to react when he grabbed her and passionately kissed her.

"You are a woman to be appreciated and admired," he whispered into her ear. "Not everyone would have stood up for me the way you did today. You deserve to be beautiful always. Say the word and it will be done."

He took her head in his hand. She squirmed, but didn't pull away. This was a completely unexpected development. Was he seducing her? She was disquieted by his advance, but it didn't feel bad. Perhaps it could work to her advantage. She laughed and then spoke in a whisper.

"Really? But I thought you didn't have any more chips?"

"It will be our secret. Together we can accomplish amazing things. Tomorrow we will work and tomorrow night we will celebrate, just you and me."

"Um, tomorrow, I…"

"Your time has come, Helene. Get what you came for."

100

Helene paused at the doorway of Justin's room and silently watched the young man who just a short time ago, it seemed, had curled in his mother's arms and hung on her every word. Now, she barely knew him. He argued about everything. It was infuriating. She felt like she was battling a combative guest on her show.

Yet if she wished anything for her son, it was that he would be an independent thinker, a man who followed his heart and chose his own path. It seemed that at least that dream had come true.

As she watched him sleep, he turned to face her. Helene walked to the edge of his bed and sat down. She tucked the covers around his chest and stroked the hair off his forehead. He was awake.

"I'm really sorry, Justin," she said with a crack in her voice.

"For what?"

"For accusing you of stuff. You're a good kid. You've always been a good kid, and you don't deserve to be mistrusted like that. You're entitled to your own opinion."

"It's okay, mom. But why do you hate God so much?"

Helene had never been asked that question before, and she wasn't quite sure how to respond. "I don't hate God, Justin. It's just that I'm not really sure there is such a thing. Sometimes people do really bad things, and then they say God said it was okay."

"So, why do you blame God for the things that people do?"

101

It was 4:45 a.m. and the Cummings household hadn't been so awake since Helene substituted on Good Morning America for the first time, many years ago. Her makeup artist rang the doorbell as the alarm went off, but Helene had been up for at least a half hour. After opening the door, she made her way to the kitchen to put on the coffee. Margie followed, rolling behind her a metal case that resembled an overnight bag.

Claire had arisen, showered, and washed her hair by the time Helene and Margie had gulped down their coffee. So Margie set up in Helene's dressing room and started working on Claire while Helene showered.

She opened the latches of the metal box to reveal a staircase of compartments containing every conceivable cosmetic and hair product. Margie was a creature of habit. She placed towels down on the dressing table in exactly the same layout she always used at the studio.

Margie watched Claire in amazement. Helene's mother was bright and alert as she sipped her coffee and talked endlessly about what she would wear. Should she wear black or navy to convey seriousness and authority or red to attract attention? Perhaps she should wear purple to keep the bad vibes away. Perhaps off white to show her sincerity. "Everyone trusts a person who's wearing white," she said.

She finally decided on a short ecru boucle jacket with a simple off white silk blouse and pearls worn over a black skirt with sheer stockings and tan shoes. She would be simple and elegant — soft in her appearance so she could be strong in her speech without offending anyone. Having a daughter with a career in television had taught her a thing or two about image management.

Even Helene, who was known for getting off to a sluggish start for early calls, was wide awake by the time she sat down for hair and makeup. Everyone knew this was an important day.

Helene closed her eyes as Margie applied foundation to her face with a sponge. Helene went over in her mind her talking points for the day:

- She was involved because the opportunity for the public good was so great.
- She could no longer hang on quietly to this incredible discovery.

- Emphasize the x-rays and scans.
- The remarkable change in her mother.
- How she too was shocked when she met Teng and could not independently verify his story.

She would have to tread lightly and maintain some degree of journalistic skepticism. Perhaps she should make her mother's tests results available for other media to scrutinize. That would take the pressure off her if something turned out to be less than what it seemed, but it could backfire if someone else spotted something fishy — that would expose her ineptitude.

"Mother?"

"Yes, Helene?"

"I need you to really concentrate on how you were feeling before — the hopelessness of your situation. Stick with how you really had no choice but to try this nanochip, and do not under any circumstances say when and where it was done. Just keep it a secret. Stick with the emotional stuff and feel free to cry."

"But..."

"And, please, do not, under any circumstances, speculate. Stick to what you know and what the doctors told you. Don't try to be an expert!"

"Fine, Helene. I'm sure you'll do most of the talking anyway." Claire left for her own room to finish dressing.

Helene carefully selected a navy blue pants suit from a row of color coordinated navy blue suits in her closet. She chose a simple beige silk blouse from a rack of beige blouses and pinned her small but lucky diamond and emerald brooch on her right lapel.

Kyle was already in the limo when it arrived to pick up Helene and Claire. Jeff Stone would join them at the studio.

"Well, Helene," Kyle said, his face expressionless. "I have the national overnight ratings here."

"And?" Helene said anxiously.

"Well..." She could tell that his hesitation was playful. "We started in a distant third place. No one was watching. But within fifteen minutes, the numbers started moving. We moved to a strong number two." Helene's face showed her disappointment. "But hang on," he continued. "By the second half hour we were number one, and at the final quarter, well...see for yourself." He handed the paper to Helene.

The numbers seemed to buzz before her eyes. The show's audience had doubled every fifteen minutes. By the end of the hour, their rating quadrupled the nearest competitor. They had blown the competition away!

"What's more," Kyle said, "look at this." He handed her a sheet with the numbers for the local New York market. "After the show, when the local stations starting breaking in with continuing coverage of Viviee's arrest, it was the only thing anyone was watching. Cable numbers plummeted. Even Barney numbers went down. I have never in my career seen anything like this."

"We did it!" Helene cried.

"Viviee did it, Helene; don't forget that," Claire said. "He's your ticket and mine. We better take good care of him."

"Oh, don't worry, mother. I will take *very* good care of Dr. Smith Viviee. *I've* made *him* a star."

102

Across town, in the suite of an eagles' nest penthouse in midtown Manhattan, Dr. Smith Viviee, admiring the strength of his face in the mirror, combed back his thick dark hair. It was a perfect face, he thought — perfect in character, attractiveness, and credibility.

He smoothed a strongly scented oil on his taught, muscular body and deeply inhaled the aroma. The scent was so strong it was putrid at first, but it softened into a barely detectable whiff of exotic spice.

He put on a medium gray one-ply cashmere Chinese style jacket with a bit more structure than his usual silk. It still contained his trademark red, dragon-embossed lining, and it draped elegantly over his matching gray cashmere pants.

He propped his foot on the unmade bed and used a shoe horn to slip on a pair of conservative black Gucci loafers over thin black silk socks. Then he walked out onto the terrace. Around him the spires of skyscrapers were gathered like worshippers. With a cool wind blowing through his hair, he looked down at a sleeping city about to awaken to a new dawn.

103

The moment they stepped out of the limos the whirlwind began. They shuttled from network morning show to network morning show, always hearing the same questions.

"How did you develop this cure? Why China? How quickly can this cure be manufactured and made available in mass quantities? Does it only work for cancer? Does it work for all cancers? Can it be used to heal other maladies? How long will people live? Is this the fountain of youth? Is immortality at hand? What happens next? Is it really possible that Dr. Viviee will go to jail? How soon can clinical trials start?"

Dr. Viviee, Helene, Claire, and Jeff Stone made a formidable team, fielding questions on the air and greeting the fans who welcomed them at every stop. The frenzy was gaining momentum. Then Dr. Viviee surprised everyone at the last interview of the morning when he said cancer wasn't the only devastating malady the nanochip could eradicate.

Helene knew that Viviee, whether by design or luck, had played it exactly right. The statement gave journalists a new angle; it intensified demand for interviews for the evening newscasts; and it ensured they would be in demand on cable for at least a week.

Kyle set up a series of interviews to take place at the TV studio.

One reporter after another filed in for one-on-one, sit-down conversations with each of them on the set of Helene's show.

When it was over, Dr. Viviee and Helene sat alone in her dressing room going over the events of the day. Helene felt as if she had been beaten down by a hurricane, but the adrenaline kept her feeling energetic.

Viviee reached over and cupped Helene's face in his right hand. "My dear Helene," he said, "you are so beautiful." He brought his lips to hers and glided his left hand down the front of her body. His hot breath on her lips made her shiver, and when he inhaled she felt as if he could suck the very life from her being.

"I can't wait to know this body," he whispered as he moved closer.

"Smith," she said, struggling to control herself, "I'm surprised at you."

"Surprised that I would find you irresistible?"

"It's just that I, well, we still have so much work to do."

He smiled and kissed her again.

"Smith, you know I really am sort of seeing Robert. Maybe this isn't such a good idea."

"Sort of seeing Robert? Aren't you a bit old to be sort of seeing someone? This isn't high school. I'm offering you so much more."

104

Robert arrived at the apartment to pick Helene up for their date, but she wasn't there. When he reached her on the cell phone she was already having dinner with Viviee at one of Manhattan's trendier restaurants.

"I'm sorry, Robert," she said. "It's business."

Robert lived his life on his instincts and his instincts told him something was terribly wrong. He woke up at dawn the next morning with a familiar feeling in the pit of his stomach. He didn't know exactly why, but he knew that time was of the essence and he must take action now.

He tossed a half empty bottle of vodka into the garbage and dug out the keys to his office from the back of his underwear drawer. He was seated behind his desk long before the office manager came to open up.

Robert Morgan had made his share of mistakes; he vowed this would not be one of them. He just wasn't buying it that a physician who made the most remarkable discovery of the twenty-first century had no profit motive, nor was he willing to accept that his patient was only coincidentally the mother of a national television personality. No, Robert knew a snake when he saw one. He was convinced that his feelings against Viviee had nothing to do with his feelings for Helene and everything to do with a man preying on the desperation of dying people.

So, as Robert began his inquires into the life of Dr. Smith Viviee he made no effort to mask his intentions; he sought no stories of bravery, brilliance, or kindness.

He placed calls to every government contact he had. He called the CIA, the FBI, an assortment of private detectives, and a few old friends whose connections to world events were unclear even to him. As the coffee pot relinquished its final cold sips and Robert watched the fiery images of the setting sun reflected on the buildings outside his window, the phone emitted its subdued electronic honk. The caller was a man referred to simply as "Horse." Robert opened his bottom drawer, pushed aside a half finished bottle of vodka, and pulled out a fresh yellow legal pad.

"Thanks, buddy, I really appreciate this," he said.

"Hey, you haven't heard what I've got to say yet. I hope it helps."

"Shoot."

Horse laughed. "Only say that when we're on the phone, pal. Listen, here's what I got for you. Dr. Lance Viviee — the father — was a bio-geneticist. He was working on controversial stuff — stem cell research, stuff like that. He was criticized by colleagues who thought he was a loose cannon, so he left town. First he went to the Cayman Islands; then he cut a deal with the Chinese and moved there to do his work. He had a son named Smith Viviee. The kid was raised by this male nanny — Teng Hao Li — and followed in the father's footsteps. The father died of old age; the kid developed a cult following in this rural town he lived in, for curing all these sick people. They think he's some sort of a god."

"Who's his mother?"

"Well, that's interesting. No one seems to know anything about his mother. There's no record of her, and no one so far has ever seen her or even knows anyone who's seen her."

"Why is that so interesting?" Robert asked.

"Well, everyone seems to know the father. It's rather interesting no one ever saw the mother, don't you think? It's like she never existed."

"When did the father die?"

"There's no record of that either. Or for that matter, exactly when the kid was born. But hey, what are you going to do? It's China. They got a billion people. They don't pay much attention to the birth records of some kid in a rice paddy."

"Do you have any photos of the father?"

"I just e-mailed them to you."

Robert swung around to his computer and opened the file. Lance Viviee looked exactly like his son, if Smith Viviee was in fact his son.

"Well, buddy," Robert said, "I think I know why there's no record of a mother."

"Why's that?" Horse asked.

"Because Junior is his father rejuvenated."

105

Cheetam was a handsome, though not particularly talented rock star who had managed to capture the imagination of a new generation by remaking old songs his fans were too young to realize were not originals. His latest digital single to hit the airwaves at number one was "I Will Live On Forever," so his business savvy manager saw it as perfect opportunity for Cheetam to show up at his Madison Square Garden concert with a bold, black copy of Teng's mark tattooed on his forehead. When the crowd saw him, they went wild, causing Cheetam to raise his fist to the air and scream "I will be an Immortal!" The photo and the phrase made the front page of the New York Post.

Justin and Madeline were in the kitchen eating their breakfast cereal when Helene brought in the newspaper.

"Can you believe this," she said, tossing the paper onto the counter.

Justin put down his orange juice; Madeline's eyes grew large.

"This is soooo huge, I can't believe it," she said. "Cheetam is the hottest thing around. I can't wait to tell everyone at school. Can I have a cup of coffee, Ms. Cummings?"

"Uh, sure, Madeline. If you'd like. What do you take in it?"

"What do you take?"

"Heavy cream," Helene said. "I hate half and half; it tastes like chemicals."

"Then let me have it with cream, please."

Helene poured Madeline a cup from the pot and handed her the cream. Madeline made her coffee almost white and took a sip.

"Mmmm. This isn't bad."

"Well, I'm glad you like it."

Justin rolled his eyes. "Come on, Mad, we're going to be late for school." He grabbed his cane and backpack. It felt terrific not to be hobbling around on the crutches anymore.

"Are you sure you're okay to walk to school, Justin?" Helene asked. "I'd feel better if you took a cab. I don't want you to over do it."

"I'm fine, mom. We'll grab a cab as soon as I get tired."

The air was brisk as Justin and Madeline hit the sidewalk. He put his arm around her to shield her from the blustery winds that had moved into the city a week ago and showed no signs of abating.

Madeline felt content in Justin's arms, though she was a bit shaky from her first cup of coffee ever. She was happy to walk it off on the way to school. She talked incessantly about Cheetam and Helene's show. It helped to slow her pace so Justin could keep up. She wondered if any of the kids at school knew what had happened.

When they arrived at school, Justin and Madeline were astounded to see their classmates milling around outside, many sporting smaller versions of the design that Cheetam had copied from Helene's show.

"Hey, Just Man, my man!" Sean yelled, extending his hand for a high five. "You're mom's a celebrity."

"Duh?"

"No, I mean a big celebrity. Cheetam has been talking about her show all morning on the radio."

"Really?"

"Well, if it isn't the loser boy," Spider said, giving Justin a slap on the back. "I've been waiting for you to get back, man. Are you up to the challenge?"

"What challenge?"

"Battle Ultimo," Spider said with a laugh. "I hear you've been practicing."

"Nah," Justin said, but as soon as the word left his mouth he reconsidered.

"Wottsa matter? You still scared? I saw 'The Just Man' made it to the top 100. You're 99 right?"

"Yeah."

"I'm 92," Spider said.

That took Justin by surprise. He had no idea Spider was ranked on the digital channel. He had assumed his game name was Spider, but now he recalled seeing a Black Widow in the game.

"You think you're smooth, but you ain't nothing against a player," Spider said. "I bet you've never even been to the Bronx."

"Stop it, Spider," Madeline said.

"And he needs his girlfriend to defend him. Losers." He spat. "Pathetic losers."

"I just don't want to play."

"I'll put up five hundred to your hundred, rich boy. I've got money on you all over town — on you losin', that is."

"Come on, Justin, you got to do it." This, from the always supportive Sean. "I know you can kick his ass. You got to do it for us, man. He's been taking our cash for months. I'll put five hundred on the 'Just Man.'"

"Yeah," Wiley piped in. "We'll go with you. Come on Justin."

"All right," Justin said. "The day after tomorrow."

"Battle in the Bronx!" Sean yelled.

106

Father David stood on the steps of the brownstone, unsure what to make of the relative quiet that had settled around the home. Gone were the television cameras and throngs of people who had lined the streets. Only a few faithful wandered into the house to pray with Holy Hazel in front of her beloved Virgin with the nuns at her side.

"May I go inside, Father?" a young woman said quietly.

"Of course. Go right in. Have you been here before?"

"No, I just came in from Florida. I wanted to see for myself."

"You picked a good day. It was much busier a day or so ago, but I guess things have quieted down now."

"Yes, I see. It looked really crowded on TV."

"It was. There are still people inside. I guess the television cameras draw as many visitors as the miracle."

"I think a new miracle has captured the people's imagination."

"What's that?"

"There's a controversial doctor who says he can cure terminal cancer patients. People are trying to show their support for him, so he doesn't get thrown in jail."

"I'm sorry, but I haven't heard anything about that."

"It's on all the TV stations. He was on the Helene Cummings Show, and he cured her mother. Just turn on the TV. I'm sure there'll be something on now."

"Thank you," Father David said.

Back inside the house he found a TV in a small back room. He settled into a well worn chair, and clicked the remote.

He stopped when he saw "Cancer Cure?" in bold letters on the screen, and watched images of Dr. Viviee, Helene Cummings, and the lawyer speaking proudly of amazing accomplishments. And then he saw Claire.

He recognized her immediately. Her hair was different, her face was almost unrecognizable, but her eyes were the same as they had been when she was twenty. Age could not diminish the gaze he had once known so well. Claire Cummings looked right into the camera as if to speak directly to Father David.

"This is a great man who gave me back my life," she said. "I owe everything to Dr. Viviee."

Could this really be the Claire Sonner he knew so long ago? It was fifty years. How could he possibly tell for sure? He tried to convince himself it really couldn't be, but her eyes, those *were* the same eyes… there couldn't be two people with those eyes. It was strange how they stood out, so strong and clear that they were unmistakable.

"In the eyes of my love," he whispered. "Dear God, no! I must find her!"

"Find who?" a voice said.

Father David turned to see a young boy staring curiously at him. He couldn't have been more than ten or eleven years old.

"I need to locate that woman on the TV," David said.

"That's easy," the boy said. "I just need a computer."

107

Throughout the city, young people picked up on Cheetam's publicity blitz. "I Will Live On Forever" played on all the hot stations; Cheetam did interviews with the popular DJ's. He claimed the ultimate move was to get the nanochip and outlive the motherfuckers trying to take down the man who would heal the sick and give them immortality. Cheetam vowed his generation would not be dictated to. As his message spread to young people all over the city, they joined the throngs of sick and elderly rallying outside the State Attorney's offices chanting "Leave Viviee alone!"

Clips of Helene's show with Viviee ran over and over again on 24 hour cable news programs, while she and Kyle planned their strategy to keep the story alive.

Claire tried to meditate, but couldn't find her peace, so she watched TV, content to live her shining moment through the eyes and images of others.

Spider hung just out of sight at the school, so he could keep an eye on the boy he aimed to defeat.

Robert worked feverishly to nail Viviee, drinking only coffee, until he slumped over his desk from exhaustion.

And Dr. Viviee sat quietly out of sight on the balcony of his penthouse, content to watch the world below work for him. He knew that his time had come, and he was ready for his destiny.

108

On the 11pm news shows, video of Helene Cummings talk show had been bumped in favor of a pretty young redhead telling an amazing story.

Robert got an old bottle of flat Pellegrino out of his refrigerator, poured himself a glass, and walked back to his bedroom.

"I was totally paralyzed," the redhead on the screen said tearfully.

"Holy shit!" Robert yelled and ran for the phone to dial Helene.

"I was told I would never walk again," the girl said, "but somewhere in my heart I knew it would happen, and I owe it all to Dr. Smith Viviee." She stood up, walked to a wheelchair, and pointed toward it as if it were a prize to be won on *The Price Is Right*.

"Helene, it's Robert. Turn on Channel 7. You're gonna want to see this."

109

Helene ran for the den with the remote in her hand.

"When did this happen?" the interviewer was asking a pretty red-haired woman.

"Oh, uh." She pasted a very serious expression onto her face. "It was definitely before the judge told Dr. Viviee he couldn't practice medicine anymore," she said.

"Smith!" Helene yelled, but he was already standing right behind her. She felt his warm breath on her neck. "Oh," she said as she turned to face him. "Why didn't you tell me?"

"Trust me, Helene," he said. "Some things are better for you not to know. It's better for your credibility."

"You did it again, against the judge's orders, didn't you?"

"Helene, I don't want you to be responsible for the many things that will happen."

"Admit it. That's the girl they brought up to you on the blanket, isn't it?"

"Yes."

"Then you've been lying. You do have more nanochips. You said you didn't have any."

"I'll make it up to you. I have one left and it's for you. Are you ready for it, my beauty?"

Helene's scowl softened into a smile. "Do you really think I should? I mean, I'm not sick or anything."

"After this, it will be a while before I'll be able to give a nanochip to anyone who isn't involved in some full scale clinical trial. Who knows what kind of controls I'll have on me then? I'll probably only be able to administer the chip to fight the gravest illnesses. Perhaps I'll never be able to get one for you. But today, at this moment, the technology is still totally in my control. You can be the first completely healthy person to receive the cure for rejuvenation purposes. You'll look like you're 30 by the end of the month."

"Well, I...."

"Tomorrow," he whispered.

He kissed her before she could answer. While gently holding her head in his left hand, he slowly moved his right hand under her skirt and caressed the inside of her thigh.

110

The news of another cure hit the city like a winter snow storm. It stopped talk of virtually everything else. This was the first known case of a paralyzed individual regaining complete movement in a matter of days. Doctors were dispatched from hospitals and research foundations all over the country; all wanted to meet and study her. But she was speaking to no one.

This young woman with the soft red curls represented the focus of the nation. As one newscaster put it, Judy Borne was either part of the most elaborate and cruel hoax ever perpetrated on this country or she was the face of hope that far exceeded even the dreams of the most optimistic medical practitioners.

Groups representing the victims of spinal cord injuries and cancer patients banded together and demanded action. Every politician was trying to figure out how to get in on the excitement, while all called for calm, careful and deliberate study. No one suggested there should be any delays.

When the prosecutor called for an emergency hearing to revoke Viviee's bond, thousands showed up at 100 Centre Street. For four hundred years New York courts had adjudicated landmark cases that shaped the nation, yet few had received the notoriety of this simple hearing.

Stone led Dr. Viviee into the courthouse, past screaming fans. Some people fainted as they saw him; others reached out to touch him. It was almost impossible for Helene to comprehend what had been created. She and Claire walked by the doctor's side down the corridor.

Everywhere Helene looked people were crying. There was hope in their tears. Goosebumps covered her arms as people reached out to touch not only Viviee, but her. She knew she was part of something bigger than her wildest ambitions. After all her years of being a celebrity, all her years of dealing with the good wishes of fans, now they were touching her as if she carried the secret that could save them. But she was a bystander. She could only imagine what they were thinking about Dr. Viviee. She was happy to be off the stage, as she took a seat in the audience. Dr. Viviee stood behind the defendants table next to Jeff Stone.

Judge Harvey Jones, cloaked in his black robe and all the majesty of the court system, looked down upon Dr. Viviee as a creature humbled before a much greater power.

Prosecutor Tim O'Neil began his argument. "Your Honor," he said walking toward the bench, "the defendant has practiced medicine in direct violation of the conditions of his release, since there is evidence he subsequently administered a nanochip to Judy Borne. Further, we believe he perjured himself when he said he was completely out of nanochips. The state moves to revoke the bond of Smith Viviee."

"Do you have evidence that he perjured himself?"

"Well, he said he was out of chips. We don't believe he just found the chip now… it would take time to…"

"Mr. O'Neil, last time you weren't even sure there was a chip, how would you know how long it would take to produce a new one?"

Helene sensed that the judge was disgusted.

Jeff Stone called Judy Borne to the stand. She marched proudly up to be sworn in. She remained standing until the judge asked her to sit down. She was bright and articulate and her eyes sparkled.

"I was completely paralyzed from the neck down. I was told I would never be able to walk again. Look at me now."

"To what to do you attribute this miraculous recovery?" Stone asked.

"Not to what, but to whom," she said. "That man right there, Dr. Smith Viviee. I will never be able to thank him."

She tearfully recounted her story. She was the victim of a drunk driver, run over in the street at the age of ten, unable even to feed herself ever since. She had won millions of dollars in a lawsuit against the driver, and now she was ready to turn it all over to Dr. Viviee so he could continue his research and make his nanochips available to everyone. All her prayers had been answered. Now she wanted to give back to the man who had given her back her life.

When O'Neil said, "Your Honor, we do not know the side effects of this nanochip," the judge interrupted him.

"Are you suggesting there is a side effect worse than death?"

"No, Your Honor."

"Is there a side effect worse than never being able to walk or feed yourself or go to the bathroom alone? Is there a side effect that is not worth enduring for the reclamation of your dignity?"

"Your Honor, the law…."

"This is beyond my jurisdiction," the judge said. "If I could order this man to go to work immediately under proper research supervision, I would do so. If I could order the medical facilities of our nation not to waste a moment before delivering this nanochip to all who need it, all the people without hope who are willing to offer themselves as guinea pigs, I would do so. But I cannot. This is beyond my jurisdiction. It's the legislature's job, or the job of the regulatory agencies.

"However, Dr. Viviee, I want you to understand this; if the court finds out you have practiced medicine again you will be arrested on new charges. Any arrest is itself a violation of the conditions of your pretrial release.

"What I can do, I will. I will not revoke your bond and I will withdraw the condition of your release relating to practicing medicine. I cannot legally permit you to practice medicine, but I also cannot morally require you to refrain from saving lives."

111

A dull anxiety gnawed in Robert's stomach as he made his way past the shops on Park Avenue. He hated when things wrapped up neatly. Murders were a messy business. They weren't meant to have neat endings. He glimpsed the reflection of his slumped over posture in the glass display windows and stood up straighter as he entered the lobby of Archibald Claiborne's building.

While the doorman confirmed he had an appointment, Robert took another look at the rows of security monitors on the desk.

"I thought the investigation was over, Mr. Morgan?" Mrs. Claiborne said when she opened the door.

"Yes. Yes, it is."

"But you're still not sure about this suspect, are you?"

"I really am sorry to trouble you, Mrs. Claiborne. I'm sure you're anxious to put this behind you. I just want to ensure there are no loose ends."

"I thought the man confessed?"

"He did. I just want to make sure I understand everything clearly."

"My husband was a good man. His death is a terrible thing. I want someone to pay for it. But I know my husband will never rest if it's the wrong person. So, you tell me what I can do to help you."

"I want to return this to you," Robert said. He slowly handed her the book on medical symbols. "Thank you for lending it to me. It was very interesting. Unfortunately it didn't lead to anything."

"We're getting ready to pack up the whole lot of them now, Mr. Morgan. My husband has so many books. Thank you for returning it."

"Mrs. Claiborne, is there anything — anything at all — you can think of that might have led Seafore to kill your husband in such a brutal fashion? The 'why' is as important as the 'how.'"

"I honestly can't imagine why anyone would ever do something like this to Archibald. Robbery is as good a motive as any."

"This handyman belongs to an unusual group. They follow UFO's and things of that kind — unexplained phenomena. Did that sort of thing interest your husband?"

"Oh, heavens no. My husband was a scientist, Mr. Morgan. Medicine and his family were the only things that interested Archibald, other than his books."

"Do you mind if I have another look around?"

"Of course not. Go right ahead."

Robert walked to the library and retraced the steps Seafore must have taken. It made no sense that he would have surprised Claiborne from behind. Robert walked the alleged route over and over.

The doorbell rang.

Robert watched the housekeeper answer the door. She let in a delivery man with a cart full of groceries. The man trekked across the polished wood floor to get to the kitchen.

"That's unusual."

"What's unusual, Mr. Morgan?"

"The delivery man came to your front door. I'm surprised they allow that in this building."

"The truth is, we never use the back door."

"So, why then do you think your husband answered it?"

"I don't know, really. He must have been in the kitchen."

"May I see it — the back door?"

"Of course."

Robert followed the trail the delivery man had taken, down a long hallway and through a large pantry. To his right, the breakfast nook was wall-papered in white and lime green bamboo; to his left the kitchen was loaded with modern, professional grade appliances, all of them matte stainless steel. The door was straight ahead. Robert watched as the delivery man unloaded bags from his cart and placed them on the white granite countertop. His red uniform reflected in the high-gloss, green paint of the door.

"Beautiful kitchen," Robert remarked. "This is such an unusual color."

"It is, isn't it? The decorator insisted. Personally, it reminds me of Palm Beach in the 1960s, but today it's considered very modern. I'm still not sure if I like it."

"It looks like you just painted."

"Yes, about a month ago."

"Did you have a good painter?"

"He seemed all right. I can get you his name if you like."

"Yes, I would definitely like his name," Robert said as he carefully examined all around the door frame. "You know, it's tough to find good help these days." He pulled a pair of glasses and a pair of gloves from an inside breast pocket and put them on. He gently ran his fingers along the door jam. "I find that very few workers take pride in their work anymore. Most of them are sloppy. They count on people not noticing details."

He took a step back.

"That's very true, Mr. Morgan."

"When the police were here, did they look at this door?"

"I think the detective looked at it and took some notes."

"But he didn't open it?"

"I don't remember."

"Do you have some tape? Any kind of tape will do."

The housekeeper pulled a roll of masking tape from a drawer. Robert taped a large "X" over the door from one wall to the other.

"I want to make sure no one opens this now," he said.

"Have you found something?"

"Come," Robert said. He handed his glasses to Mrs. Claiborne. "Take a look right here." Robert pointed to a small section of the top of the door. It was only a centimeter long, but unmistakable. The door was still painted to the door jam.

112

Greenwich Village felt like a different, more comfortable world. The streets were narrower — once they had been cowpaths — and there were few of the grand apartment buildings like the ones they lived in. Here, Justin and Madeline navigated past Federal town houses and small shops, on their way to the Little Church in the Village.

Unlike the rest of the island of Manhattan neatly laid out on a grid of numbered streets and avenues, the Village was an entity unto itself. Most of the streets were named, many slanted at odd angles, and those that were numbered were often illogical. At a famous intersection, Fourth Street intersected Twelfth Street. This perversity of layout seemed part of the rebellious spirit that had always resided in the Village and had given rise to one of the world's most famous Bohemian cultures.

The Village had been a safe haven in the1800's when the yellow fever epidemic hit Manhattan.

Justin looked forward to the upcoming meeting as a safe haven for his developing beliefs.

He squeezed Madeline's hand, and they marched into the back meeting room of the church. He immediately recognized Ezra and went to introduce himself. Ezra smiled as the pair approached.

"Hi Ezra, I'm Justin Cummings and this is my friend Madeline Quinonez. I called you…"

"Cummings as in the Helene Cummings show, right?"

"She's my mom, but I'd rather you didn't tell her I was here."

"No problem. I don't think she was too crazy about us anyway. We can speak more after the meeting."

Justin looked around the room. It was filling up with people; they chatted and laughed and drank gourmet coffees and bottled water. At last, about twenty young people, all older than Justin and Madeline, took seats in a circle of folding chairs.

A young man stood up and greeted everyone. Justin immediately recognized him as John from the video.

"I see some new faces in the crowd. Word gets around fast. I assume everyone wants to learn more about the mark of the beast, is that right?"

Several people nodded.

259

"Well," John said slowly, "according to the prophecy in the Book of Revelations, a trinity of evil will come to power in the last days, known as the devil, antichrist, and false prophet.

"I hope this wasn't too crazy bringing you here," Justin whispered to Madeline.

"It's as good a place as any to figure out what's been going on with you," she said. "Eventually this trinity will produce a mark," John said, "and that is the 666. The antichrist forces everyone 'small and great, rich and poor, free and slave, to receive a mark on his right hand or on his forehead, so that no one could buy or sell unless he had the mark, which is the name of the beast or the number of his name.' The bible also tells us, wise people should calculate the number of the beast, for it is man's number.

"Some people think it's a bar code, or maybe our social security numbers; others think it will be like a permanent credit card.

"Once you get the mark of the beast, there's no redemption. It's the ultimate unforgivable sin and everyone who gets it goes to hell."

"It's like that commercial where the guy scans his forehead at the checkout counter," another guy said. The group laughed.

"That may not be so far off," John said. "You're a business major, aren't you?"

"Yeah."

"Credit card companies are always looking for new ways to eliminate consumer fraud."

"Like optical scanners," the business student said.

"Or it could be one of those chips, like they implant in dogs so they don't get lost," a young woman sitting next to Justin said.

"Let's not forget about the idea of having a national identification system," a man who identified himself as a criminal lawyer said. "Maybe it would start with sex offenders first, so the government could keep track of them. Eventually, it would spread to other areas of the criminal population and eventually it would prove to be so convenient and simple to use, and save so much money in reducing fraud, that a new form would be developed for the rest of the population. There would be a big public relations campaign to tout all the benefits and the next thing you know, everyone has a permanent, track-able form of I.D., linked to their bank account."

"I thought Christians weren't supposed to have to worry about all this," a guy with a beard said. He looked like an aging hippie. "Aren't we supposed to be taken up in the rapture?"

"Not me," Ezra said. "The bible talks about 144,000 of God's holiest people being taken from the twelve tribes of Israel, but frankly, as much of a believer as I am, I don't think I'm gonna make *that* cut."

"But what about the sheer numbers? A third of the world's population is Christian," a young woman with long blonde hair said. She wore a tight fitting black tee-shirt with the words "Jesus First" emblazoned across the front. "That's two billion people. Do you mean to tell me there're only 144,000 who make the rapture? How can that be?"

Justin squirmed uncomfortably in his seat. He wanted to hear about angels.

"The bible says these people are virgins with no blame in them," Ezra said. "I don't know if that means they're actual virgins or just in a spiritual sense, but they're different. They're like priests."

"But how will we know when it happens?" the woman next to Justin said. "More people than that probably disappear in New York City every day."

"Not exactly," John said with a laugh. "But probably more people than that go missing every day worldwide. Maybe that's the point. It won't be obvious. Some people will know, because they'll see it happen. Or maybe the people who disappear will be so special we'll know this isn't your typical day."

"You mean like the pope suddenly doesn't show up for mass?" Madeline said.

"Exactly."

"It shouldn't be too hard to figure out who the devil is," the girl with the "Jesus First" tee-shirt said. "It's not like Americans are ever going to submit to forced worship."

"He comes like a wolf in sheep's clothing," Katrina said, "with a deception so great that most people will be fooled into thinking this guy is amazing. He is supposed to perform all kinds of miracles."

"Should we leave?" Justin whispered to Madeline.

"Miracles so great they could fool even the elect, if that were possible," Ezra said. "But it's not."

The hair on Justin's arms stood up. Madeline clutched his hand.

"That's why we have the prophecies — as a warning," Ezra said. "If anyone comes claiming to be Christ you know it's not him, because this time he comes as a God, not a man — not even a really amazing man. It's Jesus as the Messiah."

Now Justin knew he needed to stay.

When the meeting was over, Ezra approached him.

"Why did you come, Justin? What's bugging you?"

"It sounds too crazy...."

"A lot of us are going through crazy things right now. You can tell me."

"Sometimes I see things, and there's this guy — I don't know if I'm dreaming..."

"It's just a sign of the times, buddy. But you want to know who you're talking to. The devil has masqueraded as an angel of light."

113

Robert sat quietly on one of the sturdy metal chairs that lined the wall of the observation area just outside the interrogation room. Chief Lario sipped his coffee. The Chief had a flush to his cheeks — a combination of embarrassment and anger. He seemed to have to force himself to look Robert in the eye. As far as Robert was concerned, the Chief should be embarrassed.

For investigators not to have detected that the back door, through which a killer claimed he had entered the apartment, was painted shut was just plain incompetent. It was bad enough they had missed the gap in the security camera tape, but this was too much.

"I only went back there because I had to return a book," Robert said. "If I hadn't, this case would have been closed with the killer still out there."

"Oh, come on, Robert," the Chief snapped. "You never believed Seafore did it! And you didn't trust my people from the beginning. You back-tracked everything they did."

"Don't get angry at me, Chief. You've got a problem here that needs to be dealt with. You brought me in for my instincts, remember?"

Lario paced the room. He took a deep breath. "Of course I'm not angry at you. I'm just so damn pissed about this. If this ever gets out to the press — the sheer stupidity..." He pounded his fist on the wall.

"It won't. But you have to take some definitive action. I say that as a friend, and as someone who's been there before. One thing I've learned, is that you can't micromanage everyone on the force. But when something like this happens you need to make it clear it's unacceptable. I don't care what the excuse is."

"You're right, but he's one of my best cops. He's had a lot of family trouble lately, and I should have been paying more attention to his work. I thought everything would be fine after I gave him some time off to take care of his wife...."

"What's wrong with his wife?"

"She has breast cancer."

"Then a leave of absence will do him good," Robert said. "You've got to do what you've got to do."

Robert watched through the glass as an officer brought Seafore into the interrogation room. He looked even more pathetic than before as he sat down and placed his elbows on the bare table.

The cop loomed over him. "You're one of those guys who wants the glory," the cop said. "We've got a big time murder and you want the credit, so you tell everyone you did it. Is that what you were telling your buddy that came to visit you the other day? It must have felt pretty good for you to tell this big ole mother fucker that you're responsible for a big time crime. Is that what this is about?"

"Fuck off," Seafore said. "I killed him. I already told you."

"Yeah, yeah. You get your kicks confessing and your big buddy gets to tell all your friends you did it."

The officer left the room.

Seafore sat staring into space. After a few minutes he began tapping his foot. His eyes darted around the room. He jumped when Robert walked in the door.

"I knew you didn't do it," Robert said.

Seafore just stared at him.

"I told you I believed you when you said you didn't do it. So why did you change your story? Why did you lie?"

"I took an axe and chopped the rich bastard's head off. How many times do I have to tell you?" Seafore jumped and scanned the room.

"Tell me again how you got in the apartment?"

"I went up the service entrance and knocked on the door and he opened it."

"Except he didn't. And you didn't go up the service entrance."

"I did."

"Don't waste your breath or my time."

Seafore's eyes darted around the room again.

"What are you doing, chasing shadows?" Robert said.

"Leave me alone. Why are you bothering me? I already told you the truth. I confessed. Isn't that what you wanted?"

"So, tell me again. How did it happen?"

"I don't remember. I blacked out."

"Then how do you know you did it?"

"The blood on my shirt. They found it in the garbage dumpster."

"You had a visitor the other day."

"Yeah, that's my buddy."

"What's his name?"

"We call him Bull."

"That's an interesting name. Why do you call him that?"

"He's a big guy. He looks like a big bull, what can I tell ya?"

Did he have something to do with this?"

"He's just a guy from my group."

"The space alien group?"

"Yeah."

"And he told you to take the rap for someone? For him, maybe? Why would you do that? What could possibly have made you so scared that you're willing to spend life in prison rather than tell the truth? Are you involved with the mob?"

"No."

"And they threatened to get you no matter where you go? You can't run and you can't hide?" Robert got up and walked around the table. "We could talk about a witness protection program. Who is it — the Italians, Colombians, Russians, Chinese?"

Seafore let out a nervous laugh. "Protection?"

114

"These are exciting times," Ezra said. Justin and Madeline were walking with him, one on each side. "Sure it's scary, but we're living the classic story of good versus evil. Every book you ever read and every movie you ever saw is based on it. We may all be about to see it play out big time!"

Ezra led them through the Village streets to his loft.

"What did you mean when you said the devil can pretend to be an angel of light?"

"The devil *was* an angel," Ezra said, "a great beautiful angel, called Lucifer. So he's really good at taking good things and twisting them just enough to make them bad."

He opened the door. On the wall before them was a painting so immense it filled the entire 12 x 16 foot space. The colors were vivid, with dense pigments of gold, red, purple, and blue. There was so much to look at, it was hard to focus.

"Wow!" Madeline said. "That's incredible."

"It's sort of my version of the Sistine Chapel," Ezra said. "It's kind of how I like to envision it would have looked before it got all faded and everything. It's that good versus evil story that has played out in small ways for every human being since the beginning of time. *This* is the big picture. *This* is what it's all about, how it all came to be, and how it all ends.

"It starts over here with Lucifer, God's favorite angel, challenging God. He gets thrown out — his band of rebel angels turn into demons, and he turns into Satan. He changes from beautiful to hideous, but he remembers just enough of beauty to hate it. He's particularly great at telling people things they want to hear."

"Cool," Justin said, "so, why did God throw the devil to earth?"

"It's the oldest deal ever made. God gave the devil a time here. This is God here," Ezra said, trying to regain his attention. He pointed to a colorful flame that burst forth from the center of the canvas. "God is the brightness that's in all things that belong to Him."

"Like *namaste*," Justin said. "They say it in yoga. It means 'The light in me bows to the light in you.'"

"Sure God is within you and me, but He also exists independently of us. In the Judeo-Christian tradition, the most important commandment is 'You shall have no other gods before me.' It was the first commandment Moses brought down from the mountain, and Jesus said it was the most important one.

"It's a subtle distinction," Ezra said, "but it's a critical one and exactly the kind of subterfuge the devil loves."

"What's this?" Madeline said pointing to a strip of bare canvas with a circle in the center.

"The mark of the beast goes there, when I figure out what it is."

"Why the circle?"

"I don't know. It's just a circle." He walked in front of the canvas and stood on tip toes to point to the images at the top. "This is the big battle. Jesus as the Messiah vs. Satan, the beast and the false prophet. Guess who wins?" He laughed.

"He's scaring me," Madeline whispered.

115

Robert's desk was filled with papers and unopened mail. He grabbed for an overseas FedEx letter pack and ripped it open.

"Well done, old friend," he said to himself as he rummaged through the papers.

There were several pictures of Dr. Viviee. He bore an uncanny resemblance to his father, if in fact that was his father. There were pictures of the nanny as an older man, dated twenty years earlier.

And then he saw them — the photos that dashed his theory. There was a school photo of Viviee, and then a picture of him as a young boy with his father. Robert studied these, and all the other photos from the package. He couldn't get around the conclusion that Smith Viviee was not, in fact, a rejuvenated version of his father. He was his own person, just as Viviee himself had claimed.

Then he found the note. It simply said, "Still nothing on the mother."

116

Justin and Madeline got out of the cab before they reached the apartment, so they could spend time walking and talking. Justin was getting around well with the cane, and the pain in his ankle was almost completely gone. They held hands as they walked along.

"I don't know what I'd do without you right now," Justin said. "I can't imagine being able to talk to anyone else about this stuff. It's all so weird." The night air was crisp and fresh. Justin said, "You know, Ezra's cool, but he's really strange."

"All artists are a little weird. It's the creativity thing," Madeline said.

"Do you think all this stuff is true?"

"I don't know," she said. "How can God expect us to make huge decisions when our moms won't even let us stay out late?"

"That's for sure," Justin laughed.

As they approached the entrance to the building they noticed a man standing in front. He turned to Justin.

"Excuse me," the man said. "Are you Justin Cummings?"

"Who are you?" Justin asked. As they got closer, he could see a white priest's collar beneath a long black coat.

"I'm Father David Consolo."

The name was oddly familiar, but Justin couldn't place it.

"Do I know you?" he said.

"No. I'm an old friend of your grandmother Claire's."

"*Father* Consolo? She never talks about any priests… No, wait, you're David. You're David! You're the guy from the retreat Grams went on when she was a kid!" Justin was suddenly laughing with excitement.

"That's me."

"Man, she was crazy about this guy," Justin said to Madeline. "And then you ran off and became a priest. She's going to be so excited to see you. What are you waiting for? Why don't you go upstairs?"

"I was here earlier but she didn't answer when we buzzed up. The doorman said she was probably sleeping and that you would be back shortly. So I waited."

Justin was thrilled. Perhaps seeing Father David would pull Grams out of all her weird behavior.

269

"She's going to be soooo excited…" but before Justin could finish his sentence his head began to spin. He felt like he was being sucked into a vortex. There was a loud yelp, and a strong whooshing sound swept past his face…and then that awful sound — a thud, more like a splat.

"Oh my God!" Madeline screamed, as specks of blood hit her arm like tiny needles. Suddenly she was screaming and crying and shaking uncontrollably. The sound of her voice jolted Justin back. A drop of warm liquid hit his cheek. He rubbed it with his hand and saw a red smear on his palm. There was blood all over the sidewalk and a small carcass five feet away, right below Grams' window.

"What is it?" Max yelled as he ran from the lobby. Justin grabbed Madeline and held her close. He began to sob. Father David walked toward the mess — an animal's body flattened and disfigured by the force of the fall. "It looks like a dog," he said.

Justin already knew what Max would confirm. "It's Natasha," he said. Tears streamed down his cheeks, but he could feel the anger growing in his face.

Max recognized Natasha's collar and tag. "I'm so sorry," he said. "This is terrible. I can't imagine how…"

Just then Claire walked slowly out of the elevator.

"What happened?" Justin demanded. "That's your window that's open Grams, that's your window! Tell me what happened?"

"It was an accident Justin. She fell out." Claire said. "I tried to grab hold of her when I saw her on the window sill but it was too late. She slipped."

"Since when does Natasha climb on the window sill? And how would she get up there?"

"Justin!" Madeline said. "It was an accident. Don't talk to your grandmother like that."

"I moved my chair by the window," Claire said. "How was I supposed to know she would crawl up?"

"I don't believe you," he said.

Justin didn't understand the words that were coming out of his own mouth even as he was speaking them. How could he really believe that Grams could be capable of such a thing? He found himself staring at Father David. His skin was filled with deep wrinkles and lines, but his eyes seemed to understand all that Justin was feeling. Suddenly his eyes turned to Grams as she focused on Father David.

"Who are you?" Claire said, but it was obvious to Justin she knew exactly who he was.

"It's me, Claire. It's David. David Consolo."

"What do you want?"

"I saw you on TV. I was in town. I had to come see you."

"So, you've seen me. Now get out."

"Will you pray with me — for your beloved pet, your family, yourself?"

Claire turned abruptly and headed for the elevator. "Stay away from me."

"Wow!" Justin said. "I told you, Madeline, she's just not the same anymore. I'll pray with you, Father David."

Max retrieved a plastic tarp and laid it over Natasha's body. He brought Madeline some wet paper towels to wipe the blood from her arm. "I'll call your mother," Max said, "She'll know what to do."

Father David led Justin and Madeline in prayer over Natasha's body.

"Do dogs go to heaven?" Madeline said.

"I can't imagine why there wouldn't be room for all God's creatures," Father David said.

As Justin looked into Father David's eyes, a white glow began to surround the priest, until it engulfed him.

"What is it, Justin?" Madeline said. "You're having one of those things again, aren't you?"

Justin stood like a rock. He didn't feel able to move. Father David took his hand.

"Don't be afraid. He has hidden these things from the wise and learned and revealed them to little children. Tell me what you've seen, young man."

Just then Max walked out. "Someone from your vet's office is coming to pick up the body," he said. "Why don't you go upstairs. There's nothing else you can do here. I'll wait here until they come."

"I don't want to go up there right now," Justin said.

"It's getting late," Madeline said. "Father David, will you come with us?"

"Of course."

Claire was asleep in her room by the time they got upstairs. They quietly went into the den. Justin spoke hesitantly at first, and then it all came pouring out. He told Father David everything; his fears about Grams, his mother, the nanochip and his visions.

"Do you believe me?" Justin said.

"Yes, I do. God has always chosen unlikely messengers."

"This is so horrible," Madeline cried. "I can't believe what's happening."

"Why me? I didn't ask for this. I'm just a kid. I've never even done anything good in my life."

"All fall short of the glory of God, Justin. He said he will have mercy on who he has mercy and compassion on who he has compassion. It doesn't depend on your desire or effort, but on His Mercy."

"I'm afraid," Justin said.

"Of course you are. But His grace will be enough. His strength will be there when you need it. He knows what's in your heart."

Father David reached out to embrace him. "Many have waited for this day but did not see it. Blessed are you, for you will see."

Justin wiped tears on his shirt sleeve. "What day?"

"The day that no man knows the hour of. Now, let's pray for your grandmother — not that she be cured, but that she be healed and that God's will be done."

The three of them prayed together for a time, and then Justin and Madeline walked Father Consolo to the elevator. He hugged each child and blessed them.

"Don't be discouraged," Father David said. "All things are possible for those who believe." Justin and Madeline turned to walk back to the apartment. "Wait," Father David said. "I need to tell you…"

"What?" Justin said.

"That some things can only be cured through prayer. You must believe that with your whole heart, Justin."

Justin shut the door.

"You should have gotten his card," Madeline said as they walked toward the kitchen. "You know, you should have his phone number so if we need to talk to him we know how to find him."

"You're right."

Justin walked back to the door just as the grandfather clock signaled midnight, but when he opened it, Father David was already gone.

117

Justin and Madeline woke up to the familiar smell of chicken soup cooking in the kitchen.

"All right! Erbie," Justin yelled. "Erbie, are you here?"

"Right here, Mr. Justin," she said. He gave her a huge hug.

"I am so glad you're back. You have no idea. I thought you weren't coming back for another week."

"Ah, I've had enough rest. The doctors told me to just take it easy and keep taking my blood pressure medicine and there shouldn't be any more fainting episodes. But, the Lord said you needed me, so here I am."

"I do need you. Everything has gone crazy."

"I'm so sorry about Natasha. I just can't believe she's gone."

"It's more than that," Justin said.

"It's your grandmother, isn't it?"

He nodded.

"Well, let's sit down and have some soup together. You tell me all about it."

The television was on in the kitchen, and all the stations were still offering coverage of Viviee's hearing. Helene, Claire and Dr. Viviee were everywhere. Jeff Stone was making statements, and Dr. Viviee was accepting the adoration of the masses. Judy Borne excitedly told her story over and over again.

The phone rang. Justin picked it up and it was Robert. Justin placed him on speaker and began to pour out the story about his grandmother — the broken crystal vase, Max's stolen diamond ring, and his suspicions about Natasha's death. "That's not Grams!" he yelled.

"Whoa," Robert said. "I'm not sure I understand what you're saying."

"The better she's gotten the worse she is," Justin said.

"Do you believe she's doing all these things because of the nanochip?"

"Yes, that's exactly it. When she was sick she was normal. Now that she's gotten well again, she's gotten weird. It's like it's not Grams!"

"I want you to be careful. That doctor is a bad guy," Erbie said. "I feel it in my bones and my bones don't lie to me."

"Believe me, I'm no fan of Smith Viviee," Robert said. "I'm doing everything I can to find out who he really is, but I'm hitting a lot of dead ends."

"Maybe it turns off the God gene," Madeline said.

"What are you talking about?" Justin said.

"If it can tell genes that create cancer cells to stop, maybe it can turn off the God gene."

"Are you talking about the theory that there's a gene that connects people to the idea of God?" Robert said.

"Yeah. It's like spirituality is hard wired into the brain. Maybe the nano-chip breaks the connection."

Justin heard the front door and his mother's voice on the cell phone.

"We'll have to call you back later," he said.

118

Helene walked into the apartment with a cell phone on each ear and Claire at her heels. She was planning, negotiating, and arranging appearances with Kyle on one phone and Dr. Viviee on the other.

She caught a glimpse of Erbie and momentarily paused to extend her arms. "You're back! Thank you!" she mouthed silently.

Claire went to her room.

Helene went into the living room and threw herself on the silk sofa until she finished her calls.

"This is the most exciting moment of my life," she said when Justin and Madeline came in. "You can't imagine what's going on. The city is in an uproar. This is the biggest story in the world and I'm in the middle of it! We're changing the world, kids! We're changing the world!"

"Mom," Justin said soberly. "I realize this may not be the best time, but can I talk to you?"

"Sure, honey. What's the matter? You sound so glum. I know you miss Natasha. We'll get another puppy as soon as things quiet down."

"I don't want a puppy. It's about Grams."

"Grams? She did great today. Did you see her on TV? All anyone can say is how beautiful and remarkable she is."

"Yeah. I know. But have you noticed she's changed?"

"In what way, Justin? Tell me what you mean."

Justin recounted his fears to his mother, and as she listened, Helene could not imagine why he would lob such accusations at his grandmother. She was worried about him. Perhaps he needed more of her attention. So much was going on and he had no part in it.

"Trust me mom, it's that nanochip. I know it is."

"Is that what this is all about? Justin you are so dramatic sometimes."

"You're blinded by this guy and by all the attention you're getting. You can't even see what's really going on."

"And what exactly do *you* think is going on?" Helene was exhausted. She was operating on adrenaline and now the stress was getting to her. She felt herself getting angry at Justin, and the words flooded out. "Do you think it's been easy all these years without your father, trying to raise you and provide for you in a business where any moment I could be yesterday's news? You don't know what it's like to be always fighting the competition. I've lived my life in contractual increments, always knowing the next one might be my last, and then how would I provide for you? You don't know anything about that, because everything has been handed to you. I saw to that. I've been fighting all these years to stay alive and now I've made it. For the first time I truly feel they can't touch me — not even with a bunch of twenty-somethings. I don't have to fight to not get older anymore..."

"That's what this is about. You think he's going to make you young forever."

"Oh, stop it."

"That's it, isn't it? You think he has the fountain of youth, and you won't need surgery. You won't need to keep up with the latest skin care stuff, you'll just get his nanochip and be young forever."

"Well, I do it all for you."

"*What*? You mean you're going to get it? Oh my God! Has he promised you that nanochip? Mom, you can't. Please, you can't do it."

"Justin, I'm in a very competitive business. I have supported you single handedly my entire life. This is so you can go to Harvard. It's so you can follow your dreams. It's so you won't have to worry about whether you have the money to go to graduate school. If you want to join the Peace Corp and save the damn world, you'll have the money to do it. But I don't have that luxury. I have to work for my money. And make no mistake about it, I get face time because people like my face. Say what you will, appearances are everything. How much longer do you think I can hold on?"

"Oh, mom," Justin said, his eyes welling with tears. "We have enough money. I keep telling you, I don't even want to go to Harvard."

"Well, I want you to be able to."

"When are you planning on doing it?"

"I don't know, but soon."

"Please, mom. Just wait a little longer. Don't do anything yet. You're beautiful. Everybody knows you're beautiful. He's after you. You were right all along. The reason he came to Grams — everything — it was all because of you. He needed you to fight for him and put him on TV and make him a household name. He needed you to hire him a lawyer and stand beside him."

"Oh, please Justin. He doesn't need me. I need him."

"Don't you see? You give him credibility. Why are you so quick to hand that over to him? You don't really know anything about this guy or his nano-chip. What if it turns off your conscience?"

"What?"

"You heard me. What if, when it goes through you, turning genes on and turning them off, it shuts off your conscience? Please, mom, I can't lose you like I lost Grams."

119

"Yitzhak," Robert typed in on his cell phone. "I need sage advice: What do you do when the truth is in front of you, but you can't see it?"

Ever since college, Robert had been turning to his friend in times of confusion. He pressed the button to send the email and got out of the cab.

He was standing once again at the door to Claiborne's apartment. He wondered why he kept coming back. He could have taken care of this over the phone, but he couldn't stay away. It was like he was being drawn here by some magnetic force.

"Hello again, Mr. Morgan," Mrs. Claiborne said. "Come in, and I'll get you a cup of tea. Or perhaps you should be helping yourself by now?"

They both smiled.

"Thank you, I'll pass on the tea. Actually this will only take a moment."

She took a seat in the living room and Robert did the same.

"I spoke to Seafore," he said, leaning forward toward her. "I'm convinced he didn't kill your husband." Her breathing told him she was about to cry. He reached over with a comforting touch to her clasped hands. "Now I need to find out who did. Something has been troubling me, and I'm hoping you can help me with it."

She nodded.

"Do you know Dr. Jim Schultz?"

"Yes, of course." She took a long fortifying breath. "He's a fine neurosurgeon; he was my husband's personal physician."

"I don't mean to upset you, but Dr. Schultz told me your husband was dying of cancer."

"Why, that's impossible," she said sharply. "My husband was healthy as a horse." She had clearly been startled, but then she softened. "Sure, he was tired and didn't always feel well, but lately he had been feeling terrific."

"Well, that's just it. I think he might have been cured."

"Cured?"

"Have you ever heard of Dr. Smith Viviee?"

Mrs. Claiborne stared into Robert's eyes for a full five seconds without moving.

"That television show, of course, you mean that television show. Everyone is talking about it." She spoke slowly, struggling to use precisely the right words, as if she were fitting together the pieces of a puzzle. "My husband went to China." She paused. "A month and a half ago he went to China. He said it was business. I didn't want him to go because he was very weak and tired all the time. His coloring was bad and he had lost his appetite. He was losing weight. But he insisted. When he came back, he was feeling much better."

"How long was he in China?"

"A couple of days. Just long enough to fly there and back. He said it was an important medical conference he didn't want to miss. I didn't question him. That's when he got that medal. When he came back, he was wearing that caduceus medal."

120

Dr. Smith Viviee arrived at Helene's apartment with his briefcase in one hand and a bottle of vintage pink Tattinger champagne in the other.

"This will be a day we will remember forever," he said, kissing Helene on the cheek as she nervously led him into the bedroom.

Claire had gone out to dinner with some friends, and Justin and Madeline said they were going to a movie. Helene needed the house to herself.

Viviee put his briefcase on the bed and placed the bottle on the night table. He went to the bar in the living room to retrieve two champagne glasses. Helene paced the floor. He returned and popped the cork. As he poured the champagne he said, "Why don't you undress for me, so I can immortalize this moment in my mind?"

"Undress?" She knew she was blushing, but she couldn't help it.

"Oh, don't tell me you're shy. We are both adults, Helene. You are attracted to me and I am attracted to you. We are about to form a bond to which there is no foreseeable end. It's time for us to be together."

"Well, I mean it's not that I don't want to sleep with you, because I do. It's just, I don't know, the way you put it. It's just so abrupt."

"No, Helene," he said. "It's honest. Now, please, undress for me." He set about unlocking his briefcase.

As awkward as she felt, she also felt he was right. They were both adults, and she could sleep with anyone she wanted. She was too old to go steady.

She slowly removed her blouse and pants and then her undergarments. Viviee glanced up with a reassuring smile as she stood naked before him.

He readied the hypodermic needle.

"Are you sure this is safe, Smith? I mean maybe I should wait."

"For what? For the ravages of age to continue to take their toll?"

"Well, you know my son is very upset about this. He really doesn't want me to do it."

Viviee said nothing.

"He thinks my mother has changed in some way, and he's afraid there's a problem that maybe you're not aware of."

"I told you, there can be some slightly erratic behavior at first. It takes awhile for the technology to merge. You shouldn't have told him about this."

"Well, what happens if I do something erratic, as you put it, on TV?"

"You won't. Stop listening to your son. He's a child. He knows nothing. Tell him to mind his own business."

"Smith!" Helene said curtly. "Really, he's just concerned. It's hard for a kid to understand the concept of aging and death."

"So, what are you saying? He would rather have his grandmother dead? Is that the kind of thanks I get? I save the woman's life, give you the exclusive, put your show on the map, and your child is questioning the integrity of my work? Do you want to listen to a delusional fourteen-year-old or to the man who has cured hundreds of incurable diseases?"

"Hundreds?"

"Yes, hundreds."

"I never know what to believe with you, Smith. There's always a new piece of the story. And my son is not delusional."

"Believe in this," he said, holding up the hypodermic needle.

Helene caught a glimpse of her naked body in the mirror. She was tall and slim and had always been reasonably proud of her shape. She walked everywhere and worked out with a trainer as often as she could, but now all she could see was her drooping butt and saggy breasts. Her arms jiggled despite thousands of push ups, and the best salon treatments couldn't completely rid her of cellulite.

And there was Smith Viviee, facing her, fully clothed, holding up a hypodermic needle. There was something sinister in the scene. She looked into his eyes and glimpsed a part of herself she refused to acknowledge.

"You know, maybe I *will* wait." she said. "Maybe I'm just not ready, yet."

"Fine." He reopened the small case from which he had removed the needle and placed it back inside.

She walked over to him and softly stroked his hair. "Thank you for understanding. I'm just a little nervous."

"It's not a problem."

She tried to kiss him but he pulled away.

"I still want to be with you," she said. "I'm still crazy about you. I know we can make the most phenomenal team. We'll be the power couple to end all power couples."

"Helene," Viviee said, "you're a beautiful woman, but how long do you think that beauty will last? Another two or three years, maybe ten?" He tenderly caressed her outer thigh. "The cellulite will spread. Your breasts will continue to sag. Menopause will draw the elasticity out of your skin. How long will it take? You'll be an old lady. And I'll be at my peak. There is no future for us like that."

You manipulative little prick! But she didn't dare say it out loud.

121

Barrouck hunched over his computer screen. Under the light of a dull reading lamp he carefully typed ones and zeros, one finger at a time. He had been up all night, unable to sleep until his job was done. Was he truly recording the software of God? He realized the notion was absurd, yet he could not separate his mind from the urgent belief that this task must be completed.

"Take not your Holy Spirit from me," he said, quoting from Psalms.

He sat back for a moment and rubbed his eyes. Would it work? Would this series of ones and zeros, if coded into the computer properly, actually constitute a computer program? And on what would he run the program — on the Book of Daniel, Revelations, the Torah, the Bible as a whole, or some other as yet undiscovered document?

Barrouck stared at the screen. He sipped a cup of coffee. The programmer would be coming soon; he had been sent by the government without any knowledge of the significance of the task.

Barrouck saved his work and checked his email. The message from Robert asking for sage advice made him smile. He responded:

Dear Robert:

Pray not that your answers are there when you want them, but when you need them. Yitz

He enjoyed his silly nickname; it was so unlikely from someone as serious as he was. He enjoyed sending paradoxical messages; being paradoxical was very much in line with his way of thinking about everything.

It was just before 7a.m. in Jerusalem; just before midnight in New York. Within moments, there was incoming mail.

Yitzhak: Good to hear from you. Can't sleep. Puzzles annoy me and I'm stuck trying to solve a perplexing murder. But hey, here I am complaining about trying to square the books on one snuffed out life while you're working on world peace. How's it going?

Robert

Yitzhak enjoyed the element of humor in Robert's words, an indication he had emerged from his days of despair since Maria's death.

Robert: World peace is a slow and fearful business, but nonetheless, life is amazing. I am captivated by a project so special I dare not speak of it lest it disappear in a moon beam, which seems to be where it came from. The world is changing. The old order is dissolving beneath our feet and a new order is coming to pass. Hold tight my friend!

In a few minutes, the response.

Yitz

You can't leave me hanging like that! What on earth are you talking about???

Yitzak Barrouck tapped Reply and began to type.

Do you remember the Time of Jacob's Trouble, when....

122

The light from the television flickered in the dark room; the muted light from the screen of the laptop was steady. There was no other light in the room. Robert had drawn the curtains in hopes of sleep, but his mind was far from restful.

A rerun of Helene's show was playing on the TV. He missed her. He wanted her in his arms. He wasn't paying much attention to what she was talking about; he was focused on watching her walk across the stage.

"Shit," he said aloud. "Leave it to Yitzhak to throw me a brain teaser at this hour." He quickly ran a search engine on Jacob's Trouble.

The time of Jacob's Trouble in Judaism corresponded to the 70th seven year period in the Book of Daniel and the Tribulation in Christianity.

There was a quote from the Hebrew bible. Jeremiah wrote "'A sound of terror have we heard; of fear and not peace'…Woe! For that day will be momentous, there is nothing like it; it will be a time of trouble for Jacob, but he shall be saved from it."

"Of course I remember," Robert typed in. "'It will be a time of trouble for Jacob, but he shall be saved from it.' Did you think I had forgotten everything?"

A few minutes later, Yitzhak responded. "I see you looked it up," he wrote. "I fear the time is near."

Robert wrote: What's new? Frankly, I always thought you were waiting for it.

Yitzhak's response was: You **have** forgotten everything. Shall I fight for peace knowing where my efforts will lead?

Was Yitzhak really questioning the peace process? Robert needed more information.

He read: The Time of Jacob's Trouble would last seven years. It would begin with a treaty between Israel and its neighbors. Daniel and Revelations both gave the same time frame. Three and a half years into the treaty it would be violated, launching a time of great distress on earth, preceding the end.

Robert wrote again to his friend:

Yitz:

I'm surprised at you. Since when do you worry about such things? You cannot control the course of peace any easier than you can control the course of war. These prophecies have been around for centuries. Jews don't study prophecies. Life must be lived on available facts and knowledge, not some ancient writings that can mean a thousand things — or nothing. You have always been a man of logic, not just of faith. What's different now?

Robert raised the volume on the TV as he waited for a response. His mouth dropped open. It was Helene's show on Apocalyptic Youth. He laughed at the coincidence. Suddenly everyone around him was talking not only about God, but about the wrath of God. Was God trying to tell him something? Would it help him solve Claiborne's murder? Would it help him nail Viviee? No. If God was calling, Robert would have to answer another day.

A little megaphone on the computer screen indicated that Yitzhak's new message had arrived.

Robert:

The study of biblical prophecy may be shunned in common Jewish circles, but lest you forget, prophecy has long been studied in the Rabbinical schools and by students of the Zohar and Kabbalah. I realize that's extreme for most people, unless you're in Hollywood, of course, but as the time of the Messiah approaches, the mysteries are to be revealed.

And have you found one of these mysteries? Robert wrote.

Would you think I was crazy if I told you there may be a key to unlock the sealed book of Daniel? Or perhaps it is the sealed scroll of Revelations. These books are only to be opened at the time of the end.

Yitz, Robert wrote,

No, I wouldn't think you were crazy. I'd just say I would love to see it. Funny, they're talking about all that stuff on television right now. Some kids in New York think this is the beginning of the end of the world. Why does everyone seem to be talking about God these days?

Robert:

Coincidences are God's way of getting your attention. As for the 'kids' — the author of the holy Zohar, Rabbi Shimon bar Yochai, said as the time of the Messiah approaches the mysteries will be revealed to little children.

Robert laughed. He wrote:

I'll just consider this a coincidence. I don't think God is looking for me today. As Freud said, "Sometimes a cigar is just a cigar."

Freud only said that so he wouldn't be accused of smoking a phallic symbol, which it was — an object of power and masculinity. No object is without many meanings. In the same way, your coincidence can mean many things, depending on what you are willing to see. Perhaps it was Fidel Castro who said, "Sometimes a cigar is the answer to your prayers." Don't ignore signs, Robert. God speaks to you even when you're not listening.

"There are many signs and symbols that have meanings beyond what is commonly known," a voice from the television said.

"What?" Robert looked up.

One of the young men was speaking. "Versions of crosses, the Star of David, a lot of things that mean one thing to us have other meanings for people involved in the occult."

Robert felt as if he were in a three way conversation.

He typed,

I think we have some synergy going on with the TV here, buddy. Multiple meanings, but they all elude me. Robert

He looked up from the computer in time to see Helene closing the show. The volume went up slightly as the screen filled with a commercial. Robert stayed awake another fifteen minutes, but Yitzhak never responded. Robert played solitaire on line with an insomniac in Nebraska and then went to sleep.

123

Justin woke to the familiar sound of his grandmother's coughing. He hadn't heard that sound since Dr. Viviee had worked his magic, but he remembered it well.

Madeline made a pot of coffee and poured some heavy cream into a cup.

"So this is the big game, Justin. Should we cancel?"

"I *want* to play today." He was trying to hide the uneasiness that had kept him awake much of the night.

"Spider's so weird; I don't like the way he's always hanging around. I wish you hadn't agreed to this, especially since you told him you'd go to the Bronx!"

"Madeline, don't be so elitist. I can't back out now."

"I'm not being elitist. I just don't like the idea of going all the way to some unfamiliar place with this guy. I don't trust him."

"Everything is going to be fine. If I lose, I lose. It's not a big deal. Besides, it's a lock. I've cracked the game. I don't see how I can actually lose."

"Then why do I have this lousy feeling in my stomach?"

"Because you're drinking too much coffee," he said.

Another loud, deep cough exploded from Grams' room.

Justin went to his room and closed the door. He took his bible from the nightstand and sat on the bed. He closed his eyes and with his right hand randomly selected a page. Slowly and softly he dragged his finger down the page, until he stopped and opened his eyes to read.

"Before they call, I will answer; while they are still speaking I will hear."

"Justin," Madeline called out.

He closed the book. "In here."

"Grams is really coughing. We need to make sure she's okay."

They stood outside Grams' room watching her. She was lying in bed, her face contorted. She seemed to be struggling through a nightmare; she was having difficulty breathing. Madeline said they shouldn't leave her by herself.

"Are you okay, Mrs. Cummings?" she asked in a quiet voice.

Claire stirred a bit, then answered, "I don't know."

"Do you want us to do something?" Madeline said.

"I'm just feeling a little strange — a little light headed."

"You've been going crazy doing these television shows and everything," Madeline said, "Your body is probably exhausted."

"I think I'd like to be alone for awhile."

"Actually we're going out for a while. Are you going to be all right alone?"

"Of course I am. If I need anything, I'll call Dr. Viviee."

124

Robert woke up feeling better than he had in a long time. He took a deep breath and flung the sheets off his body; a cool breeze fluttered across his chest and legs. He smiled as he walked to the bathroom and splashed cool water on his face. He was a man on a mission he intended to complete.

The wood floor was cold under his bare feet. He thought about putting a rug down and wondered why he had never thought about that before. He shook his head and laughed at the sight of himself in boxer shorts heading for the refrigerator with his hair sticking up in the air. More cold air hit his chest and abdomen as he opened the door; it felt good. Unfortunately the fridge was empty except for a couple of tall bottles of Evian. He tried the freezer. He found an old can of frozen orange juice next to a half empty bottle of vodka. Thank God for small favors.

Robert took out the orange juice can and the Evian and read the instructions for mixing the juice. He pulled a pitcher from a cabinet and dumped the juice in, followed by four can-fulls of cold Evian. He stirred and stirred with a wooden spoon, watching the orange whirlpool spin in the glass pitcher. He poured himself a glass.

As he took a sip and the cold juice flooded his throat, he felt a familiar sensation rushing through his head — a familiar pain from a forgotten moment. It was a moment from a dream recalled in a split second at the kitchen sink. He looked toward the blank wall and it was transparent; he was looking through a frost covered window in Long Island at a snow covered backyard. A rabbit was making tracks through nearby bushes. Robert made orange juice from the can with tap water chilled through half frozen pipes. The phone rang; it was Maria. She was on the road. "No," he pleaded. "Don't go to the city today. We're taking these terrorist alerts very seriously."

But she laughed at the thought of being a target. "I understand completely, Robert," she said. "You think terrorists are targeting the ladies who lunch. There's something Freudian about that. Nonetheless, I will not stop living every time someone posts a terror alert. Even though we have a house in the Hamptons, we're still New Yorkers, and New Yorkers don't get scared." She laughed and the cell phone crackled. "We're resilient."

They were disconnected as she entered the midtown tunnel. An hour later, the suicide bomber struck, killing himself and a couple of dozen people. It was a ridiculously small gesture for a terrorist organization to undertake, but Robert knew it had been undertaken out of futility. Robert was so good at his job, there was no chance of their pulling off any of their grander plans. His wife died because he protected the city so well. That was the most unbearable irony.

It was the Day of Atonement. It was supposed to be a day of fasting and repentance; and for asking God's forgiveness for promises broken to Him. But it was the promise broken to Maria that shattered Robert to the bone.

In his dream, there she stood, in front of the flames, as firefighters worked frantically to douse them. "The madness has just begun, Robert. You can't save everyone. There will always be causalities, but you can create light against the darkness that will engulf the planet."

As her image began to fade into the flames he called out to her, "No, Maria, please don't leave."

"I will never leave you, Robert, but you must hold on to what you can touch. I will be here for you for as long as you need me." And she was gone.

He cupped his forehead in the palm of his right hand. "God, it's been so hard. I miss you so much, Maria." He sobbed out loud, alone, with his pain, in his apartment.

He was still crying as he gulped the orange juice and went to the front door for the newspapers. He read the headlines.

GONE AT THE STROKE OF MIDNIGHT. HOLY HAZEL PULLS A DISAPPEARING ACT. There was a full page photo of the woman kneeling in front of the statue of the Virgin. The caption read, "I left her praying. When I went back, she was gone!"

Holy Hazel had been in a trance; one of the nuns was praying beside her. The nun got up to get a drink of water. She looked at her watch, wondering how long Hazel would be in a trance this time. It was just before midnight. When she came back, Holy Hazel was gone.

Some were speculating that she had played out her ruse as long as she could sustain it and then snuck out the back way at her first opportunity. The statue of the Virgin Mary was left behind, and its miraculous tears had ceased to flow. No one had ever counted the collections and donations, so there was no way of knowing if Holy Hazel had simply taken the money and run.

"I believe God has taken her," the nun said. "I have no other explanation."

Robert flipped the page. A smaller article took him completely by surprise.

NOBEL PEACE PRIZE WINNER FEARED DEAD.

125

"Are you sure you don't want to take your cane?" Madeline said.

"I'm sure," Justin said as they made their way to the street corner. "I don't want to look weak. My ankle barely hurts anymore and I'll be mostly sitting anyway." Justin was limping only slightly, but pain shot up his leg when he walked too quickly.

They joined Sean and Whiley and flagged down a cab. They asked the driver to take them to the Bronx.

As they left the island of Manhattan, Madeline said a silent prayer.

They drove past ethnic grocery stores, small industrial plants, redeveloped housing units, and small single family homes, through neighborhoods that were undergoing resurgence after decades of decline.

None of the kids had been born in the 1970's, when the Bronx was the most devastated urban landscape in the country. Buildings in the South Bronx regularly burned down, either because the electrical wiring was so desperately frayed or because landlords were desperately looking to collect insurance money. Residents slept with their shoes on to get out fast if a fire broke out. Today everything was different, and these kids had no concept of how much fear had once plagued these neighborhoods. As Madeline looked out the window of the cab, she took comfort from the innocent faces of the children playing on the street. What had she been so worried about?

They paid the cabbie and walked to the entrance of one of the twenty-four high rises that together comprised one of the nation's largest multi-family housing developments — ten thousand units. As the kids waited to be buzzed up to Spider's apartment, Justin pointed out an egret that had wandered over from the adjacent woods.

"I'll take that as a good omen," he said.

"What the fuck are we doing here?" Sean said.

"Don't go there," Justin said sharply. "This was your idea."

Inside the pale yellow block lobby, Sean repeatedly pushed the elevator call button.

"That doesn't make it come any faster," Justin said.

The door opened and a middle aged lady got out. Justin held the door open for her, and she smiled at him.

293

They arrived at the 18th floor and made their way down a long, dimly lit corridor. They found the door to #216, and Justin knocked, hesitantly at first and then louder.

The door was opened by a huge man who filled the frame. At about 6'5" he was as wide as any two average men, and he towered over the kids.

Madeline looked closely at the large skull and crossbones tattooed on each forearm and the biceps that bulged from beneath a black tee-shirt. If Spider was looking to intimidate them, he had succeeded.

The enormous man stepped to the right, and the kids walked in.

Spider was sitting at a small chrome and glass table in the middle of a large, almost empty room. Over the table, a single light bulb hung from the ceiling. The steel gray walls and plush black carpet were a jolt after the faded yellow of the halls. Against a long wall were a couch covered in black leather, a straight chair, and a large flat screen TV.

Madeline, Sean, and Whiley took seats on the sofa. Justin took the empty chair across the glass table from Spider. The big guy stood silently next to the door, his hands folded politely in front of him.

126

Justin and Spider linked their games as the others watched the TV. Spider's playing field appeared on the top TV screen and Justin's on the bottom; the configuration was the same on their GamePad screens.

The Kings appeared in flowing robes and gold crowns, against a stormy background. Justin chose the Purple King, Spider the Red. The Kings bowed to the screen.

In One on One games, Kings simultaneously battled a game Challenger, attempting to clear the level and move on. They had one minute to do so. Kills were usually the fastest and simplest way to beat the Challenger, but Captures were more desirable since they would later fight in the Player's army at the Ultimate Battle — Armageddon.

Any player who could completely desolate an army while his own remained in tact, was known as Ruler of the Apocalypse — a rare and sought after moniker.

"Let the games begin," Spider said.

Suddenly, Molten Man Challenger was in Volcano World hurling flaming lava rocks at the Kings. Spider chose a water cannon for defense and Justin a shield. The water cannon efficiently zapped the fireballs to oblivion, and Spider quickly cleared the field, but with no Captures. Justin's shield deflected the fireballs and he eeked out a win just before his time expired, also with no Captures. The Battlefield seemed unusually hard for Level 1, and Justin hoped it was not a sign of things to come.

Then came Rock Challenger, Lions of Destruction, and Lazer Legions. Both Kings moved quickly through the Levels. They arrived at Level 4 to find themselves in One on One combat.

"Finally," Spider muttered.

They watched carefully as words appeared on their screens.

"The Kings will take a short rest as their minions fight for them. Select a Capture from your army to battle a Capture from your opponent's army. The winner earns the opposing Capture's loyalty, along with a Life Elixir."

They each chose a Capture from Lazer Legions. Spider quickly outmaneuvered Justin for the win.

Justin feared he wouldn't survive long enough to use the new trick he'd learned.

127

Helene sat in her office fielding calls from her agent and network executives all over town.

"Well, of course I would *consider* taking over the Primetime Interview show for Academy Awards nights," she said into the phone. "Obviously I would want to make some changes, and I'd need Kyle."

Kyle was seated on a beige leather sofa, beaming, but barely visible over the over-sized arrangement of flowers on her desk.

"I'm sure you'll work it out," she said to her agent, "and I think the network should do something nice for Kyle." She paused. "I know you're not his agent, but just let them know that would make me very happy. After all, if it weren't for him getting all those promos on the air, no one would have ever known to turn to us in the first place. Oh, and thank you for the roses. They're just... well, they're enormous. I would take them home but I don't think they'd fit in the cab."

Helene hung up the phone barely able to contain her glee. "We did it!" she shouted. "They are eating out of our hands."

Her assistant walked in with a bottle of champagne.

"Just put it over there," Helene said, pointing to a row of floral arrangements.

"Actually it's for Kyle. The courier just came by."

Kyle checked the card.

"Who's it from?" Helene said.

"My buddy over at CNN. Their numbers took a big spike during your interviews."

"We own this story," Helene said.

"Speaking of owning the story, no more letting Viviee go on other media outlets to make announcements. I was less than thrilled to see the redhead on the news. We should have broken that."

"You're right. I'm going to have to keep a tighter rein on the good doctor."

128

In Nam — the portion of Battle Ultimo inspired by the Vietnam War — Justin quickly defeated the first Soldier and made the Capture, but he moved his King too slowly while gathering the assault rifles and when more Soldiers emerged, time was running out. Justin was forced to Kill rather than Capture. Spider turned all Nam's Challengers into Captures.

By the time Justin and Spider made it to level 10, Justin was feeling tense and insecure. He knew he would never win if he didn't relax.

He got a burst of confidence when Brainiac appeared. The players would have to solve problems or answer questions within a designated time period. These *could* be Mensa level questions. Brainiac, though physically the weakest of the challengers, when presented at such a high level, could become an important strategic ally at Armageddon.

They had thirty seconds to answer the first question: How long did the Hundred Years War last?

a. 100 years, b. 116 years, c. no such thing.

Justin chose b. He let out a nervous laugh when the correct answer came on the screen. He had it right.

The next question was more difficult: What mathematical expression uses three of the same digits to equal 24, without using 8?

Spider quickly clocked in his answer. How could he have figured it out so fast? Justin ran numbers in his head. He couldn't concentrate. Spider was smirking at him. It had to be a double digit. Eleven? No. Twenty-two? Yes, of course: twenty-two plus two. And just in the nick of time!

Spider had also gotten it right. He winked at Justin and said, "Not so smart, are you, motherfucker?"

Justin said nothing. He just wanted to last long enough for his ship to come in, literally. He could feel his stomach tighten as a One on One Challenge appeared on the screen.

"Choose a Capture from your Opponent's army to battle a Capture your Opponent chooses from your army. Meet on the battlefield in thirty seconds. Choose wisely, for the winner will retain the loyalty of the loser."

"Shit!" Justin said unconsciously.

The safest strategy was for each player was to choose the opponent's physically weakest Capture, which in each case would be Brainiac, but Justin desperately felt he needed one of Spider's Captures from Nam, so he picked it. As soon as his finger hit the key he knew it was a mistake. It was a risk that didn't pay off.

Spider chose Brainiac to play for Justin, and Brainiac promptly lost to Nam.

Then came the level Justin had waited for. It was his only chance to make up for the loss of Brainiac.

Each King was put in an armed ship that was sailing along the coast of an island. The Natives on the island were firing bow and arrows. The King could choose a machine gun or a cannon. The common strategy was to fire the machine gun at the Natives and quickly destroy them. Instead, Justin chose the cannon. He fired it twice into the water and created a tsunami that swept all the natives instantly into the water. Within moments they would all disappear in the computer generated sea and Justin would rack up the Kill in under five seconds — bonus time — which meant he would win a Life Elixir.

Justin could hear Spider make a growling sound. As he was about to hit the complete button and move to level Thirteen, Justin paused to look at the rows of life preservers on the ship. He had never noticed them before and was unsure if they had been there all along. There was one second left for bonus time. The Purple King threw a life preserver into the water. He could hear Spider laugh. Then the Native grabbed it and became a Capture. Justin couldn't believe his luck. One by one he threw the life preservers into the sea and collected the largest single batch of Captures in the game so far.

Spider's gaze intensified.

He stood up and threw his beer bottle to the floor. Madeline gasped.

"Whoa, man," Justin said. "It's only a game."

"Shut the fuck up and play, motherfucker."

"Hey, come on, there's no need for that. You've been kicking my ass all along. I haven't said a word."

"Yeah," Sean said. "Let's all try to stay cool."

"I said, shut the fuck up and play." Spider placed his bare foot on the beer bottle and crushed it. Dark red blood oozed into the dark plush carpeting.

Justin was stunned. He stood up. He glanced over at Madeline, but the fear in her eyes was not reassuring. Everyone was looking to him for an answer, and he didn't know which way to go. He suddenly realized his dilemma — he didn't know what would happen if he won the game and he didn't know what would happen if he lost.

"You know," he said. "I think we'd better go."

Madeline, Sean, and Whiley practically leapt to their feet. The big guy took a tiny step to his left, which placed him in front of the door.

"This is a little intense for me," Justin said. "It is totally your game, man. You won." He reached for his GamePad.

Spider reached behind his back and pulled a revolver from his pants. It was a dull metallic color. Spider extended his arm until the end of the barrel was between Justin's eyes. It made an insistent pressure just at the top of his nose.

129

Erbie took to singing a hymn as she waited, and waited, and waited for one of two service elevators to take her to the Cummings apartment. The other was undergoing maintenance.

She was annoyed at the delay, but happy to be back to work — even though it was her regular day off. She was feeling strong, figured she had a lot of work to catch up on and really wanted to see the kids. She didn't know they had already gone out.

When she looked for them in their rooms, she became alarmed by the sound of Claire groaning. She checked in on Claire and noticed a slight gray pallor to Claire's skin.

"What has that Dr. Viviee done to you?" Erbie said, as she stroked Claire's forehead. "We'll find out what's going on here. Don't you worry. He's a bad man and he's not going to get away with this."

Claire moaned louder and thrashed her head about.

"Miss Claire, are you alright?" Erbie whispered, unsure if she was awake.

Claire quieted and Erbie decided it was best to let her sleep. She went about her housework. A couple of times she thought she heard noises over the sound of the vacuum cleaner, but each time she turned it off there was nothing but silence. Each time she checked on Claire, she was sleeping peacefully.

Erbie was in the kitchen when she noticed the line to the phone was illuminated, so she knew Claire was awake. Dr. Viviee's card was next to the phone. She studied the curious way he presented his name –"VIVIee". She began to prepare some food. She threw an orange peel into the now overflowing garbage and removed the bag from beneath the kitchen sink. Erbie paused and returned to look at the card. She couldn't stop staring at it. The sound of the door slamming in Claire's room brought Erbie back to the present and she exited out the back door to the stairwell. She flicked the light on and pulled down the heavy metal door to the incinerator and dumped the bag of trash down.

She was surprised to turn around and find Claire standing at the doorway in her night clothes.

"Miss Claire, you shouldn't be out of bed."

"What are you doing here?" Claire said abruptly.

"I'm working."

"Get out."

Erbie started to approach the entrance to the apartment but Claire blocked the way.

"Get out now," Claire said. "You're not wanted here."

"Well, that's up to Miss Helene. If you'd like I can get her on the phone and if she doesn't want me here I'll just leave."

"I don't want you here."

Erbie took a step to the door and again Claire blocked her.

"What would you like me to do, Miss Claire? I have to get my handbag and my things from the apartment. Do you want me to leave them here?"

Claire stepped away from the door just far enough for Erbie to slide in the doorway.

"I've made you some food," Erbie said. "You'll feel better after you eat something."

"Leave."

Erbie put her things in her bag and walked out the back door. She was trembling. She dialed Helene from her cell phone but before she could place the call the elevator door opened. She felt a presence behind her and quickly turned to see Claire staring at her from the door.

As she looked back to the elevator she realized it was the broken elevator and there was no car there, only an empty shaft. Her fingers began to tingle and she grabbed the side of the door. Her vision blurred as she looked down the long, dark, tunnel leading to the basement. Her knuckles turned white, her hands went clammy. Her knees buckled as the feeling of needles pierced her toes. She felt herself about to fall.

"Oh God," Erbie said.

Claire stepped toward her.

Erbie began to reach for her with one hand, her other still frozen to the door, but Claire lunged toward her.

"Help me, Miss Claire. I'm dizzy, I..."

Suddenly a voice shouted, "Claire!"

Erbie looked up. It was Dr. Viviee standing at the door.

Claire seemed in a daze. She looked to Dr. Viviee and her body began to shake. He leaned her against the wall and extended his hand to Erbie.

"Come on Erbie, let go of the door," he said softly.

"What have you done to her?" Erbie gasped.

"Take my hand. Trust me. Take my hand."

130

No matter how many times he read them, Robert could not absorb the words on the newspaper in front of him.

A leader in the Middle East peace process, Nobel Prize winner Yitzhak Barrouck, is missing and feared dead in Jerusalem. Israeli authorities say his disappearance comes on the eve of peace talks aimed at putting an end to the violence in the West Bank, with a compromise that has yet to be disclosed. Barrouck was said to have obtained high level support from both sides of the bargaining table for his proposal. There were, however, prominent interests that had already voiced opposition to any compromise at the present time. Barrouck's family says the historian and religious scholar had been working late into the night in his home office. His disappearance was discovered by an assistant at 8:30 a.m. A family spokesperson said those opposed to peace have frequently leveled death threats at Barrouck and may finally have succeeded in abducting him. Police continue to search his office for clues.

"Oh, dear God," Robert said. "It can't be. They finally got you, old friend."

Robert had flown to Israel three times, at the Barrouck family's request, in an effort to convince Yitzhak to employ greater security measures. Yitzhak always agreed to everything, but he never actually did anything to improve his security. Robert was overwhelmed. Why was he completely unable to help those he loved the most?

"When they're out to get you, they get you," Yitzhak used to say. "It only takes one mistake, and we all make mistakes."

Robert threw the paper to the floor and ran to the computer. He looked up the time of Yitzhak's last email. 11:58 a.m. — 6:58 a.m. in Jerusalem.

131

"You shut that game down, and I'm gonna shut you down, and all your friends," Spider said, and there wasn't an inch of Justin that didn't believe him. "No, you're gonna play, rich boy, and we're gonna up the stakes. You lose and you lose. Capice?"

Justin wanted to run, but he was paralyzed with fear. He sat down slowly. A bead of perspiration stung his eye, and he felt his heart pounding with such intensity that he feared he would hyperventilate. The last thing he wanted to do now was reveal his absolute panic. He could hear Sean whimpering in the background, and apparently so could Spider. He turned the gun to Sean, and Justin braced himself for the sound.

"Let's be cool," Justin said. "It's okay. Let's finish the game and live to play another day, huh, Spider? You're a great player. I enjoy playing you." He managed to eek out a smile, but his desperate condition deprived him of the capacity to take any pride in this achievement.

"And you're a fucking liar," Spider snapped. "Now make your move." He put the pistol down on the table in front of his screen.

The next level was a One on One Battle called Dragon Fury. Justin had never played it at such a high level, and never as a One on One Battle. Both Kings turned into Dragons. Spider's Red Dragon attacked Justin's Purple Dragon before he could orient himself. He felt helpless. The Red Dragon attacked relentlessly. Justin was totally confused. The Life Energy of his Dragon was rapidly diminishing and its movements began to slow. He hurled a powerful blow against the Red Dragon — more powerful than he had expected. He remembered what his mother said; they put in all kinds of tricks to make you do one thing when you're really supposed to do something else. Suddenly he realized that as the Life Energy of his Dragon declined, the Fury became more powerful. What if he held off, and didn't fight back. What if the Purple Dragon's Fury only increased by the beating he was taking from the Red Dragon? Justin held off his attacks. He could see a victorious smirk make its way to Spider's lips. Then, as his Life Energy was almost completely gone, he launched a single attack that took out Spider's Dragon instantly.

After that Justin played almost unconsciously — by intuition and feel — until "Armageddon: The Ultimate Battle" appeared on the screen. Blood dripped from the letters of the title. His palms were clammy. He tried to suppress his trembling.

Please, God, don't leave me now. Keep me calm. I'm really sorry about everything. Whatever you want me to do, I'll do. Just get us through this!

The armies assembled. Each player selected his best order for the Captures, now known as Soldiers. They would battle until someone lost his King.

Justin was still unsure of whether he wanted to win or lose. He wanted both. He understood, "You lose, you lose," but he wasn't sure what the ramifications would be if he won. Safety was nowhere in sight.

Spider chose first and sent out the Swordsman. Justin responded with his own Swordsman and took a hit, but quickly he rallied and defeated Spider. He then chose his Jouster, but Spider sent out Nam and defeated him. Justin retaliated with the tribe from the Tsunami. Spider sent in the Lions.

Justin moved his fingers frantically to keep up. Soon both armies and most of the weapons were gone. Justin was down to his King and two Life Elixirs. Spider had Brainiac and his King, with one Life Elixir. Justin's King moved deftly around the battlefield as Brainiac shot at him. Justin shot back. Brainiac was smart enough to anticipate Justin's moves. It was only a matter of time until he hit Justin's King. There was nowhere to go.

The Purple King jumped and delivered a karate kick to Brainiac's arm, then shot him. Brainiac fired a shot that hit the King, but wounded by the kick, he immediately dropped the gun to the ground. Justin went for his Life Elixir. He could heal his King and finish off Brainiac if he could get to the gun before Brainiac did.

Justin felt nauseated. His screen began to blur. He was about to faint. As he fought the urge to throw up, he experienced the now familiar white haze creeping before his eyes and dulling his senses. He was unable to move. He no longer even felt the sensation of breathing. His mind was in total panic. Surely Spider would shoot him now, or perhaps he already had.

"Need Life Elixir, Need Life Elixir," flashed on both screens.

Justin pushed his finger against the sensor to administer the first aid. He closed his eyes and held his breath and then stopped. Spider was not giving his Life Elixir to Brainiac. He was saving it for the Red King!

He heard his mother's voice: *they trick you into thinking you're supposed to do one thing when you're really supposed to do something else.*

Justin still had two Elixirs. The Purple King handed the first to Brainiac and took the second for himself. Brainiac was immediately healed. The whole room gasped. As Brainiac moved to pick up his weapon, he disappeared — and reappeared in Justin's army, gun in hand. He had defected! Unbelievable! Instinctively Justin moved for Brainiac to fire. The Red King dissolved into Oblivion before Spider had a chance to react.

"Noooo," Spider cried out. "This ain't possible."

Justin felt a surge of heat; it was adrenaline pumping through his body. He knew they had to get out of there quick. He leapt to his feet, and the kids on the couch did too. They were all standing, but the big guy was in front of the door, blocking the only exit.

"Spider, what's up man?" Sean said. "We're pals."

"Shut up, punk," Spider said, never taking his eyes off Justin. "Did I forget to tell you — you win, you lose?" He aimed the gun at Justin's face.

"Hey, look, man, I didn't even want to play this game. I just got lucky, that's all. Come on, we had a deal."

"You kids think you're hot shit, don't you? You think you're better than everybody else. You think you can just waltz into the Bronx and bitch slap us around. Well, you can't. This ain't your town, bros. It's mine. And I tell you when you can leave."

"Okay Spider, put the gun down," Madeline said. "Let's just chill. Maybe that was kind of rude of us to be running out like that."

"Yeah," Justin said, "Tell us what you want and we can work this out. Is it the bet? Because if that's it, I mean, you don't have to pay. Let's just consider this a friendly game. And we'll all live to play another day."

Spider let out a diabolical howl, never taking the gun off Justin.

"Do you want money?" Justin said.

"Yeah," Sean said. "I'll give you everything I got. Here." He pulled a small role of bills from his pants pocket. "Take it. Whatever you want, man. We'll just be on our way."

"You see, Bull," Spider said to the big guy, "that's the problem with these boys. They think money can buy you anything. Well it can't." He turned back to Justin. "I want your blood," he said.

132

"It's a good thing you called quickly, Claire," Dr. Viviee said, walking briskly into her bedroom, his attaché in hand. "You don't look very well."

She was lying on the bed.

"I don't feel very well either, doctor. Am I going to be okay?"

"Well, let me have a look at you." He opened the front of her dressing gown, placed his right hand on her chest, and asked her to cough. With his left hand he took her right hand and examined the mark. The circle was intact and two spokes were clearly defined. He laid her hand back on the bed.

"I'm going to be honest with you, Claire. The third spoke should have formed by now, and it has not. You're fighting the nanochip. I've told you before — if you fight the chip it will not work."

"But I'm not fighting it, Dr. Viviee. I'm so thrilled to have this opportunity. I'm not fighting the chip." She was almost in tears.

"All right, Claire. Calm down now."

"Maybe I'm just exhausted from all this publicity."

"Maybe," he said. "Why don't you tell me when you started feeling the way you feel now."

"There was an accident, with our dog the other day. She fell out the window. My window. My grandson is very upset. He thinks I did it. You don't think I did, do you, Dr. Viviee?"

"Of course not, Claire. What else happened?"

"Well, when I got downstairs someone was here to see me. I didn't want to see him and I asked him to leave. It's all been very upsetting. I didn't feel well yesterday and then when I woke up this morning I didn't feel well at all. Erbie, where's Erbie?"

"Erbie didn't come to work today. Who was it who came to visit you?"

"An old friend. Someone I haven't seen in years. I didn't even talk to him."

"Why was he here?"

"He's a priest and he saw me on TV."

"I see. You asked him to leave?"

"Yes, immediately. I didn't even speak with him. Then I woke up coughing."

"All right," Dr. Viviee said. "Now I know what to do." You're going to be fine." He opened his briefcase and took out his laptop. He connected a small round metal object to her right hand. It was attached to a thin white wire, the other end of which he plugged into the laptop.

"I'm going to need you to rest for a couple of days," he said. "It will be a deeper rest than you've had so far. I'll take you with me, so I can monitor you constantly. At this point we must facilitate the effectiveness of the nano-chip. We have to move you through the stage you're in to get you into full recovery. Until you get into full recovery there is always the possibility of a relapse. Accept it, Claire. Let the chip do its work."

133

"No Please!" Madeline screamed, but Spider cocked the pistol. Almost in unison the kids gasped. Madeline cringed and turned her head. She let out a loud "Noooooooooooooo!" but instead of a crack all they heard was a click. And then another. Spider pulled the trigger three times, but nothing happened.

"Fuck!" he yelled as he threw the gun to the floor. It discharged and the shot hit Bull in the chest. They watched as his enormous frame slid in slow motion down the door, leaving a trail of blood. He slumped to the side.

Madeline ran to him. "Call 911," she yelled. Then she realized his position against the wall left just enough room for her to open the door. "Come on," she screamed to the others. She bolted into the hall with the boys right behind. She led the way down the long, dimly lit corridor to the fire stairs, and she didn't stop running till she was at the bottom. As she reached for the fire door on the first floor, she heard Justin yell.

"Wait. Don't open the door." Sean ran into Madeline, almost pushing her into the door, but Justin grabbed him. "He's not behind us. Maybe he's waiting there."

Justin slowly moved to the window and saw the head of a shadow standing flush against the wall. He motioned with a finger to his lips to keep quiet and pointed to the others to take the stairs back up.

They moved to the second floor, huffing and puffing.

"What are we gonna do?" Sean said in a loud whisper.

"I don't know," Justin said breathlessly. "I've got to think."

"Maybe we can knock on doors," Madeline said, "and get somebody to hide us."

They heard the ding of the elevator. As they stood listening they could hear the doors open. They stayed open for a moment and then closed.

"He's checking the floors," Justin said. "Let's get out of here now." He ran down the stairs to the first floor. He looked out the window and gave the others an all clear. He grabbed Madeline's hand and pulled her out the exit door; Sean and Whiley bolted out right behind them. Madeline chanted a silent prayer at the sudden warmth of the sunlight. Justin paused to get his bearings; then he headed around another of the buildings. As they rounded the corner a hand reached out and grabbed Sean by the collar.

"Help!" he cried out.

Spider had Sean by the hood of his sweatshirt and was pointing the gun at his right temple. Even from a distance Madeline could see the terror in Justin's face.

"Run," he said to Madeline.

"I won't leave you, Justin."

"Just go," he said. But she didn't move; instead she started screaming at the top of her lungs. "Help," she bellowed over and over, as loud as she could.

Suddenly an old lady wearing a blue and white flowered dress, a straw hat, and white gloves emerged from a nondescript door and walked toward Spider. She looked like she was dressed for church. In the tone of an angry mother, she said, "You let that young man go right now!"

Spider looked at her in amazement. "Get out of here, you old bitch. This ain't none of your concern."

"Don't go talking to my mother that way, punk," a voice said.

Spider turned. He was face to face with a tall, thin black man in a cordovan colored suit, black shirt, and skinny black tie. The man was so tall that Spider had to tilt his head back to look into his stern brown eyes. He felt a push at his groin and looked down to see a small pistol pointed at his crotch.

"Hey, I ain't got no beef with you," Spider said.

"My Mama doesn't like trouble in the neighborhood."

"That's cool," Spider said. "I'll just take my business elsewhere." Still holding Sean tightly by the shirt, he began to move away, but the tall man grabbed his arm.

"Let the kid go."

"What are you doing, man?"

"Let him go, now, or I blow your dick off."

Spider let go.

"Now you run, kid," the man said to Sean. He put his arm around Spider. "While I talk to my new friend here."

134

"Robert?"

"Yes, Mrs. Claiborne?"

"I need you urgently. Can you come over right now?"

"I'm on my way."

He had barely hung up the phone when he was out the door, impatiently waiting for the elevator. It was taking too long, so he decided to take the stairs.

He flagged down a cab, but after only a block and a half he figured he could do better on foot. He was moving at a pretty good pace when, in the middle of the crowded block, he spotted the back of the little blond girl.

He gasped but continued walking toward her. She turned to face him. He looked her in the eye and picked up the pace. She stared at him, and he started running toward her.

She was standing on the corner, just across the street. If only he could reach her, he would grab a hold of her and find out if she was real. As he approached the crossing he looked into her eyes. Blood began to drip from her face.

He looked around at the busy street and started to laugh. He looked her right in the face and laughed. He didn't know why he was laughing, but he knew it was a victorious laugh. He didn't know what victory he had won.

When he reached the walkway a bus passed in front of him. When it was gone, so was the girl. Robert found himself filled with energy. He was at the entrance to Claiborne's building.

The doorman greeted him and let him in. Evelyn Claiborne answered her door immediately.

"We were cleaning," she said. She seemed on the verge of tears. "We were packing up Archibald's books and, and I honestly never imagined… oh come, let me show you."

Robert followed Mrs. Claiborne into the library. It was crowded with packing boxes. The shelves were half empty, and a handwritten catalogue lay on a chair. A stout woman, in a dress that appeared to have been constructed out of tar paper and doilies, nodded at Robert; she held a feather duster in one hand. Mrs. Claiborne walked through the doorway and turned around to face it. There was a library ladder leaning next to the doorway. She motioned to Robert, and he began to climb, just a few steps, approximately eight feet off the ground, directly across from Archibald's desk.

"Look at the shelf," she said.

It was empty. *Not on the shelf, at the shelf,* he told himself. Then he saw it. It was obvious. He was eye to eye with a camera lens, embedded in the wood, flush to the edge. It would be unnoticeable unless you knew it was there, but from this vantage point he couldn't miss it, even without his glasses.

"Sometimes the answer is right in front of your eyes."

"What?"

"Nothing," Robert said as he took a soft cloth from his pocket and gently ran it across the paneling.

He quickly climbed down and began removing books from the shelves. Mrs. Claiborne helped him.

"Look for any book that doesn't feel right," he said. "Maybe it will be too heavy, or maybe it won't be heavy enough." Together they would examine every book in the library.

Robert's heart raced. This was too good to be true. At first they neatly stacked the books in sections as they checked for abnormalities. Before long they were tossing precious rare volumes on the floor in anticipation of a finding what they were looking for. The housekeeper picked up the books and put them into separate piles.

"I've got something!" Mrs. Claiborne said excitedly. "This is *not* right."

She handed Robert a large, leather bound book, four inches thick, with two brass enclosures and "The Eagle" embossed in gold on the binding. The weight of the book should have been enormous but this felt hollowed out.

He placed the oversized volume on the ledge, flipped the latches with the end of a small pocketknife, and opened the book.

"Oh, my!" Mrs. Claiborne gasped.

Robert removed a pair of gloves from his pocket and placed them on his hands. He gently removed a disk from the recording device in the center of the hollow book.

"Do you have somewhere I can play this?"

"Of course," she said. She opened a cabinet to reveal audio and video equipment.

Robert placed the disc in the DVD player. He turned to Mrs. Claiborne. "I don't think you should look at this right now, just in case there's something on it. Let me watch first."

"Mr. Morgan, when my husband was alive he tried to shield me from all the unpleasantness of the world. I will not have him shielding me in death. Play the tape."

"It looks like the device was set up to record for 2 weeks straight and reset itself. We found it just in time."

"My husband handled all the security issues himself. It never occurred to me he would videotape his collection."

"Are you ready?" Robert said.

"Ready."

The camera provided a steady wide shot of the room. It was obvious it was motion activated. Archibald was in the library looking at his collection. Robert watched as he ripped off a necklace and let it fall to the floor, right where Robert had found the caduceus. The camera went to black and restarted with emergence of Archibald and two men, one large and one small, dressed in black hoods and trench coats.

The quality of the picture was dark and slightly grainy, but it was clear enough. Archibald sat at his desk, facing the camera. The smaller of the two men sat across from him, with his back to the camera.

The larger of the two stood off to the side. He pushed his sleeves back, exposing his forearms, but the hood was pushed forward far enough to cast a shadow that hid his face. Perhaps, with digital enhancement, the face could be captured. The sound of the voices was muffled, but the words were discernable.

"I can't go through with this," Archibald said. "I just want things to go back the way they were."

"Think of what you're saying, Archibald," the man seated across from him said. "You're not being rational. You're not thinking clearly. Give it some time. You'll see, everything is going to be fine. You worry too much. Don't make a hasty decision when so much is at stake for all of us."

"I don't care. This is an unexpected development, and I cannot continue."

A book fell off the bookcase and the large man kicked it to the side.

"Are you contemplating suicide?" the seated man said.

Archibald didn't answer.

"You were greedy. You wanted it all," the man continued. "There's nothing wrong with that. Everyone does. But you can wind up with nothing if you're not willing to pay the price."

"I've changed my mind."

"What about all your plans and dreams? What about your wife, your children, your grandchildren — the grandchildren you'll never see?"

"It doesn't matter," Claiborne said. "I can't go through with this."

"It's not that easy."

"There's got to be a way. The chip has side effects. You didn't tell me about that."

"You've already taken off the necklace," the man said. "Didn't that help?"

"No. It's like you put up a firewall. I've been completely cut off."

"Interesting observation."

"God is gone from me — completely gone. It must be because of the chip."

"Is that all you're worried about?" the man said dismissively. "Your cancer is gone. You are completely cured. You have a shot at immortality. The whole scientific world is about to grovel at your feet. It's time to give up your superstitions and grow up."

Archibald let out a nervous laugh. "I can't believe it. In my wildest dreams I never thought I would actually look *you* in the eyes. And I didn't even recognize you. How could I have been so stupid?"

"You were expecting... oh, forget it. I know exactly what you were expecting. Don't flatter yourself. You're just like everyone else. You see exactly what you want to see. In time you'll forget all about your concerns."

"I imagine I will. Once you've cut someone off it's pretty easy to get them to worship you. I mean, why not? What else is there? The mark of the beast as a dry eruption? It's really quite brilliant."

"Thank you. I think you already know the chip can't be removed. So where do we go from here?"

Archibald took a deep breath. He seemed to have gained a new resolve. "I understand now. 'Whoever loses his life will keep it.'"

The man across from him howled with laughter, then abruptly stopped. There was rage in his voice.

"He is filled with fury because he knows that his time is short," he said.

The larger man was behind Archibald in two steps. He pulled a two-bladed axe from beneath the trench coat and swung it deep into the back of Claiborne's neck, pinning him face down on the blood red leather of his George III carved mahogany library desk.

Mrs. Claiborne brought her hand to her mouth and gasped.

"I'm sorry," Robert said.

"It's from the bible."

"What?"

"'Whoever loses his life will save it.' Jesus said it to his disciples. 'Those who seek to save their life will lose it, and those who seek to lose their life on my account will save it.' My husband was a deeply religious man."

Robert could see Evelyn Claiborne was barely breathing. "Let me call a doctor. This must be a tremendous shock for you." He reached for his cell phone.

She pushed his hand away.

"'He is filled with fury because he knows that his time is short.' That's a reference to the devil and his reign at the end of the days."

135

Justin and Madeline walked quickly into Justin's building without even a nod to Max. Justin, still trembling, was pulling Madeline by the hand. He didn't want to see anyone or explain anything. His ankle was throbbing and he just wanted to get to his room and crawl into his bed and hold Madeline in his arms.

"Hang on just a minute," Max said, returning from the back room. "I have a package for your grandmother."

He stepped behind the door, pulled out a cardboard shipping box three feet long by three feet wide, and handed it to Justin.

The box was addressed to Claire Cummings from a place called Exiiol in California.

Justin held the box. They rode up in the elevator. Madeline kept her hands around Justin's waist and her head on his shoulder the whole way up to the apartment.

"You were really brave, Justin."

"So were you," he said

"No, you were really brave. He could have killed us, but you kept your cool."

"I didn't have much of a choice."

"How did you know what to do at the end of the game?"

"I don't know. I didn't know I was going to win. I think I wanted to lose. I thought he would kill us if I won."

"He wanted to kill us either way," she said. "I know how you won. Madeline squeezed his arm as the elevator came to a stop.

"You do?"

"It's your gift. You don't have to be afraid of it."

The elevator doors opened, but Justin held Madeline back. He propped the box in front of the door to keep it from closing. He kissed her.

The old door smashed against the box with enough force to put a large dent in it.

Justin and Madeline walked to the kitchen and placed the box on the countertop of the island. Justin leaned against the countertop to take the weight off his ankle and the box fell to the floor.

"Oh, shit. I hope I didn't break it."

Another box fell partially out of the broken cardboard. "Maybe you should check it."

"Hand me a knife from the drawer, please."

Madeline brought him a long sharp knife, which he used to cut open the tape on the box. The inside was filled with plastic shipping peanuts and the smaller box that had peeked out. It was about two feet long and a foot across. He slit the tape on both sides and opened it.

"What is it?"

"I have no clue."

Justin lifted out of the box what appeared to be a golden staff. It was just over a foot long; double black piping was wrapped around it in a criss-cross fashion. At the top were a stone and two white wings.

"This is weird." Justin laid the item back in the box.

"You know," Madeline said, "it kind of looks like the medical symbol."

Justin shrugged his shoulders. "Here's a card. It's from Dr. Viviee. Let's Google the return address and see what it is."

Madeline scratched out the address on a piece of paper and took it to the computer in Justin's room.

The website immediately came up. "Witchcraft and Magick Store."

"That's creepy," Madeline said. She navigated the website.

"Here." Justin said. "Ritual items, pendulums, runes, oh — here's a voodoo doll kit. Let's see, crystals. Here… ritual wands. That's what it is — a wand. Go there."

Madeline and Justin scanned a list containing a hundred different kinds of wands — a pewter dragon wand, a fairy wand, a pentagram and stag wand, the tree wand, the bloodstone wand, the energy wand….

"Here it is," Justin shouted. "The healing wand. This must be it."

Madeline double clicked on the words, but the picture was wrong. It showed a wand that was long, like a baseball bat, with a large stone embedded in the top and a ring of stones around the upper quadrant.

"Wait," Madeline said. "Here it is." She started reading: "'The wand is used to invoke spirits. The caduceus wand has two snakes entwined with a winged top. It is a symbol of power, wisdom, and healing. It represents the Greek god Hermes.' That's it. That's what's in the box. It *is* a caduceus."

Justin read: "'The central rod is a phallic symbol with writhing, coupling serpents wrapped around.' Huh?"

"The snakes are supposed to be having sex, stupid."

"Oh. 'The serpents also conduct spiritual energy in a double helix pattern.' It's a hundred bucks."

136

Spider looked up from the television set surprised to see Samantha standing in the door.

"Shit, I thought I locked that," he said.

"You must have forgotten." she said.

"I thought we weren't allowed to have contact? I guess we must be working together now. I see you leaving school and I think, *Me and that foxy lady could do some serious damage together*."

"I didn't come here to work with you, Spider."

"So what are you doing here, little lady? This ain't no place for a pretty young thing like you. Bad things can happen here, if you don't have some protection."

"You know, Spider, you're right. Bad things happen when you lose your protection. And you just lost yours."

"What are you talking about, bitch?"

"You blew it. You let the big guy down." She spoke calmly and confidently. "Let me rephrase that. You are a fucking loser!"

"Watch it, bitch!" Spider scrambled up from the sofa, but as his feet hit the ground his body collapsed backward. He didn't know what hit him. He struggled to stand, but he couldn't raise his body. He pushed with his arms, but they couldn't support his weight; he was unable to straighten his legs. In fact, he couldn't feel them. Was he drunk? Was he high? Was this a dream, a delusion, a flashback?

"Wha...wha...what the fuck!"

"Just shut up."

Samantha walked to the kitchen and pulled a glass from a cabinet. She filled it with some vodka from a bottle on the counter and took the bottle and the glass to Spider.

"Have a drink," she said, handing him the glass. He quickly drank it down. She poured him some more.

"Knock your socks off, Spider. You are a loser. Got that?"

Spider stared at her beautiful, cruel face.

"I said, Do you got that?"

"Yeah. What do you want with me bitch? What'd you do to me?"

She laughed at him. "I said you're a loser and I want to make sure you understand. You were supposed to watch the kid. You were supposed to keep him close, keep an eye out for anything the boss needed to know. You were supposed to win the game. But you didn't, because you're a loser. Now, can you comprehend that, in that wasted excuse for a brain in your head?"

"Sure, whatever you say," Spider said. *Is this really happening? I must be dreaming. This high school chick is threatening me? Wake up man. Wake up.*

"Good. Now, what do we do with losers? We tell them to disappear. So, you are out of here."

"Okay, man. I'm out of here. I'll go anywhere you want. Just tell me how to get up."

Samantha laughed, more softly this time. "Tell me you didn't really think you could just lose the game and go on selling your drugs and corrupting our youth, did you?"

"He got lucky. What was I supposed to do? I tried to shoot him. Didn't you hear I tried to shoot him? The gun didn't work. It was jammed. I don't know what happened. Somebody tampered with it. That's what happened. Somebody tampered with it. And I'm not responsible for what happened to Bull. It was an accident. The gun dropped and ...."

"I don't give a shit about Bull. You just don't get it. Do you think there are accidents? Do you think the gun just jammed? There are rules to things like this. You can't just shoot the kid. Didn't it ever occur to you *he* might have protection? You weren't supposed to kill him you were just supposed to defeat him at the game and keep him off balance. But you didn't. You lost. Now you lose again. Have you ever heard of spontaneous combustion?"

"No."

"It's quite interesting really. We don't use it very often, but when we do it has a big impact — nice and neat. It only happens — oh, I think it's been about three hundred times in the last two hundred years. No one has ever figured out what causes it and no one has ever actually witnessed it, but I'll tell *you* the secret. It's sort of like channeling your anger. Alcohol helps the process, by the way." She smiled genially. "Care for another?"

Spider let out a nervous, "No, uh, no, man."

"You need to take all that stuff that's pissing you off," she said, repeatedly poking her finger at his nose. "Think of how much I'm bothering you for instance — and take it deep down. It starts like a mild pain in your gut and then it starts to get hot." She was right up in his face. He could feel her foul breath on his cheek.

"The flame grows and grows. It's like a slow burn — from the inside out. And then *pouf*!"

Beads of perspiration dripped off Spider's forehead.

"Ashes to ashes. A nice, neat, little pile, except for maybe a stray hand or foot. Sometimes that happens. It's really quite tidy. Burns hotter than a crematorium, takes care of the bones and all but doesn't hurt the apartment. Amazing really. Of course there's a greasy kind of residue that's left on the walls. Nothing a little ammonia won't take care of. There will be a nice little hole in your sofa, but that cheap black leather is so yesterday anyway."

"You're crazy, lady. Just let me out of here and we'll work this out. Whatever you need, you know I'll take care of you."

"You think I'm kidding?"

"Come on, what did you call it? Spontaneous…"

"Spontaneous combustion," she said.

"Yeah, yeah, people burning up and such, now that's like right out of some Hollywood movie. But we ain't in Hollywood, baby."

"Oh, what's that?" she asked sweetly.

Spider looked at his torso and arms. Smoke was emanating from his skin.

"Didn't anyone ever tell you smoking is hazardous to your health? Time for me to go."

"No, please, wait. What do you want from me?"

"I just want you to feel the burn. Ta *ta*!" Laughing uproariously, she walked out the apartment door with barely a final glance at Spider, paralyzed, on the couch.

He began to pant and then his whole body screamed.

"Noooooooooooooooo!"

137

Robert held Evelyn Claiborne's hand. He was sitting on a cognac colored leather ottoman at the foot of the chair she had come to rest on. She looked so dainty and fragile, enveloped in the soft leather of the oversized chair.

An officer had taken the digital recording back to headquarters. A new detective was wrapping up his investigation of the scene. He had promised nothing would be missed this time.

"We should have something on the video shortly," he said to Robert as he headed out the door. "We'll be in touch."

Robert turned his attention to Mrs. Claiborne.

"When my wife was killed..." he said, as softly and gingerly as he could, "I went immediately to the scene of the explosion. When I arrived, the fire was still burning. At the time we only knew that a bomb had been detonated. No one knew she was there, but I felt it in my gut.

"As I ran across the street, in all the commotion, with all the people, the fire department, police and debris, I saw a small object lying on the sidewalk. It was the ring finger of her right hand. I recognized it immediately." He choked back tears. "I had held that finger in my hands so many times. I'd kissed it and caressed it, and there it was, just lying on the sidewalk like a piece of trash.

"No one should have to see something like that. Not when it's someone you love. I can't tell you how to get rid of the images you just saw, but I know it's important to focus on your husband as a living being, not a dead body. He would want that.

"I also believe I can find your husband's killer, but I need to know what he meant that taking off the necklace didn't help."

"My husband believed something had put his soul at risk. He never liked the caduceus much. He used to call it sinister. He much preferred the Staff of Asclepius."

"Is that the one with a man holding a staff and a snake?"

"That's it right there," she said, pointing to an engraving of a man wrapped in a toga holding a large wooden staff with a snake wrapped around it. It was on a faded yellow piece of parchment paper, mounted and framed in a mahogany case that hung behind Archibald's desk. To the right of the man was a document hand-written in Latin.

Robert moved in for a closer look. "Do you know what it says?"

"It's the Hippocratic Oath. It's written in Latin, translated from the original Greek, just like Hippocrates wrote it. It was my husband's prized possession."

Robert flashed back to the scene of the murder; Archibald's head pinned to the desk, beneath the oath.

"Hippocrates was the first physician," Mrs. Claiborne continued. "Doctors take the oath when they graduate from medical school. It's the pledge they take to care for the sick. Almost all the schools use some version of it."

"Tell me about the symbol, the Staff of Asclepius," Robert said.

"Medical schools originally developed out of temples dedicated to Asclepius. Homer's Iliad talks about him. The Staff of Asclepius is used a lot in Europe and by the World Health Organization. The snake in the symbol is supposed to symbolize renewal, shedding its skin.

"My husband considered it to be the true symbol. In fact, in all his collections, I don't believe he had a single caduceus, until he came back from China with that medal around his neck."

"But he did have books on it."

"Yes. I found another one when we were cleaning out his things," she said as she walked to a box in the corner. She removed a small, black, leather bound book with a caduceus — a staff, entwined by two snakes, with wings at the top — embossed on the cover.

"I seem to recall there was an occult connection to the caduceus," Robert said, putting on his glasses and opening the book.

"I know it's called the Caduceus of Hermes in Greek and the word hermetic — in addition to meaning hermetically sealed — relates to magic or alchemy. Magicians, people who practice magic, not the entertainers, call their ceremonies hermetic. Originally medicine, chemistry, pharmaceuticals, the whole thing came under the study of Alchemy. It was all magic."

"Well then, that makes sense," Robert said, "because this isn't a book on medicine, it's a book on the occult."

He placed his reading glasses on and took a seat on the floor. He read until his vision blurred and his eyes had lost their focus. He looked up at Mrs. Claiborne still quietly combing through the antique books. "According to the Romans, Hermes, or Mercury as they called him, was given the caduceus as a magic wand," Robert said. "He was the patron of thieves and gamblers and the inventor of magical incantations. It says he could control the living and the dead with the caduceus and turn anything into gold. It makes you wonder how it ever got to be our medical symbol."

"Here, it says Mercury is the guardian and guide of souls.

"A patron of thieves — just who you want guiding your soul," he said. Then, Robert turned a page and read the words that pulled it all together.

"He was the guardian of souls alright. It says here, the caduceus is used to guide the souls of the dead into Hell."

138

When Helene walked into the apartment Justin could tell she had had a very long day, but his only concern was that she would detect what had happened to him.

"Justin, I'd like to talk to you alone. Madeline, would you mind leaving us for a couple of minutes? I promise I won't be long."

"Sure, Ms. Cummings," Madeline said. She removed the box from Justin's dresser and took it to her room.

"What's in the box?"

"Uh, just some stuff for school. It's for our project."

"I see. I need to talk to you about Grams." She sat down on the bed.

"What's up?"

"She wasn't feeling that well this morning."

Helene took his hand.

"Your grandmother has taken a turn for the worst. Dr. Viviee came over and hooked her up to the machine, but he said it would be best if he took her to where he's staying. He has more equipment there. He thinks he can fix the problem, and I certainly hope he's right."

Justin couldn't believe it. "You let him take her?"

"Of course. What else was I to do?"

"Call a real doctor."

"Honey, your grandmother is committed to this process. We are all committed to it. Without the technology, she's dead. I have to respect your grandmother's wishes."

"She's not in her right mind. She's different."

"Justin, it's her only hope. Dr. Viviee says it will only take a couple of days and then she's going to be fine. He wants her to stay hooked up to the machine, and he doesn't want anyone to disturb her."

"Do you know where she is?"

"Of course. It's not like he's trying to kidnap her. I'm not going to let her just disappear. I have the address written on the card in the kitchen. I know you love your grandmother. Even if she *has* changed, so what? At least she's alive."

"You're just afraid if she dies your career is down the tubes."

"That's not fair, Justin. The bottom line is, your grandmother is giving it her best shot so she can stay and watch you grow. I think the only thing that has kept her around is her will to see you graduate from high school, go to college, and grow into a man. In many ways she's already seen you grow into a man. I don't tell you often, but I'm as proud of you as I could ever be of anyone. I used to think you were like me — but the truth is you're better. I know how much you love your grandmother, but right now you need to love her enough to let all this nonsense go."

139

Helene emerged from a long hot shower to the sound of the telephone ringing.

"Hello."

"Helene. I was rude to you the other day and I very much want to make it up to you."

"Yes, you were, Smith." She paused. "But what's a little rudeness between friends?"

"I want us to be more than friends. And I promise I won't rush you into getting the chip this time. I have only your best interests at heart."

"How's my mother?"

"She's fine. She's resting. She'll be back to normal in a day or two. I think you should come and see her. She's still sleeping, but studies have shown that even people in comas are comforted by the words of their loved ones. I believe it will help her progress if you spend a little time with her."

"Of course."

"I'm heading into a meeting right now, but I'll meet you with Claire shortly. You know how to get here...."

"I wrote it down. I'll be right over."

"And Helene…"

"Yes?"

"I have a very rare bottle of aromatherapy in a bathroom to the right of the elevator when you get off. It's in a gold bottle. Your mother might enjoy your opening it up in her room. Her room is to the left of the elevator. The fourth door down."

"Okay."

"Helene, we *will* be an incredible couple."

140

"Robert, I've got news on the video," the Chief's voice blared through the cell phone as Robert made his way through foot traffic. "We were able to digitally enhance it. It looks like we've got a positive ID on at least one of the guys."

"That's fantastic!" Robert said.

"It's only preliminary at this point, but the guy in the video matches the description of a guy we just pulled out of the East River — 6'5", 350 pounds, built like a horse. He had a skull and cross bones tattooed on his forearms and a bullet in his chest. And here's the big news: The guy in the East River is the same guy who visited Seafore in jail."

The walk sign flashed, and Robert slowed his pace. "Bingo! But I want the other guy."

"It wasn't Seafore. The voice print doesn't match. We're questioning Seafore now with the new information. He said the big guy asked him to let him in the back of the building and he did."

"What does he say about the other guy in the video?"

"He says he never saw him, but he seems awfully afraid of someone he never saw."

Robert caught a glimpse of his reflection in a store window. He looked like his old self; determined and unstoppable.

"Why do you say that?"

"He wet his pants when we were questioning him."

Robert picked up the pace. "Cut him a deal."

"We're trying."

Robert raced across 59th Street. A taxi came to a screeching halt in his path as he dashed through the crosswalk. He banged his hand on the hood. On the other side of Madison Avenue he turned downtown toward Dr. Jim Schultz's office.

He had known Schultz for a long time and always found him a reasonable man, but Robert didn't know how he would explain what he had to say in reasonable terms. The elevator was slow and the ride to the office was interminable. When he arrived on the floor he rushed past the receptionist, shouted out his name, and said he had to see Schultz urgently.

"Hang on, sir. You'll have to wait," the receptionist called out.

"I'm an old friend," Robert shouted, already at Schultz's door. He gave the door a quick tap and then opened it. "Well, pal, this is your lucky day," he said, walking in.

"Sit down Robert," Schultz said. "Let's have a drink." He was sitting in a large leather chair behind a large desk.

"No thanks. I'm not drinking."

"I have your favorite — a little Absolut." He walked over to a small sink on the wall beneath a cabinet. He opened the doors, pulled out a couple of crystal rock glasses, and filled each of them with a healthy shot of vodka from the small refrigerator beneath the sink. He placed a glass on the desk in front of Robert and held his own glass up.

"Cheers," he said.

"Yeah, cheers," Robert said, without picking up the drink. He just looked at it, and it looked good.

"Go ahead, Robert. I'm running out to a meeting, but I have a minute if you have something to tell me."

"It's about Viviee. You wanted some dirt on him, and I've got it."

"Really? What kind of dirt?"

"I believe he's connected to the Claiborne murder."

Dr. Schultz laughed abruptly. "Your friend Helene has made the guy a saint, and now you come and tell me he's a murderer. I was thinking a little financial mishandling, some ethical breach, a few medical malpractice cases, but murder? Really, Robert, that's just not to be believed." Dr. Schultz downed his drink. "Walk with me, Robert, I really have to go. I'm late already."

The men walked together out of Schultz's office, rode the elevator down, and walked out to the street. Robert grabbed the collar of his trench coat as a gust of wind blew him backwards.

"Fucking wind tunnel down here," he commented. The pair headed down toward East 49th Street, and Robert resumed his report.

"*You* told me Claiborne had terminal cancer, but it didn't show up in the autopsy. There was no sign of it. He must have had the nanochip. That's why he didn't tell anyone he was dying. That's why he thought he was going to be cured."

"So are you saying Viviee tried to give him life — or that he took it?"

"Maybe both. I think he gave him the chip and then something went wrong. Maybe Claiborne found out the chip had side effects. So Viviee killed him."

"I hope you know how crazy this sounds, Robert. Even if Dr. Viviee treated him, that doesn't mean he killed him. Besides, the police already have a confession. Why are you making waves?"

"The confession doesn't hold up."

"I just don't think I'm interested, Robert, but thank you for trying."

"I don't think you're understanding me, Jim," Robert said as they crossed the street.

"I understand, Robert. I really do. You see, our experts are now telling us there is a good chance this technology really works, and if that's true, well, we would never want to keep that from the public. I don't have to tell you the implications for the medical community."

"Yeah, it will put you out of business."

"That's antiquated thinking. We have to look to the possibilities the future holds."

"You mean you figured out how to make money on it?"

"We're all about saving lives — at a profit, of course. We want to make it happen. We can't keep something this good from the public. *That* would be murder, Robert."

"You know, you look different, Jim," Robert said. "You look great, actually. Your hair — what did you… did you get a hair transplant?"

As Robert spoke, a strong gust blew through the wind tunnel that was East 49th Street. It pushed the hair off Dr. Schultz's forehead. It was only for a moment, but it was long enough for Robert to catch a glimpse of the now famous mark, just beneath his hairline.

Dr. Schultz turned to Robert and smiled. "I'll catch you later, Robert. I'm late. And thanks for your help, but we won't be needing your assistance any longer. You can go back to protecting the city now."

Robert stopped to watch Schultz enter a revolving glass door and disappear into the mass of people moving through a lobby. As the door spun he caught his own reflection in the shiny brass framework of the intricately carved stone façade of the skyscraper. He was startled by the look of fear on his face. Slowly he backed away, looking to the heavens, as if for a sign, but instead he saw only the stone overhang of the building with its address emblazoned on it in bold brass numbers — 666.

141

Helene stepped off the elevator into the expansive penthouse apartment. "Well, I'll be damned," she said to herself as she scanned the contemporary masterpiece of urban architecture. There were thirty foot high, floor to ceiling windows that made even the surrounding skyscrapers seem ordinary by comparison. "How the hell did he come up with an apartment like this?"

She placed her handbag on a black lacquer console table, removed her trench coat, and placed it on top of her bag.

She walked down a hall of closed doors until she came to the fourth one. She knocked and, when there was no response, opened it. Her mother was sleeping in a bed in the center of the room. It had the look of a recovery room in an upscale plastic surgeon's office, only significantly more high tech.

She slid a chair next to the bed and took her mother's hand.

"Hi, mom. It's me, Helene. I just want you to know that everything is going to be just fine. Smith says you're going to be back to normal in a day or two. I can't wait to have you come home. We're going to have so much fun. As soon as this is all behind us I want to take a vacation — just you, me and Justin. We'll go skiing in Gstaad, or maybe hang out at the beach in Mustique — something fun."

Helene watched her mother's slow and rhythmic breathing.

"You know, mother, Smith thinks he and I should be together. I know that will make you happy. But I don't know… he was pretty creepy to me the other day." Helene thought back to her apartment and Viviee with his needle in hand. Suddenly she said, "Imagine that snake thinks I would be with him after the way he treated me." She hadn't meant to say it out loud. She hoped she hadn't upset Claire. *This* was not the time to piss off Viviee. Not until her mother was well and the future of her show was secure. Helene got up from the chair and headed down the hallway in search of the aromatherapy.

142

"Don't fail me now," Justin said as he clicked the crystal ball on the kitchen chandelier and rummaged through the bowl. "She said the address was here on Viviee's business card. Now where is it?" He dumped the contents of the bowl on the marble countertop.

"Here," Madeline said, pulling the card from the pile of notes, coins, cash and keys.

Justin slipped the card in the pocket of his Levi's, and they ran down to the street. Somehow his ankle didn't hurt anymore. Traffic was horrendous, so they headed east on foot.

Justin was startled by the vibrating cell phone in his pocket. He stopped running and answered. It was Robert.

"We've got to talk," Robert said.

"He's taken her, Viviee's taken her," Justin shouted. "We're on our way to find her."

"Taken her where?"

"To his clinic or something," Justin said breathlessly, "It's at 666 East 49th Street."

"Wait, wait for me, and I'll go with you."

"No, we're almost there. She's on the 50th floor. He told my mother to ask for Jamal in security in case of emergency. He has to let us up."

"I know where it is," Robert said. "I just left there. I'm stuck in traffic, but I'll turn around and meet you there."

143

Helene wandered through the large living room. A door with no doorknob automatically slid open as she approached it. Inside was what had to be Viviee's bedroom. The bed was enormous. It filled the entire room. It looked like a piece of art — beams and girders were intertwined to create an odd structure of shapes and levels. It was dark gray scarred steel, and the sheets were stark white. Imagine making love on that! It made her shudder.

Beyond the bedroom was a bathroom with a long, dark slate countertop. On it, she found a single large gold bottle the size of a liter of soda, but in the shape of a teardrop. As she raised the bottle to inspect it, it slipped from her fingers and caught on her long, double strand of pearls. The bottle crashed down on the countertop, dousing her dress with a strong smelling liquid as shards of glass flew everywhere. Simultaneously the pearls exploded off her neck — the beads danced on the floor with the sound of a hailstorm.

"Oh shit!" she yelled. When she went to pick up one of her precious pearls, a piece of the broken container cut her finger — not badly, but she bled onto the floor. Her dress was soaking wet, and the fifty or so pearls that had come loose from their string were now immersed in strong smelling fluid and broken glass. She wrapped a towel around her finger as she fumbled with a silk robe on a hanger on the back of the bathroom door. She placed her dripping dress on the hanger while she tried to figure out how to retrieve her pearls and clean up the mess. Even her Manolo's were soaking wet, but she would have to clean up the glass before she could take her shoes off.

144

J ustin and Madeline raced past store fronts and high rises. Justin was feeling a sense of apprehension and dread.

"Maybe we should wait for Robert to get here," Madeline said. "I'm a little nervous."

"Look at this place," Justin said. "It's huge," he said, trying to convince himself. "There are a million people around here. She must be in some sort of clinic or outpatient place or something. It's got to be a big office. It should be safe. But no matter what, we have to find her."

"Yeah, I guess you're right."

The pair passed through the revolving glass doors and stepped onto the black marble floors of the entrance lobby, where they came face to face with a life-sized white marble horse and rider. The rider carried a bow but no arrows.

They walked toward the elevator banks, which were protected, it seemed, by a series of bronze statues of Chinese warriors. Madeline asked one of the security guards where they could find Jamal. The man spoke into a hand piece around his neck, and after a minute a tall guard with a shiny bald head appeared from behind a granite wall. He spotted the kids and walked slowly over to them. "You were looking for Jamal," he said.

"Hey, Jamal, my grandmother is up in Dr. Viviee's clinic on the 50th floor. I have to give her something. He said to ask for you to let us up."

"Clinic? I don't know about that, but Dr. Viviee's expecting you. He said to let you up if you came."

Jamal put them into a private elevator in a corner of the lobby and with a card key illuminated the 50th floor. "This is a private residence," he said. "It's the only one in the building; most people don't even know about it."

145

Helene could feel liquid squishing in her shoes as she threw a large bath towel to the ground and picked through the glass, gathering the pearls one by one and placing them on a hand towel.

When she was finished she would take a cool blow dryer to her dress, taking care not to dry it too quickly and set the stain. Apparently there was enough alcohol in the liquid that it was already drying almost invisibly. The strong, spicy smell she would have to live with for the time being. This was going to take forever.

146

Justin looked at Madeline; she was looking back at him with a blank look on her face. The elevator whirred as it rode them swiftly up. Justin grabbed Madeline's hand and squeezed it tight. The doors opened, and Justin's fingers and toes tingled. He was looking at an enormous open space with seamless floor to ceiling windows; it looked as if the aluminum ceiling was suspended from the sky. With Madeline holding his hand, he stepped out of the elevator. The brushed chrome floor felt like solid rubber under his feet, which made absolutely no sound. There was very little furniture in the huge room — a sleek sofa, a chaise and two chairs in black and blood red velvet. In the center was a steel coffee table, surrounded by oversized, black velvet pillows. The kids took a moment to absorb their surroundings. Madeline walked to the windows and looked down on midtown Manhattan. Justin got vertigo just looking from a distance. There was a single door against the wall on the right and a hallway to the left. Justin wandered down the hallway, calling out at doors, "Hello, is anybody here?" His words returned to his ears as a cacophonous echo.

A single door was ajar. Madeline grabbed his arm.

"This is too weird," she said. "It's like he wants us here."

He pushed gently at the door, but it didn't move. He pushed harder. It opened far enough for him to see someone's feet at the end of a black lacquer platform bed.

147

"I believe we are all here," Dr. Viviee said, "so let's get started, shall we?" He looked around the shiny, dark wood conference table at the twenty-two men and women who had arrived from the summits of health care, the pharmaceutical industry, insurance, and government. They looked back at him with hostility and fear. He was changing all they knew. Their instincts said to destroy him, but Schultz said to trust him. Schultz and curiosity had brought them to this meeting. Viviee knew what they were waiting for; they wanted him to expose some great weakness from which they could fashion a noose that would hang him.

They resented his proud stance and thought his Chinese jacket was inappropriate and lame. It made him look like a dreamer, someone they should be able to crush easily beneath their collective boot. It reassured them of his weakness and their dominance. He was an outsider — not one of them.

"Ladies and gentlemen," he said, taking his seat at the head of the table, "I want to first thank you all for coming here today. I realize this is a somewhat unorthodox way of handling our differences, but I am confident we can find a mutually agreeable solution that will be of great benefit to everyone here."

"I doubt that, doctor," someone said. There were grumblings and nods from the group.

"Please, my distinguished friends, allow me to present my proposal before you reject it."

"A proposal for what? To put us out of business?"

"A proposal to share in the vast empire we will create together, something that will be greater than anything you have, something beyond your stockholders' wildest dreams of profit. But first, Mr. Studor and Dr. Schultz, I must thank you for gathering this distinguished group together. Without your efforts it could not have been done. The reason for my humbly requesting this gathering is that, as you may have heard, I have discovered the single most important medical technology of our time. You may have heard that it cures cancer and spinal cord injuries and that it retards and even reverses bodily degeneration due to the aging process. The truth is, it does all that and more."

"We want proof."

Dr. Viviee pressed a button on the speaker that was on the table before him. "Mr. Teng, can you come in please." He turned back to his audience. "Ladies and gentlemen, this is my assistant, Mr. Teng Hao Li.

Teng entered the conference room wheeling a cart on which were twenty-two small computers, each no larger than a DVD container. He walked around the table distributing them to the group. When he came to a young Asian man, the man said, "Very interesting name, Mr. Teng. You are 'the Dragon's Helper.'"

Teng bowed to the man and smiled. "Thank you," he said. He added a few words in Chinese, then continued his deliveries.

"If you will open your computers and press the green button," Dr. Viviee said, "you will see a demonstration of how the technology works."

Dr. Viviee stood, placed his hands behind his back, strode to one of the massive steel framed windows, and stared out at the city below.

"How do we know it really does work?" Block from the FDA said.

"You will have all the time in the world to study it."

"Starting when?"

"Beginning today if you like. But before you tear apart my technology and discover its secrets I want you to share in its profits. Am I now speaking your language?"

There was silence from the group.

"There are many issues that separate us. I hope that money is not one of them. You see, I am not a greedy man. I choose to share with my friends. I need simply to know who they are. Are you with me?"

He had their attention now.

"You may acquire many friends at this table, Dr. Viviee," Jim Schultz said, "if that is your approach."

"As a matter of fact, Jim, I'd like your father to be part of our initial testing. I understand he has a particularly virulent strain of lymphoma. And you, Mr. Jordan, your daughter — the repairs to her heart can be made simply and without fuss."

"How did you….?"

"I always do my homework, sir."

"I have a grandchild who has a rare form of cancer," Congressman Mitchell Hawthorne said. "I'm told there's nothing anyone can do for her. Will the technology work for her?"

"How old is she?"

"She just turned three."

"How sad. I'm afraid this can't be used on small children yet. But I am hopeful. If we can get her to age eleven, it will be safe to make the repairs."

"Why is that?" The questioner was Ms. Havari, from the AAMP.

"We don't exactly know. The nanochip is susceptible to rejection, just like any other foreign substance introduced into a human body. Children's bodies seem to reject it automatically."

"Talk to me after this is over," George Gottleib, from Tefco-Selica Pharmaceuticals, said. "Maybe we have an orphan drug for that."

"A what?"

"A treatment we've shelved due to lack of profitability. We have quite a few for rare diseases. Maybe we have one for your granddaughter."

"What I need to convey to all of you today," Viviee continued, "is that as far as profits are concerned, there will be plenty to go around. While some sources of your income will dry up, they will be replaced by many more voluminous streams. Of course, we will need legislative help." He looked directly at one of the congressmen present. "I am prepared to make sure you all share in the profits." He walked around the long conference table and placed his hand on the shoulder of each person.

"What is the time horizon you imagine for this?" Block said.

"Immediately. We will build an alliance together — this will be a global project. There is so much to do and so much to go around. The technology works, but it needs to be maintained. We will use a short term battery that needs annual maintenance. I believe you can help us with that, Ms. Wallace?" He nodded at the representative from EanCo.

"Yes, of course."

"Envision a time when every living human being will need this nanochip. The chip needs to be manufactured, maintained annually, and checked by a physician at least once a year. When was the last time, Dr. Schultz, that your physicians could say every one of their patients came in on time for their annual check up?"

"The nanochip has to be expensive," Block said. "How can you suggest that everyone will be able to afford one?"

"The price will be high at first, but as people see the results and the demand increases, it will come down. Besides, that's where our friends in the insurance industry play their part." Viviee nodded to Peter Gelson of Dubend Insurance Trust.

Gelson responded. "If the chip does all that's promised, we would be hard pressed to provide insurance to people who refuse it — provided we can cover the chip and its maintenance at a reasonable cost."

"Yes. We will make sure that happens for you, Mr. Gelson," Viviee said. "Once you have the chip, lifetime maintenance is a necessity. There will be shortages for sure. But I want you also to think outside the box about revenue sources."

"Yes, that's just what I have in mind," a woman said. "My company is in the consumer fraud business. Could this individual mark — the mark that's created by the nanochip — become a form of identification?"

"Very good, Ms. Duggan," Viviee said. "In fact it can."

There were loud whispers and nods all around the table.

"How much money are we talking about?" Studor asked.

"Ask yourselves: What price would you pay for a chance to extend your life indefinitely?"

"More importantly, what price would you pay every year?" Schultz said, to raucous laughter all around.

"But you've been attacking and vilifying us in the press." It was Michael Cordon, the head of Chemaceuticals, one of the world's largest pharmaceutical firms. "You've got everyone believing we're evil. It's unconscionable what you've done. How can we recoup the loss of public trust?"

"This country loves the lost lamb who returns to the fold. I will be your redeemer. You will all be heroes. For a chance at immortality, what belief do you think they will not give up?" He paused to look Cordon right in the face. "Wouldn't you sell your soul for a chance at immortality?"

"Fortunately I won't have to," Cordon said.

"Yes. Fortunately."

148

Justin pushed the door gently, then pushed it again. Each time he pushed, it opened a little further, until he saw his grandmother, lying on the bed. Above the headboard, a two-foot high caduceus hung on the wall. On one side of the headboard was a computer screen with a recessed removable keyboard.

A black leather executive chair on steel wheels was next to the bed. Attached to it was an airplane-seat fold-up tray table.

"Grams?" Justin said quietly. Then louder, "Grams, can you hear me?"

She didn't answer.

He shook her. The computer screen suddenly revealed her vital signs. She was breathing slowly. Her heart rate was 40 beats per minute. Her temperature was 94 degrees.

"This is really wrong," Justin said to Madeline. "Look at her heart rate. That can't be right. And her temperature is so low! We've got to get her out of here. Help me move her."

"To where? You can't take her off the machine. You don't know what will happen."

"You're right."

"Why don't you try the computer? He showed you how to use it, didn't he?"

"Sort of."

Justin pulled the keyboard from the side of the bed, sat down in the black leather chair, and extended the tray table. Madeline slid a chair over from the other side of the room and sat down. The computer screen saver appeared. It was Viviee's company logo — the mark Teng had on his hand, the mark that was almost complete on Grams. Justin was about to hit a key when Madeline grabbed his arm. "Wait. Look at the logo."

"What about it?"

"Watch."

The screen went black. Immediately a circle formed with a curved spoke extending upward. A second circle formed on top of the first, with a curved spoke extending out at 120 degrees, and then a third circle with the curved spoke at 240 degrees. The three circles merged into one and began to rotate like the bent spokes of a propeller. Viviee's name came on the screen, spelled out one letter at a time, V — I — V — I — e — e.

"Those are sixes," Madeline said. "Those lines aren't spokes; they're the stems of three distinct sixes."

They watched again, as the screen faded and started over.

"Justin," Madeline continued, "if those are sixes, then the mark on Grams' hand is the mark of the beast."

A rumble reverberated down the hall and they could hear the elevator doors opening.

"Someone's here," Justin said. He slid the keyboard back into the side of the bed. They braced themselves and watched the door, listening to the footsteps approach. It was Robert's face they saw.

"Whew! Am I glad to see you," Madeline said.

"What's going on?"

"This is the mark of the beast — the symbol on her hand, it's really three sixes. Everyone has to get it on their hand or…"

"Forehead." Robert said.

"Exactly," Madeline said.

"But if that's the mark of the beast," Justin said, "then Viviee is the antichrist. His name is supposed to be 666."

"We're supposed to calculate the number," Madeline said excitedly. "Let's add it up."

She found a piece of paper and a pen and laid out the alphabet, numbering each letter.

A-1, B-2, C-3, D-4, E-5, F-6, G-7, H-8, I-9, J-10, K-11, L-12, M-13, N-14, O-15, P-16, Q-17, R-18, S-19, T-20, U-21, V-22, W-23, X-24, Y-25, Z-26.

They tried D-4 + R-18 = 22, 2 + 2 = 4.

They tried S-19 + M-13 + I-9 + T-20 + H-8 = 69, 6 + 9 = 15, 1 + 5 = 6

V-22 + I-9 + V-22 +I-9 +E-5 +E-5 = 72, 7 + 2 = 9.

But they only came up with 469.

"Maybe it's not him," Justin said. "Maybe he's just a middle guy. Or maybe we *are* nuts and this is some teenage fantasy, like delusions of grandeur or something."

Robert said nothing.

"I do not believe we made this whole thing up just to feel important." Madeline stomped her foot like a child. "There must be something we're missing."

"In Hebrew, letters are also represented by numbers," Robert said.

"Wow," Justin said. "So do you know what a six is in Hebrew?"

"The letter *vav* is the six. It represents a v or w sound. But there are no vowels in Hebrew, so that isn't going to work for Viviee. Maybe there's another language it works in, like Sanskrit or Aramaic."

"Let's think about this," Justin said. "The antichrist is the opposite of everything that is God. Seven is considered His perfect number, because God made the world in seven days. So each six is short of the perfect number, just as Lucifer was short of God's perfection — and power."

"Wait a minute," Madeline said. "What was that Smith integer stuff? Remember the sum total...."

"If you don't remember, I certainly don't," Justin said.

"It's a number where the sum of the digits equals the sum of the digits of the prime divisors," Madeline said. She quickly began scribbling numbers on the page.

"$666 = 2 \cdot 3 \cdot 3 \cdot 37$ and $6 + 6 + 6 = 2 + 3 + 3 + 3 + 7 = 18$. So, the 666 is a Smith number — Dr. Smith Viviee!"

"Do you know how many Smith's there are in the United States?" Robert asked.

Grams began to groan quietly. It was the first time she had shown any sign of life other than breathing. Madeline went to her side and took Grams' hand in hers. She gently stroked it, stretching the wrinkles of her skin.

"Come here," Justin called out. "Look at this."

He stared at the screensaver, where V-I-V-I-ee was spelled out.

"Since when do you spell your name with a mixture of capital and lower case letters?"

"It's his logo," Robert said.

They all stared intently at the twirling symbol and then watched Viviee's name spell out underneath it on the screen.

"Well, has everyone forgotten that VI is six in Roman numerals?" Justin said. "Maybe the small 'e's mean something too."

"That's how you write *vav* in Hebrew," Robert said. "If you go to a store and buy six of something, that's how they write it. It looks like two small 'e's." He paused. "What's the most important thing about Jesus?"

"That he sacrificed himself?" Madeline said. "That he rose from the dead?"

"How about that His was a virgin birth?" Robert said. "And if you wanted to consider the opposite of that, what would it be?"

"I don't get it," Madeline said.

"The Virgin Mary was Jesus's mother, right? And God was his father. That means he had no earthly father. If you wanted to mock that, you would have no earthly mother."

"How would you do that?" Madeline said.

"He's a clone!" Justin blurted out.

"Let's get your grandmother out of here," Robert said.

When Robert reached under Grams' back and legs to lift her, a shock jolted his body. The lights flickered as the electricity sent his muscles into convulsions. Robert froze for a moment, and then his contorted body crumbled to the ground.

149

"I think I'm going to have some good news for you shortly, Chief," the detective said, pouring himself a cup of coffee.

"So what are you doing in *here?*" Chief Lario said. "Shouldn't you be with the suspect?"

"He asked if he could lie down for a minute. I've got some burgers coming for him. As soon as it gets here, I'll go back in."

"You left him alone?"

"We're watching him through the glass. He's insisting he never turned the cameras off. He claims when he let the big guy in the building, the power surged and the lights went out: that's why he never saw the other guy. It was pitch dark. He went to find a flashlight and the lights came back on. He says the two of them had already gone to Claiborne's apartment by the time he got back, so he just locked up. We offered him a sweet deal. So, we'll see what happens now."

The phone emitted an electronic sound. Chief Lario picked it up.

"The food is here," he said to the detective. "Let's get this show on the road."

Chief Lario and the detective walked the corridor to the interrogation room. The Chief stood behind the one way glass as the detective placed a greasy paper bag on the table. Lario stared at the suspect, reclining on two chairs in the corner. He watched for the suspect's breathing. Was he breathing rapidly? Was he calm? The chief's pulse quickened as the detective shook the suspect, gently at first, then harder.

The suspect fell to the floor.

"Get the paramedics!" the detective yelled, but it was already too late. The man's lifeless body slumped on the floor, with his face turned toward the one way glass. Chief Lario was startled by the look of fear frozen on Seafore's face — a permanent cry for help.

150

The moment Dr. Smith Viviee left the conference room, the noise level escalated to a dull roar.

"This guy is crazy," Gottleib from Tefco-Selica said. "Does he really think we can just reorganize multi-billion dollar companies overnight? Assuming this chip does all he says it does, it would take years to prepare it for market."

"And it will take years to study," Block said. "I don't give out approval that easily."

Gelson, from Dubend Insurance Trust was leaning back in his chair, smiling.

"Wipe that smirk off your face Peter. The medical community already hates you HMO guys," Havari from the AAMP said.

"Take it easy," Gelson said quickly sitting up. "Clearly I can foresee a new category of critical care policy, but there's plenty of time for that. So, why do you think he's being so generous?"

"What choice does he have?" the Congressman said. "He can't get anything done without the people in this room."

Lars Studor got up from his chair and began to pace the room. Arms folded in front of him, he said, "Dr. Viviee has managed to capture the trust and imagination of the public. We need to bide our time. If he fails, we don't want to go down with him, but if he succeeds, we need to be at his side. Personally, I believe anything he can produce, we can produce. I don't believe he's some Einstein that can outdo the greatest minds we have. And so, I have taken the liberty of assembling a team of professionals. They are down the hall looking over this presentation reel as we speak."

"Well, bring 'em in!" Congressman Mitchell Hawthorne said. "Let's hear what they have to say."

When the team of three men and three women entered the room the look of befuddlement on their faces was obvious, or perhaps it was awe.

The head of the team was Dr. Mitch Hannan — a tall, lanky, dark skinned man with short brown hair and a white lab coat.

"I have been working with nanotechnology in the field of cancer for years," he said. "We've gotten very good at detecting cancer in its earliest stages and bypassing biological barriers to delivering multiple treatments to cancer cells. However, this is beyond the scope of our current research."

"That's not the kind of response I'm looking for," Studor said.

Dr. Diane Deem stepped forward. Her long gray hair was tied back in a pony tail, but an errant piece fell in her eyes as she started to speak. "We know that bioconjugated quantum dots are effective in identifying multiple molecular biomarkers in cancer tissue…"

"In plain English, if you please." Studor interrupted.

She stopped speaking for a moment, brushed the hair off her face, then continued. "We have certainly talked, I should say dreamt about something similar to this. Viviee's video is surprising in its detail. It's almost a blueprint. In fact, he's claimed to confirm some of the theories that we hold as our most closely guarded secrets."

"That's more like it," Studor said.

"However," she continued, "Assuming I could independently verify his findings in our own labs, I still don't think I could produce the chip."

"Why?"

Dr. Johnson, a thin, bespectacled black man, and one of the world leaders in materials science raised his index finger to the sky.

"We're talking about molecular components that assemble themselves chemically by way of molecular recognition. We don't know what his trigger for the assembly is."

"So you'll find it," Schultz said.

No one on the team said a word.

"Alright, let's cut to the chase," Studor said. "Given unlimited resources how long would it take to replicate this chip?"

"Well, as you know, Mr. Studor," Hannan quickly said, as if suddenly inspired by the prospect, "we'd all love to get our hands on the chip and rip it apart. We are only limited by our budgets. Now, if we were to have all the necessary resources, given a reasonable amount of time, I'm sure we could do this. And if we can't — it can't be done."

"How soon?"

"Three years, maybe more."

"Unacceptable. I want every available person working on this. If you need to hire people — hire them. If you need to bring them in from the far corners of the earth do it — but I want this technology yesterday. Now, please get back to work."

He had dismissed them like a group of children. The people seated at the conference table were silent.

"I need each of your companies to invest generously in achieving our joint goal," Studor said. "In the meantime, I believe it is in our best interests to work with Dr. Viviee."

151

Justin knelt beside Robert's body. He placed his ear to his chest.

"Is he dead?" Madeline cried out.

"I don't know. I don't think so. I can feel him breathing. Call 911!"

Madeline rummaged through her purse looking for the phone; finally she dumped the contents onto the floor to retrieve it.

She dialed the number, but as soon as she hit the send button she got a 'no service' tone. She hung up and tried again and again. Justin pounded on Robert's chest with his fists. He opened his hands and pumped his chest as he had seen people do on TV, and then he listened again for a heartbeat.

"What's going on here?"

Justin quickly turned to the familiar sound of his mother's voice. His heart sank and his stomach ached at the sight of her bare feet. He hadn't heard her coming. She was wearing a thin, red silk robe, hastily tied. He didn't know if he wanted to scream or cry or both.

"Mom?" Justin said. His listened to his own voice say her name in disbelief and anger.

"What are you *doing* here?" Helene said.

"I came to see Grams. What are *you* doing here?"

Helene looked at Robert's body.

"Oh, God, you slept with Viviee!" Justin yelled.

"What are you talking about?" she said, running to Robert. "What's happened!" She knelt down to place her hand on his head.

"He got shocked!" Madeline said. "He tried to move Grams and he got shocked."

"Oh, Robert!" Helene cried. "Somebody do something. Call the police."

"We're trying," Justin said.

"I can't get a call out," Madeline said.

"Keep trying," Helene yelled as she began CPR.

Madeline moved down the hall, into the front room, and back to Grams' room, but still she could get no service.

"Where's your phone, Justin? Mine doesn't work, and I can't find a phone anywhere in this place."

"Here," he said, pulling it from his belt.

She tried it, but Justin's phone didn't work either. "There is no service!"

"Breathe, damn it!" Helene said as she took a deep breath and pressed her lips to Robert's.

"There must be a way to ring down to security," Justin said.

"I can't find a phone or an intercom," Madeline said. "I'm just gonna go down and find someone."

"Go," Helene said. "But hurry. I can barely hear his heart."

Madeline was by the elevator, nervously hitting the call button over and over. She jumped up and down, unable to contain her emotions. Tears streamed down her face. Finally she heard the inner workings of the elevator. "It's coming, Justin," she called out. "I can hear it." The elevator doors opened. She stepped inside and gasped. Dr. Viviee was standing in a darkened corner.

"Is something wrong?" He smiled as she slowly backed out of the elevator.

"Uh, oh, Doctor, oh, oh, you've got to help us," she said. She didn't know what to do. "Something's happened to Robert."

"Of course," Dr. Viviee said. He winced as he stepped into the light of the foyer. "Where is he?"

"Outside of Grams' room. We came to visit. He touched her and got shocked or something."

Madeline called out to Justin as Dr. Viviee walked down the corridor.

152

First the hair stood up on Justin's arms, then on the back of his neck. He felt every follicle on his body, from his legs to his belly to his chest, pulse with electricity. It was a feeling so viscerally uncomfortable that he feared he would vomit or pass out.

He could hear Madeline calling him in the back of his head, but his feelings of tingling pain were louder than any words. As he pulled himself to his feet, Dr. Viviee entered the room.

"What's the matter?" Viviee said to him. "You look surprised."

"Smith," Helene said, "thank goodness you're here." She gently removed Robert's head from her lap and placed it on a pillow.

"Madeline was going for help," Justin said.

"Well, then, aren't you lucky. Help is here. Let me take a look at him." Viviee bent down over Robert's lifeless body; he placed his hand to Robert's chest. He turned to Helene. "You should get dressed," he said softly. "I have this under control."

"Yes, of course," she said. She grabbed the robe tight to her chest and left the room.

Viviee reached toward the side of the bed. There was the snick of Velcro separating. He held a small black item in his hand.

"Wait!" Justin said.

"It's only a blood pressure monitor," Viviee responded. He placed it on Robert's finger. He pulled another attachment from the computer and put it on Robert's chest.

"Call an ambulance!" Justin yelled. "What are we waiting for?"

"I see you've been working on the computer," Viviee said. He got up, sat down in the chair, and hit a few keys. Then he bent down and placed another monitor on Robert's chest. "Can't you hear the traffic outside? There's a protest going on down the street. It will take an hour for an ambulance to get here."

Suddenly Helene burst breathlessly into the room. She was completely dressed, wearing her trench coat and carrying her hand bag. "Kyle just called. I'm supposed to be live on the air in fifteen minutes! The network playback machine is down. He's been trying to reach me all afternoon!"

"Go, Helene. Everything is under control. Robert's going to be fine."

"Are you sure?"

"I'm positive. He's going to be fine."

"I'll call you!" she yelled, running down the hall.

"What's wrong with him?" Justin said.

Viviee brought up a screen that showed Robert's vital signs.

"This is worse than I thought."

"What do you mean?" Madeline said. "You said he was going to be fine."

"This isn't good," Viviee said. "I'm afraid he's dying."

"No," Justin said.

"Fortunately I can save him." Viviee walked to the far corner of the room. He pulled a hypodermic needle out of a black alligator doctor's bag. It was an old fashioned bag, but it looked shiny and brand new. He held the needle up to the window in a familiar pose of compassionate medicine and poked it into a small bottle.

"What are you going to do?" Justin asked.

"He's lucky. I have one nanochip left."

"No!" Madeline yelled.

"No?" Dr. Viviee asked. "Do you want him to die?"

"He won't want the chip," Justin said. "I know he won't want it."

"He would rather die? Is that what you're telling me?"

"Yes. I mean — I don't know. He doesn't want the chip."

"How do you know?"

"We talked about it," Madeline said. "He doesn't want it."

"You talked about it? Well, you know there's a big difference between talking about something and actually doing it. No one wants to die — not today, not any day. No one wakes up and says, I think I'll die today. But every day people die. Which of those do you think would rather live? Are there any who would choose death on their deathbed? Because if there are, I've never met one." He pulled the plunger back on the hypodermic, filling it with fluid that contained the nanochip.

He walked to Robert with the needle in his hand, next to his shoulder, pointing heavenward.

"Don't do it," Madeline yelled.

"His death will be on your head," Dr Viviee said, stooping down over Robert. "How far are you willing to go to stop me?"

"We know who you are," Justin said.

Dr. Viviee stood up from Robert's failing body.

"You think you know who I am?" he said, sounding like a razor. "You don't even know who you are, Matthew." His face was contorted in anger.

The kids were frozen with fear.

"His name is Justin," Madeline said firmly.

"Stop talking, Mary!" Viviee said. "You always were an annoyance." He placed the needle on a table and walked closer to Madeline. "You were his favorite, you know." She stepped back. "But you never got any of the glory. They all saw to that." He swept his hand out wide in a gesture that included Justin. "They stole it from you."

"The glory was always God's," she said.

"What are you talking about, Madeline? Don't listen to him." Justin said. "He's trying to confuse us."

"Who was *he*?" Viviee said. "Nobody. Matthew. A glorified IRS hack — the tax collector. One of the most despised people on the planet. Ha! And they made you out to be nothing more than a prostitute. What did you get? A couple of lines? He got a whole chapter. The simple hooker — Mary Magdalene. You posed no threat to *their* legacy. They saw to that. You're a footnote!"

"It wasn't about us then, and it's not about us now."

"Madeline, what are you talking about?" Justin screamed in her face.

"Don't you remember?" Dr. Viviee said. "How quickly they forget."

"…This generation will certainly not pass away until all these things have happened," Madeline said. "He told us that. Jesus told his disciples they would see the end days."

"Madeline, he's a liar. Don't listen to him," Justin said.

"So what are you going to do with us?" Madeline asked.

"Under the circumstances, I am quite content to have you watch me fulfill my destiny."

"You're destined for destruction." Justin said.

"He sends a child to do a man's job," Viviee said, looking to the ceiling. "This is my time; it has been owed to me from the beginning."

"Too bad for you, it doesn't last long," Justin said. "And it ends badly."

"Long enough to watch you suffer, that I can promise. His fury is great for he knows that his time is short." He looked to the ceiling for a moment, then continued.

"You know, I wasn't sure if that was you at first, Matthew. Mary was easy. She's always had those eyes — so soft and sweet — like a deer at hunting season. But you, Matthew, you I didn't recognize — until I smelled your tears.

It's funny how some things stick in your head, even over the centuries. It was so sweet the way the odor curled in my nostrils." He took a deep breath. "It's like a high. And I have to say, I do derive some pleasure from our being together again. This world has grown too accustomed to my ways. It's nice to be recognized — finally."

"But it's over for you now," Justin said softly.

Viviee laughed as if Justin had just told a very funny joke. "And what will you do?" he said. "Will you tell the world I'm the big bad guy? Me, who offers them everything? And you, a fourteen year old child who offers them nothing? The spoiled offspring of a famous mother? It's a pity how money and privilege corrupts our youth. You know, your mother is a lot smarter than you think. She's absolutely right. Man is on an eternal quest for immortality, and when he finds it — the search for God becomes irrelevant."

"Other people will figure you out," Madeline said.

"I'll let you in on a secret. They don't believe in me. They think I'm a product of ghost stories and vampire movies. They mock those who do know me — the ones who hear my voice and recognize it. They call them delusional and psychotic. No, they won't figure *me* out. I'm here to heal them. I will rule the world by invitation." He paused. "That sounds even better now than when I said it the first time."

"I want my grandmother back," Justin said.

"You can't have her."

"You lied to her. She didn't know she was going to change. She didn't know what the nanochip was."

"I didn't change her. I simply blocked the channel of communication, and she accepted it willingly. It was quite easy, actually. She liked the *idea* of God, but faith can only take you so far. I have so much more to offer in the way of tangible goods."

"Well, unblock her channel of communication. Find out what she chooses now."

"I'm afraid I can't." He waited a moment. "Well, actually I can. I'll make you a deal, since you care so much for her. I'll trade you for her. In fact, I'll make it two for two. You two for her and Robert. He's still breathing. It's really very easy, Matthew. Just a simple shot and all those voices and visions that have been tormenting you will disappear in an instant."

"Don't listen to him, Justin."

"Don't you know I can squash you?" Viviee said, casually making a pinching motion with his fingers. "You're nothing but a moment's amusement to me."

"Then why don't you just do it?" Justin said. "Why bargain?"

"Because your death might ruin my plans for your mother."

Justin lost his breath; it was as if he'd been punched.

"After all, I wouldn't want to take away her will to live. I'm counting on it. Besides, having the two of you would be a coup of immeasurable proportions. Think about it. My reign is predetermined. You can watch from the sidelines, or you can join me and I can give you the world — more power and glory than you've ever dreamed of."

"Uh, that is such a cliché!" Madeline said.

"You should consider it. You could finally get your due, Mary. You could finally get the recognition you earned and deserve. We are living in increasingly interesting times, I assure you."

"We will never follow you," Madeline said.

Viviee's phone rang. "Think about my offer. It's your grandmother's only hope." He answered the call.

Through the window, Justin could see that a small cloud had drifted down to encircle the building; it looked like a footstool for an angel.

"Yes, of course," Viviee said into the phone. "I'll be right there." He smiled and with a look of great satisfaction turned to Justin. "Man is quite capable of doing the work of many demons."

153

Viviee left and a dark shadow from the window followed him as if by design.

Justin frantically dialed 911, but before he could complete the call a shadow of light gathered them all like in the wings of a dove.

Robert began to stir. He opened his eyes, but he couldn't find the strength to sit up.

"Look to the gift," Fouick's voice said. "There is truth in its meaning." This time, Madeline also heard the voice.

"The gift — the coin," Madeline said. "Justin, where did you put the coin?"

"It's right here," he said. He pulled the coin out of his pocket and clutched it tightly in his fist.

"What does it mean," Robert mumbled. He slowly sat up, holding his head in his hands.

"Robert, Robert, are you all right?" Madeline asked. She ran to hug him. Justin held them both tight.

"It means, *Render unto Caesar what is Caesar's and unto God what is God's,*" Justin said. "We need to get Grams' nanochip back to Viviee and her soul back to God. How do we do that?"

"I don't know. What happened?" Robert said.

"He's gone," Justin said. "Viviee's gone, at least for now."

Grams began to moan again, moving her head from side to side.

"Those who seek to lose their life will save it," Robert said. "Claiborne said it just before he was murdered. He gave up his life because of it, and the mark disappeared."

"I don't want her to die," Justin said.

"Get rid of the caduceus," Robert said.

"What?"

"The caduceus over the bed, get rid of it."

Madeline tried to pull it off the wall but it was plastered on.

"Get something, anything, but get it off," Robert said with as much energy as he could muster.

Madeline ran out of the room.

Justin grabbed a wooden hanger from a closet and began trying to pry up the side of the image, but nothing happened. Madeline returned with a large knife from the kitchen and a small pan. She slid the knife blade under the edge of the caduceus and banged at the knife handle with the pan.

"Here, let me do that," Justin said. He took the pan and banged over and over again on the knife.

"Why?" Madeline asked Robert. "Why are we doing this?"

"It's symbolic. In mythology, the caduceus is used to lead the souls of the dead into Hell."

Madeline gasped. At that moment, the caduceus seemed to leap from the wall. It hit the ground and crumbled into a million pieces.

Robert rose to his feet and joined Justin and Madeline in a circle around the broken caduceus. Justin stared at the shattered pieces as if some spell had been broken. They had only shattered a symbol, yet it seemed to him that any small victory was a sign that they possessed the power to defeat this foe.

154

Dr. Viviee entered the conference room to a standing ovation. For ten full seconds the most powerful men and women in medicine, stood at attention, clapping their hands, smiles pasted on their faces, lauding the man who had done what they could not.

Studor was the first to approach Viviee, still applauding, with a handshake and a pat on the back. "Welcome to the fold, doctor."

Viviee smiled. "You humble me with your gesture," he said, looking anything but humbled.

"We want you to feel welcome," Studor said.

"You have done an amazing thing," Dr. Schultz said, "and we want to express our appreciation for your brilliance and team spirit."

"We look forward to working with you," Block said.

"Let's talk about the particulars, shall we?" Studor said, motioning for Dr. Viviee to take a seat at the head of the conference table.

Viviee sat proudly and erect, his hands placed on the armrests as if he had just been seated in a great throne.

"You have made a very compelling case to us, Dr. Viviee," Studor began. "The way you have shared your knowledge and your plan with us is most generous and we are grateful to you. We like many of your ideas and would like to begin to flesh out a deal."

"I will have a formal proposal to you in twenty-four hours and we can begin our alliance next week. I want to get this to the public as soon as possible."

"As soon as possible, yes, of course, Dr. Viviee. Please keep in mind this is a huge undertaking and it's going to take some time to come to terms — you know, with the lawyers and all."

"Like I said, Mr. Studor, I am not a greedy man."

"There are other issues to be considered besides money. We need time to prepare, restructure, reorganize. You know how it is."

"How much time did you have in mind?"

"Not long. Less than a year."

"A year!" Viviee laughed out loud. Everyone else was silent. "Do you take me for a fool?"

"Of course not," Schultz said.

"With all the information I've given you, in a year, with a team of top notch researchers, perhaps you could create your own nanochip. Is that what you're thinking?"

"Well, now that you mention it, I've just learned that our research department has been developing something similar for some time now."

"You *do* take me for a fool. Well, consider this. I promise you that no matter what you do or how hard you work you will not discover the secret of the chip without actually having a chip to analyze. The only chips in existence have been implanted. You have one, Dr. Schultz."

There was loud mumbling and everyone in the room focused their gaze on Schultz.

"Perhaps you would like to volunteer as the guinea pig. Maybe one of your extremely knowledgeable scientists can figure out a way to remove it — without killing you, of course."

Schultz's lip trembled.

"Otherwise," Viviee continued, "you're all going to have to wait for someone to die and that could be a very long time — unless of course, some unforeseen tragedy should befall Dr. Schultz."

155

"The chip," Robert said. "What do we do about the chip?"

"This is nanotechnology," Madeline said. "We need to think in quantum terms. That's what governs the way small things behave. We're on the atomic level — hundreds of millions of microcircuits on maybe a couple of angstroms — one tenth of a billionth of a meter. What do we know about small things?" Now she was looking directly at Justin.

Justin's head spun, not because he was confused, but because he suddenly had a moment of clarity and was trying to find the words.

"The act of observing it... changes it. It's like light bouncing off an object. It exerts minute pressure, enough to change it. I know how to observe the nanochip!"

Justin frantically hit keys on the computer, moving through a series of screens. He saw Grams' vital signs, close-ups of her heart and lung functions, and a map of her circulatory system, but he couldn't get to the spinal cord.

"It needs a code. I saw him put it in. It was 2, 3." Justin squeezed his eyes shut tight, but he couldn't think.

"Those are the prime factors of the Smith number," Madeline cried out. "Two, three, three, three, seven."

"That's it!" Justin yelled. He keyed in the numbers, and the screen revealed the spine and Claire's neurology. The illuminated nanochip was moving through her body. The transition was almost complete, but it hadn't yet lodged in her brain.

The chip was flashing a bright blue light, pulsing rhythmically — one, two, three, four — one, two, three, four; as if to the beat of a metronome.

"Keep your eyes on it," Justin said. "Don't take your eyes off the chip."

The three of them stared at the light, hypnotized by its repetitiveness, looking for any sign that their observation was having an impact.

They watched and waited.

Grams let out a soft sigh.

"Look," Madeline said. She whispered, afraid her words would shatter the effect. "I saw a change. I definitely saw a change." As the words left her mouth the flashing nanochip resumed its rhythm.

Suddenly Grams took in a quick breath of air. The blue light began to pulse faster.

"Something is wrong," Madeline said.

The flashing light moved up the spinal cord, inching closer to the base of her brain.

"It's getting stronger," Madeline said. "This isn't working."

"We have to stop the chip," Justin yelled. "When it gets to the base of the brain it's complete and Grams is doomed." He quickly stood and paced the floor. "I don't understand. Why would God do this? Grams didn't know what she was doing. She didn't understand. This isn't fair."

"But we do understand," Robert said, "and we need to do more than change it. We need to make it go away."

"Okay, okay," Madeline said, "I don't understand this very well, but a nanochip assembles *itself*. It's too small for anybody to actually make. So it makes itself. There are enzymes and catalysts that get the atoms and molecules to organize and make something. It's supposed to work like nature."

"That's way over our heads," Justin said. He was on the verge of tears.

"Justin's right," Robert said. "We're never going to figure out how to disassemble the nanochip. It sounds like you're talking about transforming matter."

"Dear God!" Justin said, "You can't do this to her! Please don't do this to Grams. It's not fair!"

"The world isn't always fair," Robert said, putting his arm on Justin's shoulders.

"Ahhhhh, ahhhhh." The sounds coming from Grams were like a whimper; a faint cry for help.

"Energy transforms matter," Madeline said.

"It's sucking the life out of her!" Justin cried out.

"Look. The chip is slowing down," Madeline said. "It's slowing, I can see it." She began to speak excitedly. "Maybe it's *your* energy Justin. The difference between a star evaporating and its turning into a black hole with enough power to suck up the universe is a fraction of a decimal point of energy. Right now the nanochip is a black hole sucking up her universe. We need to create an energy shift."

"How do we do that?" Justin said.

"Why did he bring her here?" Robert said. "Why did he take her out of the apartment?"

360

"She was coughing this morning," Justin said.

"A priest came to visit her," Madeline said. "We prayed for her. She's been sick ever since."

"There it is again," Justin said. "The beat was off. It went away for a second, I know it did." He sat back down in front of the computer screen.

"What were you thinking? Tell me exactly what you were thinking just now," Robert said.

"I was remembering Father David's prayer," Justin said.

"Maybe that's the energy shift we need," Robert said. "Prayer will create the energy shift."

"Justin," Madeline said, "Father David said some things could only be cured by prayer. He told us we needed to remember that."

"But I've been praying since we got here!" Justin stared out the window. "No, wait. Father David said don't pray that she be cured, pray that she be healed — healed of the nanochip. I don't care if she's cured anymore. I just want her to be healed." Justin said.

Grams let out a loud groan. "She's fighting it," Justin said. His eyes filled with tears. "I know she's fighting the chip."

"If it works and the chip disappears, there's a good chance she'll die," Robert said.

"As long as the chip is inside of her, her soul can't return to God. We have to re-open those lines of communication before it gets to her brain."

Sunlight streamed in from the window. Justin followed the beam as it hit Grams' face, causing a tear on her cheek to glisten like a small flash of light.

"Okay, okay, I got it." Justin said.

"Dear Lord." He was breathless. "Madeline said when she was a little kid you used to answer all her prayers. I think that's because she really believed you would do it. And now, I really believe. You told us if we had enough faith we could do anything. So, now you have to get this chip out of her. It doesn't belong to Grams. It never did. It belongs to Viviee. Please send it back to Viviee. Her soul belongs to you. You have to take it back. It's yours. Please take it back. I know you will do this for us. You said if two or more people are gathered in your name you will be with them. Well, here we are and we need you."

He spoke with the enthusiasm of a small child. Tears began to flow from his eyes. There was innocence in his voice.

"We need you God, we really need you. You have to heal her."

The pulsing light began to slow. And so, they prayed together, sometimes silently and sometimes out loud, as they watched the nanochip on the screen, until the chip came to a complete stop.

Claire gradually began to wake up. She started to look like her old self again. Her face softened, in a way, but a deep furrow returned to her forehead, and the lines around her eyes became more prominent. Her skin grew looser and took on the awful grayish tone that Justin remembered so well from her hospital days. When she opened her eyes, she began to weep, but her lungs could hardly handle the strain. She winced in pain as she coughed, unable even to hold up her head.

"Oh Grams, I'm so sorry. I'm so sorry," Justin sobbed. "I didn't know what to do."

She struggled to reach for his hand and squeeze it. "It's all right, Justin. I understand now. I'm not alone anymore."

"I'm here Grams, and I'm not going to leave you." The tears streamed down his face.

"I've been to a very dark place. I felt so alone, but I'm not alone anymore. My time here has passed, and I'm ready to meet my maker."

"Please don't go, Grams. Maybe you don't have to die. God heard your prayers, Grams. You've got to fight this with all you have."

"He didn't hear my prayers. He heard yours. Is the mark gone from my hand yet?"

Justin wiped his eyes to see through his tears.

"Almost," he said. "It's almost gone."

"You are the prize, Justin," Claire said. "He didn't use me to get to your mother. He used me as he will use your mother — to get to you. *You* are the prize. I love you."

"I love you, Grams."

Claire looked to the ceiling and a peaceful smile came over her face. "Thank you Lord, for taking back your lost sheep."

They all looked to the computer screen as the light from the nanochip slowly faded and disappeared, as all false lights eventually do.

She looked to Justin and blew out a long, deep breath. She closed her eyes and, in her final whisper, said, "You must tell the world. Your destiny still lies ahead."

Justin and Madeline heard Fouick's voice. "Blessed are the dead who die in the Lord from now on."

And so it came to be that just as Moses turned his rod into a serpent, as Jesus turned water to wine, matter was once again transformed, fulfilling His words, that if you have faith the size of the tiny mustard seed, you can say to the mountain, "Move," and it will move.

In the end, it took a power so small that it is measured by man in the fifteenth decimal point — the power of intention — but is measured by God as among the greatest gifts he gave to man — the power to choose.

156

News that Claire Cummings succumbed to the same cancer she claimed to be cured of spread through the country like a wildfire, but not before Dr. Smith Viviee quietly slipped out of town and returned to China. That left Helene holding the bag, as the judge put it, when Dr. Viviee didn't show up for his court hearing. The judge held Helene in contempt of court, fined her show fifty thousand dollars and gave a stern lecture on the dangers of journalists overstepping the bounds of impartiality and taking an advocate's position. He threatened to send her to jail, but relented when Jeff Stone reminded the judge that he too had been swayed by Dr. Viviee.

As for her show, even Helene's fans were angry. In an attempt at garnering some positive press Helene and Kyle did a series of interviews explaining their decision to put Viviee on the air. While some viewers expressed "feeling sad" for Helene's loss of her mother, there was little sympathy for her or for her show. The pubic relations effort was a flop. The ratings took a nose dive and the network brass stood ready to cancel the program.

Throughout the ordeal, Robert stood by Helene's side — sober. He was never able to prove that the smaller man in Archibald Claiborne's final video was Viviee. Bull, the larger of the two, and Seafore were both dead, so the case was closed for all intents and purposes.

Neither Spider nor Samantha ever showed up at school again. It was rumored Samantha's father was transferred back to Texas and no one much cared what happened to Spider. His landlord was happy to keep his security deposit to cover the cleaning of a large black soot mark on the ceiling.

In desperation, Erbie did reach for Viviee's hand as she balanced precariously on the edge of the elevator shaft. When she loosened her grasp from the side of the door to grab hold with the other hand, he simply let go and stepped back.

She tumbled down the shaft until she hit the broken car stuck on the fifth floor — with a thud that echoed through the building. A worker inside pulled her body through the escape hatch just before it started running. She spent a year in the hospital and rehab, won a substantial settlement against the building and elevator company and retired to direct the chorus at her church — left with only a faded memory of falling through the darkness into a blanket of soft light; perhaps the light from the elevator car.

Robert resumed his youthful studies of the Kabbalah as he struggled to make sense of events, but never shared with Helene or anyone else, the seemingly crazy conclusions he and the kids had arrived at. He might have told his old friend Yitzhak, but Barrouck never returned to his Jerusalem home and no ransom note was ever delivered. Barrouck was presumed dead. His peace plan was abandoned.

When Father David failed to return to the Harlem brownstone the nuns there reported him missing. He was listed among hundreds on the NYPD website for missing persons until Father David's superiors at the Vatican failed to confirm he had disappeared. They had his photo withdrawn from the site and refused to discuss his whereabouts.

As far as the nuns were concerned, Father David wasn't going to be found. He had been taken up in the same holy event that Holy Hazel spoke so intently about — the rapture of the 144,000 of the purest souls on earth. The nuns surmised the event had also delivered up Holy Hazel's soul to God, along with all those people great and small, but mostly small, who disappeared at midnight eastern standard time, on a seemingly ordinary day in the course of the world — in numbers so inconsequential as to go unnoticed. The nuns, who had become media savvy through their experiences at the Harlem brownstone, considered holding a press conference to warn the world of the events that were unfolding, but they knew the Vatican would make them out to be fools. Afterall, if there had been a rapture why was the Pope still here?

They remained silent and went into seclusion, guarding their precious statue of the Virgin. After Holy Hazel disappeared the Virgin never cried again, so it was easy for most people to assume she had rigged the statue and disappeared with the faithful's donations. It was the only plausible conclusion.

One month after Viviee left town a terrorist hit Manhattan. An operative employed at a water treatment plant slipped an unidentified poison into the drinking supply. Hundreds died and thousands were taken ill — small numbers, considering the potential impact on millions; largely attributable to Robert's quick action in warning the public and the modern penchant for drinking bottled water.

Through Robert's expertise and connections, Helene was able to stay one step ahead of the other media — thus becoming the go-to source for news and information on the attack. Her ratings were restored and within a year, the Viviee episode was all but forgotten — except for by Judy Borne, the pretty young girl with the red hair.

For that year, the former paraplegic ran and danced and walked like any other able bodied woman, as members of the Research Center to Cure Paralysis quietly studied her recovery. Then, without warning, at the end of a year, without Viviee to maintain the nanochip, her condition quickly deteriorated. She ended up back in a wheelchair. As the medical community debated the cause of the sudden return of her paralysis, she took a suicidal overdose of pain medication — leading many to ponder the ethics of a temporary cure. Unlike Claire's body, in which no trace of a nanochip was ever found, the chip was located in Borne's corpse, but efforts to remove it irreparably damaged the chip, rendering it useless for study.

Justin and Madeline went about their lives as normal teenagers who under extraordinary circumstances had formed a lifelong bond. They never told anyone what happened when they were alone in that room with Dr. Smith Viviee. The drama of the moment seemed so far away and the details faded with each passing day. On rare occasion they would talk out what happened and discuss who they might have been, but their conversations always ended with a giggle and a sigh. The entire notion was so preposterous, yet in the quiet of their own hearts they believed what their rational minds were unwilling to accept. They had changed the course of the future and it didn't much matter who they might have been once. Yesterday's lessons had already been learned. Their purpose on earth was to be found today.

Fouick stopped his visits as suddenly as he had appeared. Justin missed him, but he knew Fouick would return if he ever desperately needed his guidance again. Justin believed that day was still to come.

Throughout the time the medical community was less than subtle in its disdain for Dr. Smith Viviee, often publicly gloating at his disgrace. But when efforts to retrieve the chip from both Claire's and Bourne's bodies were failures, the medical community softened it's stance on Dr. Viviee, fearing they may need to resurrect him and his chip at an appropriate time. Dr. Schultz traveled to China to work with Dr. Viviee, assuring his chip would be properly maintained. He secretly passed information back to his friends in the US, hoping someone would crack the code and free him from his unseverable tie to Viviee, but he never got close enough to the secret.

Then Teng Hao Li made an unexpected appearance at Lars Studor's office.

"Mr. Teng, what a surprise," Studor said. "What can I do for you?"

"I believe you need to learn the mystery of the chip and will pay handsomely for it."

"I have a team of the world's best researchers. If it's viable; if it's for real, we'll figure it out."

"I am living proof that it is," he said. "I have the answers to your questions right here."

Teng pulled a letter-sized white envelope from a small leather bag he carried around his neck.

"And if that were the secret, what would you want for it?" Studor said.

"A portion of the proceeds and a generous advance."

"And what does Viviee say about this?"

"He doesn't know."

"I see. You've spent your life with this man and now you're willing to just walk away? Is that what you expect me to believe?"

"I have many, many years ahead of me. Immortality is an expensive prospect, Mr. Studor. I have spent my life in servitude. I would like my new life to be a bit more luxurious. I can give you the secret to my long and healthy life, and perhaps you can share with me your taste for material goods."

"Yes, I understand." Studor said. "And do you guarantee your information?"

"Of course."

"Then I believe we will have no problem coming to terms."

He reached for the envelope from Teng with his left hand. He weighed it carefully, as if to feel the full impact of the object. He extended his right hand and Teng grasped it firmly. Teng smiled.

Studor thought it was a familiar smile.

And so, the deal with the devil was made.

THE END

Biblical Citations and Notes

All biblical references in this novel are real. All quotes are from the NIV Bible unless otherwise specified. The words of Jesus are in italics.

Scene 4

Revelation 12:3
3Then another sign appeared in heaven: an enormous red dragon with seven heads and ten horns and seven crowns on his heads.

Revelation 12:7
7And there was war in heaven. Michael and his angels fought against the dragon, and the dragon and his angels fought back. 8But he was not strong enough, and they lost their place in heaven. 9The great dragon was hurled down—that ancient serpent called the devil, or Satan, who leads the whole world astray. He was hurled to the earth, and his angels with him.

Scene 7

Romans 11:29
29for God's gifts and his call are irrevocable.

Matthew 10:26
26*"So do not be afraid of them. There is nothing concealed that will not be disclosed, or hidden that will not be made known. 27What I tell you in the dark, speak in the daylight; what is whispered in your ear, proclaim from the roofs. 28Do not be afraid of those who kill the body but cannot kill the soul. Rather, be afraid of the One who can destroy both soul and body in hell."*

Scene 9

Mark 13:27
27And he will send his angels and gather his elect from the four winds, from the ends of the earth to the ends of the heavens.

Matthew 24:31
31And he will send his angels with a loud trumpet call, and they will gather his elect from the four winds, from one end of the heavens to the other.

Corinthians 15:51

[51]Listen, I tell you a mystery: We will not all sleep, but we will all be changed— [52]in a flash, in the twinkling of an eye, at the last trumpet. For the trumpet will sound, the dead will be raised imperishable, and we will be changed.

Revelation 14:1

[1]Then I looked, and there before me was the Lamb, standing on Mount Zion, and with him 144,000 who had his name and his Father's name written on their foreheads.

Revelation 14:4

[4]These are those who did not defile themselves with women, for they kept themselves pure. They follow the Lamb wherever he goes. They were purchased from among men and offered as firstfruits to God and the Lamb. [5]No lie was found in their mouths; they are blameless.

Scene 10

Revelation 21:3

[3]And I heard a loud voice from the throne saying, "Now the dwelling of God is with men, and he will live with them. They will be his people, and God himself will be with them and be their God. [4]He will wipe every tear from their eyes. There will be no more death or mourning or crying or pain, for the old order of things has passed away."

Scene 24

Luke 12:7

[7]*"And the very hairs on your head are all numbered."*

Matthew 6:21

[21]For where your treasure is, there your heart will be also.

Matthew 24:37

[37]As it was in the days of Noah, so it will be at the coming of the Son of Man. [38]For in the days before the flood, people were eating and drinking, marrying and giving in marriage, up to the day Noah entered the ark; [39]and they knew nothing about what would happen until the flood came and took them all away. That is how it will be at the coming of the Son of Man.

Matthew 17:19

[19]Then the disciples came to Jesus in private and asked, "Why couldn't we drive it out?"

[20]He replied, *"Because you have so little faith. I tell you the truth, if you have faith as small as a mustard seed, you can say to this mountain, 'Move from here to there' and it will move. Nothing will be impossible for you.* [21]*But this kind does not go out except by prayer and fasting."*

Peter 3:8

[8]But do not forget this one thing, dear friends: With the Lord a day is like a thousand years, and a thousand years are like a day.

Scene 26

Matthew 7:7

[7] *"Ask and it will be given to you; seek and you will find; knock and the door will be opened to you.* [8]*For everyone who asks receives; he who seeks finds; and to him who knocks, the door will be opened."*

Revelation 13:16

[16]He also forced everyone, small and great, rich and poor, free and slave, to receive a mark on his right hand or on his forehead, [17]so that no one could buy or sell unless he had the mark, which is the name of the beast or the number of his name.

[18]This calls for wisdom. If anyone has insight, let him calculate the number of the beast, for it is man's number. His number is 666.

Revelation 9:6

[6]During those days men will seek death, but will not find it; they will long to die, but death will elude them.

Scene 31

Corinthians 12:7

[7]Now to each one the manifestation of the Spirit is given for the common good. [8]To one there is given through the Spirit the message of wisdom, to another the message of knowledge by means of the same Spirit, [9]to another faith by the same Spirit, to another gifts of healing by that one Spirit, [10]to another miraculous powers, to another prophecy, to another distinguishing between spirits, to another speaking in different kinds of tongues, and to still

another the interpretation of tongues. ¹¹All these are the work of one and the same Spirit, and he gives them to each one, just as he determines.

Matthew 18:10

¹⁰*See that you do not look down on one of these little ones. For I tell you that their angels in heaven always see the face of my Father in heaven.*

Scene 32

Psalm 91:11

¹¹For he will command his angels concerning you to guard you in all your ways.

Scene 49

Revelation 21:1

¹Then I saw a new heaven and a new earth, for the first heaven and the first earth had passed away, and there was no longer any sea. ²I saw the Holy City, the new Jerusalem, coming down out of heaven from God, prepared as a bride beautifully dressed for her husband. ³And I heard a loud voice from the throne saying, "Now the dwelling of God is with men, and he will live with them. They will be his people, and God himself will be with them and be their God."

Romans 11:25

²⁵I do not want you to be ignorant of this mystery, brothers, so that you may not be conceited: Israel has experienced a hardening in part until the full number of the Gentiles has come in. ²⁶And so all Israel will be saved, as it is written: "The deliverer will come from Zion; he will turn godlessness away from Jacob. ²⁷And this is my covenant with them when I take away their sins." ²⁸As far as the gospel is concerned, they are enemies on your account; but as far as election is concerned, they are loved on account of the patriarchs, ²⁹for God's gifts and his call are irrevocable.

Matthew 24:30

³⁰At that time the sign of the Son of Man will appear in the sky, and all the nations of the earth will mourn. They will see the Son of Man coming on the clouds of the sky, with power and great glory. ³¹And he will send his angels with a loud trumpet call, and they will gather his elect from the four winds, from one end of the heavens to the other.

Matthew 26:41

[41]*"Watch and pray so that you will not fall into temptation. The spirit is willing, but the body is weak."*

Acts 2:17

[17]"'In the last days, God says, I will pour out my Spirit on all people. Your sons and daughters will prophesy, your young men will see visions, your old men will dream dreams.'"

Mark 2:1

[1]A few days later, when Jesus again entered Capernaum, the people heard that he had come home. [2]So many gathered that there was no room left, not even outside the door, and he preached the word to them.

[3]Some men came, bringing to him a paralytic, carried by four of them. [4]Since they could not get him to Jesus because of the crowd, they made an opening in the roof above Jesus and, after digging through it, lowered the mat the paralyzed man was lying on. [5]When Jesus saw their faith, he said to the paralytic, *"Son, your sins are forgiven."*

[6]Now some teachers of the law were sitting there, thinking to themselves, [7]"Why does this fellow talk like that? He's blaspheming! Who can forgive sins but God alone?"

[8]Immediately Jesus knew in his spirit that this was what they were thinking in their hearts, and he said to them, *"Why are you thinking these things? [9]Which is easier: to say to the paralytic, 'Your sins are forgiven,' or to say, 'Get up, take your mat and walk'? [10]But that you may know that the Son of Man has authority on earth to forgive sins . . . ."* He said to the paralytic, [11]*"I tell you, get up, take your mat and go home."*

[12]He got up, took his mat and walked out in full view of them all. This amazed everyone and they praised God, saying, "We have never seen anything like this!"

Luke 5:17

[17]One day as he was teaching, Pharisees and teachers of the law, who had come from every village of Galilee and from Judea and Jerusalem, were sitting there. And the power of the Lord was present for him to heal the sick.

[18]Some men came carrying a paralytic on a mat and tried to take him into the house to lay him before Jesus. [19]When they could not find a way to do this because of the crowd, they went up on the roof and lowered him on his mat through the tiles into the middle of the crowd, right in front of Jesus.

[20]When Jesus saw their faith, he said, *"Friend, your sins are forgiven."*

²¹The Pharisees and the teachers of the law began thinking to themselves, "Who is this fellow who speaks blasphemy? Who can forgive sins but God alone?" ²²Jesus knew what they were thinking and asked, *"Why are you thinking these things in your hearts? ²³Which is easier: to say, 'Your sins are forgiven,' or to say, 'Get up and walk'? ²⁴But that you may know that the Son of Man has authority on earth to forgive sins...."* He said to the paralyzed man, *"I tell you, get up, take your mat and go home."*

²⁵Immediately he stood up in front of them, took what he had been lying on and went home praising God.

²⁶Everyone was amazed and gave praise to God. They were filled with awe and said, "We have seen remarkable things today."

Matthew 13:16

¹⁶*"But blessed are your eyes because they see, and your ears because they hear. For I tell you the truth, many prophets and righteous men longed to see what you see but did not see it, and to hear what you hear but did not hear it."*

Scene 59

Revelation 12:12

¹² "Therefore rejoice, you heavens and you who dwell in them! But woe to the earth and the sea, because the devil has gone down to you! He is filled with fury, because he knows that his time is short."

Scene 60

Revelation 7: 1

¹After this I saw four angels standing at the four corners of the earth, holding back the four winds of the earth to prevent any wind from blowing on the land or on the sea or on any tree. ²Then I saw another angel coming up from the east, having the seal of the living God. He called out in a loud voice to the four angels who had been given power to harm the land and the sea: ³"Do not harm the land or the sea or the trees until we put a seal on the foreheads of the servants of our God." ⁴Then I heard the number of those who were sealed: 144,000 from all the tribes of Israel.

Revelation 9:4

⁴They were told not to harm the grass of the earth or any plant or tree, but only those people who did not have the seal of God on their foreheads. ⁵They were not given power to kill them, but only to torture them for five

months. And the agony they suffered was like that of the sting of a scorpion when it strikes a man.

⁶During those days men will seek death, but will not find it; they will long to die, but death will elude them.

Scene 61

Daniel 9:24

²⁴"Seventy 'sevens' are decreed for your people and your holy city to finish transgression, to put an end to sin, to atone for wickedness, to bring in everlasting righteousness, to seal up vision and prophecy and to anoint the most holy.

²⁵"Know and understand this: From the issuing of the decree to restore and rebuild Jerusalem until the Anointed One, the ruler, comes, there will be seven 'sevens,' and sixty-two 'sevens.' It will be rebuilt with streets and a trench, but in times of trouble. ²⁶After the sixty-two 'sevens,' the Anointed One will be cut off and will have nothing. The people of the ruler who will come will destroy the city and the sanctuary. The end will come like a flood: War will continue until the end, and desolations have been decreed. ²⁷He will confirm a covenant with many for one 'seven.' In the middle of the 'seven' he will put an end to sacrifice and offering. And on a wing *of the temple* he will set up an abomination that causes desolation, until the end that is decreed is poured out on him."

Scene 79

Daniel 12:4

⁴"But you, Daniel, close up and seal the words of the scroll until the time of the end. Many will go here and there to increase knowledge."

⁵Then I, Daniel, looked, and there before me stood two others, one on this bank of the river and one on the opposite bank. ⁶One of them said to the man clothed in linen, who was above the waters of the river, "How long will it be before these astonishing things are fulfilled?"

⁷The man clothed in linen, who was above the waters of the river, lifted his right hand and his left hand toward heaven, and I heard him swear by him who lives forever, saying, "It will be for a time, times and half a time. When the power of the holy people has been finally broken, all these things will be completed."

⁸I heard, but I did not understand. So I asked, "My lord, what will the outcome of all this be?" ⁹He replied, "Go your way, Daniel, because the words are closed up and sealed until the time of the end. ¹⁰Many will be purified, made spotless and refined, but the wicked will continue to be wicked. None of the wicked will understand, but those who are wise will understand.

¹¹"From the time that the daily sacrifice is abolished and the abomination that causes desolation is set up, there will be 1,290 days. ¹²Blessed is the one who waits for and reaches the end of the 1,335 days.

¹³"As for you, go your way till the end. You will rest, and then at the end of the days you will rise to receive your allotted inheritance."

Revelation 5:1

¹Then I saw in the right hand of him who sat on the throne a scroll with writing on both sides and sealed with seven seals.

²And I saw a mighty angel proclaiming in a loud voice, "Who is worthy to break the seals and open the scroll?" ³But no one in heaven or on earth or under the earth could open the scroll or even look inside it. ⁴I wept and wept because no one was found who was worthy to open the scroll or look inside.

⁵Then one of the elders said to me, "Do not weep! See, the Lion of the tribe of Judah, the Root of David, has triumphed. He is able to open the scroll and its seven seals."

Scene 92

Matthew 24:24

²⁴*For false Christs and false prophets will appear and perform great signs and miracles to deceive even the elect—if that were possible.* ²⁵*See, I have told you ahead of time.*

Mark 13: 21

²¹*At that time if anyone says to you, 'Look, here is the Christ!' or, 'Look, there he is!' do not believe it.* ²²*For false Christs and false prophets will appear and perform signs and miracles to deceive the elect—if that were possible.* ²³*So be on your guard; I have told you everything ahead of time.*

Scene 96

Matthew 22:15

[15]Then the Pharisees went out and laid plans to trap him in his words. [16]They sent their disciples to him along with the Herodians.

"Teacher," they said, "we know you are a man of integrity and that you teach the way of God in accordance with the truth. You aren't swayed by men, because you pay no attention to who they are. [17]Tell us then, what is your opinion? Is it right to pay taxes to Caesar or not?"

[18]But Jesus, knowing their evil intent, said, *"You hypocrites, why are you trying to trap me? [19]Show me the coin used for paying the tax."* They brought him a denarius, [20]and he asked them, *"Whose portrait is this? And whose inscription?"*

[21]"Caesar's," they replied. Then he said to them, *"Give to Caesar what is Caesar's, and to God what is God's."* [22]When they heard this, they were amazed. So they left him and went away.

Scene 112

Revelation 13:16

[16]He also forced everyone, small and great, rich and poor, free and slave, to receive a mark on his right hand or on his forehead, [17]so that no one could buy or sell unless he had the mark, which is the name of the beast or the number of his name.

[18]This calls for wisdom. If anyone has insight, let him calculate the number of the beast, for it is man's number. His number is 666.

Revelation 14:11

[9]A third angel followed them and said in a loud voice: "If anyone worships the beast and his image and receives his mark on the forehead or on the hand, [10]he, too, will drink of the wine of God's fury, which has been poured full strength into the cup of his wrath. He will be tormented with burning sulfur in the presence of the holy angels and of the Lamb.

[11]And the smoke of their torment rises for ever and ever. There is no rest day or night for those who worship the beast and his image, or for anyone who receives the mark of his name."

[12]This calls for patient endurance on the part of the saints who obey God's commandments and remain faithful to Jesus. [13]Then I heard a voice

from heaven say, "Write: Blessed are the dead who die in the Lord from now on."

"Yes," says the Spirit, "they will rest from their labor, for their deeds will follow them."

2 Corinthians 11:14

[14]And no wonder, for Satan himself masquerades as an angel of light. [15]It is not surprising, then, if his servants masquerade as servants of righteousness. Their end will be what their actions deserve.

Scene 116

Matthew 11:25

[25]At that time Jesus said, "*I praise you, Father, Lord of heaven and earth, because you have hidden these things from the wise and learned, and revealed them to little children.*"

Exodus 33:19

[19]"I will have mercy on whom I will have mercy, and I will have compassion on whom I will have compassion. [20]But," he said, "you cannot see my face, for no one may see me and live."

Scene 121

Psalm 51:11

[11]Do not cast me from your presence or take your Holy Spirit from me.

Scene 122

Jeremiah 30:05 The Stone Edition Tanach

For thus said HASHEM: 'A sound of terror have we heard; of fear, and not peace. Ask now and see if a male has ever given birth. Why, (then) do I see that every man puts his hand upon his loins like a woman in child-birth, and all faces turn pallid? Woe! For that day will be momentous, there is nothing like it; it will be a time of trouble for Jacob, but he shall be saved from it. It shall be on that day — the word of HASHEM, Master of Legions — that I will break off the yoke (of conqueror) from your neck and I will tear your straps, and foreigners will no longer enslave him. They will serve HASHEM their God and David their king, whom I will establish over them. But as for you, do not fear, My servant Jacob, the word of HASHEM, and do not be afraid, Israel; for behold, I am saving you from distant places, and your descendants from the land of their captivity, and Jacob will return and be at peace and tranquil, and none will make (him) afraid.'

Scene 123

Isaiah 65:24
[24]Before they call I will answer; while they are still speaking I will hear.

Scene 134

Matthew 10:39
[39]*Whoever finds his life will lose it, and whoever loses his life for my sake will find it.*

Luke 9:24
[24]*For whoever wants to save his life will lose it, but whoever loses his life for me will save it.* [25]*What good is it for a man to gain the whole world, and yet lose or forfeit his very self?*

Revelation 12:12
[12]"But woe to the earth and the sea, because the devil has gone down to you! He is filled with fury, because he knows that his time is short."

Scene 144

Revelation 6:2
[2]I looked, and there before me was a white horse! Its rider held a bow, and he was given a crown, and he rode out as a conqueror bent on conquest.

Scene 152

Matthew 24:34
[34]*I tell you the truth, this generation will certainly not pass away until all these things have happened.* [35]*Heaven and earth will pass away, but my words will never pass away.*

Mark 9:1
[1]And he said to them, "I tell you the truth, some who are standing here will not taste death before they see the kingdom of God come with power."

Mark 13:30

30"I tell you the truth, this generation will certainly not pass away until all these things have happened. Heaven and earth will pass away, but my words will never pass away."

Luke 21:29

29He told them this parable: "Look at the fig tree and all the trees. When they sprout leaves, you can see for yourselves and know that summer is near. Even so, when you see these things happening, you know the kingdom of God is near.

"I tell you the truth, this generation will certainly not pass away until all these things have happened. Heaven and earth will pass away, but my words will never pass away."

Scene 155

Matthew 18:19

19"Again, I tell you that if two of you on earth agree about anything you ask for, it will be done for you by my Father in heaven. 20For where two or three come together in my name, there am I with them."

Matthew 17:20

20He replied, "Because you have so little faith. I tell you the truth, if you have faith as small as a mustard seed, you can say to this mountain, 'Move from here to there' and it will move. Nothing will be impossible for you."

Notes on Matthew and Mary Magdelene

Matthew was a tax collector named Levi who became one of Jesus's twelve Apostles and is the namesake of the New Testament Gospel of Matthew. It is still debated as to whether he was the actual author.

Mary Magdalene has been a source of controversy and confusion as of late. As early as the 3rd and 4th centuries Church Fathers considered her to be the Mary that was the redeemed prostitute of the New Testament. That view was changed by the Roman Catholic Church in 1969 and the prostitute is believed to have been a different Mary. A Gnostic Gospel of Mary Magdalene is at Nag Hammadi with gaps in provocative places that have led some to speculate as to the true nature of her relationship with Jesus. What the gospel does say is that Jesus favored her. She was among those who stayed with Jesus as he hung on the cross and was the first to see him at the Resurrection.

Notes on Angels

Angels are frequently cited in the Old and New Testaments as guardians, messengers and deliverers of God's wrath. There are hierarchies of angels and not all angels have wings.

Notes on antichrist and end times

The Book of Revelation refers to the trinity of evil — the beast, antichrist and false prophet — as a multi-headed dragon that would be given authority over the earth for an allotted time known as the Great Tribulation. According to the prophecy, many would be fooled into following the antichrist. He would make war against God's people, would be defeated by Jesus at the Second Coming, and thrown into an Abyss where he would remain for 1,000 years. At the end of the 1,000 years, he would be set free to deceive the nations and gather them to battle. Satan would again be defeated, the dead would be judged and a new heaven and a new earth would be created where God would dwell with his people.